EVERYMAN,
I WILL GO WITH THEE,
AND BE THY GUIDE,
IN THY MOST NEED
TO GO BY THY SIDE

The Arabian Nights II
Sindbad and Other Popular Stories

Translated by Husain Haddawy

EVERYMAN'S LIBRARY

142

This book is one of 250 volumes in Everyman's Library
which have been distributed to 4500 state schools
throughout the United Kingdom.
The project has been supported by a grant of £4 million
from the Millennium Commission.

First included in Everyman's Library, 1907
This translation first published in Everyman's Library, 1998
Copyright © 1995 by Husain Haddawy
Published by arrangement with W. W. Norton & Company, Inc.,
New York

ISBN 1-85715-142-9

A CIP catalogue record for this book is available from the
British Library

Published by David Campbell Publishers Ltd., 79 Berwick Street,
London W1V 3PF

Distributed by Random House (UK) Ltd.,
20 Vauxhall Bridge Road, London SW1V 2SA

THE ARABIAN
NIGHTS II

Contents

For Diana, Myriam, Peter, Christopher, Mark,
and for Samson of the Hebrides
and those who have the grace of turning hate to love.

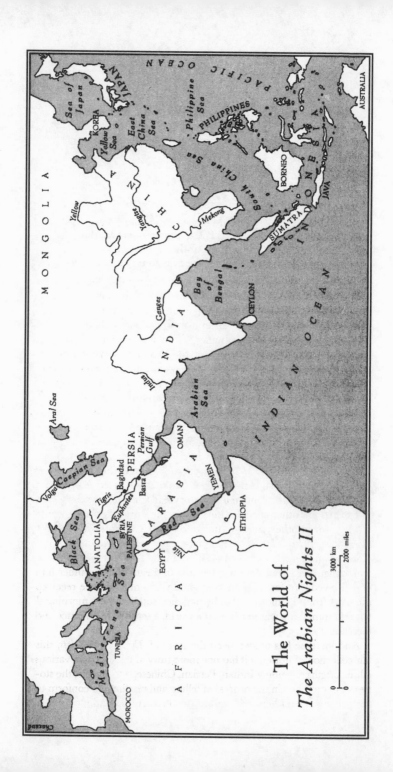

The World of
The Arabian Nights II

Introduction

"From fairest creatures we desire increase"; so have I, ever since I was a child in Baghdad. At that time, when life was desire and dreams, fulfillment was wish fulfillment, and dreams were only dreams. The main event of the season was King Kong or Flash Gordon or some Indian film, and when these came and went, we were left with our *Arabian Nights* and our favorite storytellers, men and women.

I remember my great-uncle best. He was a towering man whose eyes sparkled with kindness, an impish smile, and a child's sense of wonder. Though his wife and numerous children lived in Salman Pak, a village near Baghdad named for the Prophet's barber who lies buried there under the shadow of the great hall of Ctesiphon, the capital of the ancient Sassanian empire, my great-uncle himself spent most of his time at the Gaylani Mosque in Baghdad. He was an assistant to a diminutive holy man from Morocco to whom people came, seeking protection from harm by his talismans and charms, as in the case of his ancient predecessor, the holy Fatima, in the story of "'Ala al-Din and the Magic Lamp."

My great-uncle used to visit my grandmother, bringing walnuts grown in the Kurdish mountains or bananas imported from India, and after supper, he would tell us a story. He knew that both she and I expected this other gift from him. When the story was over, I would ask him for another, and he, unlike our other visitors who usually offered an encore that, because of its brevity, left us with a feeling of pleasure and regret, would embark on a long story that we followed with delight and gratitude. It is because of this that I remember him best. I loved him for his generosity, and when one day, we received the news from the mosque that he had died suddenly that morning, I felt that something was lost from the world, a sense of abundance and increase.

And increase has indeed been the story of *The Arabian Nights*, this fair collection of stories, if it has one more story to tell. Being of various ethnic origins, including Indian, Persian, Chinese, and Arabic, the stories were modified in the process of telling and retelling, to conform to the general life and customs of the Arab society that adopted them and to the particular conditions of that society at a particular time. Thus they circulated orally for centuries from the ninth century onward before they were collected and written down and began to be circulated in different manuscript copies, taking a path that intertwined with that of the oral tradition, until they were finally written down in a definite form in the second half of the thirteenth century, within the Mamluk domain, both in Egypt and Syria. Although that copy is now lost, its existence is attested to by the remarkable similarities in substance, form, and style among the subsequent early copies. All of them share the same nucleus of eleven stories, which persisted in all other manuscripts and which are:

"King Shahrayar and Shahrazad, His Vizier's Daughter"
"The Merchant and the Demon"
"The Fisherman and the Demon"
"The Porter and the Three Ladies"
"The Three Apples"
"The Two Viziers, Nur al-Din 'Ali al-Misri and Badr al-Din Hasan al-Basri"
"The Hunchback"
"Nur al-Din 'Ali ibn-Bakkar and the Slave-Girl Shams al-Nahar"
"The Slave-Girl Anis al-Jalis and Nur al-Din 'Ali ibn-Khaqan"
"Jullanar of the Sea"
"Qamar al-Zaman and His Two Sons, Amjad and As'ad"

All these early manuscript copies use the strategy of the frame story of Shahrayar and Shahrazad, dividing the stories into nights. Unlike later manuscripts, which contain one thousand and one nights, they contain about two hundred and eighty-two. Furthermore, the earliest versions, such as the fourteenth-century Syrian manuscript, show a certain cohesion and uniformity as a clear expression of the life, culture, and literary style of a specific historical moment, namely, the Mamluk period. I limited my first volume of translation of the *Nights* to the stories contained in this early manuscript, with a view to offering the English reader a specifically Mamluk literary work. The only exception is the omission of "The Story of Qamar al-Zaman," as that manuscript contains only a few pages.

This second volume of the *Nights* is based, however, on a different consideration, prompted by the subsequent history of the stories. As their popularity increased, editors and copiers collected stories from various sources, from both the oral and the written traditions, and wrote them down in numerous manuscripts, preponderantly Egyptian, from the mid-eighteenth through the early nineteenth centuries. They deleted, added, modified, and borrowed passages from each other and kept adding stories, to create the compendious anthology of folktales we now have under the title of *The Thousand and One Nights* or *The Arabian Nights*.

Eventually, the manuscripts became the basis for the printed editions, mostly of the nineteenth century. The first was the Calcutta edition (1814, 1818); the second, the Breslau edition (1824–43); the third, the Bulaq edition (1835), based on a late Egyptian manuscript whose editor, by adding and interpolating numerous tales, swelled the old text and subdivided the material until he had one thousand and one nights; and the fourth, the second Calcutta edition (1839–42), which was based variously on a late Egyptian manuscript, the first Calcutta, and the Breslau editions. All these editions were pieced together from various sources, not according to consistent, sound editorial principles, but solely for the purpose of producing the most compendious anthology of tales. The one notable exception is Muhsin Mahdi's recent work *Alf Layla was Layla* (Leiden, 1984). This is a painstaking, critical, and definitive edition of the fourteenth-century Syrian manuscript, but like its source, it is limited to the first ten of the nucleus stories, with the bulk of the eleventh, namely, "Qamar al-Zaman," derived from a later manuscript.

Because of the authenticity, or rather the relative purity, of the stories in the Syrian manuscript version, as well as their general qualities, I, as I said, limited my first-volume translation to this text. But that left out an entire tradition, both written and oral, spanning the fifteenth through nineteenth centuries, and comprising hundreds of stories; I was reminded of this omission by both scholars and general readers, particularly those who missed their favorites, for from fairest creatures they desired increase. But although the solution—to translate more stories—seemed easy, it posed some problems. First, to translate the massive work in its entirety was out of the question, at least for me, since there are other fair creatures in this world. Second, to turn from the Syrian version, which is the closest to what one might call the "original" version of the written tradition, a version whose qualities I enjoyed and extolled, to later versions, which are inferior from a literary point of view, as I showed in the introduction to my first volume, seemed inconsistent and hard to do. Yet, somehow, the gap had to be filled, and a fair image of the *Nights* had to be presented. Therefore, I decided to compromise, by selecting among the stories those which, by representing the essential nature of the *Nights,* have captured the popular imagination. My choices, too, were determined by the existence of a reasonably good text.

The first choice was "Qamar al-Zaman," thus giving me the opportunity to complete the nucleus by translating the eleventh story. After that, it was not difficult to decide on "Sindbad the Sailor," " 'Ala al-Din (Aladdin) and the Magic Lamp," and " 'Ali Baba and the Forty

Thieves." The choice of text, however, proved more problematic. For "Qamar al-Zaman" and "Sindbad," I chose the Bulaq edition over the second Calcutta, which is its rival among critics as the "standard edition," simply because the Bulaq is less of a quilt, having fewer accretions and fewer random additions. To be sure, the editor of the Bulaq, following eighteenth- and nineteenth-century editorial practices, modified considerably the content and especially the style of the text, which was derived either from an oral version or from an older written version or both. For example, whereas the early versions vary in style from the colloquial to the literary from one story to another and even within the same story, the Bulaq is uniformly literary in style. But literary here does not necessarily mean superior, for what the style gains in "polish," it loses in freshness and vigor. Such drastic editing reflected the biases of the Arab literati of the eighteenth and nineteenth centuries; these readers, including the editors themselves, regarded the tales with condescension, judging them to be entertaining in substance but "vulgar" in style, and appointed themselves to the task of "improving" them. Fortunately, the tales, in spite of any loss they may have suffered by being "improved," have nevertheless maintained much of their beauty and vigor.

The choice of text for "'Ala al-Din" and " 'Ali Baba" was much more problematic, for no available standard Arabic manuscript or printed edition contains these two stories, and no authentic source has yet been found. I therefore resorted to the French version of Antoine Galland, *Mille et Une Nuits* (1704–17). Galland, according to his diaries, first heard "'Ala al-Din" from Hanna Diab, a Maronite Christian from Aleppo, who may have subsequently written it down and given it to him for his translation. The first time the story appeared in Arabic was in 1787, in a manuscript by Dionysius Shawish, alias Dom Denis Chavis, a Syrian Christian priest living in Paris. This manuscript was designed to complete the missing portions of the fourteenth-century Syrian manuscript that Galland used for the first part of his translation of the *Nights*. The story appeared again in a manuscript written between 1805 and 1808, in Paris, by Mikhail Sabbagh, a Syrian collaborator of Sylvestre de Sacy. Sabbagh claimed to have copied it from a Baghdad manuscript written in 1703. However, careful examination of Sabbagh's and Chavis's versions, in light of the general styles of the *Nights* and of Galland's version, leads to the conclusion that they are not authentic. As evident from his French syntax and turns of phrase, Chavis fabricated his text by translating Galland back into Arabic; and Sabbagh perpetuated the hoax by improving Chavis's translation and claiming it to be a Baghdad version.

" 'Ali Baba" has a similar history. Galland heard the story from

Diab and wrote it down in French. Subsequently, an Arabic manuscript written by one Yuhanna ibn-Yusuf Warisi was acquired by the
Bodleian in 1860. Although it is written in a pseudo-grammatical Arabic, with some mistakes and colloquial words, as well as purple
patches, verses, and rhyming phrases alien to Galland's version, a
close examination reveals that it is a modified translation of Galland. It
is no more of Arabic origin than its author Jean Varsi, a Frenchman
attached to the French mission in Egypt. (For further details concerning "'Ala al-Din" and " 'Ali Baba," see Muhsin Mahdi's Arabic introduction to *Alf Layla was Layla*, Leiden, 1984, and the discussion in his
forthcoming third English volume.)

All four stories in this volume have been translated from Arabic into
English before. Having dealt at length with the history and quality of
the other translations in the introduction to my first volume, I will
limit myself here to some relevant aspects of the versions which are
still more or less current. These are Edward Lane's (1839–41),
Richard Burton's (1885–86), and N. J. Dawood's (Penguin, Revised
Edition 1973). Lane and Burton include both "Qamar al-Zaman" and
"Sindbad," while Dawood, whose selections contain less than three of
the nucleus stories, includes only "Sindbad." Lane includes neither
"'Ala al-Din" nor " 'Ali Baba," while Burton includes both stories,
and Dawood includes only "'Ala al-Din." Both Burton and Dawood
unknowingly based their translations on the fake Arabic versions.

Typically, Lane, Burton, and Dawood follow the practice of their
predecessors, the Arab literati and editors of the eighteenth and nineteenth centuries, by taking liberties with the text. Dawood omits all
the verse passages. Lane translates his sentences closely, but, ever sen-
sitive to Victorian sensibilities, he omits many words and passages he
considers inappropriate or offensive, passages or words that not only
lend the Arabic original color and piquancy, but also reveal the spirit
in which it was written. Burton, on the other hand, revels in and pre-
serves the peculiarities of the style of the Arabic original, declaring in
his introduction that he has "carefully Englished the picturesque turns
and novel expressions of the original in all their outlandishness." But
for Burton, preserving these peculiarities meant exaggerating them,
by creating an ornate pseudo-archaic style that is alien both to the
style of the Arabic original and to any recognizable style in English
literature.

Consider the fate of the following passage from "Qamar al-
Zaman":

> And when she saw that he was without pants, she placed her
> hand under his shirt and felt his legs, and as his skin was very

smooth, her hand slipped and touched his penis, and her heart ached and pounded with desire, for the lust of women is greater than the lust of men, and she felt embarrassed.

Lane omits it altogether, while Burton translates it as follows:

Then she thrust her hand into his breast and, because of the smoothness of his body, it slipped down to his waist and thence to his navel and thence to his yard, whereupon her heart ached and her vitals quivered and lust was sore upon her, for that the desire of women is fiercer than the desire of men, and she was ashamed of her own shamelessness.

This example of Burton is mild by comparison with his other flights. For instance, a passage from his literal translation of Galland's "'Ala al-Din," which he gives in an appendix, reads,

In this action of joining his hands, he rubbed the ring which the magician put on his finger, and of which he knew not yet the virtue, and immediately a genie of an enormous size and frightful look rose out of the earth, his head reaching the vault, and said to him, "What wouldst thou have with me? I am ready to obey thee as thy slave, and the slave of all who have the ring on thy finger; I, and the other slaves of that ring."

Yet in his translation of Sabbagh's manuscript, which is basically a plain translation of Galland, no more ornate than Burton's own cited rendering, the passage reads,

And whilst he implored the Lord and was chafing his hands in the soreness of his sorrow for that had befallen him of calamity, his fingers chanced rub the Ring when, lo and behold! forthright its Familiar rose upright before him and cried, "Adsum; thy slave between thy hands is come! Ask whatso thou wantest, for that I am the thrall of him on whose hand is the Ring, the Signet of my lord and master." Hereat the lad looked at him and saw standing before him a Márid like unto an Ifrít of our lord Solomon's Jinns. He trembled at the sight; but, hearing the Slave of the Ring say, "Ask whatso thou wantest, verily, I am thy thrall, seeing that the signet of my lord be upon thy finger, he. . . . "

It is useful to compare this passage with Dawood's translation of Sabbagh:

Whilst he was wringing his hands together, he chanced to rub the ring which the Moor had given him as protection. At once a great black ifrit, as tall as one of Solomon's jinn, appeared before him.

"I am here, master, I am here!" the jinnee cried. "Your slave is at your service. Ask what you will, for I am the slave of him who wears my master's ring."

The sight of this apparition struck terror to Aladdin's heart.

Burton and Dawood stand poles apart; Burton is flamboyant, while Dawood is serviceable and plain.

Compared with the following faithful translation of Galland, Dawood, as is typical of his translation throughout, seems to be somewhat lacking in vividness and immediacy.

In clasping his hands, he rubbed, unaware, the ring which the magician had placed on his finger and of which he knew not the power. As soon as he did so, a demon of enormous size and dreadful look rose before him, as if out of the earth, with his head reaching the vault, and said to him, "What do you wish? Here I am, ready to obey you, as your slave and the slave of all who wear the ring, I and the other slaves of the ring."

A similar difference may be seen in Lane's and Burton's respective treatments of the verse passages, which are a peculiarity of the *Nights* and which are interspersed with the prose narrative. They are inserted by a given editor or copyist to suit the occasion, and whether adding color to the description of a place or person, expressing joy or grief, complimenting a lady, or underscoring a moral, they are intended to heighten the action, raise the literary level, and intensify the emotional effect. Lane omits them for the most part, and when he includes them, he gives them in an abbreviated form and translates them in a flat, literal style. Dawood omits them altogether because, according to him, they "obstruct the natural flow of the narrative" and because they are "devoid of literary merit." He forgets that at least half of these passages come from some of the most prominent classical Arab poets. Burton, on the other hand, again translates them in an inflated style that is often awkward and forced. For example, the passage which reads,

> Resisting women is obeying God,
> For they will not thrive who lend them their ears.
> They will hinder them on perfection's way,
> Though they may study for a thousand years,

Lane translates as follows,

> Oppose women; for so wilt thou obey [God] becomingly
> since the youth will not prosper who give them
> his rein.

> They will hinder him from attaining perfection in
> his excellencies though he pass a thousand
> years in the study of science.

And Burton translates this section as follows:

> Rebel against women and so shalt thou serve Allah
> the more.
> The youth who gives women the rein must forfeit all
> hope to soar.
> They'll balk him when seeking the strange device,
> Excelsior,
> Tho' waste he a thousand of years in the study of
> science and lore.

If Lane and Burton fail in their translations, it is not simply due to their tampering with the text; it is due to the kind of tampering and the nature of the text itself. The genius of the *Nights* and the secret of their appeal lie in their reconciliation of opposites. Whether they are fables, fairy tales, romances, or comic as well as historical anecdotes, they interweave the unusual, the extraordinary, the marvelous, and the supernatural into the fabric of everyday life, in which both the usual incidents and the extraordinary coincidences are but the warp and weft of divine Providence, a fabric in which the sacred and profane meet. Their meeting place is in the details—the unabashed, straightforward, matter-of-fact details that secure the reader's willing suspension of disbelief and open the way to a mysterious yet immediate world of wonder and wish fulfillment. Both Lane and Burton violate this place of equilibrium and thus spoil the effect, Lane by censoring the details, Burton by exaggerating them.

Nowhere is the essential quality of the *Nights* more apparent than in the four stories of this volume, which is why I have scrupulously tried to adhere to both the spirit and the letter of the original text. This means that, on the one hand, I have endeavored to be as literal as possible within the limits of idiomatic English and, on the other, that I have used a style designed to produce on the English reader as much as possible the aesthetic effect produced on the Arabic reader by the original. There are two notable differences between my first volume of translations and the present one. First, the reader will not find, except in some sections of "Qamar al-Zaman," that the style modulates between colloquial and literary. This is because both the editor of the Bulaq edition and Galland have cultivated the terrain and smoothed out the differences. Second, the reader will not find the frame dialogue between Shahrayar and Shahrazad and consequently the divisions into nights, for the Bulaq edition uses a different sequence

from that of the Syrian manuscript I used for my first volume, and
Galland does not divide the stories into nights. To impose an arbitrary
order, therefore, would have been an inconsistent consistency or an
unseemly mannerism. It should be noted, moreover, that in "'Ala al-
Din," Galland permits himself to forget that Shahrazad is the story-
teller. He often deviates from the omniscient third-person narrator
and editorializes in the first person. Throughout, the reader will miss
Shahrazad, but then I miss her too.

Finally, I am presenting these four stories without any special claim
to authenticity or uniqueness. My sole aim in offering this volume is to
fill a literary gap and, like my more generous great-uncle who told me
more than four tales in Baghdad, to entertain the reader in the hope
that, in time, others will do the same, with versions of their own, more
suited to their time, "that thereby beauty's rose might never die."

HUSAIN HADDAWY
Reno 1994

HUSAIN HADDAWY is Professor of English at the University of
Nevada at Reno. He was born and brought up in Baghdad and
has lived in both the United States and the Middle East.

Acknowledgments

My thanks are to Robert Merrill, Patty Peltekos, Julia Reidhead, and Vonnie Rosendahl for their generous help with the manuscript, and to Anna Karvellas for her fine supervision of virtually every stage of production.

A Note on the Transliteration

For the transliteration of Arabic words, the Library of Congress system is used, without diacritical marks except for the " ' ", as in " 'Ali," which is an "a" pronounced from the back of the throat.

الف ليـــلة وليلة

The
Arabian Nights II

THE STORY OF
SINDBAD THE SAILOR

There lived in Baghdad, in the time of the Commander of the Faithful, the Caliph Harun al-Rashid, a man called Sindbad the Porter, who was poor and who carried loads on his head for hire. One day, he was carrying a heavy load, and as it was very hot, he became weary and began to perspire under the burden and the intense heat. Soon he came to the door of a merchant's house, before which the ground was swept and watered, and the air was cool, and as there was a wide bench beside the door, he set his load on the bench to rest and take a breath. As he did so, there came out of the door a pleasant breeze and a lovely fragrance; so he remained sitting on the edge of the bench to enjoy this and heard from within the melodious sounds of lutes and other string instruments accompanying delightful voices singing all kinds of eloquent verses. He also heard the sounds of birds warbling and glorifying the Almighty God, in various voices and tongues, turtledoves, nightingales, thrushes, doves, and curlews. At that he marveled to himself and felt a great delight. He went to the door and saw inside the house a great garden and saw pages, servants, slaves, and attendants, the likes of whom are found only with kings and sultans. And through the door came the aromas of all kinds of fine delicious foods and delicious wine.

He raised his eyes to heaven and said, "Glory be to You, o God, Creator and Provider! You bestow riches on whomever You wish, without reckoning. O Lord, I ask Your forgiveness of all sins and repent to You of all faults. O Lord, there is no argument with Your judgment or Your power. You are not to be questioned on what You do, for You are omnipotent in every thing. Glory be to You! You enrich whomever You wish and impoverish whomever You wish. You exalt whomever You wish and humble whomever You wish. There is no god but You. How great is Your majesty, how mighty Your dominion, and how excellent Your government! You have bestowed favors on one you have chosen of your servants, for the owner of this place is in the height of comfort, enjoying all kinds of pleasant perfumes, delicious foods, and fine beverages. You have foreordained and apportioned to Your creatures what You wish, so that among them some are weary, some comfortable, and some enjoy life, while some, like me, suffer extreme toil and misery." Then he recited the following verses:

> How many wretched men toil without rest,
> And how many enjoy life in the shade!
> My weariness increases every day;
> 'Tis strange, how heavy is the burden on me laid!
> Others are prosperous and live in ease,
> Having never my heavy burden known,
> Living in luxury throughout their life,
> Enjoying food and drink and pleasure and renown.
> Yet all God's creatures are of the same species;
> My soul is like this one's and his like mine,
> And yet we are so different, one from one,
> As different as is vinegar from wine.
> And yet, o Lord, I impugn not Thy ways,
> For Thou art wise and just, and all judgment is Thine.

When the porter finished reciting his verses and was about to carry his load and continue on his way, a young page with a handsome face, fine build, and rich clothes, came out of the door, took his hand, and said, "Come in and speak with my master, for he is asking for you." The porter wanted to refuse but could not. He left his load with the doorkeeper in the hallway and went into the house with the page. He found it to be a handsome mansion, stately but cheerful. Then he came to a great hall in which he saw noblemen and great lords and saw all kinds of flowers and fresh and dried fruits and a great variety of exquisite foods and wines of the finest vintage. And he saw musical instruments and all kinds of beautiful slave-girls, all arranged in the proper order. At the upper end of that hall sat a venerable and majestic man whose beard was turning gray on the sides. He had a handsome appearance and a comely face, and he had an aspect of dignity, reverence, nobility, and majesty. When Sindbad the Porter saw all this, he was confounded and said to himself, "By God, this place is one of the spots of Paradise, or else it is the palace of a king or a sultan." Then he assumed a respectful posture, saluted the assembly, invoked a blessing on them, kissed the ground before them, and stood with his head bowed in humility. The master of the house asked him to sit near him, welcomed him, and spoke kindly to him. Then he set before Sindbad the Porter various kinds of fine, exquisite, and delicious foods. Sindbad the Porter invoked God, then ate until he was satisfied and said, "Praise be to God." Then he washed his hands and thanked the company.

The master of the house then said, "You are welcome, and your day is blessed. What is your name, and what do you do for a living?" The porter answered him, "Sir, my name is Sindbad the Porter, and I carry on my head people's goods for hire." The master of the house smiled and said to him, "Porter, your name is like mine, for I am called Sindbad the Sailor. I would like you to let me hear the verses you were reciting when you were at the door." The porter was ashamed and said, "For God's sake, don't reproach me, for fatigue, hardship, and poverty teach a man ill manners and impudence." The host said to him, "Do not be ashamed, for you have become a brother to me. Recite the verses, for they pleased me when you recited them at the door." The porter recited to him those verses, and when he heard them, he was pleased and delighted. Then he said, "Porter, my story is astonishing, and I will relate to you all that happened to me before I attained this prosperity and came to sit in this place, where you now see me, for I did not attain this good fortune and this place save after severe toil, great hardships, and many perils. How much toil and trouble I have endured at the beginning! I embarked on seven voyages, and each voyage is a wonderful tale that confounds the mind, and everything happened by fate and divine decree, and there is no escape nor refuge from that which is foreordained."

The First Voyage of Sindbad

Gentlemen, my father was one of the most prominent men and richest merchants, who possessed abundant wealth and property. When I was a little boy, he died and left me many buildings and fields. When I grew up, I seized everything and began to eat and drink freely, associated with young friends, wore nice clothes, and passed my life with my friends and companions, believing that this way of life would last forever and that it would benefit me. I lived in this way for a length of time but finally returned to my senses and awoke from my heedlessness and found that my wealth had gone and my condition had changed. When I came to myself and found that I had lost everything, I was stricken with fear and dismay, and I remembered a saying I had heard before, a saying of our Lord Solomon, the son of David, that three things are better than three: the day of death is better than the day of birth; a living dog is better than a dead lion; and the grave is better than the palace. Then I gathered all I had of effects and clothes and sold them, together with what was left of my buildings and property and netted three thousand dirhams, thinking that I might travel abroad and recalling what some poet said:

A man must labor hard to scale the heights,
And to seek greatness must spend sleepless nights,
And to find pearls must plunge into the sea
And so attains good fortune and eminent be.
For he who seeks success without labor
Wastes all his life in a futile endeavor.

I made my resolve and, having been inclined to take a sea voyage, I bought goods and merchandise, as well as provisions and whatever is needed for travel, and embarked with a group of merchants on a boat bound downstream for Basra. From there, we sailed for many days and nights from sea to sea and from island to island, and sold, bought, and bartered until we came to an island that seemed like one of the gardens of Paradise. There the captain docked, cast anchor, and put forth the landing plank. Then all those who were on the ship landed on that island. They set up wood stoves, lighted fires in them, and busied themselves with various tasks, some cooking, some washing, some sightseeing. I myself was among those who went to explore the place, while the passengers assembled to eat and drink and play games and amuse themselves.

While we were thus engaged, the captain, standing on the side of the ship, cried out at the top of his voice, "O passengers, may God preserve you! Run for your lives, leave your gear, and hurry back to the ship to save yourselves from destruction. For this island where you are is not really an island but a great fish that has settled in the middle of the sea, and the sand has accumulated on it, making it look like an island, and the trees have grown on it a long time. When you lighted the fire on it, it felt the heat and began to move, and it will soon descend with you into the sea, and you will all drown. Save yourselves before you perish."

When the passengers heard the captain's warning, they hurried to get into the ship, leaving behind their woodstoves, copper cooking pots, and their other gear, together with their goods. Some made it to the ship, but some did not. The island had moved and sunk to the bottom of the sea with everything that was on it, and the roaring sea with its clashing waves closed over it. I, being one of those left behind on the island, sank in the sea with those who sank, but God the Almighty saved me from drowning and provided me with a large wooden tub that the passengers had been using for washing. I held on to it for dear life, got on it, and began to paddle with my feet, while the waves tossed me to the right and left. Meanwhile, the captain spread the sails and pursued his voyage with those who had made it to the ship, without regard for those who were drowning. I kept looking at the ship until it disappeared from my sight, and as night descended, I became sure of perdition. I remained in this condition for a day and a night, but with the help of the wind and the waves, the tub landed me under a high island, with trees overhanging the water. I seized a branch of a tall tree, clung to it, after I had been on the verge of death, and climbed it to the land. I found my feet numb and my soles bore the marks of the nibbling of fish, something of which I had been unaware because of my extreme exhaustion and distress.

I threw myself on the ground like a dead man and, overcome by stupefaction, lost consciousness till the next day, when the sun rose and I woke up on the island. I found that my feet were swollen and that I was reduced to a helpless condition. So I began to move, sometimes dragging myself in a sitting position, sometimes crawling on my knees, and found that the island had abundant fruits and springs of sweet water. I ate those fruits, and after several days I recovered my strength, felt refreshed, and was able to move about. I reflected and, having made myself a crutch from a tree branch, walked along the shores of the island, enjoying the trees and what the Almighty God had created.

I lived in this manner until one day, as I walked along the shore, I saw an indistinct figure in the distance and thought it a wild beast or one of the creatures of the sea. I walked toward it, without ceasing to look at it, and found that it was a magnificent mare tethered by the seashore. I approached her, but she cried at me with a loud cry, and I was terrified, and as I was about to retreat, a man emerged suddenly from the ground, called to me and pursued me, saying, "Who are you, where do you come from, and what brings you here?" I said to him, "Sir, I am a stranger, and I was on a ship and sank in the sea with some other passengers, but God provided me with a wooden tub, and I got on it and floated until the waves cast me on this island." When he heard my words, he took me by the hand and said, "Come with me." I went with him, and he descended with me to a subterranean vault. We entered a large chamber, and he seated me at the upper end of the chamber and brought me food. I was hungry, and I ate until I was satisfied and felt good. Then he inquired about my situation and what had happened to me. I told him my story from beginning to end, and he marveled at it.

When I finished my story, I said to him, "Sir, I have told you all the particulars of my situation and all that has happened to me. For God's sake, pardon me, for I would like you to tell me who you are, why you live in this subterranean chamber, and why is the mare tethered by the seashore?" He said to me, "I am one of a group of men scattered on this island. We are the grooms of King Mihrajan, in charge of all the horses. Every month, at the new moon, we bring the best mares that have not been bred before and hide in the subter-

ranean chamber, so that no one may see us. Then one of the sea
horses comes out to the shore after the scent of the mares and, looking
and seeing no one around, mounts one of them. When he finishes with
her and dismounts her, he wishes to take her with him, but she cannot
follow him, because she is tethered. Then he begins to cry out at her
and batter her with his head and hoofs. When we hear his cries, we
know that he has dismounted, and we run out, shouting at him, and
frighten him back into the sea. Then the mare conceives and bears a
mare or a filly worth a fortune, one whose like is not to be found on
the face of the earth. This is the time of the coming of the sea horse
and, God the Almighty willing, I will take you to King Mihrajan and
show you our country. Had you not met us, you would not have found
anyone else on this island, and you would have died miserably, and
no one would have known of you, but I will save your life and return
you to your country." I invoked a blessing on him and thanked him
for his help and kindness.

While we were in conversation, a sea horse suddenly came out of
the sea and, letting out a great cry, leapt on the mare. When he finished with her, he dismounted and tried to take her with him but
could not, as she resisted, neighing at him. The groom took a sword
and buckler and ran out, shouting to his companions, "Run to the sea
horse," as he hit the buckler with the sword. Then a group of them
came out, shouting and brandishing spears. The sea horse, frightened
by them, ran away, plunged into the water like a buffalo, and disappeared. As the groom sat down to rest for a while, his companions
came, each leading a mare. When they saw me with him, they
inquired about my situation, and I repeated to them what I had told
him. Then they drew near me and, spreading the table, ate and
invited me to eat; so I ate with them. Then they rode the mares and
gave me one to ride, and we traveled until we reached the city of King
Mihrajan.

Then they went in to see him and acquainted him with my story,
and he sent for me, and they led me in and made me stand before
him. I saluted him, and he returned my salutation, welcomed me,
greeted me in a courteous manner, and inquired about my situation. I
related to him what had happened to me and what I had seen from
beginning to end, and he marveled at my story, saying, "By God, my
son, you have had an extraordinary escape, and had you not been destined to a long life, you would not have escaped from these difficulties, but God be praised for your safety." Then he treated me kindly
and honored me and, seating me near him, engaged me in friendly
conversation. Then he made me his agent to the port and registrar of
all the ships that landed. I stood in his presence to transact his affairs,
and he treated me generously, bestowed a fine, rich suit on me, and

rewarded me in every way. I became a person of high esteem with him, interceding for the people and facilitating their business.

I remained with him for a long time, but whenever I went to the port, I used to ask the merchants and the sailors about the direction of the city of Baghdad, hoping that someone might inform me and I go with him and return to my country, but no one knew it, nor knew anyone who went there. I was perplexed, and I had grown weary of my long absence from home, and I continued to feel this way for some time.

One day I went in to see King Mihrajan and found with him a group of Indians. I saluted them and they returned my salutation, welcomed me, and asked me about my country. Then I asked them about theirs, and they told me that they consisted of various races. One is called the Kshatriyas, who are the noblest of their races and who oppress no one, nor inflict violence on anyone. Another is called the Brahmans, who abstain from wine but live in joy, sport, merriment, and prosperity, possessing horses, camels, and cattle. They told me, moreover, that the Indians consist of seventy-two castes, and I marveled at that.

Among other things, I saw in the dominion of King Mihrajan an island called Kabil, on which the beating of drums and tambourines is heard all night long and whose inhabitants are reported by travelers and neighboring islanders to be people of judgment and serious pursuits. I saw in the sea a fish four hundred feet long and saw fish with faces that resembled the faces of owls. During that voyage, I saw many strange and wonderful things, which would take too long to relate to you.

I continued to divert myself with the sights of those islands until one day, as I stood in the port, with a staff in my hand, as was my custom, a large ship approached, carrying many merchants. When it entered the harbor and reached the pier, the captain furled the sails, cast anchor, and put forth the landing plank. Then the crew brought out to shore everything that was in the ship and took a long time in doing so, while I stood writing their account. I said to the captain, "Is there anything left in the ship?" He replied, "Yes, sir, I have some goods in the hold of the ship, but their owner drowned at one of the islands during our voyage here; so his goods remained in our charge, and our intention is to sell them and keep a record, so that we may give the money to his family in the city of Baghdad, the Abode of Peace." I asked the captain, "What was the name of the merchant, the owner of the goods?" He said, "His name was Sindbad the Sailor." When I heard these words, I looked carefully at him and, recognizing him, cried out loudly, saying, "Captain, I am the owner of the goods; I am that Sindbad who landed from the ship on the island, with the other merchants, and when the fish moved, and you called out to us, some of us got into the ship, and the rest sank. I was among those who sank, but God the Almighty preserved me and saved me from drowning by means of a wooden tub that the passengers had used for washing. I got on the tub and paddled with my feet, and the wind and the waves brought me to this island, where I landed and where, with the help of the Almighty God, I met the grooms of King Mihrajan, who brought me with them to this city and took me to the king, to whom I related my story, and he treated me generously and made me clerk of the harbor of this city, and he appreciated my services and rewarded me accordingly. These goods in your charge are my goods and possessions."

The captain said, "There is no power and no strength, save in God, the Almighty, the Magnificent. There is neither conscience nor trust left among men." I said to him, "Captain, why those words, after you heard me telling you my story?" The captain replied, "Because you heard me say that I have with me goods whose owner has drowned, you are trying to take them without any rightful claim, and this is unlawful. We saw the owner drown with many other passengers, none of whom escaped. How can you claim that you are the owner of the goods?" I said to him, "Captain, listen to my story and try to understand, and you will discover my veracity, for lying is the mark of a hypocrite." Then I enumerated to him everything I had with me, from the time I left Baghdad with him until we reached that island, where we sank in the sea, and I mentioned to him some incidents that had occurred between him and me. The captain and the other merchants then became convinced of my veracity, and they recognized me and congratulated me on my safety. All of them said, "We never believed that you had escaped from drowning, but God has granted you a new life." Then they gave me my goods, and we found my name written on them, and nothing was missing. Then I opened them and took out something precious and costly, and the crew of the ship carried it with me to the king as a gift. I told him that this ship is the one in which I had been a passenger and that all my goods were intact and in perfect order and that this present was a part of them. The king was amazed and was even more convinced of my truthfulness in everything I had told him. He felt a deep affection for me, treated me with great generosity, and gave me many presents in return for mine.

Then I sold my goods and all my other property and made a great profit. Then I bought goods, gear, and provisions from that city, and when the merchants were about to depart, I loaded everything I had on the ship and went in to see the king. I thanked him for his kindness and generosity and asked his permission to return to my country and family. He bade me farewell and gave me a great many of the products of that country for my voyage. I bade him farewell and embarked. Then we set sail with the permission of the Almighty God, and fortune served us and fate favored us, as we journeyed day and night until we reached Basra safely.

After staying in Basra for a short time rejoicing in my return to my country, I headed for Baghdad, the Abode of Peace, carrying with me an abundance of merchandise, provisions, and gear of great value. I went to my quarter and entered my house, and all my relatives and friends came to see me. Then I acquired a great number of servants and attendants and concubines and bought slaves, both black and white. Then I bought houses and other properties that exceeded what I had had before. And I associated with friends and companions, exceeding my former habits, and forgot all I had suffered of toil, exile, hardship, and perils, indulging for a long time in amusements and pleasures and delicious food and fine drink. This was my first voyage. Tomorrow, the Almighty God willing, I will tell you the story of the second of my seven voyages.

Then Sindbad the Sailor had Sindbad the Porter dine with him and gave him a hundred pieces of gold, saying to him, "You have cheered us today." The porter thanked him, took his present, and went on his way, meditating and marveling at the events that befall mankind. He spent that night at home, and as soon as it was morning, he went to the house of Sindbad the Sailor, who welcomed him, spoke courteously to him, and asked him to sit. When the rest of his companions arrived, he set food and drink before them, and when they were cheerful and merry, he said to them:

The Second Voyage of Sindbad

Friends, as I told you yesterday, I lived a most enjoyable life of unalloyed pleasure until it occurred to me one day to travel abroad, and I felt a longing for trading, seeing other countries and islands, and making profit. Having made my resolve, I took out a large sum of money and bought goods and travel gear, packed them up, and went down to the shore. There I found a fine new ship, with sails of good cloth, numerous crewmen, and abundant equipment. I loaded my bales on it, as did a group of other merchants, and we sailed on the same day.

We sailed under fair weather and journeyed from sea to sea and from island to island, and wherever we landed, we met merchants, high officials, and sellers and buyers, and we sold, bought, and bartered.

We continued in this fashion until fate brought us to a beautiful island abounding with trees, ripe fruits, fragrant flowers, singing birds, and clear streams, but there was not a single inhabitant nor a breathing soul around. The captain anchored the ship at the island, and the merchants and other passengers landed there, to divert themselves with the sight of the trees and birds and to glorify the One Omnipotent God and wonder at the power of the Almighty King. I landed with the rest and sat down by a spring of pure water among the trees. I had with me some food, and I sat there eating what the Almighty God had allotted me. The breeze was cool, and the place was pleasant; so I dozed off and rested there until the sweetness of the breeze and fragrance of the flowers lulled me into a deep sleep.

When I awoke, I did not find a single soul around, neither man nor demon. The ship had sailed with all the passengers and left me behind, none of the merchants or the crew taking any notice of me. I searched right and left, but found no one but myself. I felt extremely unhappy and outraged, and my spleen was about to burst from the severity of my anxiety, grief, and fatigue, for I was all alone with nothing of worldly goods and without food or drink. I felt desolate and despaired of life, saying to myself, "Not every time the jar is saved in time. If I escaped safely the first time, by finding someone who took me with him from the shore of that island to the inhabited part, this time I am very far from the prospect of finding someone who will deliver me out of here." Then I began to weep and wail for myself until I was completely overcome by grief, blaming myself for what I had done and for having embarked on the hardships of travel, after I had been reposing peacefully in my own house and in my own country, happily enjoying good food and good drink and good clothes, without need for money or goods. I regretted leaving Baghdad on this sea journey, especially after the hardships I had endured on the first and after my narrow escape from destruction, saying, "We are God's and to God we return." I felt like a madman.

At last, I arose and began to walk on the island, turning right and left, for I was unable to sit still in any one place. Then I climbed a tall tree and looked to the right and left but saw nothing but sky and water and trees and birds and islands and sands. Then I looked closely and saw a large, white object. I climbed down and walked in its direction until I reached it and found it to be a huge white dome of great height and circumference. I drew closer and walked around it but found that it had no door, and because of its extreme smoothness, I had neither the power nor the nimbleness to climb it. I marked the spot where I stood and went around the dome to measure its circumference and found it to be a good fifty paces. I stood, thinking of a way to get inside, as the day was about to end and the sun was about to set. Suddenly, the sun disappeared, and it grew dark. I therefore thought that a cloud had come over the sun, but since it was summer, I wondered at that. I raised my head to look at the object and saw that it was a great bird, with a huge body and outspread wings, flying in the air and veiling the sun from the island. My wonder increased, and I recalled a story I heard from tourists and travelers that there is on certain islands an enormous bird, called the Rukh, which feeds its young on elephants, and I became certain that the dome I saw was one of the Rukh's eggs and wondered at the works of God the Almighty.

While I was in this state, the bird alighted on the egg and brooded over it with its wing and, stretching its legs behind on the ground, went to sleep. Glory be to Him who never sleeps! I unwound my turban, twisted it with a rope and, girding my waist with it, tied it fast to the bird's feet, saying to myself, "Perhaps, this bird will carry me to a land where there are cities and people. That will be better than staying on this island." I spent that night without sleep, fearing that the bird might fly with me while I was unaware. When dawn broke and it was light, the bird rose from its egg, uttered a loud cry, and flew with me up into the sky. It soared higher and higher until I thought that it had reached the pinnacle of heaven. Then it began to descend gradually until it alighted with me on the ground, resting on a high place. As soon as I reached the ground, I hastened to unbind myself, and, loosening my turban from its feet, while shaking with fear, although it was unaware and took no notice of me, I walked away. Then it picked up something with its talons from the ground and flew high into the sky. When I looked at it carefully, I saw that it was an enormous serpent, which the bird had taken and flown with toward the sea. And I wondered at that.

Then I walked about the place and found myself on a crest overlooking a large, wide, and deep valley at the foot of a huge and lofty mountain that was so high no one could see the top nor climb to it, so I blamed myself for what I had done, saying, "I wish that I had stayed on the island, which is better than this desolate place, for there I might at least have eaten of its various fruits and drunk from its streams, whereas this place has neither trees nor fruits nor streams. There is no power and no strength save in God the Almighty, the Magnificent. Every time I escape from a calamity, I fall into one that is greater and more perilous." Then I arose and, gathering my strength, walked in that valley and saw that its ground was composed of diamonds, with which they perforate minerals and jewels, as well as porcelain and onyx, which is such a hard and dense stone that neither stone nor steel has any effect on it and which nobody can cut or break except with the leadstone. Moreover, the valley was full of serpents and snakes, each as big as a palm tree, indeed so huge that it could swallow an elephant. These serpents came out at night and hid themselves during the day, fearing that the Rukh or eagles might carry them away and cut them in pieces, for a reason of which I was unaware. I stood there, regretting what I had done and saying to myself, "By God, I have hastened my own destruction."

As the day was waning, I walked in that valley and began looking for a place to spend the night, being afraid of the serpents, forgetting my food and drink and subsistence, and thinking only of saving my life. Soon I saw a cave nearby. It had a narrow entrance, and when I went in I saw a big stone lying by that entrance. I pushed the stone and closed the entrance from the inside, saying to myself, "I am safe here now, and as soon as it is day, I will go out and see what fate will bring." But when I took a look inside, I saw a huge snake brooding over its eggs. My hair stood on end, and I raised my head, committing myself to fate and divine decree. I spent the entire night without sleep, and as soon as it was dawn, I removed the stone with which I had closed the entrance of the cave and went out, like a drunken man, feeling dizzy from excessive hunger, sleeplessness, and fear.

I walked in the valley in this condition, when suddenly a big slaughtered sheep fell before me, but when I saw no one else around, I was amazed, and I recalled a story I used to hear a long time ago from some merchants, tourists, and travelers that the mountains of the diamonds are so perilous that no one can gain access to them, but that the merchants who deal in diamonds employ a device to get them. They take a sheep, slaughter it, skin it, cut up the meat, and throw it from the top of the mountain into the valley. When the meat falls, still fresh, the diamonds stick to it. Then they leave it there till midday, when the eagles and vultures swoop down on it, pick it up with their talons, and fly with it to the top of the mountain. The merchants then rush, shouting at them, and scare them away from the meat. Then the merchants come to the meat, take the diamonds sticking to it, and carry them back to their country. No one can obtain diamonds except by this method.

When I saw that slaughtered sleep and recalled that story, I approached the carcass and began to pick a great number of diamonds and to put them into my pockets and the folds of my clothes, and I continued to fill my pockets, my clothes, my belt, and my turban. While I was thus engaged, another carcass suddenly fell before me. I bound myself to it with my turban and, lying on my back, placed it on my chest and held on to it. Thus it was raised above the ground. Suddenly, an eagle swooped down on it, caught it with his talons, and flew up into the air with it and with me clinging to it. The eagle continued to soar until it reached the top of the mountain and, alighting there, was about to tear off a piece of meat, when suddenly a loud cry and the sound of clattering with a piece of wood came from behind the eagle, who took fright and flew away.

I unbound myself from the carcass, with my clothes stained with its blood, and stood by its side. Suddenly, the merchant, who had shouted at the eagle, approached the carcass and saw me standing there, but he did not utter a word, for he was frightened of me. Then he came closer to the carcass, and when he turned it over and found nothing on it, he uttered a loud cry and said, "What a disappointment! There is no power and no strength, save in God the Almighty, the Magnificent. May God save us from Satan the accursed," and he kept expressing regret, wringing his hands and saying, "What a pity! How did this happen?" I went to him, and he said to me, "Who are you, and what brings you to this place?" I said to him, "Don't be afraid, for I am a human being, and one of the best men. I was a merchant, and I have a strange and extraordinary tale to tell, and the reason for my coming to this valley and this mountain is marvelous to relate. Don't worry, for you will receive from me what will please you. I have with me a great deal of diamonds, each one better than what you would have gotten, and I will give you a portion that will satisfy you. Don't fear and don't worry." When he heard this, he thanked me and invoked a blessing on me, and we began to converse.

When the other merchants, each of whom had thrown down a slaughtered sheep, heard me conversing with their companion, they came to meet me. They saluted me, congratulated me on my safety, and took me with them. I told them my whole story, relating to them what I had suffered on this voyage and the cause of my coming to this valley. Then I gave the merchant, to whose slaughtered sheep I had attached myself, a large portion of diamonds, and that made him happy, and he thanked me and invoked a blessing on me, and the merchants said to me, "By God, you have been granted a new life, for no one has come to this place before and escaped from it, but God be praised for your safety." They spent the night in a pleasant and safe place, and I spent the night with them, extremely happy for my safe escape from the Valley of Serpents and my arrival in an inhabited place.

When it was morning, we arose and journeyed along the ridge of the high mountain, seeing many snakes in the valley below, and we continued walking until we came to a large and pleasant island with a grove of camphor trees, each of which might provide a hundred men with shade. When someone wishes to obtain some camphor, he makes a perforation in the upper part of the tree with a piercing rod and catches what descends from it. The liquid camphor, which is the juice of that tree, flows and later hardens, like gum. Afterwards, the tree dries and becomes firewood. We also saw in that island, besides cattle, a kind of beast called the rhinoceros, which pastures as cows and buffaloes do in our country, and feeds on the leaves of trees, but the body of that beast is bigger than that of a camel. It is a huge beast, with a single horn in the middle of its head, thick and twenty feet long and resembling the figure of a man. Travelers and tourists on land and in the mountains report that this beast called the rhinoceros carries a huge elephant on its horn and grazes with it in the island and on the shores, without feeling its weight, and when the elephant dies on the horn, its fat melts under the heat of the sun and flows on the head of the rhinoceros and, entering his eyes, blinds it. Then it lies down by the shore, and the Rukh picks it up with its talons and carries it together with the elephant to feed to its young. I also saw in that island a great number of a certain kind of buffalo, the like of which is not seen among us.

The merchants exchanged goods and provisions with me and paid me money for some of the diamonds I carried in my pockets from the valley. They carried my goods for me, and I journeyed with them, from town to town and from valley to valley, buying and selling and viewing foreign countries and what God has created until we reached Basra, where I stayed for a few days, then headed for Baghdad. When I reached my quarter and entered my home, with a great quantity of diamonds and a considerable amount of goods and provisions, I met with my family and other relatives and gave alms and distributed presents to all my relatives and friends. Then I began to eat and drink well and wear handsome clothes, associating with friends and companions and forgetting all I had suffered, and I continued to lead a happy, merry, and carefree life of sport and merriment. And all who heard of my return came to me and inquired about my voyage and the countries I saw, and I told them, relating to them what I had seen and what I had suffered, and they were amazed at the extent of my hardships and congratulated me on my safety. That was the end of the second voyage. Tomorrow, the Almighty God willing, I will tell you the story of my third voyage.

When Sindbad the Sailor finished telling his story to Sindbad the Porter and the other guests, they all marveled at it. After they had supper, he gave Sindbad the Porter a hundred pieces of gold, which he took and, after thanking Sindbad the Sailor and invoking a blessing on him, went on his way, marveling at what Sindbad had suffered. The following day, as soon as it was light, the porter arose, and after performing his morning prayer, came to the house of Sindbad, as he had bidden him. The porter went in, wished him good morning, and Sindbad welcomed him and sat with him until the rest of his friends and companions arrived. After they had eaten and drunk and enjoyed themselves and felt relaxed and merry, Sindbad the Sailor began his story.

The Third Voyage of Sindbad

Friends, the story of my third voyage is more amazing than the two you have already heard, and God in His wisdom knows best what He keeps hidden. When I returned from my second voyage, I led a life of ease and happiness, rejoicing in my safety, having gained great wealth, for God had compensated me for everything I had lost, as I had related to you yesterday. I lived in Baghdad for some time, in prosperity and peace and happiness, until my soul began to long for travel and sightseeing and commerce and profit, and the soul is naturally prone to evil. Having made my resolve, I bought a great quantity of goods suited for a sea voyage, packed them up, and journeyed with them from Baghdad to Basra. Then I went to the seashore where I found a large ship in which there were many merchants and other passengers who seemed to be good people—men of rectitude, piety, and kindness. I embarked with them on that ship, and we sailed, relying on the blessing and aid and favor of the Almighty God, feeling happy in the expectation of a safe and prosperous voyage. We sailed from sea to sea and from island to island and from city to city, buying and selling and diverting ourselves with the sights and feeling exceedingly content and happy until one day we found ourselves in the middle of a roaring, raging sea. The captain stood at the side of the ship and examined the sea in all directions. Then he slapped his face, furled the sails, cast the anchors, plucked his beard, tore his clothes, and uttered a loud cry. When we asked him, "Captain, what is the matter?" he said, "O fellows, may God preserve you. The wind has prevailed against us and forced us into the middle of the sea, and fate and our ill fortune have brought us to the Mountain of the Apes. No one has ever come here and escaped safely." I was sure that we were all going to perish, and no sooner had the captain finished his speech than the ship was surrounded by ape-like creatures who came in great number, like locusts, and swarmed on the boat and on the shore. We were afraid that if we killed, struck, or chased away any of them, they would easily kill us because of their number, for numbers prevail over courage. We also feared that they would plunder our goods and provisions. They are the ugliest of beasts, with a terrifying appearance, covered with hair like black felt. They have black faces, yellow eyes, and small size, no more than four spans. No one understands their language nor knows who they are, for they shun the society of men. They climbed up the anchor cables of the ship, on every side, and cut them with their teeth, and they cut likewise all the ropes; so the ship swerved with the wind and stopped on the shore, below the mountain. They seized all the merchants and the other passengers and, landing us on the island, took the ship with everything in it and disappeared into an unknown place, leaving us behind.

We stayed on the island, eating of its vegetables and fruits and drinking of its streams until one day we saw a stately mansion, situated in the middle of the island. We walked in its direction, and when we reached it, we found it to be a strong castle, with high walls and a gate of ebony, with two leaves, both of which were open. We entered and found inside a large courtyard, around which there were many high doors, and at the upper end of which there was a large, high bench, on which rested stoves and copper cooking pots hanging above. Around the bench lay many scattered bones. But we saw no one and were very much surprised. Then we sat down in the courtyard for a while and soon fell asleep and slept from mid-morning till sundown, when suddenly we felt the earth trembling under us, heard a rumbling noise in the air, and saw descending on us from the top of the castle a huge figure in the likeness of a man, black in color and tall in stature, as if he were a huge palm-tree, with eyes like torches; fangs like the tusks of a boar; a big mouth, like the mouth of a whale; lips like the lips of a camel, hanging down on his breast; ears like two barges, hanging down on his shoulders; and nails like the claws of a lion. When we saw him, we fainted, like men stricken dead with anxiety and terror.

When he descended, he sat on the bench for a while, then he got up and, coming to us, grabbed my hand from among my fellow merchants and, lifting me up in the air, turned me over, as I dangled from his hand like a little morsel, and felt my body as a butcher feels a sheep for the slaughter. But finding me feeble from grief, lean from the toil of the journey, and without much meat, he let me go and picked up one of my companions, turned him over, felt him, as he had done with me, and released him. He kept turning us over and feeling us, one after one, until he came to the captain of our ship, who was a fat, stout, and broad-shouldered man, a man of vigor and vitality. He was pleased by the captain, and he seized him, as a butcher seizes an animal he is about to slaughter, and, throwing him on the ground, set his foot on his neck and broke it. Then he fetched a long spit and thrust it through the captain's mouth until it came out from his posterior. Then he lit a big fire and set over it the spit on which the captain was spitted, turning it over the coal, until the flesh was roasted. Then he took the spit off the fire and, placing the body before him, separated the joints, as one separates the joints of a chicken, and proceeded to tear the flesh with his nails and eat it until he devoured all the flesh and gnawed the bones, and nothing was left of the captain except some bones, which he threw on one side. Then he sat on the bench for a while and fell asleep, snoring like a slaughtered sheep or cow, and slept till morning, when he got up and went on his way.

When we were sure that he was gone, we began to talk with one another, weeping for ourselves and saying, "We wish that we had drowned in the sea or been eaten by the apes, for that would have been better than being roasted on the coals. By God, this is a vile death, but what God wills comes to pass, and there is no power and no strength save in God the Almighty, the Magnificent. We will die miserably, and no one will know, for there is no escape from this place." We got up and walked in the island to look for a means of escape or a place to hide, feeling that death was lighter to bear than being roasted on the fire. But we failed to find a hiding place, and as the evening overtook us, we returned to the castle, driven by great fear.

No sooner had we sat down than the earth began to tremble under us, and that black creature approached us and began to turn us over and feel us, one after one, as he had done the first time, until he found one he liked, seized him, and did to him what he had done to the captain, on the first day. Then he roasted him and, after eating him, lay down on the bench and slept, snoring all night, like a slaughtered beast. In the morning, he got up and went on his way, leaving us, as usual.

We drew together and said to one another, "By God, if we throw ourselves into the sea and drown, it will be better than dying by fire, for this is a horrible death." One of us said, "Listen to me! Let us find a way to kill him and rid ourselves of this affliction and relieve all Muslims of his aggression and tyranny." I said to them, "Listen, friends! If we have to kill him, let us transport these planks of wood and some of the firewood and make for ourselves a raft and, after we find a way to kill him, embark on the raft and let the sea take us wherever God wishes. Then we will sit there until a ship passes by and picks us up. And if we fail to kill him, we can still embark on the raft and set out in the sea, even though we may drown, in order that we may escape from being slaughtered and roasted on the fire. If we escape, we escape, and if we drown, we die like martyrs." They all replied, "By God, this is a good plan," and we agreed to carry it out; so we carried the wood out of the castle, built a raft, tied it to the seashore and, after putting some food on it, returned to the castle.

When it was evening, the earth trembled under us, and in came the black creature, like a raging dog. He proceeded to turn us over and to feel us, one after one, until he picked one of us and did to him what he had done to his predecessors. Then he ate him and lay to sleep on the bench, snoring like thunder. We got up, took two of the iron spits of those set up there, and put them in the blazing fire until they became red-hot, like burning coals. Then, gripping the spits tightly, we went to the black creature, who was fast asleep, snoring, and, pushing the spits with all our united strength and determination, thrust them deep into his eyes. He uttered a great, terrifying cry. Then he got up resolutely from the bench and began to search for us, while we fled from him to the right and left, in unspeakable terror, sure of destruction and despairing of escape. But being blind, he was unable to see us, and he groped his way to the door, and went out, as his screams made the ground tremble under us and made us quake with terror. When he went out, we followed him, as he went searching for us. Then he returned with a female, even bigger than he and more hideous in appearance. When we saw him and saw that his female companion was more horrible than he, we were in utmost terror. When the female saw us, we hurried to the raft, untied it and, embarking on it, pushed it into the sea, while the two stood, throwing big rocks on us until most of us died, except for three, I and two companions.

The raft conveyed us to another island. There, we walked till the end of the day, and, when it was night, we went to sleep. We were barely asleep when we were aroused by an enormous serpent with a wide belly. It surrounded us and, approaching one of us, swallowed him to his shoulders, then swallowed the rest of him, and we heard his ribs crack inside its belly. Then it went on its way, leaving us in utter amazement and grief for our companion and fear for our lives, thinking to ourselves, "By God, this is amazing, for each death is more terrible than the preceding one. We rejoiced at our escape from the black creatures, but our joy did not last. There is no power and no strength, save in God. By God, we have escaped from the black creature and from drowning, but how shall we escape from this accursed monster?"

Then we walked in the island, eating of its fruits and drinking of its streams, and when it was evening, we found a huge, tall tree, climbed it, and went to sleep there, I myself being on the highest branch. As soon as it was dark, the serpent came and, looking right and left, headed for the tree on which we were, and climbed until it reached my companion. Then it swallowed him to his shoulders, coiled with him around the tree, as I heard his bones crack in its belly, then swallowed him whole, while I looked on. Then it slid down from the tree and went on its way.

I stayed on the tree for the rest of the night, and when it was day-light, I climbed down, like a man stricken dead with terror. I thought of throwing myself into the sea and delivering myself from the world. But I could not bring myself to do it, for life is dear. So I tied a wide piece of wood crosswise to my feet, tied two similar ones to my right side, to my left side, and to my chest, and tied another, very wide and long, crosswise to my head. Thus I was in the middle of these pieces of wood which surrounded me and, having fastened them tightly to my body, I threw myself on the ground and lay, with the wood enclosing me like a closet.

When it was dark, the serpent came, as usual, saw me, and headed for me, but it could not swallow me with the wood surrounding me. Then it began to circle around me, while I looked on, like a man stricken dead with terror. Then the serpent began to turn away from me and come back to me, and every time it tried to swallow me it was prevented by the wood that was tied to me on every side, and it continued in this fashion from sunset to sunrise. When it was light, it went its way, in the utmost vexation and rage. Then I moved my hands and untied myself from the pieces of wood, feeling almost dead from what I had suffered from that serpent.

I then walked in the island until I reached the shore and, happening to look toward the sea, saw a ship on the waves, in the distance. I took a big branch and began to make signs with it and call out to the passengers. When they saw me, they said to each other, "We must see what this is, for it may be a man." They came closer, and when they heard my cries for help, they came to me and took me with them in the ship. Then they inquired about my situation, and I related to them what had happened to me, from beginning to end, and what hardships I had suffered, and they marveled at that. Then they gave me some of their clothes to make myself decent and offered me some food and some cool sweet water. I ate and drank until I had enough, and I felt refreshed, relaxed, and very comfortable, and my vigor returned. God the Almighty had brought me to life after death, and I thanked Him and praised Him for his abundant blessings, after I had been certain of destruction, thinking that I was in a dream.

We sailed, with God's permission, with a fair wind, until we came to an island called the Salahita Island. The captain cast anchor there, and all the merchants and other passengers landed with their goods to sell and buy. Then the captain turned to me and said, "Listen to me! You are a poor stranger who has, as you told us, suffered many horrors, and I wish to benefit you with something that will help you to return to your country, so that you will pray for me." I replied, "Very well, you will have my prayers." He said, "There was a passenger with us whom we lost, and we don't know whether he is alive or dead, for he has left no trace. I would like to give you his goods, and you will take charge of them to sell them in this island, and we will pay you an amount commensurate with your work and trouble and take the rest with us back to Baghdad, find his family, and give it to them, together with the proceeds of the sale. Will you receive the goods and take them to the island to sell them, like the other merchants?" I replied, "Sir, I hear and obey, with gratitude and thanks," and I invoked a blessing on him and thanked him. He then ordered the porters and sailors to carry the goods to the island and deliver them to me. The ship's clerk said to him, "What are those bales that the porters and sailors are carrying out and in whose merchant's name shall I register them?" The captain replied, "Register them in the name of Sindbad the Sailor, who was with us on that island and who drowned, without leaving any trace. I wish this stranger to sell these goods, and I will give him an amount commensurate with his work and trouble and keep the rest of the money with us until we reach Baghdad and, if we find Sindbad, give it to him and, if we don't, give it to his family." The clerk replied, "This is a good and wise plan." When I heard the captain mention that the goods were in my name, I said to myself, "By God, I am Sindbad the Sailor who was lost on that island!"

Then I controlled myself and waited patiently until the merchants came back to the ship and assembled to chat and consult on the affairs of buying and selling. I approached the captain and said to him, "Sir, do you know anything about the man whose goods you gave me to sell?" The captain replied, "I know nothing about him, except that he was a man from Baghdad, called Sindbad the Sailor. We cast anchor at one of the islands, and he was lost, and we have not heard anything about him to this day." I uttered a great cry and said, "O captain, may God preserve you! I am Sindbad the Sailor. When you cast anchor at that island, and the merchants and the rest of the passengers landed, I landed with them. I took with me something to eat, and sat in a place, enjoying myself; then I dozed off and fell into a deep sleep." When the merchants and the other passengers heard my words, they gathered around me, some believing me, some disbelieving. Soon, one of the merchants, hearing me mention the valley of diamonds approached me and said to them, "Listen to what I have to say, fellows! When I related to you the most extraordinary events that I encountered in my travels and how the merchants threw the slaughtered sheep into the valley of diamonds, and I threw mine with theirs, as was my habit, and how I found a man attached to my slaughtered sheep, you did not believe me and thought that I was lying." They said, "Yes, you did tell us that story, and we did not believe you." The merchant said, "This is the very man who gave me the unmatched expensive diamonds, compensating me with more than I would have gotten from my slaughtered sheep, and who traveled with me as my companion until we reached Basra, where he bade us farewell and headed to his city, while we returned to ours. This is the very man who told us that his name was Sindbad the Sailor and related to us how the ship had left, while he was sitting in that island. This man has come to us, in order that you may believe my story. All those goods are his property, for he informed us of them when he first met us, and the truth of his words is evident." When the captain heard the merchant's words, he stood up and, coming up to me, stared at me for a while and asked me, "What is the mark on your bales?" I said, "The mark is such and such," and when I informed him of a matter that had occurred between us when I embarked in the ship, in Basra, he became convinced that I was indeed Sindbad the Sailor, and he embraced me, saluted me, and congratulated me on my safety, saying, "By God, sir, your story is extraordinary and wonderful. God be praised for reuniting you with us and returning your goods and property to you."

Afterwards, I disposed of my goods, according to the best of my skill, and made a great deal of profit, and I felt exceedingly happy and congratulated myself on my safety and the recovery of my property. We continued to sell and buy in the islands until we reached the Indus Valley, where we likewise sold and bought and enjoyed the sights. I saw in the sea there many wonders and strange things. Among the things I saw was a fish in the form of a cow and a creature in the form of an ass. I also saw a bird that comes out of a seashell, lays its eggs on the surface of the water, and hatches them there but never comes up from the sea to the land.

Then we continued our voyage, with God's permission, until, with the aid of a fair wind, we reached Basra, where I stayed for a short time and headed for Baghdad. I went to my house, where I greeted my family and my friends and companions, rejoicing in my safe return to my country and city and home and family. I gave alms and gifts and clothed the widows and the orphans. Then I gathered around me my friends and companions and began to enjoy myself with them, eating well and drinking well, and diverting and entertaining myself, and I forgot all that had happened to me and all the hardships and perils I had suffered. On that voyage, I gained what cannot be numbered or calculated. These then were the most extraordinary events of that voyage. Tomorrow, God willing, come to me, and I will tell you the story of the fourth voyage, which is more wonderful than those of the preceding voyages.

Then Sindbad the Sailor gave the porter a hundred pieces of gold, as usual, and ordered that the table be spread. After the table was spread, and the guests dined, still marveling at that story and its events, the porter took the money and went on his way, marveling at what he had heard. The porter spent the night in his house, and as soon as it was morning, he performed his morning prayer and headed to Sindbad the Sailor. He went in and saluted him, and Sindbad received him with gladness and cheer and sat with him until the rest of his companions arrived. When food was served, and they ate and drank and felt merry, Sindbad began his story, saying:

The Fourth Voyage of Sindbad

Friends, when I returned to Baghdad and to the society of my family and friends and companions, I lived in the utmost happiness, pleasure, and ease and forgot what I had experienced, because of my great profit and my immersion in sport and mirth in the society of friends and companions. Thus I lived a most delightful life until my wicked soul suggested to me to travel to foreign countries, and I felt a longing for meeting other races and for selling and gain. Having made my resolve, I purchased precious goods, suited for a sea voyage, and, having packed up more bales than usual, journeyed from Baghdad to Basra, where I loaded my bales in a ship and embarked with some of the chief merchants of the town.

We set out on our voyage and sailed, with the blessing of the Almighty God, in the sea, and the journey was pleasant, as we sailed, for many nights and days, from sea to sea and island to island until one day a contrary wind rose against us. So the captain cast the ship's anchors and brought it to a standstill, fearing that it would sink in midocean. While we were praying and imploring the Almighty God, a violent storm suddenly blew against us, tore the sails to pieces, and threw the people, with all their bales, provisions, and possessions, into the sea. I too was submerged like the rest. I kept myself afloat half the day, and when I was about to give up, the Almighty God provided me with one of the wooden planks of the ship, and I and some other merchants climbed on it, and we paddled with our feet, with the aid of the wind and the waves, for a day and a night. On the midmorning of the following day, a squall blew, and the waves rose, casting us on an island, almost dead from lack of sleep, exhaustion, hunger, thirst, and fear.

We walked along the shores of that island and found abundant vegetation, of which we ate a little to stay our hunger and to sustain ourselves. We spent the night on the shore, and when it was daylight, we
arose and wandered in the island to the right and left until we saw a
building in the distance. We walked toward that building and kept
walking until we stood at its door. While we stood there, out came a
group of naked men, who, without speaking to us, seized us and took
us to their king. He ordered us to sit, and we sat. Then they brought us
some strange food, the like of which we had never seen in our lives.
My stomach revolted from it, and unlike my companions, I refrained
from eating it, and my refraining was, by the favor of the Almighty
God, the cause of my being alive till now. For when my companions
ate of that food, they were dazed and began to eat like madmen, and
their states changed. Then the people brought them coconut oil, and
gave them to drink from it and anointed them with it. When they
drank of that oil, their eyes rolled in their heads, and they proceeded
to devour an unusual amount of food. When I saw them in that condition, I was puzzled and felt sorry for them, and I became extremely
anxious and fearful for myself from these naked men. I looked at them
carefully and realized that they were Magians and that the king of
their city was a demon. Whenever someone came to their country, or
they spotted him or chanced to meet him in the valley or on the roads,
they brought him to their king, gave him of that food to eat and
anointed him with that oil, so that his belly would expand and he
would overeat, feeling stupefied, losing judgment, and becoming like
an idiot. Then they gave him more and more of that food to eat and of
that oil to drink, and when he became fat and stocky, they slaughtered
him, roasted him, and gave him to their king to eat, while they themselves ate the flesh without roasting it or cooking it.

When I realized the situation, I was extremely anxious for myself
and my companions, who, in their stupefaction, did not know what
was being done to them. They were committed to a man who took
them out every day and let them pasture on that island, like cattle. In
the meantime, I wasted away and became emaciated from hunger and
fear, and my skin shriveled on my bones. When the Magians saw me
in this condition, they left me alone and forgot me, not one of them
taking any notice of me, until one day I found a way to slip out of the
building and walked away. Then I saw a herdsman sitting on something elevated in the middle of the sea, and when I looked at him, I
realized that he was the man to whom they had committed my companions to be taken out to pasture. With him there were many men
like them. As soon as the man saw me, he knew that I was in possession of my reason and that I was not afflicted like my companions. He
signed to me from afar, saying, "Turn back, and take the road on your

right, and it will lead you into the king's highway." I turned back, as
he had told me and, finding a road on my right, began to follow it,
sometimes running from fear, sometimes walking slowly, in order to
catch my breath, and I kept following the road until I disappeared
from the sight of the man who had directed me to it, and we were no
longer able to see each other.

By then, the sun had set, and it had become dark. I sat down to rest
and tried to sleep, but I could not sleep that night because of my
extreme fear, hunger, and fatigue. When the night was half spent, I
rose and walked in the island until it was daylight, and the sun rose
over the tops of the hills and over the plains. I was tired, hungry, and
thirsty; so I ate of the herbs and the plants that were on that island
until I had enough to allay my hunger. Then I walked the whole day
and the next night, and whenever I felt hungry, I ate of the plants to
stay my stomach, and I walked on like this for seven days and nights.

On the morning of the eighth day, I happened to cast a glance and
saw a vague object in the distance. I walked toward it and kept walking until I reached it, after sunset. I stood scrutinizing it from a distance, still fearful because of what I had suffered the first and the
second time, and found that it was a group of men gathering pepper-
corn. When I approached them, and they saw me, they hastened to
me and, surrounding me on all sides, asked me, "Who are you, and
from where do you come?" I said to them, "Fellows, I am a poor
stranger," and I informed them of my case and how I had suffered
hardships and horrors. When they heard my words, they said, "By
God, this is extraordinary, but tell us how you escaped from these
black men and how you slipped by them, when they are so numerous
on this island, and they eat people?" So I related to them what had
happened to me with them and how they had given my companions
the food I refrained from eating. They congratulated me on my safety
and marveled at my story.

They seated me among them until they finished their work. Then
they brought me some good food, which I ate, being hungry, and
rested for a while. Then they took me and embarked with me in a ship
and went to their island and their homes. There, they presented me to
their king, and I saluted him, and he welcomed me, treated me with
respect, and asked me about my case. I related to him all that had
happened to me, from the day I left Baghdad until I came to him, and
he, as well as all those present in his assembly, marveled greatly at my
story. Then he asked me to sit and gave orders to bring the food, and
I ate until I had enough, washed my hands, and offered thanks to the
Almighty God and praised him for His favor. Then I left the presence
of the king and went sightseeing in his city and found it flourishing,
populous, and prosperous, abounding with food, markets, and buyers

and sellers. I rejoiced in my arrival in that city and felt at ease there, as I made friends with its people who, together with their king, favored me and honored me more than even the chief men of that city.

I saw that all the men, great and small, rode fine horses, but without saddles, and wondered at that, so I said to the king, "My lord, why don't you ride on a saddle, for it offers the rider comfort and greater control?" He asked, "What kind of thing is a saddle, for I have never seen nor used one in all my life." I said to him, "Will you permit me to make you a saddle to ride on and experience its quality?" He said, "Very well." I said, "Let them fetch me some wood," and he gave orders to bring me everything I required. Then I asked for a skilled carpenter and sat with him and showed him the construction of the saddle and how to make it. Then I took some wool, carded it, and made a felt pad out of it. Then I brought leather and, covering the saddle with it, polished it and attached the straps and the girth. Afterwards, I brought a blacksmith and showed him how to make the stirrups, and he forged a great pair of stirrups which I filed and plated with tin and to which I attached fringes of silk. Then I brought one of the best of the king's horses, saddled him, attaching the stirrups to the saddle; bridled him; and led him to the king, who was pleased by the saddle and received it with approval and thanks. He seated himself on the saddle and was greatly pleased with it and gave me a large reward for it.

When his vizier saw that I had made the saddle, he asked me for one, and I made one like it. Moreover, all the leading men and high officials began to order saddles, and I kept making them and selling them, having taught the carpenter and blacksmith how to make saddles and stirrups. Thus I amassed a great deal of money, and was highly esteemed and greatly loved, and I continued to enjoy a high status with the king and his entourage, as well as the leading men of the city and the lords of the state.

One day, I sat with the king, in the utmost happiness and honor, when he said to me, "You are honored and loved among us, and you have become one of us, and we cannot part from you, nor can we bear your departure from our city. I wish you to obey me in a certain matter, without contradicting me." I said to him, "What does your majesty desire of me, for I cannot deny you, since I am indebted to you for your favors, benefits, and kindness, and, praise be to God, I have become one of your servants." He said, "I wish to marry you among us to a lovely, elegant, and charming woman, a woman of beauty and wealth, and you shall reside with us and live with me in my palace. Therefore, do not deny me or argue with me." When I heard the king's words, I remained silent, for I was too embarrassed to say anything. He said, "Son, why don't you answer me?" I replied, "My lord and king of the age, the command is yours." So he immediately summoned the judge and the witnesses and married me to a fine lady of high rank, noble birth, great lineage, surpassing beauty, and abundant wealth, possessing a great many buildings and dwellings. Then he gave me a great, beautiful house, standing alone, and gave me servants and attendants, and assigned me stipends and supplies. So I lived in the utmost ease, contentment, and happiness and forgot all the weariness, trouble, and hardship I had suffered. I said to myself, "If I ever go back to my country, I will take her with me. But whatever is predestined to happen will happen, and no one knows what will befall him," for I loved her and she loved me very much, and we lived in harmony, enjoying great prosperity and happiness.

One day, God the Almighty caused the wife of my neighbor, who was one of my companions, to die, and I went to see him to offer my condolences for the loss of his wife and found him in a sorry plight, anxious, weary, and distracted. I offered my condolences and began to comfort him, saying, "Don't mourn for your wife. God the Almighty will compensate you with a better wife and will grant you a long life, if it be His will." He wept bitterly, saying, "O my friend, how will God compensate me with a better wife, when I have only one day to live?" I said, "Friend, be rational and do not prophecy your own death, for you are well and in good health." He said, "By your life, brother, tomorrow you will lose me and never in your life will you see me again." I asked, "How so?" He said, "Today, they will bury my wife and bury me with her in the tomb, for it is the custom of our country, when the wife dies, to bury the husband alive with her, and when the husband dies, to bury the wife alive with him, in order that neither of them may enjoy life after the other." I said to him, "By God, this is a most vile custom, and no one should endure it."

While we were conversing, most of the people of the city came, offered their condolences for the death of my friend's wife and his own death, and began to prepare her, according to their custom. They brought a coffin and, placing the woman in it, carried her and took her husband with them, outside the city, until they reached a place in the side of a mountain by the sea. They advanced to a spot and lifted from it a large stone, revealing a stone-lined well. They threw the woman down into that well, which seemed to lead into a vast cavern beneath the mountain. Then they brought the husband and, tying a rope of palm fibers under his armpits, let him down the well, with a jug of sweet water and seven loaves of bread. When he was down, he undid the rope, and they drew it up, covered the mouth of the well with that large stone as it was before, and went on their way, leaving my friend with his wife in the cavern.

I said to myself, "By God, this death is worse than the first." Then I went to the king and said to him, "O my lord, why do you bury the living with the dead in your country?" He replied, "It is the custom of our country, when the husband dies, to bury his wife alive with him, and when the wife dies, to bury her husband alive with her, so that they may always be together, in life and in death. This custom we have received from our forefathers." I asked him, "O king of the age, will you do to a foreigner like me as you have done to that man, if his wife dies?" He replied, "Yes, we bury him and do to him as you have seen." When I heard his words, I was galled, dismayed, stricken with grief for myself, and dazed with fear that my wife might die before me and they bury me alive with her. Then I tried to divert my mind, by keeping busy, and to console myself, thinking, "Maybe I will die before her, for no one knows who will go first and who will follow."

But a short time later, my wife fell ill, and a few days later died. Most of the people of the city came to offer their condolences for her death to me and to her relatives. The king too came to offer his condolences, as was their custom. Then they brought a woman to wash her, and they washed her and arrayed her in her richest clothes and gold ornaments, necklaces, and jewels. Then they put her in the coffin and carried her to the side of the mountain and, removing the stone from the mouth of the well, they threw her in. Then all my friends and my wife's relatives turned to me to bid me the last farewell, while I was crying out among them, "I am a foreigner, and I cannot endure your custom." They did not pay any attention to my words, but, seizing me, they bound me by force and let me down the well into the large cavern beneath the mountain, with seven loaves of bread and a jug of sweet water, as was their custom. Then they said to me, "Untie yourself from the ropes," but I refused, and they threw the ropes down on me, covered the opening of the well, and departed.

I saw in that cavern many dead bodies that exhaled a putrid and loathsome smell, and I blamed myself for what I had done, saying to myself, "By God, I deserve everything that has happened to me." I could not distinguish night from day, and I sustained myself with very little food, not eating until I felt the pangs of hunger, nor drinking until I became extremely thirsty, fearing that my food and water would be exhausted. I said to myself, "There is no power and no strength, save in God the Almighty, the Magnificent. What possessed me to marry in this city? Every time I say to myself that I have escaped one calamity, I fall into a worse one. By God, this death is a vile death. I wish that I had drowned in the sea or died on the mountain; that would have been better than this horrible death." And I continued to blame myself. Then I threw myself down on the bones of the dead, begging, in the extremity of my despair, the Almighty God for a speedy death, but found it not, and I continued in this state until my stomach was lacerated by hunger, and my throat was inflamed with thirst. So I sat up and, groping for the bread, ate a little morsel and drank a mouthful of water. Then I stood up and began to explore that cavern. I found that it was wide and empty, except that its floor was covered with dead bodies and rotten bones from long ago. I made myself a place in the side of the cavern, far from the fresh bodies, and went to sleep there. Eventually my provisions dwindled until I had only a very little left. During each day, or more than a day, I had eaten only a morsel and drunk only a mouthful, fearing that the food and water would run out before my death.

I remained in this situation until one day, while I sat wondering what I would do when I ran out of food and water, the rock was suddenly removed from its place, and the light beamed on me. I said to myself, "I wonder what is happening," and saw people standing at the opening of the well who let down a dead man and a living woman, weeping and wailing for herself, and they let down with her food and water. I kept staring at the woman, without being seen by her, while they covered the mouth of the well with the stones and went on their way. Then I took the shinbone of a dead man and, going to the woman, struck her on the crown of the head, and she fell down unconscious. I struck her a second and a third time until she died. She had on her plenty of apparel, ornaments, necklaces, jewels, and precious metals, and I took all she had, together with the bread and water, and sat in the place I had made for myself in the side of the cavern where I used to sleep, and continued to eat only a little of that food, just enough to sustain me, for fear that it would be exhausted quickly and I would die of hunger and thirst.

I remained in the cavern for some time, and whenever they buried a dead person, I killed the living one who was buried with him and took his food and water to sustain myself until one day I woke up from my sleep and heard something rummaging in the side of the cavern. I said to myself, "What can it be?" Then I got up and, with a shinbone in my hand, I walked toward the noise and found out that it was a wild beast which, when it became aware of me, ran away and fled from me. I followed it to the far end of the cavern and saw a spot of light, like a star, now appearing, now disappearing. When I saw it, I walked toward it, and the closer I got to it, the larger and brighter it became until I was certain that it was an opening in the cavern leading to the open air. I said to myself, "There must be an explanation for this. Either it is a second opening, like the one from which they let me down, or it is a fissure in the rock." I stood reflecting for a while; then I advanced toward the light and found that it was a hole in the side of the mountain which the wild beasts had made and through which they entered the cavern and ate of the dead bodies until they had their fill and went out as they came.

When I saw the hole, I felt relieved from my anxiety and worry, certain of life, after having been on the verge of death, and as happy as if I had been in a dream. Then I tried until I succeeded to climb out of the hole, finding myself on the side of a great mountain overlooking the sea and acting as a barrier between the sea, on the one side, and the island and the city, on the other, so that none could come to that part from the city. I praised and thanked the Almighty God, feeling extremely happy and regaining my courage. Then I returned through the hole to the cavern and brought out all the food and water I had saved. Then I changed my clothes, putting on some of the clothes of the dead, and gathered a great many of all kinds of necklaces of pearls and precious stones, ornaments of gold and silver set with gems, and other valuables I found on the corpses and, using the clothes of the dead to pack the jewelry in bundles, carried them out through the hole to the side of the mountain and stood on the seashore.

Every day I went into the cavern and explored it, and whenever they buried someone alive, I killed him, whether he was male or female, took his food and water and, coming out of the cavern, sat on the seashore to wait for deliverance by the Almighty God, by means of a passing ship. For some time, I kept gathering all the jewelry I could find, tying it up in bundles in the clothes of the dead, and carrying it out of the cavern.

One day, as I was sitting on the seashore, thinking about my situation, I saw a ship passing in the middle of a roaring, surging sea. I took a white shirt that I had taken from one of the dead, tied it to a stick, and ran along the seashore, making with it signals to the people on the ship, until, happening to glance in my direction, they saw me and turned toward me, and when they heard my cries, they sent a boat with a group of men. When they came close to me, they said, "Who are you, and why are you sitting in this place, and how did you reach this mountain, for in all our lives we have never known anyone who has reached it?" I said, "I am a merchant, who had been shipwrecked, and I saved myself by getting on a wooden plank, together with my belongings, and, with God's help and by my own exertions, skill, and great toil, I landed at this place, with my belongings." They took me with them in the boat, carrying all I had taken from the cavern, bundled in the clothes and shrouds of the dead, embarked in the ship, and took me with all my belongings to the captain.

The captain said to me, "Fellow, how did you reach this great mountain, which bars the shore from the great city behind it, for I have been sailing in this sea and passing by this mountain all my life, but I have never seen anyone here, except the birds and the wild beasts?" I replied, "I was a merchant on a large ship that was wrecked, and I was thrown into the sea with all my merchandise, which consisted of the fabrics and clothes that you see. But I placed them on one of the wide wooden planks of the ship, and fate and fortune aided me, and I landed on the mountain, where I have been waiting for someone to pass by and take me with him." I did not tell them, however, about what had happened to me in the city or in the cavern, for fear that they might have with them on the ship someone from that city. Then I took out a good portion of my property and presented it to the captain, saying, "Sir, you are the cause of my rescue from this mountain. Take this gift in gratitude for what you have done." But he refused my gift, saying, "We take nothing from anyone, and when we see a shipwrecked man on the seashore or on an island, we take him with us, feed him and give him to drink, and if he is naked, clothe him, and, when we reach a safe harbor treat him with kindness and charity and give him a present, for the sake of the Almighty God." When I heard his words, I offered prayers, wishing him a long life.

We sailed from sea to sea and from island to island, while I anticipated my deliverance and rejoiced in my safety, but every time I recalled my stay with my dead wife in that cavern, I almost lost my mind. At last, with the help of the Almighty God, we arrived safely in Basra, where I stayed for a few days, then headed for Baghdad. There, I came to my quarter, entered my house, and met my relatives and friends, inquiring about their condition, and they rejoiced and congratulated me on my safe return. Then I stored all I had brought with me in my storerooms, gave alms and clothed the widows and the orphans, and bestowed gifts. I felt extremely joyful and happy and returned to my former habit of associating with friends and companions and indulging in sport and pleasure. These, then, are the most extraordinary events of my fourth voyage. Dine with me now, brother, and come back tomorrow, as usual, and I will tell you the story of what happened to me on the fifth voyage, for it is more extraordinary and more wonderful than the preceding one.

Then Sindbad the Sailor gave the porter a hundred pieces of gold and ordered that the table be spread, and after the guests dined, they went their way, in great amazement, for each story was more extraordinary than the preceding one. Sindbad the Porter went to his house, where he spent the night in the utmost joy, happiness, and wonder. As soon as it was daylight, he got up, performed his morning prayer, and walked until he came to Sindbad the Sailor. He walked in, wished him good morning, and Sindbad welcomed him and asked him to sit with him until the rest of his companions arrived. They ate and drank, enjoyed themselves, and felt merry, and when they turned to conversation, Sindbad the Sailor began his story saying:

The Fifth Voyage of Sindbad

Friends, when I returned from the fourth voyage, I indulged in sport, pleasure, and delight, rejoicing greatly in my gains, profits, and benefits, and forgot all I had experienced and suffered until I began to think again of traveling to see foreign countries and islands. Having made my resolve, I bought valuable merchandise suited to a sea voyage, packed up my bales, and journeyed from Baghdad to Basra. I walked along the shore and saw a large, tall, and goodly ship, newly fitted. It pleased me and I bought it. Then I hired a captain and crew, over whom I set some of my slaves and pages as superintendents, and loaded my bales on the ship. Then a group of merchants joined me, loaded their bales on the ship, and paid me the freight. We set out in all joy and cheerfulness, rejoicing in the prospect of a safe and prosperous voyage, and sailed from sea to sea and from island to island, landing to see the sights of the islands and towns and to sell and buy.

We continued in this fashion until one day we came to a large uninhabited island, waste and desolate, except for a vast white dome. The merchants landed to look at the dome, which was in reality a huge Rukh's egg, but, not knowing what it was, they struck it with stones, and when they broke it, much fluid ran out of it, and the young Rukh appeared inside. They drew it out of the shell, slaughtered it, and took from it a great deal of meat. While this was going on, I was on the ship, uninformed and unaware of it until one of the passengers came to me and said, "Sir, go and look at that egg, which we thought to be a dome." I went to look at the egg and arrived just when the merchants were striking it. I cried out to them, "Don't do this, for the Rukh will come, demolish our ship, and destroy us all." But they did not heed my words.

While they were thus engaged, the sun suddenly disappeared, and the day grew dark, as if a dark cloud was passing above us. We raised our heads to see what had veiled the sun and saw that it was the Rukh's wings that had blocked the sunlight and made the day dark, for when the Rukh came and saw its egg broken, it cried out at us, and its mate came, and they circled above the ship, shrieking with voices louder than thunder. I called out to the captain and the sailors, saying, "Push off the ship, and let us escape before we perish." The

captain hurried and, as soon as the merchants embarked, unfastened
the ship and sailed away from the island. When the Rukhs saw that we
were on the open sea, they disappeared for a while.

We sailed, making speed, in the desire to leave their land behind
and escape from them, but suddenly they caught up with us, each carrying in its talons a huge rock from a mountain. Then the male bird
threw its rock on us, but the captain steered the ship aside, and the
rock missed it by a little distance, and fell into the water with such
force that we saw the bottom of the sea, and the ship went up and
down, almost out of control. Then the female bird threw on us its
rock, which was smaller than the first, but as it had been ordained, it
fell on the stern of the ship, smashed it, sent the rudder flying in twenty
pieces, and threw all the passengers into the sea.

I struggled for dear life to save myself until the Almighty God provided me with one of the wooden planks of the ship, to which I clung
and, getting on it, began to paddle with my feet, while the wind and
the waves helped me forward. The ship had sunk near an island in
the middle of the sea, and fate cast me, according to God's will, on
that island, where I landed, like a dead man, on my last breath from
extreme hardship and fatigue and hunger and thirst. I threw myself
on the seashore and lay for a while until I began to recover myself and
feel better. Then I walked in the island and found that it was like one
of the gardens of Paradise. Its trees were laden with fruits, its streams
flowing, and its birds singing the glory of the Omnipotent, Everlasting
One. There was an abundance of trees, fruits, and all kinds of flowers.
So I ate of the fruits until I satisfied my hunger and drank of the
streams until I quenched my thirst, and I thanked the Almighty God
and praised Him.

I sat in the island until it was evening, and night approached, without seeing anyone or hearing any voice. I was still feeling almost dead
from fatigue and fear; so I lay down and slept till the morning. Then I
got up and walked among the trees until I came to a spring of running water, beside which sat a comely old man clad with a waistcloth
made of tree leaves. I said to myself, "Perhaps the old man has landed
on the island, being one of those who have been shipwrecked." I drew
near him and saluted him, and he returned my salutation with a sign
but remained silent. I said to him, "Old man, why are you sitting
here?" He moved his head mournfully and motioned with his hand,
meaning to say, "Carry me on your shoulders, and take me to the
other side of the stream." I said to myself, "I will do this old man a
favor and transport him to the other side of the stream, for God may
reward me for it." I went to him, carried him on my shoulders, and
took him to the place to which he had pointed. I said to him, "Get

down at your ease," but he did not get off my shoulders. Instead, he wrapped his legs around my neck, and when I saw that their hide was as black and rough as that of a buffalo, I was frightened and tried to throw him off. But he pressed his legs around my neck and choked my throat until I blacked out and fell unconscious to the ground, like a dead man. He raised his legs and beat me on the back and shoulders, causing me intense pain. I got up, feeling tired from the burden, and he kept riding on my shoulders and motioning me with his hand to take him among the trees to the best of the fruits, and whenever I disobeyed him, he gave me, with his feet, blows more painful than the blows of the whip. He continued to direct me with his hand to any place he wished to go, and I continued to take him to it until we made our way among the trees to the middle of the island. Whenever I loitered or went leisurely, he beat me, for he held me like a captive. He never got off my shoulders, day or night, urinating and defecating on me, and whenever he wished to sleep, he would wrap his legs around my neck and sleep a little, then arise and beat me, and I would get up quickly, unable to disobey him because of the severity of the pain I suffered from him. I continued with him in this condition, suffering from extreme exhaustion and blaming myself for having taken pity on him and carried him on my shoulders. I said to myself, "I have done this person a good deed, and it has turned evil to myself. By God, I will never do good to anyone, as long as I live," and I began to beg, at every turn and every step, the Almighty God for death, because of the severity of my fatigue and distress.

I continued in this situation for some time until one day I came with him to a place in the island where there was an abundance of gourds, many of which were dry. I selected one that was large and dry, cut it at the neck and cleansed it. Then I went with it to a grapevine and filled it with the juice of the grapes. Then I plugged the gourd, placed in it the sun, and left it there several days until the juice turned into wine, from which I began to drink every day in order to find some relief from the exhausting burden of that obstinate devil, for I felt invigorated whenever I was intoxicated.

One day he saw me drinking and signed to me with his hand, meaning to say, "What is this?" I said to him, "This is an excellent drink that invigorates and delights." Then I ran with him and danced among the trees, clapping my hands and singing and enjoying myself, in the exhilaration of intoxication. When he saw me in that state, he motioned to me to give him the gourd, in order that he might drink from it. Being afraid of him, I gave it to him, and he drank all that was in it and threw it to the ground. Then he became enraptured and began to shake on my shoulders, and as he became extremely intoxicated and sank into torpor, all his limbs and muscles relaxed, and he began to sway back and forth on my shoulders. When I realized that he was drunk and that he was unconscious, I held his feet and loosened them from my neck and, stooping with him, I sat down and threw him to the ground, hardly believing that I had delivered myself from him. But, fearing that he might recover from his drunkenness and harm me, I took a huge stone from among the trees, came to him, struck him on the head as he lay asleep, mingling his flesh with his blood, and killed him. May God have no mercy on him!

Then I walked in the island, feeling relieved, until I came back to the spot on the seashore where I had been before. I remained there for some time, eating of the fruits of the island and drinking of its water and waiting for a ship to pass by, until one day, as I sat thinking about what had happened to me and reflecting on my situation, saying to myself, "I wonder whether God will preserve me and I will return to my country and be reunited with my relatives and friends," a ship suddenly approached from the middle of the roaring, raging sea and continued until it set anchor at the island, and its passengers landed. I walked toward them, and when they saw me, they all quickly hurried to me and gathered around me, inquiring about my situation and the reason for my coming to that island. I told them about my situation and what had happened to me, and they were amazed and said, "The man who rode on your shoulders is called the Old Man of the Sea, and no one was ever beneath his limbs and escaped safely, except yourself. God be praised for your safety." Then they brought me some food, and I ate until I had enough, and they gave me some clothes, which I wore to make myself decent. Then they took me with them in the ship, and we journeyed many days and nights until fate drove us to a city of tall buildings, all of which overlooked the sea. This city is called the City of the Apes, and when night comes, the inhabitants come out of the gates overlooking the sea and, embarking in boats and ships, spend the night there, for fear that the apes may descend on them from the mountains.

I landed, and while I was enjoying the sights of the city, the ship sailed, without my knowledge. I regretted having disembarked in that city, remembering my companions and what had happened to us with the apes the first and the second time, and I sat down, weeping and mourning. Then one of the inhabitants came to me and said, "Sir, you seem to be a stranger in this place." I replied, "Yes, I am a poor stranger. I was in a ship that anchored here, and I landed to see the sights of the city, and when I went back, I could not find the ship." He said, "Come with us and get into the boat, for if you spend the night here, the apes will destroy you." I said, "I hear and obey," and I got up immediately and embarked with them in the boat, and they pushed it off from the shore until we were a mile away. We spent the night in the boat, and when it was morning, they returned to the city, landed, and each of them went to his business. Such has been their habit every night, and whoever remains behind in the city at night, the apes come and destroy him. During the day, the apes go outside the city and eat of the fruits in the orchards and sleep in the mountains until the evening, at which time they return to the city.

This city is located in the farthest parts of the land of the blacks. One of the strangest things I experienced in the inhabitants' treatment of me was as follows. One of those with whom I spent the night in the boat said to me, "Sir, you are a stranger here. Do you have any craft you can work at?" I replied, "No, by God, my friend, I have no trade and no handicraft, for I was a merchant, a man of property and wealth, and I owned a ship laden with abundant goods, but it was wrecked in the sea, and everything in it sank. I escaped from drowning only by the grace of God, for He provided me with a plank of wood on which I floated and saved myself." When he heard my words, he got up and brought me a cotton bag and said, "Take this bag, fill it with pebbles from the shore, and go with a group of the inhabitants, whom I will help you join and to whom I will commend you, and do as they do, and perhaps you will gain what will help you to return to your country."

Then he took me with him until we came outside the city, where I picked small pebbles until the bag was filled. Soon a group of men emerged from the city, and he put me in their charge and commanded me to them, saying, "This man is a stranger. Take him with you and teach him how to pick, so that he may gain his living and God may reward you." They said, "We hear and obey," and they welcomed me and took me with them, and proceeded, each carrying a cotton bag like mine, filled with pebbles. We walked until we came to a spacious valley, full of trees so tall that no one could climb them. The valley was also full of apes, which, when they saw us, fled and climbed up into the trees. The men began to pelt the apes with the pebbles from the bags, and the apes began to pluck the fruits of those trees and to throw them at the men, and as I looked at the fruits the apes were throwing, I found that they were coconuts.

When I saw what the men were doing, I chose a huge tree full of apes and, advancing to it, began to pelt them, while they plucked the nuts and threw them at me. I began to collect the nuts as the men did, and before my bag was empty of pebbles I had collected plenty of nuts. When the men finished the work, they gathered together all the nuts, and each of them carried as many as he could, and we returned to the city, arriving before the end of the day. Then I went to my friend, who had helped me join the group, and gave him all the nuts I had gathered, thanking him for his kindness, but he said to me, "Take the nuts, sell them, and use the money." Then he gave me a key to a room in his house, saying, "Keep there whatever is left of the nuts, and go out every day with the men, as you did today, and of what you bring with you separate the bad and sell them, and use the money, but keep the best in that room, so that you may gather enough to help you with your voyage." I said to him, "May the Almighty God reward you," and did as he told me, going out daily to gather pebbles, join the men, and do as they did, while they commended me to each other and guided me to the trees bearing the most nuts. I continued in this manner for some time, during which I gathered a great store of excellent coconuts and sold a great many, making a good deal of money, with which I bought whatever I saw and liked. So I thrived and felt happy in that city.

One day, as I was standing on the seashore, a ship arrived, cast anchor, and landed a group of merchants, who proceeded to sell and buy and exchange goods for coconuts and other commodities. I went to my friend and told him about the ship that had arrived and said that I would like to return to my country. He said, "It is for you to decide." So I thanked him for his kindness and bade him farewell. Then I went to the ship, met the captain, and, booking a passage, loaded my store of coconuts on the ship. We set out and continued to sail from sea to sea and from island to island, and at every island we landed, I sold and traded with coconuts until God compensated me with more than I had possessed before and lost.

Among other places we visited, we came to an island abounding in cinnamon and pepper. Some people told us that they had seen on every cluster of peppers a large leaf that shades it and protects it from the rain, and when the rain stops, the leaf flips over and assumes its place at its side. From that island I took with me a large quantity of pepper and cinnamon, in exchange for coconuts. Then we passed by the Island of the 'Usrat, from which comes the Comorin aloewood, and by another island, which is a five-day journey in length and from which comes the Chinese aloewood, which is superior to the Comorin. But the inhabitants of this island are inferior to those of the first, both in their religion and in their way of life, for they are given to lewdness and wine drinking and know no prayer nor the call to prayer. Then we came to the island of the pearl fishers, where I gave the divers some coconuts and asked them to dive, and try my luck for me. They dived in the bay and brought up a great number of large and valuable pearls, saying, "O master, by God, you are very lucky," and I took everything they brought up with me to the ship.

Then we sailed until we reached Basra, where I stayed for a few days, then headed for Baghdad. I came to my quarter, entered my house, and saluted my relatives and friends, and they congratulated me on my safety. Then I stored all the goods and gear I had brought with me, clothed the widows and the orphans, gave alms, and bestowed gifts on my relatives, friends, and all those dear to me. God had given me fourfold what I had lost, and because of my gains and the great profit I had made, I forgot what had happened to me and the toil I had suffered, and resumed my association with my friends and companions. These then are the most extraordinary events of my fifth voyage. Let us have supper now, and tomorrow, come, and I will tell you the story of my sixth voyage, for it is more wonderful than this.

They spread the table, and the guests dined, and when they finished Sindbad gave the porter a hundred pieces of gold, which he took and went on his way, marveling at what he had heard. He spent the night in his house, and as soon as it was morning, he got up, performed his morning prayer, and went to the house of Sindbad the Sailor. He went in and wished him good morning and Sindbad the Sailor asked him to sit and talked to him until the rest of his friends arrived. They talked for a while, then the table was spread, and they ate and drank and enjoyed themselves and felt merry. Then Sindbad the Sailor began the story of the sixth voyage, saying:

The Sixth Voyage of Sindbad

Dear friends, after I returned from my fifth voyage, I forgot what I had suffered, indulging in sport, play, and merriment and leading a life of the utmost joy and happiness until one day a group of merchants came by, showing signs of travel. Their sight reminded me of the days of my return from my travel and my joy at seeing my country again and reuniting with my relatives and friends and dear ones. So I felt a longing for travel and trade, and I resolved to undertake another voyage. I bought valuable, rich merchandise suited to a sea voyage, packed it up in bales, and traveled from Baghdad to Basra. There, I found a large ship, full of prominent people and merchants with valuable goods, and I loaded my bales in the ship, and we departed from Basra peacefully.

We sailed from place to place and from city to city, selling and buying, seeing the sights of the different countries and enjoying our voyage and our good luck and profit. We continued in this way until one day the captain suddenly cried out, screaming, threw down his turban, slapped his face, plucked his beard, and fell down in the hold of the ship, in extreme anguish and grief. All the merchants and other passengers gathered around him and asked, "Captain, what is the matter?" He said, "We have strayed from our course and entered a sea of which we don't know the routes. If God does not provide us with a means of escape from this sea, we will all perish. Pray to the Almighty God to save us from this predicament." Then he climbed the mast, in order to loosen the sails, but a strong wind blew against the ship, driving it backward, and the rudder broke, near a high mountain. The captain came down from the mast and said, "There is no power and no strength save in God the Almighty, the Magnificent, and no one can prevent that which has been decreed. By God, we have fallen into a great peril, from which there is no escape." The passengers wept for themselves and bade each other farewell, having given themselves up for lost. Soon the ship veered toward the mountain and smashed against it, so that its planks scattered, and all that was in it sank into the sea. The merchants fell into the sea, and some of them drowned, while others held onto the mountain and landed on it. I was among those who landed.

That mountain was on a large island whose shores were strewn with wrecked ships and an abundance of goods, gear, and wealth that dazzled the mind, cast there by the sea from the ships that had been destroyed and whose passengers had drowned. I climbed to the upper part of the island, began to explore, and saw a stream of sweet water that issued from one side of the mountain and entered from the other. Then all the other passengers climbed to the upper part and wandered in the island, like madmen, for their minds were confounded by the profusion of goods and wealth they saw strewn on the shores.

I saw in that stream a great many rubies and royal pearls and all kinds of jewels and precious stones, which covered the bed of the stream like gravel, so that all the channels, which ran through the fields, glittered from their profusion. I saw also in that island an abundance of the best Chinese as well as Comorin aloewood. Moreover, in that island there is a gushing spring of some sort of crude ambergris, which flows like wax under the intense heat of the sun, and flows in a stream down to the seashore, where the sea beasts come up, swallow it, and return with it into the sea. When it gets hot in their stomachs, they eject it from their mouths into the water, and it rises to the surface, where it congeals and changes its color. Then the waves throw it on the shore, and the travelers and merchants who know it take it and sell it. As for the crude ambergris that is not swallowed, it flows over the side of that spring and congeals on the ground. When the sun rises, it flows, and its scent fills the whole valley with a musk-like fragrance, and when the sun sets, it congeals again. But that place where the ambergris is found, no one can reach, for the mountains surround the whole island, and no one can climb them.

We continued to wander in that island, marveling at the riches that the Almighty God had created there, but feeling perplexed in our predicament and sorely afraid. We had collected on the shore of the island a small amount of food, which we used sparingly, eating only every day or two, worried that the food would run out and we would die of starvation and fear. Whenever one of us died, we washed him, wrapped him in a shroud from the clothes cast on the shore by the sea, and buried him until most of us had died, except for a few who were weakened by a stomach ailment contracted from the sea. It was not long before all my friends and companions died, one by one.

I was left all alone in the island, with very little food. I wept for myself, thinking, "I wish that I had died before my companions, for they would have at least washed me and buried me. There is no power and no strength save in God the Almighty, the Magnificent." A little while later, I arose and dug for myself a deep hole on the shore, saying to myself, "When I grow weak and feel that I am about to die, I will lie in this grave and die in it, and the wind will blow the sand on me and cover me, and I will have my burial." I blamed myself for my lack of sense in leaving my country and city and traveling to foreign countries, after all I had suffered during the first, the second, the third, the fourth, and the fifth voyages, each marked by greater perils and horrors than the preceding one, each time hardly believing in my narrow escape. And I repented and renounced the sea and all travel in the sea, especially since I had no need of money, of which I had enough and, indeed, so much more that I could not spend or exhaust even half of it for the rest of my life.

After a while, however, I reflected and said to myself, "By God, the stream must have a beginning and an end, and it must lead to an inhabited part. The best plan will be to make a little raft, big enough to sit in, take it down, launch it on the stream, and drift with the current. If I find a way out, I will escape safely, the Almighty God permitting, and if I don't, it is better to die in the stream than in this place," and I sighed for myself.

Then I got up and proceeded to gather pieces of Comorin and Chinese aloewood from the island and tied them together on the shore with the ropes of wrecked ships. Then I took from the ships planks of even size and fixed them firmly on the wood. In this way, I made me a raft, which was a little narrower in width than the width of the stream. Then I attached a piece of wood on each side, to serve as oars, and launched it on the stream. Then I took some of the jewels, precious stones, and pearls that were as large as gravel and some of the best crude, pure ambergris, as well as other goods, together with whatever was left of the food, loaded everything on the raft, and did what the poet said:

> If you suffer injustice, save yourself
> And leave the house behind to mourn its builder.
> Your country you'll replace by another,
> But for yourself, you'll find no other self.
> Nor be too fretful at the blows of fate,
> For every misfortune begins and ends,
> And he who in a certain place his death impends,
> Will in no other place suffer that fate.
> Nor for your mission trust another man,
> For none is as loyal as you yourself.

I drifted with the stream, wondering what would happen to me, until I came to the place where the stream entered beneath the mountain and took the raft with it. I found myself in intense darkness, and the raft bore me with the current through a narrow tunnel beneath the mountain, and the sides of the raft began to rub against the sides of the tunnel, and my head began to rub against the roof. I was unable to go back, and I blamed myself for what I had done to myself and said, "If this tunnel becomes any narrower, the raft will not pass through, and since it cannot go back, I will inevitably perish miserably here." I prostrated myself on the raft, because of the narrowness of the channel, and continued to drift, not knowing night from day, because of the darkness beneath the mountain, and feeling concerned for myself and terrified that I might perish. In this condition, I continued my course along the stream, which sometimes widened and sometimes narrowed, until the intensity of the darkness and distress wearied me, and I fell asleep as I lay prostrate on the raft, which drifted, while I slept in utter oblivion.

When I awoke and opened my eyes, I found myself in the light, in the open air, and found the raft moored to an island, in the middle of a group of Indians and blacks. As soon as they saw me rise, they approached me and spoke to me in their language, but I did not understand what they said and kept thinking that I was still asleep and that this was a dream occasioned by my grief and distress. When they spoke to me, and I did not reply, not knowing their language, one of them came to me and said in Arabic, "Peace be on you, friend! Who are you, from where do you come, and what is the reason for your coming here? We are the owners of these lands and fields, which we came to irrigate, and we found you asleep on the raft. So we held it and moored it here, waiting for you to rise at your leisure. Tell us what is the reason for your coming here?" I said, "For God's sake, sir, bring me some food, for I am hungry. After that ask me what you wish." He hastened and brought me food, and I ate my fill until I felt satisfied and relaxed, and my spirit revived. I praised the Almighty God and rejoiced in my escape from that stream and in my finding them. Then I told them my story from beginning to end and how I had suffered from the narrowness of that stream.

They talked among themselves, saying, "We must take him with us and present him to our king, so that he may tell him his story." Then they took me, together with the raft and all that was on it of goods, jewels, precious stones, and gold ornaments, presented me to their king, and acquainted him with what had happened. He saluted me, welcomed me, and inquired about my condition and what I had experienced. I told him my story from beginning to end, at which he marveled exceedingly and congratulated me on my safety. Then I fetched from the raft a large quantity of jewels, precious stones, ambergris, and aloewood and presented them to the king, who accepted them, treated me very courteously, and gave me a lodging in his palace, where I stayed permanently. I associated with the best and most prominent people, who treated me with great respect. The visitors to that island came to me and questioned me about the affairs of my country, and I told them, and I, in turn, questioned them and was informed about the affairs in their own countries. One day the King himself questioned me about the conditions in my country and the way the caliph governs in Baghdad, and I told him about the caliph's just rule. The king marveled at that and said, "By God, the caliph's methods are wise and his ways praiseworthy, and you have made me love him. Therefore, I would like to prepare a present and send it with you to him." I said, "I hear and obey, my lord. I will convey the present to him and inform him that you are his sincere friend."

I continued to live with the king in great honor, consideration, and contentment for some time until one day, sitting in the king's palace, I heard that a group of people from the city had prepared for themselves a ship, with the intention of sailing to the environs of Basra. I said to myself, "I cannot do better than to travel with these people." I arose at once and, kissing the king's hand, informed him of my wish to travel with that group in the ship they had prepared, for I longed for my country and my family. The king said, "The decision is yours, yet if you wish to stay with us, we will be very glad, for we have enjoyed your company." I said, "By God, my lord, you have overwhelmed me with your kindness and your favors, but I long for my country and my family and friends." When he heard my reply, he summoned the merchants who had prepared the ship, commended me to them, paid my fare, and bestowed on me a great many gifts. He also entrusted me with a magnificent gift for the Caliph Harun al-Rashid in Baghdad. Then I bade the king, as well as my frequent companions, farewell and embarked with the merchants in the ship.

We sailed with a fair wind, committing ourselves to the care of the Almighty and Glorious God, and continued to travel from sea to sea and from island to island until, with the permission of the Almighty God, we reached Basra safely. I disembarked and spent a few days there to equip myself and pack up my goods. Then I headed for Baghdad, the Abode of Peace, and went to the Caliph Harun al-Rashid and conveyed the king's gift to him. Then I came to my quarter, entered my house, and stored my goods and gear. Soon my relatives and friends came to see me, and I bestowed gifts on all, and gave alms.

A little while later, the caliph summoned me and asked me the reason for the gift and from where it came. I said, "By God, O Commander of the Faithful, I do not know the name of the city from which this gift came, nor do I know the way to it. When the ship I was in was wrecked, I landed on an island, where I made me a raft and launched it on a stream in the middle of that island." Then I related to him what had happened to me on my journey and how I had escaped from the stream and reached that city safely. I also related to him what had happened to me in that city and explained the reason for the gift. The caliph marveled exceedingly, and he ordered the historians to record my story and deposit it in his library, so that whoever reads it might be edified by it, and he treated me very generously.

I resumed my former way of life in Baghdad and forgot all that I had experienced and suffered, living a life of sport, play, and pleasure. This, then, friends, is the story of my sixth voyage. Tomorrow, God the Almighty willing, I will tell you the story of my seventh voyage, for it is stranger and more wonderful than all the others.

Sindbad ordered that the table be spread, and the guests dined with him. Then Sindbad the Sailor gave Sindbad the Porter a hundred pieces of gold, and the porter took the money and went on his way, as did the rest of the company, all marveling exceedingly at that story. Sindbad the Porter spent the night at his house, and as soon as he performed his morning prayer, he went to the house of Sindbad the Sailor. Then the rest of the group began to arrive, and when they were

all assembled, Sindbad the Sailor began to tell them the story of his
seventh voyage, saying,

The Seventh Voyage of Sindbad

Fellows, after I returned from my sixth voyage, I resumed my former
way of life and continued to lead a life of contentment and happiness,
indulging day and night in play, diversion, and pleasure, having
secured great gains and profits, until I began to long again to sail the
seas, associate with fellow merchants, see foreign countries, and hear
new things. I made my resolve and, packing up a quantity of precious
goods suited to a sea voyage, carried them from Baghdad to Basra,
where I found a ship ready to set sail, with a group of prominent merchants. I embarked with them, and we became friends, as we sailed
with a fair wind in peace and good health until we passed by a city
called the City of China, and while we were in the utmost joy and
happiness, talking among ourselves about travel and commerce, a violent head wind blew suddenly, and a heavy rain began to fall on us
until we and our babies were drenched. So we covered the bales with
felt and canvas, fearing that the goods would be spoiled by the rain,
and began to pray and implore God the Almighty to deliver us from
the peril we were in. Then the captain, girding his waist and tucking
up his clothes, climbed up the mast and began to look to the right and
left. Then he looked at the people in the ship and began to slap his
face and pluck his beard. We asked him, "Captain, what is the matter?" And he said, "Implore the Almighty God for deliverance from
the peril we are in, and weep for yourselves and bid each other
farewell, for the wind has prevailed against us and driven us into the
farthest of the seas of the world." He then descended from the mast,
opened a chest, and took out of it a cotton bag. Then he untied the
bag, took out of it some dust, like ashes, wetted it with water, and,
waiting a little, smelled it. Then he took out of the chest a small book
and began to read in it. Then he said to us, "Passengers, in this book
there is an amazing statement that whoever comes to this place will
never leave it safely and will surely perish, for this region is called the
Province of the Kings, and in it is the tomb of our Lord Solomon, the
son of David (peace be on him), and there are huge, horrible-looking
whales, and whenever a ship enters this region, one of them rises from
the sea and swallows it with everything in it."

When we heard the captain's explanation, we were dumbfounded,
and hardly had he finished his words when the ship suddenly began to
rise out of the water and drop again, and we heard a great cry, like a

peel of thunder, at which we were struck almost dead with terror, sure of our destruction. Suddenly we saw a whale heading for the boat, like a towering mountain, and we were terrified and wept bitterly for ourselves and prepared for death. We kept looking at that whale, marveling at its terrible shape, when suddenly another whale, the most huge and most terrible we had ever seen, approached us, and while we bade each other farewell and wept for ourselves, a third whale, even greater than the other two, approached, and we were stupefied and driven mad with terror. Then the three whales began to circle the ship, and the third whale lunged at the ship to swallow it, when suddenly a violent gust of wind blew, and the ship rose and fell on a massive reef, breaking in pieces, and all the merchants and the other passengers and the bales sank in the sea.

I took off all my clothes, except for a shirt, and swam until I caught a plank of wood from the ship and hung on to it. Then I got on it and held on to it, while the wind and the waves toyed with me on the surface of the water, carrying me up and down. I was in the worst of plights, with fear and distress and hunger and thirst. I blamed myself for what I had done and for incurring more hardships, after a life of ease, and said to myself, "O Sindbad the Sailor, you don't learn, for every time you suffer hardships and weariness, yet you don't repent and renounce travel in the sea, and when you renounce, you lie to yourself. I deserve my plight, which had been decreed by God the Almighty to cure me of my greed, which is the root of all my suffering, for I have abundant wealth." I returned to my reason and said to myself, "In this voyage, I repent to the Almighty God with a sincere repentance, and I will never again embark on travel, nor mention it, nor even think of it, for the rest of my life." I continued to implore the Almighty God and to weep, recalling my former days of play and pleasure and cheer and contentment and happiness.

I continued in this condition for a whole day and a second, at the end of which I came to a large island abounding in trees and streams. I landed and ate of the fruits of those trees and drank of the waters of those streams until I felt refreshed and regained my strength and recovered my spirit. Then I walked in the island and found on the other side a great river of sweet water, running with a strong current, and I remembered the raft I had made last time and said to myself, "I must make me a raft like that one; perhaps I will get out of here. If I get out safely, I will have my wish and vow to the Almighty God to foreswear travel, and if I perish, I will find rest from toil and misery."

Then I gathered many pieces of wood from the trees, which were of the finest sandalwood, the like of which does not exist anywhere else, although I did not know it at the time. Then I found a way to twist grasses and twigs into a kind of rope, with which I bound the raft, say-ing to myself, "If I escape safely, it will be by the grace of God." Then I got on the raft and proceeded along the river, leaving that part of the island behind. I lay on the raft for three days. I did not eat, but I drank from the water of the river, to quench my thirst, until I was giddy like a young bird from extreme weariness, hunger, and fear.

At the end of this time, the raft brought me to a high mountain, beneath which ran the river. When I saw this, I was frightened, recall-ing what I had suffered from the narrowness of that other stream dur-ing my preceding voyage. I tried to stop the raft and get off on the side of the mountain, but the current overpowered me and drew the raft, with me on it, beneath the mountain. I was sure that I would per-ish and said, "There is no power and no strength save in God the Almighty, the Magnificent," but after a short distance, the raft emerged in a wide space, a great valley, through which the river roared with a noise like thunder and ran with a swiftness like that of the wind. I held on to the raft, for fear of falling, while the waves tossed it to the right and left in the middle of the river. The raft con-tinued to descend with the current, along the valley, while I was unable to stop or steer it toward the bank, until it brought me to a large, well-built, and populous city. When the people saw me on the raft, descending in the middle of the river with the current, they cast a net and ropes on the raft and drew it ashore.

I fell among them like a dead man, from extreme hunger, lack of sleep, and fear. Soon there approached me from among the people a venerable old man, who welcomed me and threw over me an abun-dance of handsome clothes, which I put on to make myself decent. Then he took me to the bath and brought me refreshing cordials and sweet perfumes. After the bath, he took me to his house, and his fam-ily received me joyfully. Then he seated me in a pleasant place and prepared sumptuous food for me, and I ate my fill and thanked the Almighty God for my safety. Then his pages brought me hot water, with which I washed my hands, and his maids brought me silk towels, with which I dried them and wiped my mouth. Then he prepared for me a private apartment in a part of his house and charged his pages and maids to wait on me and fulfill my needs, and they served me attentively. I stayed in the guest apartment for three days, enjoying delicious food and drink and sweet scents, until my fear subsided, my energy returned, and I felt at ease.

On the fourth day, the old man came to me and said, "Son, we have enjoyed your company, and God be praised for your safety. Would you like now to go down with me to the bank of the river and sell your goods in the market? Perhaps with the money you get, you will buy something with which to traffic." I remained silent for a while, thinking to myself, "What goods do I have, and what does he mean?" He added, "Son, don't worry and don't think too much about it. Let us go to the market, and if we find anyone who will offer a price that will content you, I will receive the money for you, and if we don't, I will keep them for you in my storerooms until the days of buying and selling arrive." I thought about it and said to myself, "Let me do what he asks and see what these goods are." Then I said to him, "Uncle, I hear and obey. I cannot contradict you in anything, for what you do has God's blessing." So I went with him to the market and found out that he had taken the raft apart and delivered the sandalwood, of which it was made, to the broker who was announcing it for sale. The merchants came and opened the bidding, and they increased their offers until the bidding stopped at one thousand dinars. Then the old man turned to me and said, "Listen, son, this is the price of your goods at the present time. Would you like to sell them at this price, or would you like to wait and let me keep them for you in my storerooms to sell them for a higher price at the right time?" I replied, "Sir, I leave it to you; do as you wish." He said, "Son, will you sell me this wood for a hundred dinars above what the merchants have offered?" I said, "Yes, it is done." Then he ordered his servants to carry the wood to his storerooms, and we returned to his house, where we sat, and he counted the money in payment for the wood and, fetching bags, put the money in them, locked them up with an iron lock, and gave me the key.

Some days later, the old man said to me, "Son, I would like to propose something to you, and I hope that you will comply." I said, "What is it?" He replied, "Son, I am a very old man, and I am without a son, but I do have a daughter who is young and charming and endowed with great wealth and beauty. I would like to marry her to you, so that you may live with her here in our country. Then I will give you all I have, for I have become an old man, and you will take my place." I remained silent, and he added, "Son, accept my proposal, for I wish you good. If you obey me, I will marry my daughter to you, and you will be as my son and will possess all I have. If you wish to travel to your country and engage in trade, no one will prevent you. This is your property, at your disposal, to do with it what you wish and choose." I said to him, "By God, uncle, you have become as a father to me. I have suffered many horrors that have rendered me bewildered and lacking in judgment. It is for you to decide as you wish." Then he ordered his pages to bring the judge and witnesses, and when they came, he married me to his daughter, celebrating with a great entertainment and a great feast. When I went in to my wife, I found her extremely beautiful, with a graceful figure and a lovely gait, clad in rich apparel and covered with gold ornaments, necklaces, jewels, and precious stones, worth thousands of thousands of dinars and beyond the means of anyone. When I saw her, she pleased me, and we loved one another. I lived with her for some time, leading an extremely happy and joyful life. Soon her father died and was admitted to the mercy of God. We prepared him and buried him, and I took possession of all his property, and his servants became my servants to serve me at my bidding. Then the merchants appointed me to his office, for he was their chief, and that meant that none of them purchased anything without his knowledge and permission.

When I mingled with the people of the city, I noticed that they were transformed at the beginning of each month, in that they grew wings with which they flew to the upper region of the sky, and no one remained in the city except women and children. I said to myself, "When the first day of the month comes, I will ask some of them to carry me with them to where they go." When the day came, and their colors and shapes changed, I went to one of them and said, "For God's sake, carry me with you, so that I may divert myself and then return." He said, "This is not possible," but I pressed him until he granted me the favor. So I went with them, without telling any of my family or servants or friends, and he took me on his back and flew with me up into the air and kept flying upward until we were so high that I heard the angels glorifying God in the vault of heaven. I marveled at that and exclaimed, "Glory be to God, and His is the praise."

Hardly had I finished my prayer when a fire came out of heaven and almost consumed us. They flew down and, dropping me on a high mountain, departed, feeling very angry with me, and left me alone. I blamed myself for what I had done and said to myself, "There is no power and no strength, save in God the Almighty, the Magnificent. Every time I escape from a calamity, I fall into a worse one."

I sat on the mountain, not knowing where to go, when suddenly two young men passed by. They were like twin moons, each holding a walking staff of red gold. I approached them and saluted them, and they returned my salutation. Then I asked them, "For God's sake, tell me who and what you are." They replied, "We are servants of the Almighty God," and, giving me a walking staff of gold, like the ones they had with them, went on their way and left me. I walked along the ridge of the mountain, leaning on the staff and wondering about the two young men, when suddenly a serpent emerged from beneath the mountain, with a man in its mouth, whom it had swallowed to his navel, while he was screaming and crying out, "Whoever delivers me, God will deliver him from every difficulty." I went close to the serpent

and struck it on its head with the gold staff, and it threw the man from
its mouth. Then he approached me and said, "Since you have saved
me from this serpent, I will never leave you, and you have become my
companion on this mountain."

Soon a group of people approached us, and when I looked, I saw
among them the man who had carried me on his shoulders and flew
up with me. I approached him and, speaking courteously to him,
offered my apologies and said, "Friend, this is not the way friends treat
friends." He replied, "It was you who almost destroyed us by glorifying God on my back." I said, "Excuse me, for I had no knowledge of
this, and I will never utter another word again." Finally, he consented
to take me with him, on condition that I would refrain from mentioning the name of God or glorifying Him on his back. Then he carried
me and flew up with me, as he had done before, until he brought me
to my house.

My wife met me, greeted me, and, congratulating me on my safety,
said, "Beware of going out again or associating with those people, for
they are brothers of the devils and do not worship God." I asked her,
"But how did your father then get along with them?" She replied,
"My father was not one of them, nor did he as they did. Now that he
is dead, I think that you should sell all our possessions, buy goods with
the money, and go back to your country and family, and I will go with
you, for I have no reason to stay in this city, since both my father and
mother are dead." So I sold my father-in-law's property, little by little,
and waited to find someone who would go to Baghdad, so that I might
go with him.

Soon, a group of men in the city decided to travel and, failing to
find a ship, bought wood and built for themselves a large one. I
booked passage with them, paying them the fare in full, and embarked
with my wife and all we could carry of our property, leaving our land
and buildings behind. We set out and sailed with a fair wind from sea
to sea and from island to island until we reached Basra, where, without tarrying, I booked passage on a boat and, loading our belongings,
headed for Baghdad. Then I came to my quarter, entered my house,
and met my family and friends and loved ones, and stored in my storerooms all the goods I had brought with me. My family had given up
hope of my return, for when they calculated the time of my absence
during the seventh voyage, they found that it was twenty-seven years.
When I related to them all my experiences, they marveled exceedingly
and congratulated me on my safety.

Then I vowed to the Almighty God never to travel again by land or
sea, after the seventh voyage, which was the one to end all voyages. I
also refrained from indulging my appetites and thanked the Almighty
and Glorious God and praised Him and glorified Him for having

brought me back to my native country and to my family. Consider, O Sindbad the Porter, what I had gone through.

Sindbad the Porter said to Sindbad the Sailor, "For God's sake, pardon me the wrong I did you," and they continued to enjoy their fellowship and friendship, in all cheer and joy, until there came to them death, the destroyer of delights, sunderer of companies, wrecker of palaces, and builder of tombs.

THE STORY OF 'ALI BABA
AND THE FORTY THIEVES

In one of the cities of Persia, there lived two brothers, one named Qasim and the other 'Ali Baba. As they shared equally the little their father left them, it seemed that their means should have been equal. But luck had it otherwise, for Qasim married a woman who, shortly after their marriage, inherited a well-stocked shop, a storehouse filled with fine goods, and much wealth buried in the ground. Thus Qasim became a wealthy man, one of the richest merchants of the city. 'Ali Baba, on the other hand, married a woman who was as poor as he was and lived in great poverty, and his only means to earn a living and support himself and his children was to cut firewood in a neighboring forest and sell it in town, loaded on three asses, which were his only possessions.

One day, 'Ali Baba was in the forest, having cut enough wood to load his asses with, when he saw a great cloud of dust rising high in the air and moving toward him. When he looked closely, he saw a troop of horsemen advancing rapidly. Although there had not been any mention of bandits in these parts, 'Ali Baba thought that these horsemen might well be. Thinking only of saving himself, without considering what might happen to his asses, he climbed a large tree, whose branches, at some height from the ground, fanned out in a circle, leaving very little space between each other. He positioned himself in between, with all the more assurance, since he could see without being seen, especially since that tree grew beside a solitary and much higher rock, which was so steep that no one could climb it from any side.

The horsemen, big, strong, well-armed, and doughty riders, came close to the rock and dismounted, and 'Ali Baba, who observed that they were forty in number, was convinced by their demeanor and outfits that they were bandits. He was not mistaken, for they were in fact robbers who, refraining from doing any harm in that vicinity, carried out their robberies in faraway places and came back to meet at that place, and what 'Ali Baba saw them do convinced him of that. Each horseman unbridled his horse, hung around his neck a bag of barley, which he had carried on the back of the horse, and all carried their bags, most of which seemed to 'Ali Baba to be so heavy that he concluded that they were full of coins of gold and silver. The man who seemed to be the captain, carrying his bag like the others, approached the rock and came very close to the large tree where 'Ali Baba was hiding, and after he went through some shrubs, 'Ali Baba distinctly heard him utter these words, "Open, sesame!" As soon as the captain pronounced these words, a door opened, and after he let all the men pass and go in before him, he too went in, and the door closed.

The robbers remained inside the rock for a long time, and 'Ali Baba, who feared that if he left his hiding place to escape, one of the men or all of them might come out, was forced to stay on the tree and wait patiently. He was tempted, however, to climb down, take two horses, mounting one and leading the others by the bridle, and ride to the city, driving on his three asses before him. But the uncertainty of the outcome made him take the safest course of action. At last, the door opened, and the forty thieves came out, but the captain, who had gone in last, came out first, and after watching them file past him, he closed the doors by pronouncing these words, "Shut, sesame!" Then each thief returned to his horse, bridled it, and, fastening his saddle bags, mounted. When the captain saw at last that they were all ready to depart, he rode at their head and took the road by which they had come.

However, 'Ali Baba did not come down from the tree, saying to himself, "They may have forgotten something, which may force them to return, and I will find myself trapped." He followed them with his eyes until he lost sight of them, and he did not climb down until much later, for greater security. As he had memorized the words by which the captain of the thieves had opened and closed the door, he was curious to find out whether, if pronounced by him, they would have the same effect. He went through the shrubs and saw the door, which was hidden behind. He stood in front of it and said, "Open, sesame!" and instantly the door flew wide open.

'Ali Baba had expected to find a dark and gloomy place, but he was surprised to see a well-lighted, large, and spacious place, carved by hand out of the rock, with a high vault through which the light streamed through an opening made on top of the rock for that purpose. He saw a great deal of provisions, piles of bales of valuable merchandise, such as silk fabrics and brocades and precious carpets, and above all, a great quantity of gold and silver coins in large bags and leather purses piled on each other. In seeing all this, it seemed to him that this cavern had been serving as a hiding place, not for years, but for centuries, for generation after generation of thieves.

'Ali Baba did not hesitate about what to do. He went into the cavern, and as soon as he was inside, the door closed. But this did not worry him, for he knew the secret of opening it. He paid no attention to the silver, but occupied himself mainly with the gold coins, particularly those that were in the bags, from which he kept taking out as much as he could carry until he had what his three asses could bear. He gathered the asses, which were scattered, and when he brought them near the rock, he loaded them with the bags, which he hid under some firewood in such a way that no one could see them. When he finished, he stood before the door, and no sooner had he said, "Shut, sesame," than it closed, for it closed by itself each time he entered, and it remained open each time he went out.

Then 'Ali Baba took the road to the city, and when he came home, he took his asses into a small courtyard and closed the door very carefully. Then he set down the wood with which he had covered the bags and took them into the house, placing and arranging them before his wife, who was sitting on a sofa.

His wife felt the bags and, finding them full of money, suspected that her husband had stolen them, so that when he finished bringing all of them in, she could not prevent herself from saying to him, "Could you have been so wretched, as to . . . ?" But he interrupted her, saying, "Nonsense, wife, I am not a thief, unless one is considered so for taking away from thieves. You will cease to have such an opinion of me, when I acquaint you with my good fortune." Then he emptied the bags, which were full of gold, which dazzled his wife. He then related to her his adventure from beginning to end and concluded by asking her to keep it secret.

His wife, having recovered from fear, rejoiced with her husband at their good fortune and wanted to count piece by piece all the gold coins before her, but 'Ali Baba said to her, "Wife, you are not wise; what do you intend to do, and when will you finish counting? I will dig a hole and hide the coins in it. We don't have time to lose." His wife replied, "It is good to have at least some idea of the amount. I will fetch a small scale from the neighbors, and I will weigh the gold while you dig the hole." 'Ali Baba said, "Wife, what you wish to do is useless. If you believe me, you will desist. Do as you please, but remember to keep the secret."

To satisfy herself, 'Ali Baba's wife went to the house of her brother-in-law Qasim, which was nearby. As he was not at home, she addressed herself to his wife, asking her to lend her a scale for a few moments. Her sister-in-law asked her whether she wanted a large or a small one, and 'Ali Baba's wife replied that she wanted a small one. The sister-in-law said, "Gladly! Wait a moment, while I bring it." Then she went to look for it and found it, but as she was aware of 'Ali Baba's poverty, she was curious to know what kind of grain his wife wanted to weigh. So she decided to grease the pan of the scale. After she did so, she returned and gave it to 'Ali Baba's wife, excusing her delay by telling her that she had difficulty in finding it.

'Ali Baba's wife went home and, setting the scale on the pile of gold, began to fill it and empty it aside on the sofa until she weighed it all and was pleased with the large amount, of which she informed her husband, who had just finished digging the hole. While he was hiding the gold, his wife, in order to show her sister-in-law her punctuality and diligence, took back the scale, without noticing that a gold coin was stuck to it. She gave her the scale, saying, "Sister-in-law, you see that I did not keep your scale for long; here it is. I am much obliged." No sooner had she turned her back, than Qasim's wife inspected the pan of the scale, and when she found the gold coin, she was inexpressibly surprised and forthwith stricken with envy. She said to herself, "What! 'Ali Baba has gold in quantity, and where did the wretched fellow get it from?"

As has been mentioned, her husband Qasim was not at home; he was at his shop, from which he was not supposed to return till evening. So the time she spent waiting for him seemed to her like a century, because of her great impatience to tell him the news, which should surprise him no less than it surprised her. When he came home, she said to him, "Qasim, you think that you are rich, but you are wrong. 'Ali Baba has infinitely more wealth than you. He does not count his gold as you do; he weighs it." Qasim asked her to explain this mystery, and she explained, telling him by what means she had found out and showing him the piece of gold she had found stuck to the pan of the scale. It was a piece so ancient that the name of the king inscribed on it was unknown to him. Far from feeling happy at his brother's good fortune, which would deliver him from his misery, Qasim felt a mortal jealousy and spent almost the entire night without sleeping.

The next day, before sunrise, he went to the house of his brother, whom he had not treated as a brother and whose mention he had forgotten ever since his marriage to the rich widow. He went up to him and said, " 'Ali Baba, you are quite discreet in your affairs. You pretend to be poor, miserable, and destitute, yet you weigh your gold." 'Ali Baba replied, "Brother, I don't know what you are talking about. Explain yourself." Qasim said, "Don't pretend to be ignorant," and, showing him the piece of gold, put it in his hand, adding, "How many pieces do you have similar to this one that my wife found stuck to the pan of the scale your wife came to borrow from her yesterday?"

At these words, 'Ali Baba realized that Qasim and his wife, thanks to his own wife's hardheadedness, had already found out what he was very much interested in keeping secret, but the mistake was made, and he could not remedy it. So, without showing his brother any signs of surprise or regret, he admitted the fact and told him by what chance he had discovered the thieves' hiding place and where it was, offering, if he would keep the secret, to share the treasure with him. Qasim replied arrogantly, "I do, very much," adding, "But I want to know precisely the place where this treasure is and the signs and marks, as well as how I can get in by myself, when I want to; otherwise, I will denounce you to the authorities. If you refuse, you will lose, not only any hope for it, but also the part you have already taken, which I will receive as a reward for denouncing you." 'Ali Baba, driven more by his good nature than by the insolent threats of a barbarous brother, told him clearly all he wanted to know, even the words he had to use for getting in and out of the cavern.

Qasim asked no more questions of 'Ali Baba. He left him, determined to get to the treasure first, and, full of hope to get it all for himself, he departed the next day, before dawn, with ten mules loaded with large chests he intended to fill, planning to take a greater number on a second trip, according to the amount he would find in the cavern. He took the road 'Ali Baba had told him to take, and when he came near the rock, he recognized the signs and the tree in which 'Ali Baba had hidden himself. He looked for the door and found it, and, in order to open it, he pronounced the words, "Open, sesame." The door opened, and as soon as he entered, it closed. He examined the cavern and was struck with great admiration to find even greater riches than he had expected from 'Ali Baba's account, and his admiration grew even greater as he examined each thing by itself. Being greedy and fond of riches, he spent the day feasting his eyes on so much gold, so much so that he forgot that he had come to take it and load it on the ten mules. At last, he picked as many bags as he could carry, but when he came to the door to open it, with his mind preoccupied with all sorts of ideas, save what mattered most, he found that he had forgotten the necessary words, and, instead of saying, "sesame," he said, "Open, barley," and was very much surprised to find that the door, far from opening, remained shut. He named several other grains, save the one he had to name, but the door did not open.

Qasim had not expected this outcome. In the great peril in which he found himself, he was seized by fear, and the more effort he made to recall the word "sesame," the more muddled his memory became until it was as if he had never heard this word before. He threw down the bags he was carrying and began to pace nervously inside the cavern, from one side to another, without being moved by any of the riches by which he was surrounded. He deplored his fate, but he did not deserve any pity.

Toward noon, the thieves returned to their cavern, and when, from some distance they saw Qasim's mules around the rock, loaded with chests, they were upset by this unusual sight. They advanced at a gallop and drove away the mules, which Qasim had neglected to tie and which for this reason ran freely, in such a way that they scattered here and there, far into the forest, and were soon out of sight. The thieves did not bother to run after them, for they were more interested in find-ing the person to whom they belonged. While some of them rode around the rock, looking for him, the captain dismounted with the rest and, going directly to the door, with his sword in his hand, pro-nounced the words, and the door opened.

Qasim, who heard the sound of the horses from the middle of the cavern, did not doubt the arrival of the thieves, nor his impending destruction. Determined to make at least an effort to escape from their hands and save himself, he stood, ready to jump outside, as soon as the door opened. No sooner did he see the door open, after he heard the word "sesame," which had escaped his memory, than he lunged out, so brusquely that he knocked the captain down. But he did not escape the other thieves, who too had their swords in their hands and who killed him on the spot.

After the execution, the thieves' first concern was to go into the cav-ern, where they found near the door the bags that Qasim had begun to carry, in order to take them out and load them on his mules. They put the bags back in their place, without noticing those which 'Ali Baba had taken before. In deliberating and consulting together on this event, they understood well how Qasim was able to come out of the cavern, but they could not guess how he was able to get in. It occurred to them that he could have descended from the top of the cavern, but the opening from which the light came was so high, and the top of the rock was so inaccessible from the outside, besides the fact that there was no indication that he had done it, that they all agreed it was beyond their imagination. That he went in through the door was something they could not believe, unless he knew the secret of opening it, but they thought for certain that they were the only ones who knew it. In this they were of course mistaken, being unaware that 'Ali Baba, who had spied on them, knew it.

No matter how it was done, since their joint riches seemed still intact, they agreed to quarter Qasim's body and to keep it inside the cavern, near the door, placing two pieces on one side and two on the other, in order to scare anyone who might be bold enough to make a similar attempt. They also agreed not to return to the cavern until the stench of the corpse was gone. Having made this decision, they carried it out, and when they no longer had anything to keep them there, they carefully shut the door of their hiding place, mounted their horses, and went to scour the countryside, taking the routes frequented by caravans, in order to attack them and rob them, as usual.

Meanwhile, Qasim's wife was terribly worried when she saw that it was late at night and her husband had not returned. She went to 'Ali Baba's house in alarm and said to him, "Brother-in-law, I believe that you know that your brother Qasim has gone into the forest and for what reason. It is late, and he has not returned yet, and I fear that some mishap might have happened to him." 'Ali Baba, who, after his conversation with his brother, had suspected that he would go on this trip, and, for this reason, had refrained from going into the forest that day, in order not to antagonize him, without voicing any reproach that might offend her or her husband, if he was still alive, said to her that it was too early to be alarmed and that Qasim must have thought it proper not to return to the city until late at night.

Qasim's wife agreed, all the more easily when she considered how important it was for her husband to carry out his mission secretly. She returned to her house and waited patiently till midnight. But, beyond that point, her alarms redoubled, with an agony all the more acute, since she could not give it vent or relieve it with cries that might reveal the secret cause to her neighbors. In case her mistake proved irreparable, she regretted her foolish curiosity and reprehensible desire to meddle into the affairs of her brother-in-law and sister-in-law. She spent the night crying, and, as soon as it was dawn, she ran to them and announced to them what had brought her there, by her tears, rather than her words.

'Ali Baba did not wait for his sister-in-law to ask him to be so good as to go and see what happened to his brother. He departed immediately and went into the forest with his three asses, after he advised her to calm herself. He saw neither his brother nor his ten mules on the road, and when he approached the rock, he was surprised to see blood spilled near the door and had a bad premonition. He went to the door and pronounced the words, and when it opened, he was struck by the sad sight of the quartered body of his brother. He did not hesitate on what he had to do to perform his last duties toward his brother, forgetting how little fraternal love his brother had shown him. He found in the cavern something with which to wrap up the four pieces of his brother's body, which he wrapped up in two bundles, loaded on one of his asses, and hid under some firewood. Then, without losing any time, he loaded the two other asses with bags full of gold and firewood on top, as he had done the first time. As soon as he finished and commanded the door to close, he took the road back to the city, taking the precaution to stop for some time at the forest exit, in order not to enter the city until it was night. When he arrived, he took inside only the two asses loaded with the gold, and, after he left to his wife the task of unloading them and telling her in a few words of Qasim's fate, he led the other ass to his sister-in-law.

'Ali Baba knocked at the door, and it was opened by Marjana. This Marjana was a clever slave-girl, knowledgeable and full of resources for coping with the most difficult tasks, and 'Ali Baba knew her to be so. When he entered the courtyard, he unloaded the firewood and the two bundles and, taking Marjana aside, said to her, "Marjana, the first thing I ask of you is an inviolable secret. You will see how necessary it is, as much for your mistress as for myself, when you see the body of your master in these two bundles. We must bury him as if he has died of natural causes. Let me speak to your mistress, and listen carefully to what I will say to her."

Marjana announced him to her mistress, and 'Ali Baba, who followed her, entered. The sister-in-law asked 'Ali Baba with great impatience, "Well, brother-in-law, what news do you bring of my husband? I see nothing in your face to comfort me." 'Ali Baba replied, "Sister-in-law, I cannot tell you anything before you promise to listen to what I have to say, from beginning to end, without interrupting me. It is no less important for you than for me, in the light of what has happened, to keep strict secrecy, for your peace and welfare." The sister-in-law said, without raising her voice, "Ah! This introduction tells me that my husband is dead, yet I realize the necessity for the secrecy you demand. I must force myself. Tell me; I am listening."

'Ali Baba informed his sister-in-law of the outcome of his trip till his arrival with Qasim's body, adding, "Sister-in-law, this is a painful event for you, all the more so, since you had not expected it to be as bad. Although the harm is irremediable, if anything is capable of consoling you, I offer to marry you and join the little God has given me with yours, and I assure you that my wife will not be jealous and that you will be able to live together. If you find my proposition agreeable, we must plan to proceed so as to make it appear that my brother died of natural causes. It seems to me that this is a matter you can entrust to Marjana and to which I, for my part, will contribute all I can."

What better course of action could Qasim's widow take but that which 'Ali Baba proposed, she who, after the death of her first husband, who left her much wealth, found another husband who was richer than she, and who, by his discovery of the treasure, could become even richer? She did not refuse the proposal, but, on the contrary, looked on it as a means of consoling herself. By wiping off her tears, which she had begun to shed profusely, and by suppressing the cries normal for women who have lost their husbands, she gave 'Ali Baba a sufficient sign that she had accepted his offer.

'Ali Baba left Qasim's widow in this state, and after he reminded Marjana to take good care of her charge, he returned home with his ass. Marjana did not forget; she left at the same time as 'Ali Baba and went to a druggist's shop, which was in the neighborhood. She knocked at the door, and when it was opened, she asked for some kind of tablets very effective against the most dangerous diseases. The druggist gave her some, according to the money she gave him, and asked her who was ill in her master's house. She replied with a deep sigh,

"Ah! It is Qasim himself, my good master. We don't know a thing about his sickness; he neither speaks nor wishes to eat." With these words, she carried the tablets, which, in truth, Qasim was no longer in a condition to make use of.

The next day, Marjana went to the same druggist and, with tears in her eyes, asked for an extract that people usually gave to the sick as a last resort and despaired if this extract did not revive them. She received the drug from the hand of the druggist, saying in deep pain, "Alas! I am very much afraid that this drug will not be any more effective than the tablets. Ah, that I should lose a good master!" Furthermore, as people saw 'Ali Baba and his wife go all day long back and forth to Qasim's house, with a sad demeanor, they were not surprised to hear toward evening the pitiful cries of Qasim's wife and especially Marjana, who announced that Qasim had died.

The next day, as soon as it was daylight, Marjana, who knew that there was on the square a cobbler who was a good man, very advanced in age, who every day was the first to open his shop, much earlier than the others, went out to see him. She went up to him and, wishing him good morning, put a gold coin in his hand. Baba Mustafa, who was known to everyone by this name and who was cheerful by nature and always had a ready word for banter, squinted at the coin, because it was not light yet, and, seeing that it was gold, said, "Good first gift of the day! What do you want? Here I am, ready to serve you." Marjana said, "Baba Mustafa, take whatever you need for sewing and come quickly with me, but on condition that I put a bandage over your eyes when we come to such and such a place." At these words, Baba Mustafa pretended to be difficult, saying, "Oh, oh! you want me to do something against my conscience and my honor!" Marjana put another gold coin in his hand and said, "God forbid that I should ask you to do anything you could not do honorably. Just come, and fear nothing."

Baba Mustafa followed Marjana, who, after bandaging his eyes with a handkerchief at the place she had indicated, led him to the house of her deceased master, and she did not remove the handkerchief until they were in the room where she had put the body, placing each quarter in its proper place. When she removed the handkerchief, she said to him, "Baba Mustafa, I brought you here, so that you may sew together these pieces. Don't lose any time, and when you finish, I will give you another gold coin." When Baba Mustafa finished his work, Marjana again put the bandage over his eyes, in the same room, and after giving him the third gold coin, which she had promised him, and asking him to keep the secret, led him back to the same place where she had first placed the bandage over his eyes. There, after she removed the bandage again, she let him return to his shop, following him with her eyes until he disappeared from sight, lest he should be curious to retrace his steps, in order to spy on her.

Marjana had heated some water to wash Qasim's body. So 'Ali Baba, who arrived just as she returned, washed it, perfumed it with incense, and wrapped it in a shroud, with the usual ceremonies. Then the joiner brought the coffin that 'Ali Baba had taken care to order. In order to prevent him from noticing anything, Marjana received the coffin at the door and, after paying him and sending him on his way, assisted 'Ali Baba in placing the body inside. After 'Ali Baba nailed down the top planks firmly, she went to the mosque to say that all was ready for the burial. The men at the mosque, whose function it was to wash the body, offered to perform the task, but she told them that it had been done already, and she had hardly returned when the religious leader and other clergymen from the mosque arrived. Four neighbors, who had assembled there, carried the coffin on their shoulders and followed the leader, as he recited his prayers, to the cemetery.

As for Qasim's wife, she stayed at home, grieving and uttering pitiful cries with the women of the neighborhood, who, according to custom, went to her house during the funeral and joined her with their lamentations, filling with grief the whole neighborhood and beyond. In this way, the baleful manner of Qasim's death was hidden, and 'Ali Baba, his widow, and Marjana kept the secret so well, that, far from knowing it, no one in the whole city had the slightest suspicion of it.

Three days after Qasim's burial, 'Ali Baba moved the little furniture he had, together with the money he had taken from the thieves' treasure, which he carried only at night, to the house of his brother's widow, to live there. This made known his marriage to his sister-in-law, and, as such marriages were not unusual, according to their religion, no one was surprised. As for Qasim's shop, 'Ali Baba had a son, who had for some time finished his apprenticeship with another prominent merchant, who had always testified to his good conduct, and 'Ali Baba gave him the shop, with the promise that, if he continued to conduct himself wisely, he would marry him as well as he deserved.

Let us leave 'Ali Baba, enjoying the early fruits of his good fortune, and let us speak of the forty thieves. They returned to their hiding place in the forest at the appointed time, but they were very much surprised not to find Qasim's body and even more surprised to see that the bags of gold had diminished. Their captain said, "We are exposed and lost, and if we are not careful, and if we don't look immediately for a remedy, we will slowly lose the great riches that our ancestors and we have amassed with great toil and trouble. All we can assess of the damage done to us is that the thief, whom we took by surprise, knew the secret of opening the door and that we arrived luckily at the appointed time, just as he was leaving. However, he was not the only one, for another must know it too. The removal of his body and the diminishing of our treasure are incontestable proof of it, and since there is no indication that more than two knew the secret, having killed one, we must also kill the other. What do you say, brave men? Don't you agree with me?"

The captain's proposal was found by his comrades to be so sensible that they all approved of it and agreed that they had to forego all other enterprises, devoting themselves only to this one and not abandoning it until they succeeded. The chief said, "I had expected no less of your courage and boldness, but, above all, one of you, who is hardy, clever, and enterprising, must go into the city, unarmed and disguised as a foreign traveler, and must use all his skill to find out if there is any mention of the strange death of the man whom we slaughtered as he deserved, as well as who he was and where he lived. It is important for us to know this beforehand, in order not to do anything that we may regret later or to expose ourselves in a country where we have been undetected for such a long time and where it is in our great interest to remain so. But in order to give an incentive to the one among you who will volunteer for this mission and to prevent him from making a mistake by bringing us back a false report, instead of a true one, which could cause our ruin, I ask you whether you don't consider it proper that in this case he should submit to the penalty of death?"

Without waiting for the others to express their opinions, one of the thieves said, "I submit, and I glory in risking my life by accepting this commission. If I don't succeed, you will at least remember that I lacked neither the willingness nor the courage for the common good of the group." This thief, after receiving the lavish praises of the captain and his comrades, disguised himself in such a way that no one could guess what he was. He left the company and set out at night, taking such measures that he entered the city just as it was beginning to get light. He advanced until he reached a square where he saw only one shop open. It was the shop of Baba Mustafa.

Baba Mustafa was seated on his chair, with the awl in his hand, ready to work. The thief went up to him and wished him good morning and, noticing his advanced age, said to him, "Fellow, you start work very early in the morning, but it is not possible that you can still see clearly, old as you are, and even when it gets clearer, I doubt whether your eyes are good enough for sewing." Baba Mustafa replied, "Whoever you may be, you must not know me. Old as I seem to you, I still have excellent eyes, and you will no longer doubt it when I tell you that, not long ago, I sewed up a dead man, in a place where it was not any lighter than it is now." The thief was overjoyed at his discovery, by coming at the outset to a man, who, without being asked and all by himself gave him, without doubt, the information that had brought him there. He asked in astonishment, "A dead man?" and, in order to make Baba Mustafa talk, he added, "Why sew up a dead man? You apparently mean to say that you sewed the shroud in which he was wrapped." Baba Mustafa replied, "No, no, I mean what I am saying. You want to make me talk, but you will get nothing more out of me."

The thief did not need any further explanation to be convinced that he had found out what he had come for. He pulled out a gold coin and, putting it in Baba Mustafa's hand, said to him, "I don't wish to share your secret, even though I can assure you that I would not have divulged it, if you had revealed it to me. I only ask you to do me a favor and tell me or take me to the house where you sewed up the dead man." Baba Mustafa replied, holding the gold coin and about to give it back, "Even if I have the desire to accede to your wish, I assure you that I cannot do it; take my word. The reason is that I was led to a certain place where a bandage was placed over my eyes, and from there I was led to the house from where, after I finished what I had to do, I was led back in the same way to the same place. You see how impossible it is to help you." The thief said, "You can at least remember partly the way you took while the bandage was placed over your eyes. Come with me; I beg you. I will place a bandage over your eyes at that place, and we will walk together, taking the same streets and the same turns you are able to recall, and since every effort deserves a recompense, here is another gold coin. Come, do me this favor I ask of you." So saying, he put a gold coin in Baba Mustafa's hand.

The two pieces of gold tempted Baba Mustafa, who held them in his hand, looking at them for some time, without saying a word, as he deliberated on what he should do. At last, he pulled out his purse from his breast and, putting the coins inside, said to the thief, "I cannot guarantee you that I can remember the exact road they made me take, but since you desire it, let us go, and I will do what I can to remember." He got up, to the great satisfaction of the thief, and, without closing his shop, in which he had nothing of consequence to lose, took the thief with him to the place where Marjana had placed the bandage over his eyes. When they arrived, he said, "It is here where they placed the bandage, and I was turned around, as you see." The thief, who had his handkerchief ready, bandaged his eyes with it and walked beside him, sometimes leading him and sometimes letting him go by himself, until he stopped and said, "It seems to me that I did not go any further." He was indeed standing before Qasim's house, where 'Ali Baba was living at that time. Before removing the handkerchief from his eyes, the thief quickly marked the door with a piece of chalk, which he had ready in his hand, and, when he removed the handkerchief, he asked him whether he knew to whom the house belonged. Baba Mustafa replied that he was not from that quarter and therefore could not tell him. Seeing that he could not learn anything more from Baba Mustafa, the thief thanked him for his trouble and headed to the forest, convinced that he would be well-received.

Shortly after the thief and Baba Mustafa parted, Marjana went out of 'Ali Baba's house on some errand, and when she returned, she noticed the mark the thief had made and stopped to examine it, saying to herself, "What is the meaning of this mark? Does someone intend to harm my master, or has he made it in jest?" adding, "Whatever the intention, it is a good idea to take precaution against all eventualities." So she too took a piece of chalk, and as two or three doors up and down the street were similar, she marked them in the same spot and returned to the house, without telling her master and mistress what she had done.

Meanwhile, the thief, who continued his journey, arrived in the forest and rejoined his companions at an early hour and reported on the success of his journey, overstating his good fortune to have found at the outset a man by whom he had found out what he had gone to look for, something that no one but he could have done. His comrades listened to him with great satisfaction, and the captain, after praising his diligence, addressed them, saying, "Comrades, we have no time to lose. Let us go well-armed, without showing it, and after we enter the city in separate groups, in order not to arouse any suspicion, let us meet in the great square, some of us on one side and some on the other, while I myself go with our comrade, who has brought us such good news, to inspect the house and decide on the best course of action."

They applauded his statement and were soon ready to depart. They filed out two by two and three by three and, traveling at a little distance from each other, entered the city without arousing any suspicion. The captain and the man who had gone into the city that morning were the last to enter. He led the captain to the street where he had marked 'Ali Baba's house, and when he was before one of the doors which had been marked by Marjana, he showed it to him, saying that that was the house. But, as they continued walking, without stopping, in order not to arouse suspicion, the captain, noticing that the next door was marked with the same mark and in the same spot, showed it to his guide and asked him whether the house was this one or the first. The guide was confused and did not know what to say, and he was even more confused when he saw with the captain that the four or five other doors that followed had also the same mark. He assured the captain, swearing that he had marked only one, adding, "I don't know who could have marked the other doors with very similar marks, but in this confusion I confess that I cannot tell which is the one I marked."

The chief, seeing his plan aborted, went to the great square, where he informed his men, through the first he met, that they had wasted their efforts, that their journey was in vain, and that they had nothing else to do but to return to their common hiding place. He set the example, and the rest followed, in the same order as when they had come. When they reassembled in the forest, the captain explained to them why he had made them return, and they all declared that the guide deserved to be put to death. Even he condemned himself, by admitting that he should have taken better precautions, and he offered his neck resolutely to the man who came forward to cut off his head.

Since the preservation of the group required that the man's error not be left unpunished, the punishment was meted out, and another thief, promising to be more successful than the one who had been punished, came forward and asked the favor of being chosen. They agreed, and he departed and, as the first had done, bribed Baba Mustafa, who, with the bandage over his eyes, took him to 'Ali Baba's house, which the thief marked with red in a less noticeable spot, thinking that this was a sure way of distinguishing it from those marked with white. But shortly afterward, Marjana came out of the house as she had done on the previous day, and when she returned, she did not fail to detect the red mark with her sharp eyes, nor did she fail to mark the neighboring doors with a red pencil and on the same spot.

The thief, on his return to his companions in the forest, did not fail to value as infallible the precaution he had taken to distinguish 'Ali Baba's house from all the others. The captain and his men, agreeing with him that this should succeed, went to the city, in the same order and with the same precautions as before, armed and ready to strike. When they arrived, the captain and the thief went to 'Ali Baba's street, and as before, met with the same difficulty. The chief was indignant, and the thief was in as great a confusion as the man who had preceded him on the same mission. So the captain was again forced to withdraw that day with his men, with as little satisfaction as the day before, and the thief, as the man responsible for the error, was condemned to the same fate, to which he submitted willingly.

The captain, who saw his troop lose two brave men, feared that he might lose more if he continued to send them to find for certain 'Ali Baba's house. The example of the two convinced him that, on such occasions, planned attack was better than impulsive action. He took charge of the thing himself; he went into the city, and, with the aid of Baba Mustafa, who rendered him the same service he had rendered his two volunteers, he, without bothering to make any mark by which to recognize 'Ali Baba's house, examined it so carefully, going back and forth, in front of it so many times, that he could not possibly mistake it again.

The captain, satisfied with his journey for having found what he wanted, returned to the forest, and when he went into the cavern where his men were waiting for him, he said, "Comrades, at last, nothing will prevent us from exacting full vengeance for the damage we have suffered. I know for sure the house of the guilty one on whom it should fall, and on the way back, I thought of the means of making him taste it, in such an effective way, that no one will ever again know the secret of our hiding place or our treasure, for this is the aim we should endeavor to pursue in our enterprise; otherwise, our efforts, instead of being useful, would be fatal." The captain continued, "In order to accomplish this, here is what I think, and after I explain it to you, if any of you knows of a better way, he may tell us." He then explained to them what he proposed to do and asked them to disperse in the small market towns, the surrounding villages, and even the cities and to buy as many as nineteen mules and thirty-eight leather jars for transporting oil, one full with oil and the others empty. Within two or three days, the thieves collected everything. As the empty jars were a little too narrow at the neck for carrying out the captain's plan, he had them enlarged, and after he made each of his men go inside a jar with the weapons he considered necessary, and after he opened some seams in order that they might breathe freely, he closed the jars in such a way that they appeared to be full of oil, and, in order to disguise the jars better, he rubbed them with oil taken from the jar that was full.

After these preparations, the mules were loaded with the thirty-seven thieves, except for the captain, each hiding in a jar, together with the jar that was full of oil, and the captain, as the driver, took the road to the city at the time he had decided on and arrived there at dusk, an hour after sunset, as he had intended. He entered the city and went directly to 'Ali Baba's house, planning to knock at the door and ask to spend the night there, with his mules, as a favor from the master of the house. He did not have to knock, for he found 'Ali Baba at the door, enjoying the fresh air after supper. He halted his mules and, addressing 'Ali Baba, said, "Sir, I am bringing oil, as you see, from a faraway place, to sell tomorrow at the market, and I don't know where to find lodging at this late hour. If it does not inconvenience you, do me a favor and let me spend the night in your house, and I will be grateful to you."

Although 'Ali Baba had seen and even heard in the forest the man who spoke to him, how could he have recognized him as the captain of the forty thieves, under his disguise as an oil merchant? He said to him, "You are welcome; come in." So saying, 'Ali Baba made room to let him in with his mules. At the same time 'Ali Baba called a slave of his and ordered him, after the mules were unloaded, not only to shelter them under a cover in the stable, but also to give them hay and barley. He even took the trouble of going into the kitchen and ordering Marjana to offer supper to the guest and to prepare a bed for him in one of the rooms.

'Ali Baba did even more. When he saw that the captain of the thieves had unloaded the mules and that they had been taken into the stable, as he had ordered, 'Ali Baba, wishing to accommodate him as well as possible and looking for a place to spend the night in the open air, went to take the captain into the hall where he received his guests, saying to him that he himself would not mind sleeping in the courtyard. The captain protested strongly, but, in reality, only in order to carry out more freely what he had planned, and he did not yield to 'Ali Baba's offer until after many entreaties.

'Ali Baba, not wishing to sit down with the man who wanted to take his life until Marjana served him supper, went on to chat with him about several subjects he thought might please him and did not leave him until he finished his rich meal, saying to him, "I leave you as the master here; all you have to do is to ask for whatever you may need; there is nothing in my house that is not at your disposal." The captain rose at the same time and accompanied him to the door, and while 'Ali Baba went into the kitchen to speak with Marjana, he went into the courtyard, on the pretext that he was going to the stable to see whether his mules needed anything.

'Ali Baba again asked Marjana to take good care of the guest and not to let him lack anything, adding, "Tomorrow, I will go to the bath before dawn. See to it that my bath linen is ready and give it to 'Abd Allah (that was the name of his slave), and make me some good broth to drink on my return," and, having given her these orders, he retired to go to bed.

Meanwhile, the captain went as far as the entrance to the stable to tell his men what they had to do. From the first jar to the last, he said to each man, "When I throw small stones from the room where I will be staying, be sure to free yourself by tearing open the jar with the knife you are supplied with and coming out, and as soon as you do, I will be with you." The knife he referred to was pointed and sharpened for that purpose. Then he returned to the house, and as he stood at the kitchen door, Marjana took a lamp and led him to the room she had prepared for him, and in which she left him, after asking him whether he needed anything else. Then in order not to arouse any suspicion, he put out the light shortly after he lay down in his clothes, ready to get up after a short nap.

Marjana did not forget 'Ali Baba's orders. She prepared his bath linens, gave them to 'Abd Allah, who had not yet gone to bed, and put the pot on the fire to prepare the broth. While she was skimming the foam, the lamp went out, and as there was no more oil or candles in the house, what was she to do, while she needed to see clearly, in order to skim the broth? She expressed her predicament to 'Abd Allah, who said to her, "Here you are, at a loss. Go and take some oil from one of the jars in the courtyard." Marjana thanked him for his advice, and while 'Abd Allah went to sleep near 'Ali Baba's room, in order to follow him to the bath, she took the oil pitcher and went into the courtyard. As she approached the nearest jar, the thief who was hiding inside asked in a whisper, "Is it time?" Although he spoke in a whisper, Marjana heard the voice clearly, since the captain, as soon as he had unloaded his mules, had opened not only this jar, but all the others, to let in more air for his men, who were extremely ill at ease, although they were able to breathe.

Any other slave but Marjana, as surprised as she was to find a man in a jar instead of the oil she was looking for, would have made an uproar that might have caused a great mishap. But Marjana was above that; she understood instantly the importance of keeping secret the imminent danger to 'Ali Baba and his family, as well as to herself, and the necessity of finding a prompt and quiet remedy, to which, with her intelligence, she immediately found the means. She recovered at once and, pretending to be the captain of the thieves, she replied to the question, without showing any emotion, "Not yet, but soon." She went to the next jar, and the same question was asked, and the same answer given, and so on until she reached the jar with the oil.

Marjana realized that her master 'Ali Baba, who thought that the man he had invited to stay with him was merely an oil merchant, had actually invited thirty-eight thieves, including their captain, the fake merchant. She quickly filled her pitcher with oil, which she took from the last jar, and returned to the kitchen, where, after filling the lamp with oil and lighting it, she took a large boiling pan, returned to the courtyard, and filled the pan with oil from the jar. Then she brought it back and put it on the fire, which she stocked with more firewood, for the sooner the oil boiled, the sooner she could carry out what would contribute to the common salvation of the household, which could not bear any postponement. When the oil finally began to boil, she took the pan and, going out again, poured into each jar enough boiling oil to choke the thieves and kill them.

After this deed, which was worthy of Marjana's courage, was carried out as quietly as she had intended, she returned to the kitchen and closed the door. Then she put out the great fire that she had lighted, leaving only what was needed to finish cooking the broth for 'Ali Baba. She then put out the lamp and remained very quiet, determined not to go to sleep until she saw, through a kitchen window overlooking the courtyard, and as much as the darkness permitted, what would happen next.

It was no more than a quarter of an hour later when the captain woke up and, getting up, opened the window and looked out, and as he saw no light and heard nothing but peace and quiet in the house, he gave the signal, by throwing little stones, of which several fell on the jars, as he was certain from the sound he heard. He listened, but he neither heard nor saw anything to indicate that his men were making any move. Beginning to worry, he threw the stones a second and a third time. They fell on the jars, but not a single thief gave the slightest sign of life, and he could not understand why. He went down into the courtyard in alarm, as quietly as he could. Again, he approached the first jar, and when he was about to ask the thief, whom he thought to be alive, whether he was asleep, he smelled the odor of hot and burnt oil coming from the jar and realized the failure of his enterprise against 'Ali Baba and his plan to kill him, plunder his house, and, if possible, carry back the gold he had taken from the group. He went to the next jar and to the others and found out that all his men had perished in the same way, and, from the diminishing of the oil in the jar, which was full when he brought it, he understood the means taken to deprive him of the assistance he had expected. In his despair at the failure of his attempt, he slipped through the door of 'Ali Baba's garden, which adjoined the courtyard, and, going over the fences, from garden to garden, he escaped.

When Marjana waited for some time but did not hear any sound and did not see the captain come back, she had no doubt what course of action he had taken, instead of trying to escape through the main door, which was secured with a double bolt. Thus, satisfied and overjoyed to have so well succeeded in ensuring the safety of the entire household, she finally lay down and went to sleep.

Meanwhile, 'Ali Baba left before daybreak and went to the bath, followed by his slave, without knowing anything of the surprising turn of events that took place in his house while he slept. For Marjana did not deem it proper to awaken him about it, with all the more reason, since she had no time to lose while the danger lasted, and since it would have served no purpose to disturb his peace after she had averted that danger. When 'Ali Baba returned from the bath and entered his house, the sun was already up, and he was very surprised to see that the oil jars were still in their place and that the merchant did not go with his mules to the market and asked for an explanation from Marjana, who had come to open the door for him and who had left everything as it was, in order to show him the spectacle and explain to him more effectively what she had done to save him.

Replying to 'Ali Baba, Marjana said, "My good master, may God preserve you, you and all your household! You will understand better what you wish to know, when you see what I have to show you. Please, come with me." 'Ali Baba followed Marjana who, after closing the door, led him to the first jar, saying, "Look inside, and see if there is any oil." 'Ali Baba looked, and when he saw a man inside the jar, he drew back in fright and uttered a loud cry. Marjana said, "Fear nothing, for the man you see will not do you any harm. He did some damage, but he is no longer in a condition to do more, neither to you nor to anyone else; he is no longer alive." 'Ali Baba cried out, "What do you mean to say by showing me this? Explain!" Marjana replied, "I will explain it, but control your amazement and don't arouse the neighbors' curiosity to find out about something that is very important for you to keep hidden. Look first in all the other jars." 'Ali Baba looked in them, one after another, from the first to the last that had the oil, noticing that the oil had appreciably diminished, and when he finished, he remained motionless, looking sometimes at the jars, sometimes at Marjana, without saying a word, for so great was his astonishment. At last, as if he had recovered his speech, he asked, "And the merchant, what has become of him?" Marjana replied, "The merchant is as much of a merchant as I am. I will tell you what he is and what has become of him, but you will hear the whole story more conveniently in your room, for it is time, for the sake of your health, to drink some broth after coming out of the bath." While 'Ali Baba returned to his room, Marjana went into the kitchen to get the broth. When she brought it, 'Ali Baba, before drinking it, said to her, "Satisfy my impatience, and start telling me this very strange story, in all its details."

Obeying 'Ali Baba, Marjana said, "Sir, last night, when you retired to go to bed, I prepared your bath linens, as you had ordered me, and gave them to 'Abd Allah. Then I put the pot on the fire for the broth, and as I was skimming the broth, the lamp, running out of oil, suddenly went out. As there was not a drop left in the oil pitcher, I looked for some bits of candles and found none. So 'Abd Allah, who saw me perplexed, reminded me of the jars in the courtyard, which he as well as I and you yourself thought to be full of oil. I took the pitcher and ran to the nearest jar, but as I came near, a voice came out, asking, 'Is it time?' I was not startled, but immediately realized the malice of the false merchant and replied, without hesitation, 'Not yet, but soon.' Then I went to the next jar, and another voice asked me the same question, to which I gave the same answer. I went to the other jars, one after another, hearing the same question and giving the same answer, and it was not until I came to the last jar that I found oil, with which I filled my pitcher. When I considered that there were thirty-seven thieves in the middle of your courtyard, waiting for a signal or an order from their captain, whom you had taken for a merchant and to whom you had given such a fine reception, poised to tear the house down, I lost no time. I brought back the pitcher and lighted the lamp, and after I took the largest boiling pan in the kitchen, I went and filled it with oil. I then put it on the fire, and when the oil began to boil, I went and poured it into every jar in which the thieves were hiding, as I had to, to prevent them from carrying out the wicked plan that had brought them here. When the thing was done, as I had planned, I returned to the kitchen, put out the lamp, and, before going to sleep, watched quietly from the window, to see what the fake oil merchant was going to do. A short time later, I heard him signaling by throwing from his window some small stones, which fell on the jars. He threw some more, a second and a third time, but as he did not detect or hear any movement, he went down, and I saw him go from jar to jar, until I lost sight of him in the darkness. I kept watching for some time, and when I saw that he did not return, I was sure that he must have escaped through the garden, in his despair after his great failure. Thus, convinced that the house was safe, I went to sleep."

In finishing, Marjana added, "This is the story you asked me to tell you, and I am convinced that it is the sequel of something I observed two or three days ago and which I did not think I should tell you about, namely, that when I returned from the city, one early morning, I noticed that the main door bore a white mark, and the following day, I noticed that it bore a red mark beside the white one, and each time, without knowing for what purpose it could have been marked, I made the same mark in the same spot on two or three doors of our neighbors, up and down the street. If you add that to what has happened, you will realize that all this had been engineered by the thieves from the forest. Of these forty thieves, two were left out for a reason I don't understand, but whatever it may be, there are now three left. This shows that they have sworn to destroy you and that it is better for you to be on guard, as long as it is certain that there is even one left in the world. For my part, I will do everything to remain vigilant for your preservation, as my duty requires."

When Marjana finished, 'Ali Baba, realizing his great indebtedness to her, said, "I will not die before rewarding you as you deserve. I owe you my life, and, to begin, I give you a token of my gratitude by granting you your freedom, from this moment, in anticipation of rewarding you fully, later on, in the manner I intend. I am convinced like you that the forty thieves planned this ambush for me and that God has delivered me at your hands. I hope that He will continue to protect me from their wickedness and that, in warding them off me, He will save the world from their persecution and their evil breed. What we

have to do now is to bury forthwith the bodies of these infernal speci-
mens, with great secrecy, so that no one will have any suspicion of
their fate, and this is what I will work on with 'Abd Allah."

As 'Ali Baba's garden was very long, ending with large trees, he,
without hesitation, went with his slave and dug a hole under these
trees, long and wide enough for the bodies he had for burial. Since
the ground was soft and loose, it did not take them long to finish the
work. They then pulled the bodies out of the jars and, putting aside
the arms with which the thieves had been supplied, they transported
the bodies to the far end of the garden and arranged them in the hole.
Then they covered them with some of the earth they had dug up and
scattered the rest about, in such a way that the ground seemed the
same as before. 'Ali Baba then hid the oil jars and the arms carefully.
As for the mules, he sent them in several installments to the market,
where they were sold by his slave.

While 'Ali Baba took every measure to hide from the public the
means by which he had become rich in such a short time, the captain
of the forty thieves was back in the forest, in a state of unimaginable
humiliation, and, in his agitation, or rather confusion, after an outcome so unfortunate and so contrary to his expectation, he returned to
the cavern, without having reached any resolution on the way, as to
what he should or should not do to 'Ali Baba. The solitude in which
he found himself in this gloomy place was very disagreeable. He cried
out, "O companions of my vigils, my journeys, and my labors, where
are you? What will I do without you? Have I chosen you and assembled you, only to see you destroyed at once by a fate so deadly and so
unworthy of your courage? I would have grieved less, had you died
with your swords in your hands, as valiant men. When will I put
together another group of capable men like you? And if I wish, can I
do it, without exposing so much gold, so much silver, and so much
wealth to the mercy of the man who has already enriched himself with
one part of it. I cannot, and I must not think of it, before I take his
life. What I was not able to do with such a mighty assistance, I will do
by myself alone, and when I will see to it in that way that the treasure
will no longer be subject to plunder, I will see to it that it will stay neither without successors nor without a captain after me, in order to
preserve it and to increase it for all posterity." Having reached this
resolution, he was not worried about finding a means of carrying it
out, and so, full of hope and peace of mind, he went to sleep and spent
the night peacefully.

The next day, the captain woke up early, as he had intended, put
on clothing appropriate for his plan, and went to the city, where he
took lodgings at an inn. As he thought that what took place at 'Ali
Baba's house might have made a commotion, he asked the door-

keeper, while chatting with him, whether there was anything new in the city. The doorkeeper responded by telling him about all kinds of things, except that which mattered to him most. From this, the captain concluded that the reason 'Ali Baba guarded such a great secret was that he did not wish to reveal his knowledge of the treasure or the means of getting to it, knowing that it was for that reason that an attempt had been made on his life. This prodded the captain to do all he could to get rid of 'Ali Baba with the same secrecy.

He got a horse and used it to bring to his lodging several kinds of rich fabrics and fine canvas, by making several trips to the forest, with the necessary precautions to keep secret the hiding place where he went to take them from. When he had amassed what he considered to be an appropriate amount to sell as merchandise, he looked for a shop and, finding one, rented it from the owner, stocked it, and settled there. As it turned out, the shop opposite his used to belong to Qasim and had been recently occupied by 'Ali Baba's son.

The captain, who had taken the name of Khawaja Husain, did not fail to pay his neighbors the customary courtesies expected of new arrivals. But since 'Ali Baba's son was young, handsome, and not lacking in intelligence, and since he had more opportunity to speak to him and converse with him than with the others, they soon became friends. He even undertook to cultivate him more attentively and assiduously, when, three or four days after opening the shop, he recognized 'Ali Baba, who came to see his son and speak with him, as he used to from time to time, and when the captain learned from the son, after 'Ali Baba left, that he was his father. So the captain increased his overtures toward him, flattering him, giving him little presents, entertaining him, and inviting him several times to eat with him.

'Ali Baba's son did not wish to owe many obligations to Khawaja Husain without reciprocating his favors, but his place was limited, and he did not have the wherewithal to entertain him in the same manner as he wished. He spoke of his desire to his father, 'Ali Baba, saying that it would not be proper for him to defer much longer repaying the courtesies of Khawaja Husain. 'Ali Baba was pleased to undertake the task of entertaining him, saying, "Son, tomorrow is Friday, and since it is a day on which the prominent merchants, like Khawaja Husain and you, keep their shops closed, make an appointment with him to go for an after-dinner walk, and arrange it in such a way as to make him pass by my house and to bring him in. It will be better to do it in this way than if you were to invite him formally. I will order Marjana to prepare supper and to keep it ready."

On Friday, 'Ali Baba's son and Khawaja Husain met, after dinner, at the appointed place, and went on their walk. On their return, as 'Ali Baba's son had arranged to pass with Khawaja Husain through the street where his father's house was located, stopped before the house, and knocked at the door, saying to him, "This house belongs to my father, who, when he heard from me of the friendship with which you have honored me, asked me to procure him the honor of making your acquaintance. I beg you to add this favor to all the others to which I am indebted to you."

Although Khawaja Husain was about to get what he wanted, to enter 'Ali Baba's house and take his life without risking his own by making any commotion, he excused himself and seemed about to take his leave, when 'Ali Baba's slave opened the door, and the son, taking him obligingly by the hand and going in before him, pulled him and somewhat forced him to go in, as if in spite of himself.

'Ali Baba received Khawaja Husain with a cheerful mien and with all the welcome he could wish for. He thanked him for the favors he had done for his son, adding, "The debt he and I owe you is all the more great, since he is a young man who has not yet learned the ways of the world and since you do not find it beneath you to contribute to his education." Khawaja Husain paid 'Ali Baba compliment for compliment, assuring him that if his son had not yet acquired the experience of certain old men, he had the intelligence to serve him in place of the experience of an infinite number of other men.

After a short conversation on indifferent subjects, Khawaja Husain wished to take his leave, but 'Ali Baba stopped him, saying, "Sir, where do you wish to go? I beg you to do me the honor of having supper with me. The meal I will offer you is very much below what you deserve, but, such as it is, I hope that you will accept it from me, as willingly as I offer it to you." Khawaja Husain replied, "Sir, I am convinced of your kindness, and, if I ask you the favor not to find it amiss that I leave without accepting your obliging offer, I beg you to believe that I do it neither out of disrespect nor discourtesy, but due to a reason you would approve of, if you knew it." 'Ali Baba asked, "Sir, may I ask you what that reason is?" Khawaja Husain replied, "Yes, I can tell you. It is because I eat neither meat nor stew cooked with salt. Judge for yourself my abstinence at your table." 'Ali Baba insisted, saying, "If this is your only reason, it should not deprive me of the honor of prevailing on you to have supper with me, unless you do not wish it for some other reason. First, there is no salt in the bread we eat here; as for the meat and stews, I promise you that there will be no salt in those that will be served before you. I will give the order. Therefore, do me the favor and stay, and I will return in a moment."

'Ali Baba went to the kitchen and ordered Marjana not to put any salt on the meat to be served and to prepare without salt two or three other kinds of stew, in addition to those he had ordered. Marjana, who was ready to serve the meal, could not prevent herself from showing her displeasure at this new order and said to 'Ali Baba, "Who is this difficult man who does not eat salt? Your supper will be spoiled, if I serve it later." 'Ali Baba replied, "Don't be angry, Marjana. He is a decent man. Do what I tell you."

Marjana obeyed, but against her will. She was curious to see this man who did not eat any salt. So when she finished, and 'Abd Allah set the table, she helped him in carrying the dishes, and when she looked at Khawaja Husain, she recognized him at once as the captain of the thieves, in spite of his disguise, and when she examined him carefully, she saw that he had a dagger hidden under his clothes. She said to herself, "I am no longer surprised that the villain does not wish to eat salt with my master, his implacable enemy, whom he wants to assassinate, but I will prevent him."

Marjana finished serving and let 'Abd Allah serve, and while they were still having supper, she took the time to make the necessary preparations for a most daring strike, finishing by the time 'Abd Allah came to tell her that it was time to serve the fruits. She carried the fruits, and as soon as 'Abd Allah cleared the table, she served them and then placed near 'Ali Baba a little table on which she put the wine and three cups. She left, taking 'Abd Allah with her, as if they were going to have supper together and giving 'Ali Baba, according to custom, the liberty to enjoy drinking and having a pleasant conversation with his guest.

At that moment, Khawaja Husain, or rather the captain of the forty thieves, thought that the favorable opportunity for killing 'Ali Baba had come, and said to himself, "I will make them drunk, both the father and the son, so that the latter, whose life I am very willing to spare, may not prevent me from plunging the dagger into his father's heart, and I will escape through the garden, as I did earlier, before the cook and the slave finish eating or go to sleep in the kitchen."

However, Marjana, who had guessed the intention of the false Khawaja Husain, did not give him the time he needed for the execution of his evil plan. She dressed in the attire of a dancer, with the proper headdress, girded herself with a gilded silver belt, to which she attached a dagger, of which the case and the handle were of the same metal, and finally put a very beautiful mask over her face. When she finished putting on this guise, she said to 'Abd Allah, "'Abd Allah, take your tambourine, and let us go to entertain the guest of our master and of his son, by performing for him as we do sometimes." 'Abd Allah took the tambourine and began to play, walking before Marjana, as he entered the hall. Marjana, entering after him, took a deep bow, in a deliberate air, to make herself noticed and as if asking for permission to perform. As 'Abd Allah saw that 'Ali Baba wished to speak, he stopped playing the tambourine. 'Ali Baba said, "Come in,

Marjana, come in. Khawaja Husain will judge your skill and tell us what he thinks of it," and, turning to Khawaja Husain, he said to him, "Do not think that it is costing me anything to offer you this entertainment. I have it at home, for as you see, it is performed by my slave and by my cook and servant. I hope that you will not find it disagreeable."

Khawaja Husain, who had not expected 'Ali Baba to add this entertainment to the supper, feared that he would lose the opportunity he thought he had found. Should that happen, he thought, he would console himself with the hope of finding it again, by continuing to cultivate the friendship of the father and the son. Thus, although he would have preferred 'Ali Baba to spare him the entertainment, he pretended to be grateful for it and complacently indicated that what pleased 'Ali Baba would please him too. When 'Abd Allah saw that 'Ali Baba and Khawaja Husain stopped talking, he began to play the tambourine again, singing a dancing song, while Marjana, who was as good as any professional dancer, danced in a manner worthy of admiration, not only by this company for which she was performing, but by any other, save perhaps the false Khawaja Husain, who paid little attention. After she performed several dances with the same energy and delight, she finally pulled out the dagger and, holding it in her hand, performed a dance in which she excelled, by the different figures, the light movements, the astonishing leaps, and the marvelous efforts with which she danced, sometimes thrusting the dagger forward as if to stab someone, sometimes thrusting it backward as if to stab herself in the chest. Finally, out of breath, she took the tambourine from 'Abd Allah with her left hand and, holding the dagger in her right hand, went to present the tambourine by its hollow to 'Ali Baba, in imitation of the professional male and female dancers who used it to solicit liberal donations from the spectators.

'Ali Baba threw a gold coin in the tambourine, and Marjana went to his son, who followed his father's example. Meanwhile, Khawaja Husain, who saw that she was coming to him, pulled out his purse from his breast, in order to tip her, and he was putting his hand out when Marjana, with a courage worthy of the firmness and resolution she had shown till then, plunged the dagger into his heart, and kept it there until he was dead. 'Ali Baba and his son, terrified by this action, let out a loud cry, and 'Ali Baba cried out, "Ah! wretched girl, what have you done? Do you wish to destroy me and my family?" Marjana replied, "I did not do it in order to destroy you; I did it to save you." Then she opened Khawaja Husain's robe and showed him the dagger with which he was armed, saying, "See what an implacable enemy you have been dealing with; look at his face carefully, and you will recognize the false oil merchant, the captain of the forty thieves. Don't you know why he did not want to eat salt with you? Do you need further proof to convince you of his evil intention? I suspected him even before I saw him, from the moment you told me that you had such a company. Then I took a look at him, and now you see that my suspicion was not without foundation."

'Ali Baba, realizing the new debt he owed Marjana for having saved his life a second time, embraced her and said, "Marjana, when I gave you your freedom, I told you at that time my gratitude would not stop there and that I would soon reward you fully. The time has come, and I will make you my daughter-in-law." Then, addressing his son, he added, "Son, I think that you are a good enough son not to find it strange that I give you Marjana for a wife, without consulting you. You are no less indebted to her than I. You see that Khawaja Husain has sought your friendship, only the better to succeed in his plan to take my life by treachery, and, if he had succeeded, you should not doubt that he would have sacrificed you too to his vengeance. Consider, furthermore, that in marrying Marjana, you will marry the mainstay of my family, as long as I live, and the support of yours, to the end of your days."

The son, far from showing any displeasure, indicated that he consented to this marriage, not only because he did not wish to disobey his father, but also because he was driven to it by his own inclination. Then they started thinking of burying the body of the captain, and they buried him near the bodies of the thirty-seven thieves, so quietly that nobody found out about it until after many years, when no one was any longer interested in talking about this memorable event.

A few days later, 'Ali Baba celebrated the wedding of his son and Marjana with a solemn ceremony and a sumptuous banquet, accompanied with the usual dances, spectacles, and entertainments. He had the satisfaction to find that the friends and neighbors whom he had invited, without letting know the true motive for the marriage, but who recognized Marjana's good and lovely qualities, praised him highly for his generosity and good-heartedness.

After the wedding, 'Ali Baba, who had refrained from going back to the cavern after he had taken out and carried back the body of his brother Qasim on one of the three asses, together with the gold he had loaded them with, continued to refrain from going back, even after the death of the thirty-seven thieves and their captain, for fear that he would find the thieves or be taken by surprise by them there, supposing that the two other thieves, whose fate was unknown to him, were still alive. But after one year, when he saw that nothing happened to cause him any concern, he was seized by curiosity and decided to go back, taking all the precautions necessary for his safety. He mounted his horse, and when he came near the cavern, he saw it as a good omen to find no trace of men or horses there. He dismounted, went to the door, and said, "Open, sesame!" words that he did not forget. The door opened, and when he entered, the state in which he found everything in the cavern convinced him that since the time the false Khawaja Husain had come to rent a shop in the city, no one had entered there, and that therefore, since that time, all forty thieves must have been dispersed and exterminated. He had no longer any doubt that he was the only one in the world who knew the secret of opening the cavern and that the entire treasure was at his disposal. As he had a bag with him, he filled it with as much gold as his horse could carry and returned to the city. From that time on, 'Ali Baba and his son, whom he took with him to the cavern and to whom he told the secret of opening it, using their fortune with moderation, continued to live, they and their descendants, to whom they passed the secret, in great splendor and were honored as the leading dignitaries of the city.

THE STORY OF
'ALA AL-DIN (ALADDIN)
AND THE MAGIC LAMP

In one of the large and rich kingdoms of China, whose name I do not recollect, there lived a tailor named Mustafa, who had no other distinction save that of his profession. He was very poor, and his labor produced hardly enough to support him, his wife, and a son whom God had given him. The son, who was named 'Ala al-Din, had been brought up in a very careless manner that led him to acquire many vicious habits. He was nasty, obstinate, and disobedient to his father and mother, who, as soon as he was a little grown up, could not keep him at home. He would go out in the morning and spend the day playing in the streets and public places with street children who were even younger than he. When he was old enough to learn a trade, his father, who was in no position to make him learn any other trade but his, took him into his shop and began to show him how to use a needle, but neither by sweet talk nor the fear of punishment was the father able to curb the flightiness of his son. He could not make him control himself and remain as attentive and committed to his work as he wished. As soon as he had his back turned, 'Ala al-Din would disappear for the rest of the day. The father did punish him, but 'Ala al-Din was incorrigible, and Mustafa, to his great regret, was obliged to abandon his son to his delinquent ways. This caused him much pain, and his grief at not being able to make his son stick to his work caused him such a persistent illness that he died within a few months.

'Ala al-Din's mother, who saw that her son did not learn his father's trade, closed the shop and sold all the implements of that trade, and with the little she gained from spinning cotton, she tried to support herself and her son. 'Ala al-Din, who was no longer restrained by the fear of a father and who cared so little for his mother that he even had the temerity to threaten her at the slightest remonstrance she made, gave himself entirely to his delinquent ways. He associated increasingly with children of his own age and never ceased to play with them, even with more abandon than before. He continued this way of life until he was fifteen years old, without being mindful of anything and without reflecting on what might become of him one day.

One day, as he was in this situation, playing as usual with a group of

81

street children, in the middle of a square, a stranger, who was passing by, stopped to look at him. This stranger was a famous magician, called by the author of this story the African magician, a name I will more readily use as he was actually a native of Africa, having arrived from there two days before. Whether or not this magician, who was a skilled physiognomist, saw in 'Ala al-Din's face all that was absolutely necessary to carry out the purpose of his journey, he inquired artfully about 'Ala al-Din's family, who he was, and what were his inclinations. When he had learned all he desired to know, he approached the young man and, taking him a few steps aside from his comrades, asked him, "Son, was not your father called Mustafa the tailor?" 'Ala al-Din replied, "Yes, sir, but he has been dead a long time." At these words, the African magician threw his arms around 'Ala al-Din's neck, embraced him, and kissed him several times, sighing and with tears in his eyes. 'Ala al-Din, who noticed his tears, asked him why he was weeping. The African magician cried out, "Alas, my son, how can I help it? I am your uncle, and your father was my good brother. I have been traveling abroad for many years, but no sooner do I come home with the expectation of seeing him rejoice in my return than you inform me that he is dead. I assure you that it is a deep sorrow for me to be deprived of the solace I was anticipating. But what comforts me in my affliction is that as far as I can remember him, I recognize his features in your face, and I see that I was not mistaken in approaching you." Then putting his hand on his purse, he asked 'Ala al-Din where his mother lived, and as soon as 'Ala al-Din informed him, he gave him a handful of small change, saying, "Son, go find your mother, give her my compliments, and tell her that if my time permits, I will come to see her tomorrow, in order to have the satisfaction of seeing the place where my brother lived for such a long time and where he ended his days."

As soon as the African magician left his newly designated nephew, 'Ala al-Din ran to his mother, overjoyed at the money his uncle had given him. When he arrived, he said to her, "Mother, please, tell me whether I have an uncle." She replied, "No, son, you have no uncle, neither by your father's side nor mine." 'Ala al-Din said, "Yet I have just met a man who claims to be my uncle by my father's side, assuring me that he is his brother. He even embraced me and wept when I told him that my father was dead." He added, showing her the money he had received, "To show you that I am telling the truth, here is what he gave me. He also charged me to give you his greetings and to tell you that tomorrow, if he has the time, he will come to greet you himself and at the same time see the house in which his brother lived and died." The mother said, "Son, it is true that your father had a brother, but he died a long time ago, and I never heard him say that he had another." They said nothing more about the African magician.

The following day, the African magician approached 'Ala al-Din a second time, while he was playing in another part of the town with some other children. He embraced him, as he had done on the previous day, and, putting two pieces of gold in his hand, said to him, "Son, take these to your mother, tell her that I will come to see her this evening, and ask her to get something for supper, so that we may eat together, but first tell me where to find the house." 'Ala al-Din told him, and the African magician let him go. 'Ala al-Din took the two pieces of gold to his mother, and when he told her of his uncle's wishes, she went out accordingly and returned with good provisions, and since she lacked some plates, she went and borrowed them from her neighbors. She spent the whole day preparing the supper and at night, when everything was ready, she said to 'Ala al-Din, "Son, perhaps your uncle does not know how to find our house. Go look for him, and bring him if you meet with him."

Although 'Ala al-Din had told the magician how to find the house, he was about to go, when somebody knocked at the door. When he opened it, he recognized the African magician, who came in, loaded with bottles of wine and all kinds of fruits which he brought for the supper.

After the African magician handed 'Ala al-Din what he brought, he saluted 'Ala al-Din's mother and asked her to show him where his brother Mustafa used to sit on the sofa. When she showed him, he immediately bent down and kissed the place several times and, with tears in his eyes, cried out, "O my dear brother, how unfortunate I am not to have arrived soon enough to embrace you one more time before your death." Although 'Ala al-Din's mother invited him to sit down in the same place, he refused, saying, "No, I would rather not, but allow me to sit facing it, so that, if I am deprived of the satisfaction of seeing in person the father of the family, so dear to me, I may at least look there as if he was present." 'Ala al-Din's mother pressed him no further but left him at liberty to sit where he pleased.

When he sat down at the place he desired, he began to converse with 'Ala al-Din's mother. He said, "My good sister, do not be surprised at never having seen me the whole time you were married to my brother Mustafa, of happy memory. Forty years ago, I left this country, which is mine, as well as my late brother's. After I traveled in India, Persia, Arabia, Syria, and Egypt, and lived in the most beautiful cities of these countries, I went to Africa where I made a longer stay. At last, as it is natural for a man never to forget his native land and that of his relatives and those with whom he had been raised, no matter how far away he may be, I was seized by a strong desire to see mine again and to embrace my dear brother. Feeling that I still had the strength and courage to undertake such a long journey, I did not tarry in making my preparations and setting out. I will not tell you the length of time it took me, all the obstacles I encountered, and all the burdens I endured to come here. I will only say to you that nothing has afflicted me and mortified me in all my travels so much as hearing of the death of a brother for whom I have always had brotherly love and friendship. I observed his features in the face of my nephew, your son, and I was able to distinguish him from among all the children he was with. He must have told you how I received the sad news that my brother was no longer in this world, but we must praise God for all things, for I find comfort to see him again in a son who has his most remarkable features."

The African magician, perceiving that 'Ala al-Din's mother was moved by her renewed grief at the remembrance of her husband, changed the subject and, turning to 'Ala al-Din, asked him his name. He replied, "I am called 'Ala al-Din." The magician asked, "Well, 'Ala al-Din, what do you do? Do you have a profession?" At this question, 'Ala al-Din looked down, feeling disconcerted, but his mother answered, " 'Ala al-Din is an idle fellow. His father, when he was alive, did all he could to teach him his trade, but failed. Since his father's death, in spite of what I say to him, he does no work, but wastes his time playing with the children, as you saw him, without considering that he is no longer a child. If you do not make him ashamed of it and realize that it will do him no good, I despair of his amounting to anything. He knows that his father has left him nothing, and he sees that by spinning cotton all day long, as I do, I can hardly earn enough to buy us bread. I am determined to throw him out one of these days, and let him fend for himself."

When 'Ala al-Din's mother finished her speech, bursting into tears, the African magician said to 'Ala al-Din, "Nephew, this is not good. You must think of helping yourself and making a living. There are all kinds of professions. See if there is one to which you are more inclined. Perhaps your father's trade displeases you, and you would be more suited for another. Do not hide your feelings on this, for I only wish to help you." When he saw that 'Ala al-Din did not reply, he continued, "If you find it repugnant to learn any trade, and if you wish to be an honest man, I will take a shop for you and stock it with fine fabrics and linens and set you up to sell them, and with the money you make, you will buy other goods, and by this means you will live honorably. Consider this on your own, and tell me frankly what you think of it. You will always find me ready to keep my word."

This proposal greatly flattered 'Ala al-Din, who disliked manual labor, all the more since he had enough sense to know that shops selling such goods were esteemed and frequented and that their owners were well-dressed and respected. He told the African magician that he looked at him as his uncle, that his inclination was more in this direction than any other, and that he would be indebted to him all his life for his kindness. The African magician said, "Since this profession is agreeable to you, I will take you with me tomorrow and have you dressed in the fine clothes appropriate to one of the prominent merchants of the city, and after tomorrow, we will think of opening the shop I have in mind."

'Ala al-Din's mother, who never till then believed that the African magician was her husband's brother, no longer doubted it, after all the favors he promised her son. She thanked him for his good intentions, and after having exhorted 'Ala al-Din to make himself worthy of the favors his uncle had promised, she served the supper. They continued to talk about the same subject during the entire meal, until, perceiving that it was getting late, the African magician took his leave of the mother and son and departed.

The following morning, he came again to the widow of Mustafa the tailor, as he had promised, and took 'Ala al-Din with him to a great merchant who sold only ready-made clothes of fine fabrics for all ages and ranks. He asked to see some that fitted 'Ala al-Din, and having set aside those he liked and having rejected the others, which he did not find as beautiful, he said to 'Ala al-Din, "Nephew, choose from among these the one you like best." 'Ala al-Din, charmed with the generosity of his new uncle, chose one, which the magician bought, together with all the accoutrements that went with it, and paid for it, without haggling.

When 'Ala al-Din saw himself so sumptuously dressed from head to toe, he offered his profuse thanks to his uncle, who repeated his promise never to abandon him, and to keep him always with him. He took 'Ala al-Din to the most frequented places in the city, particularly those in which the shops of the most prominent merchants were located, and when they were in the street where the richest fabrics and finest linens were sold, he said to 'Ala al-Din, "Since you will soon become a merchant like these, it is proper that you frequent these shops and become acquainted with them." He also showed him the largest and finest mosques and took him to the inns where the foreign merchants stayed and to all the parts of the king's palace he was allowed to enter. At last, after they visited together the most beautiful spots in the city, they came to the inn where the magician had taken lodgings. There they met some merchants with whom he had become acquainted since his arrival and whom he assembled together, in order to entertain them and at the same time make them acquainted with his pretended nephew.

The entertainment lasted till night, when 'Ala al-Din wished to take leave of his uncle and go home, but the African magician, refusing to let him go alone, took him to his mother, who, when she saw her son so finely dressed, was transported with joy and continued to invoke a thousand blessings on the magician for having spent so much on her son. She said to him, "Generous relative, I don't know how to thank you for your generosity. I know that my son does not deserve your favors and that he would be completely unworthy of them if he failed to thank you and to behave properly in response to your good intention of setting him up in such a fine business." She added, "For my part, I thank you again with all my heart, and I wish that you may live long enough to witness my son's gratitude, which he cannot show better than by conducting himself according to your good advice." The African magician replied, " 'Ala al-Din is a good boy and listens to me well enough, and I believe that we will do very well. One thing bothers me, however, which is that I will not be able to carry out tomorrow what I promised him, because it is Friday, and the shops will be closed, and we will not be able to rent or stock one while the merchants are busy entertaining themselves. We will, therefore, postpone the matter till Saturday, but tomorrow I will come and take him with me for a walk in the gardens, where the fashionable people are usually found. Perhaps he has never seen these amusements, for till now he has associated only with children, but now he must see men." Then he took leave of the mother and the son and departed. 'Ala al-Din, who was overjoyed to see himself so well dressed, anticipated the pleasure of walking in the gardens that lay around the city, for he had never been outside the city gates nor seen the surroundings, which were very beautiful and pleasant.

The following day, he rose and got dressed early in the morning, in order to be ready to go when his uncle came to fetch him. After having waited what seemed to him a long time, he became impatient and waited for the magician at the door, and as soon as he saw him, he told his mother and, taking leave of her, shut the door and ran to meet him. The African magician caressed 'Ala al-Din and said to him with a laugh, "Come along, my dear child. Today, I want to show you some beautiful things." He led him through one of the gates of the city to some large, beautiful houses, or rather magnificent palaces, each of which had beautiful gardens open to the public. At every palace they came to, he asked 'Ala al-Din whether he thought it beautiful, and 'Ala al-Din, anticipating the question, when they came to another, would cry out, "Uncle, here is one that is more beautiful than any we have seen." Meanwhile, they advanced farther and farther into the countryside, and the cunning magician, who had intended to go farther in order to execute his plan, took an opportunity to enter one of the gardens. He sat down by a large basin into which poured clear water from the mouth of a bronze lion. Pretending to be tired and wishing to let 'Ala al-Din rest, he said to him, "Nephew, you must be as tired as I am. Let us rest here, in order to recover our strength and have more energy to continue our walk."

After they sat down, the African magician pulled out from a wrapping cloth attached to his belt several cakes and all kinds of fruits, which he had brought with him as provisions, and laid them on the edge of the basin. He divided one of the cakes between himself and 'Ala al-Din and left him at liberty to choose the fruits he liked best. During this little meal, he talked with his pretended nephew, giving him advice and exhorting him to forsake the company of children and seek that of wise and prudent men, in order to listen to them and profit from their conversation. He said to him, "Soon you will grow up to be a man like them, and you cannot learn soon enough to speak as well as they do." After they finished the little meal, they got up and continued their walk through the gardens, which were separated from one another only by little ditches that marked their borders without impeding access. Such was the good faith of the inhabitants of this city that they took no further measures to safeguard their interests. Thus the African magician led 'Ala al-Din imperceptibly far beyond the gardens and crossed the open country until they almost reached the mountains.

'Ala al-Din, who had never been so far in his life, felt very tired after such a long walk and said to the African magician, "Uncle, where are we going? We have left the gardens very far behind us, and I see nothing but mountains. If we go much farther, I don't know whether I will have enough strength to return to the city." The fake uncle replied, "Take courage, nephew. I want to show you a garden that surpasses all the ones you have seen. It is not far off, just a step from here. When we get there, you yourself will tell me whether you would not have been sorry not to have seen it, after you had been so close." 'Ala al-Din was persuaded, and the magician led him much farther, telling him many entertaining stories, to make the way seem less tedious and the fatigue more bearable.

At last they came to a place between two mountains of moderate height, separated by a narrow valley. It was the place where the African magician had intended to bring 'Ala al-Din, in order to carry out the grand plan that had brought him from the farthest reaches of Africa to China. He said to 'Ala al-Din, "We will not go any farther. I want to show you here some extraordinary things unknown to any man, and when you see them, you will thank me for having seen so many marvels, unseen by anyone in the world but you, but while I strike fire, gather the most dry sticks you can find for kindling."

There was such a great quantity of kindling sticks that 'Ala al-Din soon gathered a more than sufficient pile, while the magician was still lighting a match. The magician set them on fire, and as soon as they began to blaze, he threw in some incense he had ready, raising a heavy cloud of smoke, which he dispersed on each side, while pronouncing some magic words of which 'Ala al-Din understood nothing.

At that very moment, the earth trembled a little and opened before the magician and 'Ala al-Din, revealing a rectangular stone about one and a half feet wide and one foot high, laid horizontally, with a brass ring fixed into the middle, to raise it with. 'Ala al-Din, frightened by what he saw, was about to run away, but as he was needed for that mysterious business, the magician caught hold of him, scolded him, and gave him such a hard blow that he knocked him down and almost pushed his teeth into his mouth, which was bleeding. Poor 'Ala al-Din, trembling and with tears in his eyes, cried out to the magician, "Uncle, what have I done to deserve such a harsh beating by you?" The magician replied, "I have my reasons for it. I am your uncle, acting in place of your father, and you ought not to answer back." Then softening, he added, "But, child, don't be afraid of anything. I ask nothing of you, except that you obey me exactly, if you wish to profit and be worthy of the great advantages I wish to offer you." These fair promises of the magician somewhat calmed 'Ala al-Din's fears and resentment, and when the magician saw that he had become completely reassured, he said to him, "You see what I have done by virtue of my incense and the words I pronounced. You should now know that under the stone there is a hidden treasure that is destined for you and which will make you one day richer than the greatest king in the world. Indeed, there is no one in the world, save you, who is permitted to touch this stone and to lift it, in order to enter. Even I myself am forbidden to touch it and to set foot in this treasure when it is opened. For this reason, you should, without fail, follow point by point what I shall ask you to do, for it is a matter of great consequence, both to you and to me."

'Ala al-Din, still astonished at what he saw and what he heard from the magician about the treasure, which was supposed to make him happy forever, forgot the beating and, getting up, said to the magician, "Well, uncle, what is to be done? Command me; I am ready to obey you." The African magician embraced him and said, "I am delighted, child, to see you make this decision. Come, take hold of the ring and lift the stone up." 'Ala al-Din said, "Uncle, I am not strong enough to lift it up; you have to help me." The African magician replied, "No, you don't need my help. If I help you, we will accomplish nothing. You must lift it up by yourself. Only pronounce the names of your father and grandfather while you take hold of the ring, and lift it up, and you will find that it will come easily." 'Ala al-Din did what the magician told him and lifted up the stone with ease and laid it aside.

When the stone was removed, there appeared a cavity three or four feet deep, with a little door and steps for descending further. The African magician said to 'Ala al-Din, "Son, follow exactly what I am going to tell you. Go down into this cavity, and when you are at the bottom of these steps, you will find an open door that will lead you into a large vaulted place, divided into three large halls, adjacent to each other. In each hall, you will see four large brass vessels, placed to the left and right, full of gold and silver, but be careful not to touch them. Before you enter the first hall, lift your gown and wrap it tightly about you. When you are in, go into the second and third, without stopping. Above all, be careful not to go near the walls or touch them even with your gown, for if you do, you will die instantly. It is for this reason that I have told you to wrap your gown tightly about you. At the end of the third hall, there is a door that will lead you into a garden planted with fine trees loaded with fruits. Walk directly across the garden by a path that will lead you to a staircase with fifty steps that will bring you to a terrace, where you will find before you a niche in which there is a lighted lamp. Take the lamp and put it out, and when you have thrown away the wick and poured out the liquid, put the lamp in your breast and bring it to me. Don't be afraid that your clothes will be spoiled, for the liquid is not oil, and the lamp will be dry, as soon as the liquid is poured out. If you desire any of the fruits of the garden, you may gather as many as you please, for you are allowed to do so."

After these words, the African magician drew a ring off his finger and put it on one of 'Ala al-Din's, telling him that it was a protection against all the harms that might befall him while he carefully followed all the instructions. Then the magician said to him, "Go down boldly, child, and we shall be rich, you and I, all our lives."

'Ala al-Din leapt lightly into the cavity and, going down the steps, found the three halls the African magician had described to him. He went through them with all the precaution inspired by the fear of death, if he failed to follow carefully all he had been instructed to do. He crossed the garden without stopping, went up to the terrace, took the lamp from the niche, threw out the wick and the liquid, and, finding the lamp dry, as the magician had told him, put it in his breast. When he came down from the terrace, he stopped in the garden to look at the fruits, of which he had only had a glimpse in crossing it. Each tree was loaded with extraordinary fruits of different colors. Some were white, and some transparent and shiny like crystals; some were pale red and some deeper; and some were green, blue, violet, and light yellow, as well as all sorts of other colors. The white were pearls; the transparent and shiny were diamonds; the dark red were rubies; the pale red were spinels; the green were emeralds; the blue were turquoise; the violet were amethyst; and the light yellow were sapphire, and so of the rest. All these fruits were so large and perfect that the like of which was never seen in the world. 'Ala al-Din was still too young to realize their quality and value and was, therefore, unimpressed by them and would have preferred figs, grapes, or the other fine fruits that were abundant in China. He thought that all these fruits were nothing but colored glass of little value. Nevertheless, the diversity of so many beautiful colors and the beauty and extraordinary size of each fruit made him desire to pick one of each kind. In fact, he took several of each color and kind, filling his two pockets and his two new purses, which the magician, wishing him to have only new things, had bought for him with the clothes, and as he could not put the purses in the pockets that were already full, he attached them to each side of his belt. He even tucked some fruits securely in his belt, which was made of silk and had several folds. Nor did he overlook to cram some in his breast, between the shirt and the gown he had wrapped about him.

Thus loaded with riches, without knowing it, 'Ala al-Din proceeded to make his way back through the three halls with all speed, in order not to make the African magician wait too long. After crossing the halls with the same precaution as before, he went up the steps and arrived at the mouth of the cave, where the African magician was waiting for him impatiently. As soon as 'Ala al-Din saw him, he said, "Please, uncle, give me your hand to help me out." The African magician replied, "Son, give me the lamp first. It may burden you." 'Ala al-Din said, "Excuse me, uncle! It is not burdensome; I will give it to you, as soon as I come up." The African magician persisted in demanding that 'Ala al-Din hand him the lamp before coming out of the cave, and 'Ala al-Din, who had buried the lamp under all the fruits with which he was loaded, absolutely refused to give it before he was out of the cave. The African magician, despairing of overcoming the resistance of the boy, flew into a terrible rage. He threw a little of his incense into the fire, which he had taken care to keep, and no sooner had he pronounced two magic words than the stone, which had closed the mouth of the cave, moved by itself into its place, with the earth over it, in the same manner as it lay at the arrival of the African magician and 'Ala al-Din.

The African magician was of course not the brother of Mustafa the tailor, as he had boasted, nor consequently the uncle of 'Ala al-Din. It is true that he came from Africa, where he was born, and since Africa is a part of the world where people are more dedicated to magic than anywhere else, he had applied himself to it from his youth; and after about forty years' experience in magic, geomancy, and fumigations, and reading of magic books, he had found out that there was somewhere in the world a magic lamp, the possession of which would make him more powerful than any king in the world, if he could obtain it. Later, by an operation of geomancy, he found out that this lamp was in a subterranean place in the middle of China, in the spot and the circumstances already described. Fully persuaded of the truth of this discovery, he set out from the farthest part of Africa, as has been mentioned before, and after a long and hard journey, he came to the town nearest to this treasure. But, although he knew for certain where the lamp was, he was not permitted to take it himself nor to enter the subterranean place where it was. Someone else had to go down, take it, and hand it to him. For this reason, he approached 'Ala al-Din, who seemed to him to be a boy of no consequence and very fit to serve his purpose. He was resolved that as soon as he got the lamp he would sacrifice poor 'Ala al-Din to his greed and wickedness, in order to have no witness of the matter, by making the fumigation, mentioned before, and by pronouncing the two magic words that produced the effect we have seen.

The blow he gave 'Ala al-Din and the authority he assumed over him were only meant to make him fear him and obey him readily, so that 'Ala al-Din would give him the magic lamp as soon as he asked for it. But the opposite of what he had expected happened, and he ended by getting rid of poor 'Ala al-Din, driven by his wicked eagerness and the fear that if they argued any longer, someone might hear them and reveal what he wished to keep secret.

When the African magician saw his great hopes frustrated forever, he had no other choice but to return to Africa, and he did so that very day. He took a roundabout route in order to avoid going through the town from which he had set out with 'Ala al-Din, for fear lest some people who may have seen him go for a walk with the boy, should now see him returning without him.

According to all appearances, 'Ala al-Din was no more to be heard of. But the magician, who thought that he was rid of him forever, had overlooked the ring he had put on 'Ala al-Din's finger and which could and did in fact save 'Ala al-Din, who was totally unaware of its power, and it is surprising that the loss of the ring, as well as that of the lamp, did not drive the magician to the depths of despair. But magicians are so much used to misfortunes and events contrary to their wishes that, as long as they live, they never cease to feed on smoke, chimeras, and dreams.

'Ala al-Din, who did not expect this ill-treatment from his false uncle, after all the caresses and the favors he had done him, was stricken with such a great surprise that it is easier to imagine it than to describe it with words. When he found that he was buried alive, he called out to his uncle a thousand times, telling him that he was ready to give him the lamp, but it was all in vain, since his cries could not be heard, and thus he remained in that dark place. At last, after several bursts of tears, he descended to the bottom of the steps in order to go to the garden through which he had walked earlier and where it was light, but the wall, which was opened before by magic, was now shut by the same means. He groped before him left and right, again and again, but found no opening. So he redoubled his cries and tears and sat down on the steps, without any hope of ever seeing the light again and with the sad certainty of his passing from the present darkness into that of the death to come.

'Ala al-Din remained in this state for two days without eating or drinking. On the third day, he regarded death as inevitable and, raising his hands and clasping them in resignation to the will of God, cried out, "There is no power and no strength, save in God the Almighty, the Magnificent." In clasping his hands, he rubbed, unaware, the ring that the magician had placed on his finger and of which he knew not the power. As soon as he did so, a demon of enormous size and dreadful look rose before him, as if out of the earth, with his head reaching the vault, and said to him, "What do you wish? Here I am, ready to obey you, as your slave and the slave of all those who wear the ring, I and the other slaves of the ring." At another time and occasion, 'Ala al-Din, who was not used to such sights, would have been so frightened that he would not have been able to speak at the sight of such an extraordinary figure, but being preoccupied solely by the danger he was in, he responded without hesitation, "Whoever you are, get me out of this place, if you can." No sooner had he pronounced these words than the earth opened, and he found himself outside the cave, on the very spot where the magician had first brought him.

It is not surprising that 'Ala al-Din, who had spent such a long time in total darkness, should have found it hard to bear the bright light. He let his eyes get used to it little by little, and when he began to look around him, he was very much surprised not to find the earth open and could not comprehend how he had got so suddenly out of its bowels. He saw only the place where the sticks had been kindled, and by that, he could nearly tell where the cave was. Then, turning in the direction of the town, he soon saw it in the midst of the gardens that surrounded it and recognized the way by which the African magician had led him. So he took it back, thanking God to find himself once more in the world, after he had despaired of every coming back. When he reached the town, he dragged himself with difficulty to his home, and when he went in to his mother, the joy of seeing her again, together with his weakness, caused by not having eaten for almost three days, made him faint for some time. His mother, who had mourned him, thinking that he was lost or dead, seeing him in this condition, did everything she could to bring him to himself again. At last, he recovered, and the first words he spoke were, "Please, mother, first give me something to eat, for I have not had any food for three days." His mother brought him what she had and, placing it before him, said, "Son, don't eat too fast, for it is dangerous. Eat little by little, at your ease, and take care of yourself, for you are very much in need of it. I don't want you even to talk to me. You will have enough time to tell me what happened to you, when you are fully recovered. It is a great comfort to me to see you again, after the agony I have endured since Friday, and the pains I have taken to learn what had become of you, ever since I saw that it was night and you failed to return."

'Ala al-Din followed his mother's advice and ate unhurriedly, little by little, and drank moderately. When he finished, he said, "I would have made serious complaints about you for abandoning me so easily to the discretion of a man who had the intention of killing me and who at this very moment thinks my death certain, doubting not that I am either dead already or about to die soon. But you believed that he was my uncle, and I believed it too, for could we have entertained any other thoughts of a man who lavished on me caresses and favors and promised me many advantages? But, mother, he is nothing but a treacherous, wicked swindler, who did me favors and made me all those promises only to achieve his purpose and then kill me, as I have told you, leaving you and me unable to guess the reason. For my part, I can assure you that I never gave him any cause to deserve the least ill-treatment. You shall understand it yourself, when you hear exactly all that had happened, from the time I left you to the time he came to the execution of his evil plan."

Then 'Ala al-Din began to tell his mother all that had happened to him from Friday, when the magician took him to see the palaces and the gardens situated outside the city, and what happened to him on the way until they came to the place between the two mountains where the magician was to perform his prodigious feat. He told her how with some incense thrown into the fire and a few magic words, the earth opened instantly, revealing a cave that led to an inestimable treasure. He did not forget to mention the blow he had received from the magician, nor how, after softening a little, the magician had engaged him, by making great promises and putting the ring on his finger, to go down into the cave. He did not omit the least detail of what he saw in passing and returning through the three halls, the garden, and the terrace from which he had taken the magic lamp, which he pulled out from his breast and showed to his mother, together with the transparent fruits, as well as those of different colors, which he had gathered in the garden on his return, adding the two full purses, which he gave to his mother, who cared little for them. For although these fruits were precious stones, which shone like the sun, vying with the lamp that lighted the room, and which should have therefore led them to realize their great value, 'Ala al-Din's mother had no more knowledge of their worth than her son. She had been brought up in poverty, and her husband did not have the means to give her such things; nor had she seen any at her relatives or neighbors. Therefore, it is not surprising that she looked on them as things of little value and only pleasing to the eye by the variety of their colors. So 'Ala al-Din simply put them behind one of the cushions of the sofa on which he was sitting.

Then he resumed the story of his adventure, telling her that when he returned and presented himself at the mouth of the cave, ready to come out, the magician asked him to give him the lamp, which he wanted, but upon refusing, the magician, by throwing some incense into the fire and pronouncing some words, instantly caused the entrance to the cave to close again. 'Ala al-Din could not, without bursting into tears, go on to describe to her the miserable condition in which he found himself buried alive in that deadly cave, until by touching the ring, whose power he had not yet learned, he came out of the cave, properly speaking, came to life again. When he finished his story, he said to his mother, "There is no need to say more; you know the rest. This is my adventure and the danger I have faced, since you last saw me."

'Ala al-Din's mother listened patiently, without interrupting this surprising and wonderful story, which was at the same time painful to a mother who loved her son tenderly, in spite of his faults. Yet in the most touching parts, which clearly revealed the perfidy of the African magician, she could not help showing, by marks of her indignation, how much she detested him, and when 'Ala al-Din finished his story, she broke out into a thousand reproaches against that imposter. She called him perfidious, treacherous, barbarian, assassin, deceiver, magician, and enemy and destroyer of mankind, adding, "Yes, son, he is a magician, and they are a plague to the world, and by their magic and sorcery have commerce with the devil. Bless God for wishing to preserve you from the total effect of his infamous wickedness. You should thank Him for the mercy He has shown you, for your death would have been inevitable if you had not thought of Him and implored His assistance." She said a great deal more against the magician's treachery against her son, but while she spoke, she sensed that 'Ala al-Din, who had not slept for three days, needed to rest. So she put him to bed, and soon after went to bed herself.

'Ala al-Din, who had not had any rest while he was in the subterranean place where he was buried and left to die, slept soundly the whole night and did not wake up until very late the next day. When he got up, the first thing he said to his mother was that he wanted something to eat and that she could not do him a greater favor than to give him breakfast. His mother replied, "Alas, son, I don't have even a piece of bread to give you; you ate up all the food I had in the house last night, but have a little patience, and it will not be long before I will bring you some. I have some cotton yarn that I have spun. I will go and sell it, in order to buy bread and something for our dinner." 'Ala al-Din replied, "Mother, keep your cotton yarn for another occasion, and give me the lamp I brought yesterday. I will go and sell it, and the money I will get for it will buy us breakfast and dinner, and perhaps supper."

'Ala al-Din's mother fetched the lamp, saying to her son, "Here it is, but it is very dirty. If it was cleaned, I believe it would bring more." She took water and a little fine sand to clean it, but no sooner had she begun to rub the lamp than a hideous demon of gigantic size appeared instantly before her and her son and said to her with a thundering voice, "What do you wish? Here I am, ready to obey you as your slave and the slave of all those who have the lamp in their hands, I and the other slaves of the lamp."

'Ala al-Din's mother was in no condition to reply, for she could not bear the sight of this hideous and terrifying demon, and her terror was so great, from the very first words he uttered, that she fainted away. 'Ala al-Din, who had already seen a somewhat similar apparition in the cave, without losing time on reflection, promptly snatched the lamp from his mother's hand and, acting as her deputy, spoke for her, replying boldly, "I am hungry; bring me something to eat." The demon disappeared and in an instant returned, carrying on his head a large silver basin containing twelve covered silver plates full of excellent food; six large loaves of bread, as white as snow, placed on the plates; and two bottles of delicious wine; and holding in his hand two silver cups. He placed all this before the sofa and disappeared.

This was done in such a short time that 'Ala al-Din's mother had not yet regained consciousness before the demon disappeared for the second time. 'Ala al-Din, who had been throwing water on her face, without success, redoubled his efforts to bring her to herself, and whether her lost consciousness returned by itself or was somewhat aroused by the aroma of the food the demon had brought, she soon recovered. 'Ala al-Din said to her, "Mother, don't mind this. Get up, and come and eat. Here is what will revive you and at the same time satisfy my extreme hunger. We should not let such fine food get cold; let us eat."

'Ala al-Din's mother was extremely surprised to see the large basin, the twelve plates, the six loaves, and the two bottles and cups, and to smell the delicious aroma that wafted from the plates. She asked 'Ala al-Din, "Son, from where did we get this abundance and to whom do we owe this great generosity? Has the king learned of our poverty and had compassion on us?" 'Ala al-Din replied, "Mother, let us sit down and eat; you need food as much as I do. I will answer your questions after we eat." They sat down and ate with great relish, since both mother and son had never before sat at such a sumptuous table. Throughout the meal, 'Ala al-Din's mother could not stop looking at and admiring the basin and plates, even though she could not tell exactly whether they were silver or some other metal, for she was little accustomed to seeing such things. In fact, being ignorant of their value, it was only the novelty that aroused her admiration. 'Ala al-Din himself knew no more about them than she did. 'Ala al-Din and his mother, who had expected to eat a simple breakfast, ate until it was dinnertime. The excellent food aroused their appetite, and while it was still warm, they thought it best to combine the two meals. After they finished, they found that they had enough left not only for supper, but for two full meals for the following day.

After 'Ala al-Din's mother cleared the table and put aside the food that was not touched, she went and sat down on the sofa next to her son and said to him, " 'Ala al-Din, I want you now to satisfy my impatience to hear the explanation you had promised." 'Ala al-Din related to her exactly all that had happened between him and the demon, from the time she lost consciousness to the time she recovered. She was in great amazement at what her son told her and at the appearance of the demon and said to him, "Son, what have we to do with your demons? In all my life, I never heard that any of my acquaintances had ever seen one. By what misadventure did that demon address himself to me, and why me and not you, since he had already appeared to you in the cave of the treasure?" 'Ala el-Din replied, "Mother, the demon you saw is not the same who appeared to me; they are similar in a way, particularly in their gigantic size, but they are completely different in features and clothes, and they belong to different masters. If you remember, the one I saw said that he was the slave of the ring, which I have on my finger, while the one you saw said that he was the slave of the lamp, which you had in your hand. But I believe that you did not hear him, for you fainted as soon as he began to speak." The mother cried out, "What! Was it your lamp then that made that wicked demon speak to me, rather than you? Ah! my son, take it out of my sight, and put it where you please. I don't want to touch it again. I would rather see you throw it out or sell it than run the risk of being frightened to death by touching it, and if you would listen to me, you would also get rid of the ring. You should have nothing to do with demons, for, as our Prophet has told us, they are devils."

'Ala al-Din replied, "Mother, with your permission, I shall be careful now not to sell a lamp, as I was ready to do, which will be useful both to you and to me. Haven't you seen what it has procured us? It will continue to provide us sustenance and maintenance. You must assume, as I do, that my false and wicked uncle went to such lengths and undertook such a long and hard journey just to take possession of this magic lamp, which he preferred above all the gold and silver that he knew were in the halls, as he told me, and which I have seen with my own eyes. He knew too well the merit and value of this lamp not to prefer it to a great treasure. Since chance made us discover its power, let us use it to our advantage, in a discreet manner that will not bring upon us the envy and jealousy of our neighbors. Because the demon frightens you so much, I am quite willing to take it out of your sight and to put it in a place where I can find it when I need it. As for the ring, I cannot resolve to get rid of it either, for without it, you would never have seen me again, and though I am alive now, I may not be a few moments after it is gone. Allow me then to keep it and to wear it always on my finger, very carefully. Who knows whether we may not face other dangers, which neither you nor I can foresee and from which the ring can deliver us." As 'Ala al-Din's arguments were just, his mother had no reply, except to say, "Son, do as you please; as for myself, I will have nothing to do with demons. I will wash my hands of them and never say anything more about them."

The following night, after they had eaten supper, there was nothing left of the good provisions the demon had brought. So the following day, 'Ala al-Din, who did not wish to wait until he got very hungry, took one of the silver plates under his gown and went out early in the morning to sell it. He approached a Jew whom he met on the street and, taking him aside, showed him the plate and asked him if he wished to buy it. The Jew, who was experienced and cunning, took the plate and examined it, and as soon as he found that it was good silver, he asked 'Ala al-Din how much he valued it at. 'Ala al-Din, who did not know the value and never trafficked in such merchandise, told him that he himself knew very well how much it was worth and that he would trust in his good faith. The Jew was confounded by 'Ala al-Din's simplicity, and being uncertain whether or not 'Ala al-Din knew the material or the value, he took out of his purse a piece of gold, which was only a seventy-second of the value of the plate, and gave it to him. 'Ala al-Din took the money very eagerly and, as soon as he had it in his hand, left so hurriedly that the Jew, not content with the exorbitant profit of this purchase, was angry with himself for not realizing that 'Ala al-Din did not know the value of what he had sold him and that he could have paid him much less. He was about to run after the young man, in order to get some change back, but 'Ala al-Din had run so fast and got so far that it would have been very difficult for the Jew to overtake him.

On his way back to his mother, 'Ala al-Din stopped at a bakery, where he bought some bread for his mother and himself, paying with the piece of gold and receiving the change. When he arrived, he gave the change to his mother, who went to the market and bought enough provisions to sustain the two of them for several days. In this manner, they continued to live, as 'Ala al-Din sold all the plates to the Jew, one after another and in the same way as he had sold the first. The Jew, who had paid a piece of gold for the first plate, did not dare to offer him less for the others, for fear of losing such a windfall, and so paid him the same amount for each plate. When the money from the last plate was spent, 'Ala al-Din had recourse to the basin, which alone weighed ten times more than each plate. He would have carried it to the usual purchaser, but its heavy weight prevented him; therefore, he was obliged to look for the Jew and bring him to his mother's house. The Jew, after assessing the weight of the basin, laid down, on the spot, ten pieces of gold, and 'Ala al-Din was satisfied.

They used the money for some time to pay for their daily expenses. 'Ala al-Din, who had been used to an idle life, had stopped playing with the boys of his own age ever since his adventure with the African magician. He spent his days in walking about and talking with people with whom he had gotten acquainted. Sometimes he would stop at the shops of the prominent merchants which people of distinction frequented, on business or for a rendezvous, and he would listen to their conversation, by which he gained, little by little, a smattering of knowledge of the world.

When all the money was gone, 'Ala al-Din had recourse to the lamp. He took it in his hand, looked for the spot which his mother had rubbed, and, finding it by the mark the sand had left on it, rubbed it, as she had done, and the demon immediately appeared before him, but since 'Ala al-Din had rubbed the lamp more lightly, the demon spoke to him with a gentler voice, saying, as before, "What do you wish? Here I am, ready to obey you as your slave and the slave of all those who have the lamp in their hands, I and the other slaves of the lamp." 'Ala al-Din replied, "I am hungry; bring me some food." The demon disappeared and, a very short time later, returned, carrying a table service similar to the one he had brought the first time. He put it before the sofa and disappeared instantly.

'Ala al-Din's mother, warned of the plan of her son, had gone out on some errands, on purpose, in order not to be at home when the demon appeared. When she returned, a little time later, she found the table very well furnished and was as much astonished as before at the prodigious effect of the lamp. 'Ala al-Din and his mother sat down to eat, and after they finished, enough food was left to last them two more days.

As soon as 'Ala al-Din saw that nothing was left in the house, neither bread nor other provisions nor any money to buy them with, he took a silver plate and went to look for the Jew he knew, in order to sell it to him. On his way, he passed by the shop of a goldsmith who was of venerable age, a man of honesty and great probity. When the goldsmith saw him, he called him, invited him into his shop, and said, "Son, I have often seen you go by, loaded as you are now, to meet a certain Jew and come back a short time later, carrying nothing. I assume that you carry something that you sell to him, but perhaps you don't know that the Jew is a cheat, indeed, even more so than all the other Jews, and that none of those who know him wishes to do any business with him. I am telling you this for your own good. If you wish to show me what you are carrying now, and if it is for sale, I will pay you its exact value, if I can afford it. If I cannot, I will direct you to other merchants who will not cheat you."

The hope of getting more money for the plate induced 'Ala al-Din to pull it out from under his gown and show it to the goldsmith. The old man, who knew at first sight that it was made of fine silver, asked him whether he had sold similar plates to the Jew and how much he had gotten for it. 'Ala al-Din told him plainly that he had sold twelve and that he had received only one piece of gold for each. The goldsmith cried out, "Ah! the thief!" adding, "Son, what is done is done, and you should forget about it. But when I tell you the value of your plate, which is made of the finest silver we use in our shops, you will realize how much the Jew has cheated you."

The goldsmith took a pair of scales and weighed the plate, and after explaining to 'Ala al-Din how much an ounce of silver, as well as its fractions, contained, he told him that according to its weight the plate was worth seventy-two pieces of gold, which he paid him immediately, saying, "This is the fair value of your plate. If you doubt it, you may go to any of our goldsmiths you please, and if he tells you that it is worth more, I promise to pay you twice as much, for we make money only on the workmanship of the silver goods we buy, and this is something that even the fairest Jews don't do." 'Ala al-Din thanked him very much for his fair treatment, which was so much to his advantage.

Afterwards, he went to no other person but him, and sold him all the plates, as well as the basin, receiving the fair value, according to their weight. Though 'Ala al-Din and his mother had an inexhaustible source of money from the lamp and might have had as much as they wanted whenever the money was spent, they nevertheless continued to live with the same frugality as before, for 'Ala al-Din spent just enough to support himself modestly and to provide for the needs of the household. As for his mother, she did not spend on her clothes more than what she earned from her cotton spinning. Considering their simple way of life, it is easy to figure out how much the money 'Ala al-Din received from the goldsmith for the plates and the basin, according to their weight, lasted. They lived in this way for many years, by the good use 'Ala al-Din made of the lamp from time to time.

During this time, 'Ala al-Din never failed to be often in the company of persons of distinction who met at the shops of the most prominent merchants of cloth of gold and silver, silk fabrics, and the most delicate linens, as well as jewelry, and with whom he sometimes joined in conversation. Thus he matured slowly and acquired all the manners of the people of fashion. By his acquaintance with the jewelers, he discovered his error in thinking that the transparent fruits he had gathered in the garden when he went to get the lamp were nothing but colored glass, as he found out that they were stones of great value. For as he had seen all sorts of jewels bought and sold in their shops, he came to know their quality and value, and as he saw nothing there that equaled his in beauty or size, he realized that he possessed, not pieces of glass, which he had considered as trifles, but an inestimable treasure. However, he had the prudence not to say anything of it to anyone, not even to his mother, and there is no doubt that it was this reticence that brought him the great fortune, as we are about to see from the following account.

One day, as he was strolling in one quarter of the city, he heard a crier proclaim with a loud voice an order of the king, commanding people to close their shops and houses and stay indoors, while Princess Badr al-Budur, the king's daughter, went to the baths and came back. This public order aroused in 'Ala al-Din the curiosity to see the face of the princess; however, he could not do it without entering the house of some acquaintance and looking through shutters. But this did not satisfy him, because, according to custom, the princess had to cover her face with a veil when she went to the baths. He therefore devised a way that succeeded. He went and placed himself behind the door of the baths, which was so situated that he could not fail to see her face. He did not have to wait long before the princess came, and he was able to see her through a large crack in the door, without being seen. She was accompanied by a great number of her female attendants and eunuchs, who walked on each side as well as behind her. When she was within three or four steps from the door of the baths, she took off her veil, which had bothered her very much, giving 'Ala al-Din the opportunity to see her clearly as she came toward him.

Until that moment, 'Ala al-Din had never seen any woman's face except his mothers', who was old and who never had such beautiful features as to make him think that other women were beautiful. He might very well have heard that there were some women of astonishing beauty, but whatever words are used to praise a beautiful woman, they never make the same impression as the woman herself. But as soon as he saw Princess Badr al-Budur, he changed his belief that all women looked more or less like his mother; his attitude changed considerably, as his heart could not resist the inclinations aroused by such a charming object. For indeed, the princess was the most beautiful brunette in the world. Her eyes were large, sparkling, and striking, her looks modest and sweet, her nose justly proportioned and without blemish, her mouth small, her lips vermillion and charmingly symmetrical—in short, all the features of her face were perfectly proportioned. One should therefore not be surprised that 'Ala al-Din, who had never seen such a combination of charms, was dazzled and beside himself. In addition to all these perfections, the princess had so stately a figure, and so majestic an air, that the mere sight of her commanded the respect due her.

After she went into the baths, 'Ala al-Din remained for some time in a state of amazement and a kind of ecstasy, retracing and imprinting deeply in his mind the image of one who had charmed him and penetrated deep into his heart. At last, considering that the princess was gone past him and that it would be useless for him to stay behind the door in order to see her again, since when she came out of the baths, her back would be turned toward him and she would be veiled, he resolved to quit his post and go home.

When he arrived, he could not conceal his uneasiness and anxiety, so that his mother noticed and was surprised to see him much more preoccupied and melancholy than usual. She asked him whether something had happened to him or whether he was not feeling well. 'Ala al-Din made no reply, but slumped on the sofa and remained in that state, full of the charming image of Princess Badr al-Budur. His mother, who was preparing supper, pressed him no further. When it was ready, she set it near him, before the sofa, and sat down to eat, but seeing that he paid no attention to it, she asked him to eat, and it was with difficulty that she persuaded him to leave his place and come to the table. But he ate much less than usual, with his eyes cast down and with such a profound silence, that his mother could not get a single word out of him in answer to all the questions she asked him to find the reason for such an extraordinary alteration. After supper, she asked again the reason for such a deep melancholy, but she could find out nothing, and 'Ala al-Din decided to go to bed rather than give her the slightest satisfaction.

Without going into how 'Ala al-Din spent the night, captivated by the beauty and charm of Princess Badr al-Budur, I shall only say that as he sat the following day on the sofa, facing his mother, who was spinning cotton as usual, he spoke to her in these words, "Mother, I am breaking the silence that I have kept ever since my return home yesterday and which, I know, has troubled you. I was not ill, as I assume you thought, nor am I ill now, but I can tell you that what I felt then and what I feel now is worse than any disease. I don't know what to call this affliction, but I have no doubt that when you hear what I will tell you, you will know what it is." 'Ala al-Din continued, "It was not known in this quarter of town, and therefore you yourself could not know, that yesterday, Princess Badr al-Budur, the king's daughter, was to go to the baths after dinner. I heard the news, as I was strolling in the city, and an order was proclaimed that all the shops should be closed and everybody should stay indoors, in order to pay the princess her due respect and to leave the streets free for her. Since I was not far from the baths, the curiosity of seeing her face unveiled gave me the idea to go and stand behind the door of the baths, supposing that she would remove the veil when she was about to enter. You know the position of the door, and you could judge for yourself that I could see her easily, if what I had supposed happened, and indeed, as she entered, she removed the veil, and I had the good fortune of seeing this lovely princess, with the greatest satisfaction in the world. This, mother, was the main cause of the state in which you saw me, when I came in yesterday, and the reason for the silence I have kept till now. I love the princess with a love so intense that I cannot express it to you, and as my lively and ardent passion increases every moment, I know that it will be satisfied only by the possession of the lovely princess, Badr al-Budur. I have therefore decided to ask the king for her hand in marriage."

'Ala al-Din's mother listened attentively to what her son told her, but when she heard of his desire to ask for the hand of Princess Badr al-Budur in marriage, she could not help interrupting him with a loud burst of laughter. 'Ala al-Din wanted to continue, but she interrupted him again, saying, "Ah! son, what are you thinking of? You must be mad to talk like this." 'Ala al-Din replied, "Mother, I assure you that I am not mad, but in my right mind. I expected you to accuse me of folly and extravagance, but your reproaches will not stop me from asking the king for the princess's hand in marriage."

The mother replied very seriously, "Really, son, I can't help telling you that you have completely forgotten yourself, but even if you still wish to carry out this decision, I don't see whom you will venture to ask to make this proposition on your behalf to the king." 'Ala al-Din replied immediately, "You yourself." The mother cried out in surprise and astonishment, "I? To the king? Ah! I will be very careful not to engage in such an enterprise." She added, "And who are you, son, to have the temerity to think of your king's daughter? Have you forgotten that you are the son of a man who was a tailor, one of the poorest in the capital, and a woman who is of no better pedigree? Don't you know that kings don't condescend to marry their daughters even to the sons of kings, unless they expect to rule one day as kings like themselves?" 'Ala al-Din replied, "Mother, I have already told you that I had foreseen all that you have said or can say. Neither your speech nor your remonstrances will make me change my mind. I have told you that through your mediation, I will demand Princess Badr al-Budur in marriage; this is a favor I ask of you, with all the respect I owe you, and I beg of you not to refuse me, unless you would rather see me die than give me life a second time."

'Ala al-Din's mother was very embarrassed when she saw how stubbornly her son persisted in pursuing such a foolish plan. She said to him again, "Son, I am your mother, and as a good mother who brought you into the world, there is nothing reasonable or appropriate that I would not readily do out of my love for you. If it was a question of marriage with one of the daughters of one of our neighbors, whose circumstances were equal or similar to ours, I would do all I can with all my heart, and even then, you would need to have some property, income, or profession. When poor people like us wish to marry, the first thing they ought to think about is how to earn a living. But without reflecting on the meanness of your birth or the little merit and the few possessions you have, you aspire to the highest degree of fortune, and your pretensions are no less than to demand in marriage the daughter of your sovereign, who with one single word can crush you and destroy you. I leave aside what concerns you, for it is for you to consider what you ought to do, if you have some sense. I come now to consider what concerns me. How could such an extraordinary thought come into your head, that I should go to the king and propose to him to give you his daughter the princess in marriage? Suppose I had, not to say the boldness, but the impudence to present myself before his majesty and make such a foolish request, to whom should I address myself to introduce me to him? Do you think that the first person I would speak to would not take me for a madwoman and drive me away indignantly, as I should deserve? Suppose there is no difficulty in having an audience with his majesty; I know that there is none for those who go to him to demand justice, which he grants readily to his subjects; I also know that when people ask him for a favor, he grants it gladly, when he sees that they deserve it and are worthy of it. But is that your case, and do you think that you have deserved the favor you wish me to ask for you? What have you done for your king or country?

How have you distinguished yourself? If you have done nothing to deserve such a great favor, nor are worthy of it, with what face can I demand it? How can I open my mouth to make the proposal to the king? His majestic presence and his dazzling court would immediately silence me, I who used to tremble before my late husband, your father, when I asked him for the slightest thing. There is another reason, son, which you don't think of and which is that one never presents oneself before the king to ask for a favor without a present, for a present has at least one advantage, and that is that if for whatever reason he refuses the favor, the demand will at least be heard. But what do you have to offer? And if you had any present worthy of the least attention of such a great king, how commensurate would it be with the favor you wish to ask of him? Reflect on it yourself, and realize that you aspire to something that is impossible to attain."

'Ala al-Din listened very calmly to all that his mother could say to dissuade him from his plan, and after he reflected on all the points of her remonstration, he at last replied, "I admit, mother, that it is very rash of me to presume to carry my pretensions so far, and very inconsiderate to ask you with so much ardor and urgency to make the proposal of my marriage to the king, without first taking the proper measures to secure you an audience and a favorable reception, and I therefore beg your pardon. But don't be surprised that, in the intensity of my passion, I did not at first think of everything necessary to procure me the happiness I seek. I love Princess Badr al-Budur beyond all you can imagine, or rather I adore her and shall always persevere in my plan to marry her. It is a thing that is determined and fixed in my mind. I am grateful to you for the suggestion you have given me, and I look on it as the first step toward procuring me the happy success I promise myself.

"You say that it is not customary to go to the king without a present and that I have nothing worthy of him. As to what you say about the necessity of a present, I agree with you, and I admit that I never thought of it, but as to what you say that I have nothing fit to present to him, don't you think, mother, that what I brought home with me the day on which I was delivered from an inevitable death may be very pleasing to the king? I am speaking of what I brought in the two purses and in the belt, which you and I both took for colored glass. But now I know that I was wrong, and I tell you, Mother, that they are jewels of inestimable value, fit only for the greatest kings; take my word for it. I discovered their worth by frequenting the jewelers' shops. All the jewels I saw at the jewelers' shops cannot compare to those we have, neither in size nor beauty, yet they offer them at excessive prices. In truth, neither you nor I know the full value of ours, but whatever it may be, as far as I know from my little experience, they will please the king very much. You have a large porcelain dish, large enough and of a shape fit to hold them; fetch it, and let us see how they look, after we arrange them according to their different colors."

'Ala al-Din's mother brought the dish, and he took the jewels out of the two purses and arranged them in the dish. The effect they made in the bright daylight, by the variety of their colors and by their luster and brilliance, was so great that both mother and son were dazzled and greatly astonished, for until then they had only seen them in the light of a lamp. It is true that 'Ala al-Din had seen them before, each kind hanging on its tree, like fruits, a sight that must have been delight-ful, but since he was only a boy, he looked on them as nothing but trinkets to play with.

After admiring for some time the beauty of the jewels, 'Ala al-Din said, "Mother, now you can no longer excuse yourself from going to the king, on the pretext that you have no present to give him. Here is one that, I think, will gain you the most favorable reception." Even though 'Ala al-Din's mother, despite the beauty and luster of the jew-els, did not think the present to be as valuable as her son esteemed it, she nevertheless thought that it might please the king. But although she knew very well that she had nothing to say against it, she kept pondering the proposal that 'Ala al-Din wished her to make to the king, by favor of the present, and which worried her very much. She said to him, "Son, I have no difficulty conceiving that your present will have an effect and that the king will look on me favorably, but I am sure that when I attempt to make the proposal you wish me to make, I will not have the power to open my mouth. Thus I will not only lose my labor, but the present, which, according to you, is of an extraordinary value, and I will return home in confusion, to tell you that your hopes are dashed. I have already told you this, and you ought to believe me." She added, "But I will exert myself to please you, and I wish that I may find the power to dare make the proposal you wish me to make. The king will certainly either laugh at me and send me back as a madwoman, or justifiably be in a great rage, of which both you and I will surely be the victims." She presented other arguments to her son in her attempt to persuade him to change his mind, but the charms of Princess Badr al-Budur had made too great an impression on his heart to dissuade him from his plan. He persisted in asking his mother to carry out his resolution, and she, as much out of tenderness as out of fear that he might resort to some violent or offensive measure, overcame her reluctance and submitted to his wish.

As it was now very late, and the time for an audience with the king had already passed, it was postponed till the next day. The mother and son talked of nothing else for the rest of the day, and 'Ala al-Din took a great deal of pain to tell her whatever he could think of, to encourage her in the resolution, which she finally took, to go to the king. But in spite of all his arguments, his mother could never convince herself that she would succeed in this affair, and in truth, one must admit that she had enough reason for doubt. She said to 'Ala al-Din, "Son, if the king receives me as favorably as I wish, for your sake, if he listens calmly to the proposition you wish me to make, and if, after this kind reception, he should think of asking me where are your possessions, your riches, and your estate, for he will sooner inquire after that than after your person; if, I say, he should ask, what do you wish me to tell him?" 'Ala al-Din replied, "Mother, let us not worry in advance about something that may never happen. First, let us see how the king receives you and what answer he gives you. If it should happen that he wishes to be informed of all that you mention, I will think of an answer to give him, for I have confidence that the lamp, which has sustained us for many years, will not fail me in time of need."

'Ala al-Din's mother had nothing to say in reply to what her son said. She thought that the lamp might be capable of performing greater wonders than simply providing them with sustenance. This thought satisfied her and at the same time removed all the objections that might have dissuaded her from undertaking the mission to the king, which she had promised her son. 'Ala al-Din, who guessed what she was thinking, said, "Above all, mother, remember to keep the secret, for on that depends all the success both you and I expect in this affair." 'Ala al-Din and his mother parted to go to bed. But his intense love and his great expectations of such an immense fortune had taken such a hold of 'Ala al-Din that he could not rest as well as he might have wished. He got up at dawn and went immediately to wake up his mother, pressing her to get dressed as soon as she could, to go to the king's palace, and to enter as soon as the gate was opened, and the grand vizier, the other viziers, and all the high officers of state went into the audience hall where the king always presided in person.

'Ala al-Din's mother did all that her son wished. She took the porcelain dish that contained the jewels, wrapped it in two wrapping cloths, one more delicate and cleaner than the other, which she tied at four corners, in order to carry the dish more easily. At last she departed, to 'Ala al-Din's great satisfaction, and took the road to the palace. When she arrived at the gate, the grand vizier, the other viziers, and the most distinguished lords of the court had already gone in. The gate was opened, and she went in with the great crowd of people who had business at the court. When she entered, she found herself in a long, spacious, and beautiful hall, the entrance to which was grand and magnificent. She stood, placing herself directly before the king, the grand vizier, and the lords, who sat in the council to the left and right of the king. The cases were called, one after the other, according to their order, and they were pleaded and judged until the time the council usually adjourned. Then the king rose, dismissed the council, and retired to his apartment, where he was followed by the grand vizier. Then the other viziers and the officers of state departed, as also did those who were there on business, some pleased with winning their case, others dissatisfied with the judgment rendered against them, and the rest in the expectation of having their cases heard at the next council.

'Ala al-Din's mother, seeing the king rise and retire and all the people depart, concluded rightly that he would not come again that day and decided to go home. When 'Ala al-Din saw her return with the present meant for the king, he did not know at first what to think of the success of her mission, and, fearing that she might have some bad news for him, he did not have the courage to ask her any question. The good woman, who had never before set foot in the king's palace and who did not have the slightest knowledge of how business was normally conducted there, relieved her son of his uncertainty, saying to him with great simplicity, "Son, I have seen the king, and I am very convinced that he has seen me, too, for I placed myself directly before him, and no one could prevent him from seeing me, but he was so busy with all those who spoke on all sides of him, that I pitied him for the pains he took to listen patiently to all of them. This lasted so long that he finally became weary, for he rose unexpectedly and retired suddenly, not wishing to hear the great many persons who were waiting for their turn to speak. Nevertheless, I was very pleased, for I was losing patience and getting extremely tired from standing for such a long time. But there is no harm done. I will go back tomorrow; perhaps the king may not be as busy."

Although 'Ala al-Din's love was very intense, he was forced to be satisfied with this excuse and to brace himself with patience. He had at least the satisfaction to find that his mother had taken the most difficult step, namely, to have seen the king, and he hoped that she would be emboldened by the example of those whom she saw speak to him and no longer hesitate to carry out her commission when a favorable opportunity to speak to the king offered itself.

The following day, 'Ala al-Din's mother went to the king's palace, with the present, as early in the morning as the day before, but she went for nothing, for she found the audience hall closed and discovered that the council convened every other day, and, therefore, she had to come back the following day. She went back with this news to her son, who had no choice but to remain patient. She went back to the palace on the appointed day, six more times, placing herself always directly before the king, but again with as little success as the first time, and she might have perhaps gone a hundred times, all to no avail, if the king himself, who saw her at each session standing before him, had not taken notice of her. For it is very probable that only those who had petitions to present and who waited in line approached the king, in order to plead their cases, each in his turn, and 'Ala al-Din's mother was not one of them.

At last, after the council had adjourned, and the king had retired to his apartment, he said to his grand vizier, "For some time now, I have noticed a certain woman, who comes every day I hold a council. She carries something wrapped in a wrapping cloth and remains standing up, from the beginning to the end of the session, deliberately placing herself directly before me. Do you know what she wants?" The grand vizier, who knew no more than the king what she wanted, but who did not wish to seem curt, replied, "My lord, your majesty knows that women often form complaints based on trifles. Perhaps this woman comes to complain to your majesty that someone has sold her some bad flour, or to complain about some other wrong, equally trivial." The king was not satisfied with this explanation and said to the grand vizier, "If this woman comes again on the next council day, do not fail to call her, in order that I may hear what she has to say." The grand vizier replied by kissing his hand and lifting it above his head, indicating that he was ready to lose his head if he failed to carry out the king's order.

'Ala al-Din's mother had by now become so much accustomed to going to the council and standing before the king that she did not think it any trouble, as long as her son knew that she did all she could to comply with his wishes. So the next council day, she went to the audience hall and as usual stood at the entrance, directly before the king. The grand vizier had not yet reported on any business when the king noticed her and, feeling compassion for her for having waited so patiently, said to the grand vizier, "First of all, lest you should forget, there stands the woman I spoke to you about. Bid her approach, and let us hear her and dispatch her business first." The grand vizier, pointing out 'Ala al-Din's mother to the chief of the officers, who stood awaiting orders, commanded him to go to her and bring her before the king. The chief of the officers went to 'Ala al-Din's mother, and at a sign he gave her, she followed him to the foot of the king's throne, where he left her and went back to his place near the grand vizier.

'Ala al-Din's mother, following the example of the great many others whom she saw approach the king, prostrated herself, with her forehead touching the carpet that covered the steps of the throne, and remained in that position until the king bid her rise. When she rose, he said to her, "For a long time now, I have seen you come to my audience hall. What business brings you here?" When she heard these words, she prostrated herself a second time, and when she rose, she

replied, "O King of Kings, before I reveal to your majesty the extraordinary and almost incredible business that brings me before your
sublime throne, I beg you to pardon the boldness or rather the impudence of the demand I am going to make, for it is so uncommon, that
I tremble and feel ashamed to propose it to my king." In order to give
her complete freedom to explain herself, the king ordered everyone,
except the grand vizier, to leave the audience hall; then he told her
that she might now speak without fear.

'Ala al-Din's mother, not content with this favor of the king in saving her from the pain of speaking before so many people, wished furthermore to save herself from the anger, which, she feared, would be
his response to her unexpected proposal. She said, "My lord, I implore
your majesty, in case you find my demand offensive or injurious, to
assure me first of your pardon and forgiveness." The king replied,
"Whatever it may be, I will forgive you, and no harm shall come to
you. Speak freely."

After 'Ala al-Din's mother took all these precautions for fear of the
king's anger at a proposition as delicate as the one she was about to
make, she related to him faithfully how 'Ala al-Din had seen Princess
Badr al-Budur, the intense love that fatal sight had aroused in him,
the declaration he had made to her, and all that she had said to him to
dissuade him from a passion, no less injurious to his majesty than to
the princess, his daughter, adding, "But my son, instead of benefiting
from my advice and recognizing his rashness, persevered obstinately,
to the point of threatening me with some desperate act if I refused to
come and demand the princess in marriage from your majesty, and it
was not until he was extremely violent with me that I was forced to
humor him by coming to you, an act for which I beg your majesty
once more to pardon, not only me, but also my son 'Ala al-Din, for
having the temerity to aspire to such a high alliance."

The king listened to this speech very gently and kindly, without
showing any sign of anger or indignation and without jeering at her
proposal. But before he gave this good woman any answer, he asked
her what she had brought in that wrapping cloth. She immediately
took the porcelain dish, which she had set down at the foot of the
throne before prostrating herself and, unwrapping it, presented it to
the king. One can hardly describe the king's surprise and amazement
when he saw so many jewels, so perfect, so brilliant, and of a size the
like of which he had never seen before, collected in that dish. He
remained for some time motionless with admiration. When he
regained his composure, he took the present from 'Ala al-Din's
mother's hand, crying out with great delight, "Ah! how beautiful and
how rich!" After he had admired and handled virtually all the jewels,
one by one, examining each from its most striking angle, he turned to

the grand vizier and, showing him the dish, said, "Look here, and admit that one has never seen anything more rich and more perfect." The grand vizier was charmed by them. The king continued, "Well, what do you say of such a present? Is it not worthy of the princess, my daughter? And ought I not to give her to the one who demands her at such a price?"

These words put the grand vizier into a strange agitation. The king had some time before told him of his intention to give in marriage the princess, his daughter, to one of the vizier's sons; therefore, he feared, not without foundation, that the king, dazzled by such a rich and extraordinary present, might change his mind. He approached the king and, whispering in his ear, said, "My lord, I cannot but admit that the present is worthy of the princess, but I implore your majesty to grant me three months before you come to a decision. I hope that before that time, my son, on whom the princess looks favorably, as she herself has given me reason to believe, will give her a more valuable present than that of 'Ala al-Din, who is a stranger to your majesty." Although the king was convinced that it was not possible for his grand vizier to provide his son with so valuable a present for the princess, he listened to him and granted him that favor. So, turning to 'Ala al-Din's mother, he said, "Good woman, go home, and tell your son that I accept the proposal that you have made me on his behalf, but I cannot marry the princess, my daughter, until I have some furniture made for her, which will take three months. At the end of that time, come again."

'Ala al-Din's mother returned home with a greater joy than she had expected, for she had first considered her access to the king impossible, and besides, she obtained a very favorable response, instead of the rebuff and resulting confusion she had expected. When 'Ala al-Din saw her enter, two things led him to conclude that she brought him good news. The first was that she returned sooner than usual; the second, that her countenance was relaxed and happy. He said to her, "Well, mother, should I entertain any hope, or should I die of despair?" After she pulled off her veil and sat down beside him on the sofa, she said to him, "Son, in order not to keep you in suspense, I will begin by telling you that, instead of thinking of dying, you have every reason to be satisfied." Then she went on to tell him how she had an audience, before everybody else, a circumstance that enabled her to come home so soon. She told him about the precautions she took, in case the king took offense at the proposal of marriage between him and Princess Badr al-Budur, and about the entirely favorable answer she heard from the king's own mouth. She told him that, as far as she could tell from the king's expression, it was, above all, the powerful effect of the present which induced him to give her that favorable answer. She added, "I had expected much less, for as he was about to give me an answer, the grand vizier whispered in his ear, and I was afraid that he might dissuade him from his good intentions toward you."

At hearing this news, 'Ala al-Din considered himself the most happy of men and thanked his mother for all the troubles she had taken in pursuit of this affair, the successful outcome of which was of such great importance for his happiness. Although three months seemed to him an extremely long time in his impatience to enjoy the object of his desire, he nevertheless conditioned himself to wait with patience, relying on the king's word, which he considered to be irrevocable. But he counted not only the hours, days, and weeks, but every moment, while he waited for the time to expire. About two months passed, when, one evening, his mother, going to light the lamp, found that there was no oil in the house. So she went out to buy some, and when she came into the city, she saw public celebrations. The shops, instead of being closed, were open, and they were decorated with boughs and lights, every shop owner striving to outdo the other displays in pomp and magnificence, the better to show his zeal. Indeed, everyone showed signs of happiness and rejoicing. The streets were crowded with officers dressed in ceremonial uniforms and mounted on horses with rich trappings and surrounded by a great number of attendants on foot, milling about. 'Ala al-Din's mother asked the oil merchant what was the meaning of all this activity, and he said to her, "Where did you come from, good woman? Don't you know that the grand vizier's son is to marry Princess Badr al-Budur, the king's daughter, tonight? She will soon return from the baths, and these officers you see are assembled to assist at the procession to the palace, where the ceremony is to take place."

'Ala al-Din's mother did not wish to hear any more. She hurried back, so fast, that when she entered, she was out of breath. When she saw her son, who little expected the sad news she brought him, she cried out, "Son, you have lost everything; you have relied on the fine promises of the king, but they will come to nothing." 'Ala al-Din, who was alarmed at these words, asked, "Mother, in what way did the king break his promise to me, and how do you know?" She replied, "Tonight, the grand vizier's son is to marry Princess Badr al-Budur, in the palace." Then she related to him how she had found out and the circumstances that left no doubt about it. At this news, 'Ala al-Din remained motionless, as if struck by lightning. Any other man would have been completely overwhelmed, but a deep jealousy aroused him, and he soon thought of the lamp, which had till then served him well, and without venting his anger in empty words against the king, the grand vizier, or his son, he only said, "Mother, perhaps the grand vizier's son may not be as happy tonight as he expects. While I go into my room for a moment, prepare us some supper."

'Ala al-Din's mother guessed that her son was going to make use of the lamp to prevent, if possible, the consummation of the marriage between the grand vizier's son and the princess, and she was not wrong. For when 'Ala al-Din entered his room, he took the magic lamp, which he had hidden from his mother after the appearance of the demon had caused her such great terror. He rubbed it in the same spot as before, and immediately the demon appeared and said to him, "What do you wish? Here I am, ready to obey you, as your slave and the slave of all those who have the lamp in their hands, I and the other slaves of the lamp?" 'Ala al-Din replied, "Listen, you have till now brought me whatever food I needed, but now I have a business of the greatest importance. I have asked the king for his daughter Princess Badr al-Budur in marriage. He promised her to me, but he asked for a three months' delay; however, instead of keeping his promise, he is marrying her tonight to the grand vizier's son, before the expiration of the time. I have just heard this, and I have no doubt about it. What I demand of you is that, as soon as the bride and bridegroom are in bed, you carry them and bring them both here in their bed." The demon replied, "Master, I will obey you. Do you have any other command?" 'Ala al-Din replied, "None at present," and the demon disappeared immediately.

'Ala al-Din went back to his mother and had supper with her, with his usual calm. After supper, he talked with her for some time about the princess's marriage, as if it was an affair that no longer troubled him. Then he returned to his room, while his mother went to bed; however, he himself did not sleep but waited for the return of the demon and the execution of his order.

Meanwhile, everything in the king's palace was magnificently prepared to celebrate the princess's wedding, and the evening was spent with ceremonies and festivities till midnight, when the grand vizier's son, at a signal given him by the chief of the princess's eunuchs, retired forthwith and was taken by that officer into the princess's apartment and led to the room where the wedding bed was prepared. He lay in bed first, and in a little while, the queen, accompanied by her women and those of the princess, her daughter, brought in the bride, who, as is usual with brides, made great resistance. The queen helped to undress her, put her into bed, as if by force, and, after kissing her and bidding her good night, departed with all the women, and the last woman to leave shut the door.

No sooner was the door shut than the demon, as faithful slave of the lamp and punctual in executing the commands of those who had it in their hands, without giving the bridegroom any time to make the

slightest caress to his bride, lifted the bed with the bride and bridegroom, to their great amazement, and transported it in an instant to
'Ala al-Din's room, where he set it down. 'Ala al-Din, who was waiting
impatiently for this moment, could not bear to see the grand vizier's
son stay long in bed with the princess. He said to the demon, "Take
this bridegroom, and lock him up in the toilet, and come back tomorrow morning, a little after daybreak." The demon immediately lifted
the grand vizier's son out of the bed and carried him in his shirt to the
place where 'Ala al-Din bid him take him, and after blowing a breath
on him, which he felt from head to toe and which prevented him from
moving, the demon left him there.

Although 'Ala al-Din's love for Princess Badr al-Budur was great,
he did not say much to her when he found himself alone with her, but
only said passionately, "Fear nothing, adorable princess; you are safe
here, for ardent as my love is for your beauty and charm, it shall never
go beyond the bounds of the profound respect I owe you." He added,
"If I have been forced to this drastic measure, it was not with the
intention of offending you, but to prevent an unjust rival from possessing you, contrary to the promise of the king, your father, in my
favor." The princess, who knew nothing of these particulars, paid very
little attention to what 'Ala al-Din said, and she was in no condition to
respond. For the fright and amazement of such an unexpected adventure had put her in such a state that 'Ala al-Din could not get one
word out of her. He therefore did not persist, but undressed and lay in
the place of the grand vizier's son, with his back turned toward the
princess, after he took the precaution of putting a sword between him
and her, to indicate that he deserved to be punished if he attempted
anything against her honor. 'Ala al-Din, satisfied to have thus
deprived his rival of the happiness he had flattered himself to enjoy
that night, slept very quietly, while Princess Badr al-Budur, on the
contrary, never spent a night so bad and so disagreeable in all her life.
And if one considers the place and condition in which the demon had
left the grand vizier's son, one may conclude that the bridegroom
spent it in a much worse way.

The following day, 'Ala al-Din did not have to rub the lamp to call
the demon. He came by himself at the appointed hour, just when 'Ala
al-Din had finished dressing himself, and said to him, "Here I am;
what are your commands?" 'Ala al-Din replied, "Go, and bring the
grand vizier's son from the place where you put him, and put him in
this bed again, and carry it back to the king's palace, from where you
brought it." The demon went to fetch the grand vizier's son, and when
he returned, 'Ala al-Din took up his sword, and the demon laid the
bridegroom by the princess and in an instant carried the wedding bed
back to the same room in the king's palace, from where he had

brought it. It should be observed that all this time, the demon was seen neither by the princess nor the grand vizier's son. His hideous form would have made them die of fear. They did not even hear the talk between him and 'Ala al-Din. They only perceived the shaking of the bed and their transportation from one place to another, which, one may well imagine, was enough to frighten them.

No sooner had the demon set down the wedding bed in its place, than the king, curious to know how the princess, his daughter, had spent her wedding night, entered her room to wish her good morning. The grand vizier's son, who had almost died of the cold he suffered all night and who had not yet had time to warm himself, no sooner heard the door open, than he got out of bed and ran into the closet where he had undressed himself the previous night. The king approached the bed, kissed the princess between the eyes, according to custom, wished her good morning, and asked her with a smile how she had spent the night. But lifting up her head and looking at her more closely, he was extremely surprised to see that she was in a deep melancholy and that neither by a blush nor any other sign could she satisfy his expectation. She only cast at him a most sorrowful look that expressed great affliction or great dissatisfaction. He said a few words to her, but, finding that he could not get her to speak, thought that she was silent out of modesty and departed. Nevertheless, he remained worried that there was something extraordinary in her silence. So he went immediately to the queen's apartment and told her in what a state he had found the princess and how she had received him. The queen said to him, "My lord, this should not surprise your majesty. There is no bride who does not show the same reserve on the morning after her wedding. This will change in two or three days, and then she will receive the king, her father, as she ought to." She added, "I will go and see her, and I am very mistaken if she receives me in the same manner."

As soon as the queen was dressed, she went to the apartment of the princess, who was still in bed. She approached the bed, wished her good morning, and kissed her. But she was extremely surprised, not only because the princess made no reply, but also, because in looking at her, the queen saw that she was in a state of deep dejection, which led her to conclude that something she did not understand must have happened to her. The queen asked her, "Daughter, why do you respond so poorly to my caresses? Ought you to treat your mother in this manner, and do you think that I do not know what happens to someone in your situation? I believe that this is not what is bothering you and that something else must have happened to you. Tell me frankly, and do not keep me any longer in painful suspense."

At last Princess Badr al-Budur broke her silence, with a deep sigh, and cried out, "Ah! my lady and most honored mother, forgive me if I failed to show the respect I owe you. My mind is so full of the extraordinary things that happened to me last night that I have not yet recovered from my amazement and fright, and I scarcely know myself." Then she told her in vivid details how, the instant after she and her husband were in bed, the bed was lifted up and transported in a moment into a dark, dirty room, where she found herself alone and separated from her husband, without knowing what became of him, and where she saw a young man, who, after saying a few words to her, which her fright prevented her from understanding, lay beside her in the place of her husband, after he put a sword between them; and how her husband was brought back to her, and the bed was transported back to its place, again in a very little time. She said, "All this had just happened, when the king my father entered my room. I was so overwhelmed with grief that I did not have the power to respond even with a simple word, and I have no doubt that he is offended by the manner in which I received the honor he did me, but I hope that he will forgive me when he knows my sad adventure and the pitiful state I am in at present."

The queen listened very calmly to what the princess told her but did not believe it, and said to her, "Daughter, you did well not to speak of this to the king, your father. Be careful not to say anything about it to anyone, for people will think that you are mad if they hear you talk this way." The princess replied, "My lady, I can assure you that I am in my right mind. Ask my husband, and he will tell you the same thing." The queen said, "I will ask him, but if he talks like you, I will not believe it any more than I do now. Rise, and rid yourself of this delusion. It will be a fine story, if you spoil by such a dream the festivities planned for your wedding, which are supposed to continue for several days, not only in the palace, but in the entire kingdom. Do you not hear the fanfares and the sounds of trumpets, drums, and tambourines? All this should inspire you with joy and pleasure and make you forget all the fantasies you tell me of." Then the queen called the princess's women, and, after seeing the princess get up and begin to groom herself, went to the king's apartment and told him that her daughter did actually entertain some delusions but that there was nothing to them. Then she sent for the grand vizier's son to inquire from him about what the princess had told her, but the grand vizier's son, who considered himself extremely honored by his alliance with the king, decided to be secretive. The queen said to him, "Son-in-law, are you as stubborn as your wife?" He said, "My lady, may I be so bold as to ask in what regard do you ask me this question?" The queen replied, "That is enough; I do not wish to inquire any further; you are wiser than she."

The celebrations in the palace lasted all day, and the queen, who never left the princess, did all she could to entertain her and make her take part in the various diversions and shows prepared for her. But the princess was so struck by the recollection of what had happened the previous night that it was easy to see that her thoughts were preoccupied with it. The grand vizier's son suffered no less as a result of that bad night, but his ambition made him disguise his condition so well that no one who saw him doubted he was a happy bridegroom.

'Ala al-Din, who was well informed of what was going on in the palace, never doubted that the newlyweds would be together again that night, in spite of the misadventure of the previous night, and he had no desire to leave them in peace. Therefore, when it was night, he had recourse to the lamp, and the demon appeared immediately and paid 'Ala al-Din the usual compliments and offered his services. 'Ala al-Din said to him, "The grand vizier's son and Princess Badr al-Budur will lie together again tonight. Go, and as soon as they are in bed, bring it here, as you did yesterday." The demon obeyed 'Ala al-Din as faithfully and punctually as on the previous day. The grand vizier's son spent the night as disagreeably as he did before, and the princess felt the same humiliation to have 'Ala al-Din as her bedfellow, with the sword placed between them. The next morning, the demon, following 'Ala al-Din's orders, came back and, bringing the bridegroom and laying him beside his bride, lifted up the bed with the newlyweds and transported it back to the room in the palace from where he had taken it.

The king, who, after the reception Princess Badr al-Budur had given him the previous day, was anxious to know how she passed the second night and whether she would give him the same reception, went into her room as early as the previous morning. The grand vizier's son, more ashamed and humiliated by the ill success of the second night, no sooner heard the king coming than he got up and rushed into the closet. The king approached the princess's bed and wished her good morning, and after caressing her as he did the previous morning, he asked her, "Well, daughter, are you in a better mood than you were yesterday morning? Tell me how you passed last night." But the princess was again silent, and the king saw that she was even more troubled and more despondent than before, and he had no doubt that something extraordinary must have happened to her. So, irritated by her for keeping him mystified, he said to her angrily, with his sword in his hand, "Daughter, either you tell me what you are hiding, or I will cut off your head immediately."

At last, the princess, more frightened by the tone and menaces of the offended king than by the sight of the drawn sword, broke her silence. She cried out, with tears in her eyes, "My dear father and king, I beg forgiveness of your majesty, if I have offended you; and I hope that out of your goodness and mercy, you will let your compassion replace your anger, when I give you the faithful account of the sad and miserable condition in which I spent last night and the night before." After this preamble, which appeased the king and moved him a little, she related to him faithfully all that had happened to her during the two unfortunate nights. She spoke in a manner so touching that the king, who loved her and felt tenderness toward her, grieved deeply for her. She concluded with these words, "If your majesty has the slightest doubt concerning my account, you may inquire from the husband you gave me. I am sure that he will testify to the same thing."

The king felt readily the extreme pain such a surprising misadventure must have caused the princess. He said to her, "Daughter, you made a great mistake by not telling me yesterday about the strange affair, which concerns me as much as yourself. I did not marry you to make you miserable, but with the intention of making you satisfied and happy and able to enjoy all the good fortune you deserve and expect with a husband who seemed to me to suit you. Forget these troublesome thoughts. I will see to it that you shall have no more such disagreeable and unbearable nights."

As soon as the king returned to his own apartment, he sent for his grand vizier and said to him, "Vizier, have you seen your son, and has he said anything to you?" When the grand vizier replied that he had not seen him, the king repeated to him all that Princess Badr al-Budur had related to him, concluding, "I have no doubt that my daughter has told me the truth; nevertheless, I would feel better to have it confirmed by your son. Go and ask him about it."

The grand vizier went immediately to his son, acquainted him with what the king had told him, and asked him to conceal nothing from him, but to tell him whether all this was true. The son said, "Father, I will hide nothing from you. Everything the princess said to the king is true, but she could not describe to him the ill treatment I myself received. Ever since my wedding, I have spent the two most cruel nights imaginable, and I do not have the words to describe to you in exact detail everything I have suffered. I will not describe to you my fright to feel my bed lifted up four times and transported from one place to another, without being able to see who was doing it or guess how it was done. I will leave it to you to judge the miserable condition I was in to spend two nights, standing in nothing but my shirt in a kind of small toilet, unable to stir from the place where I was put or make the slightest movement, although I could not see any obstacle to prevent me. More than this, there is no need to tell you of my sufferings. Yet I must tell you that none of this has in any way lessened my love, respect, and the gratitude that the princess, my wife,

deserves. But I must confess in all sincerity that in spite of all the honor
and the splendor that attend me to have married the daughter of my
sovereign, I would rather die than endure any longer such a high
alliance, if I must undergo such a disagreeable treatment. I have no
doubt that the princess feels the same way and that she will readily
agree that our separation is no less necessary for her peace than it is
for mine. Therefore, father, I beg you, by the same tenderness for me
that led you to procure for me such a great honor, to get the king's
consent to have our marriage declared annulled."

Great as the grand vizier's ambition was for his son to be the son-in-
law of the king, the firm resolution his son expressed to be separated
from the princess convinced him that it was not a good idea to propose to him to have a little patience for a few more days, to see
whether this predicament would not come to an end. He left him and
went to report to the king, telling him in all candor that, according to
what he had heard from his son, all was true. And without waiting
until the king himself, whom he found very much disposed to it, spoke
of breaking the marriage, the grand vizier begged him to permit his
son to leave the palace and live with him, giving the king the excuse
that it was not fair to leave the princess exposed a moment longer to
such a terrible persecution for the sake of his son. The grand vizier
had no difficulty in obtaining what he requested. The king, who had
already made up his mind, immediately gave orders to stop the festivities in the palace, the city, and all parts of his kingdom, counter-
manding his first orders, and in a short time, all signs of rejoicing and
public celebration in the city and the entire kingdom ceased.

This sudden and unexpected change gave rise to various specula-
tions. People asked each other what caused this mishap, but none of
them had any explanation except to say that they had seen the grand
vizier leave the palace and retire to his home with his son, both seeming very dejected. Nobody but 'Ala al-Din knew the secret and he
rejoiced within himself in the happy success his lamp brought him.
Thus, having heard for certain that his rival had left the palace and
that the marriage between him and the princess was broken off, he no
longer had any need to rub the lamp to summon the demon in order
to prevent the consummation of the marriage. But what is most peculiar is that neither the king nor the grand vizier, who had forgotten
'Ala al-Din and his demand, had the slightest idea that he had any
hand in the enchantment that caused the dissolution of the marriage.

'Ala al-Din, however, waited for the expiration of the three months'
period requested by the king before the marriage between him and
Princess Badr al-Budur was to take place. He counted every day very
carefully, and when the time came, he sent his mother the next day to
the palace, to remind the king of his promise. She went to the palace,

as her son had asked her, and stood at the entrance of the audience hall, in the same place as before. As soon as the king saw her, he recognized her and remembered her proposal to him and the date to which he had put her off. He therefore interrupted the grand vizier, who was reporting to him on some matter, and said, "Vizier, I see the good woman who, a few months ago, made me such a fine present. Bring her to me, and after I hear what she has to say, you may resume your report." The grand vizier, looking toward the entrance of the hall, saw 'Ala al-Din's mother and immediately called the chief of the officers and, pointing her out to him, ordered him to bring her.

'Ala al-Din's mother came to the foot of the throne and prostrated herself, as usual, and when she rose up again, the king asked her what she wished. She said to him, "My lord, I stand again before the throne of your majesty to point out, on behalf of my son 'Ala al-Din, that your three months' postponement of the proposal I had the honor to present to you has expired, and to beg you to remember your promise." The king, when he demanded a three months' delay before fulfilling his promise to this good woman the first time he saw her, little thought of hearing any more of marriage, which he considered unsuitable to the princess his daughter, simply in view of the low class and poverty of 'Ala al-Din's mother, who had appeared before him in very ordinary clothes. Yet her urgent request to him to keep his promise was embarrassing to him, and he did not deem it appropriate to give an immediate reply. So he consulted his grand vizier, expressing to him his repugnance to marry the princess to a stranger whose fortune he supposed to be very mean. The grand vizier did not hesitate to tell him his thoughts on the matter and said to him, "My lord, I think that there is a sure way to avoid such an ill-matched union, without giving 'Ala al-Din, even if he were better known to your majesty, any grounds for complaint. Set such a high price on the princess that no matter how great his riches may be, he cannot meet it. This will make him desist from such a bold, not to say, rash pursuit, about which he undoubtedly did not think much before embarking on it."

The king, approving of the grand vizier's advice, turned to 'Ala al-Din's mother and, after a few moments of reflection, said to her, "Good woman, kings ought to keep their word, and I am ready to keep mine and make your son happy by marrying the princess, my daughter, to him. But since I cannot marry her before I know that she will be better provided for, tell your son that I will fulfill my promise as soon as he sends me forty large basins of heavy gold, full to the brim of the same things you have already given me on his behalf, and carried by a similar number of black slaves, led by forty white slaves, young, handsome, well-built, and magnificently dressed. These are the conditions on which I am ready to give him the princess, my daughter. Go, good woman, and I will wait until you bring me his response."

'Ala al-Din's mother prostrated herself before the king's throne and retired. On her way home, she laughed within herself at her son's foolish imagination and said to herself, "Where will he find so many gold basins and such a quantity of colored glass to fill them? Will he go back to that subterranean place, the entrance to which is stopped up, and gather them from the trees? And where will he get all the slaves, such as the ones demanded by the king? All of this is beyond his reach, and I think that he will not be satisfied with my embassy." When she came home, full of such thoughts that led her to believe that 'Ala al-Din's case was hopeless, she said to him, "Son, I advise you to give up all thought of marriage with Princess Badr al-Budur. The king received me very kindly, indeed, and I believe that he had good intentions toward you, but, if I am not mistaken, the grand vizier made him change his mind, as you will agree after you hear my account. After I reminded his majesty that three months had expired and begged him on your behalf to remember his promise, I noticed that he talked in a whisper for some time with his grand vizier, before he gave me the reply that I shall repeat to you." She then gave her son an exact account of what the king had said and the conditions on which he consented to the marriage between him and the princess, his daughter. Then she said, "Son, he awaits your answer, but, between us," she continued with a smile, "I believe that he will have to wait a long time." 'Ala al-Din replied, "Not so long as you think, mother, and the king is mistaken to think that by these exorbitant demands he can prevent me from desiring Princess Badr al-Budur. I had expected even more insurmountable difficulties and thought that he would even set a much higher price on this incomparable princess, but now I am satisfied, and what he demands is little, compared to what I could have done for her in order to have her. But while I think of satisfying his demand, go and get us something for dinner, and leave the rest to me."

As soon as 'Ala al-Din's mother went out to the market, 'Ala al-Din took the lamp and rubbed it, and in an instant the demon appeared before him and asked him in the usual terms what he wished, expressing his readiness to serve him. 'Ala al-Din said, "The king is giving me the princess, his daughter, in marriage, but first he demands of me forty large basins of heavy gold, full of the fruits I gathered from the garden from where I took the lamp that you are slave to. He also demands of me that these forty basins be carried by forty black slaves, led by forty white slaves, young, handsome, well-built, and richly dressed. Go, fetch me this present, as soon as possible, so that I may send it to the king, before the council adjourns." The demon told him that his command would be carried out forthwith and disappeared.

The demon returned a little while later with forty black slaves, each carrying on his head a large basin of twenty marks' gold, full of pearls, diamonds, rubies, and emeralds, all better chosen and larger and more beautiful than those presented to the king before, and each basin was covered with a silver cloth, embroidered with flowers of gold. All these slaves, as many black as white, and these gold basins virtually filled the entire house, which was very small, as well as the little court in front and the little garden in the back. The demon asked 'Ala al-Din whether he was satisfied and whether he had any other demands, and when 'Ala al-Din replied that he had none, the demon disappeared again.

When 'Ala al-Din's mother returned from the market and entered the house, she was greatly surprised to see so many people and such great riches. When she laid down the provisions she had brought, she was about to pull off her veil, but 'Ala al-Din stopped her, saying, "Mother, there is no time to lose. Before the king adjourns the council, you should return forthwith to the palace, and take with you this present as the dowry he demanded for Princess Badr al-Budur, so that he may judge, by my diligence and punctuality, my ardent zeal and sincerity to procure the honor of entering this alliance with him." Without waiting for his mother to make a reply, 'Ala al-Din opened the street door and made the slaves file out, a white slave followed always by a black one carrying a gold basin on his head. When they all were out, and the mother followed the last black slave, 'Ala al-Din shut the door and sat calmly in his room, in the hope that the king, after receiving the present he required, would at last consent to receive him as his son-in-law.

The first white slave who went out of 'Ala al-Din's house made all the passersby who saw him stop, and before all eighty white and black slaves were out of the house, the street was crowded with people who rushed from all parts to see this magnificent and extraordinary spectacle. The dress of each slave was so rich, both in fabric and jewels, that those who were most knowledgeable valued each at more than a million. The extreme neatness and perfect fit of each dress; the good grace, noble air, and uniform and elegant shape of each slave; their stately march, at an equal distance from each other; the luster of their jewels, which were extremely large and set in a beautiful symmetry in their belts of heavy gold; and the glitter of the insignias of jewels in their hats, which were of a particular style, struck the crowds of spectators with such a great admiration that they never wearied of gazing at them and following them with their eyes, as far as possible. The streets were so crowded with people that everyone was forced to stay in place.

As the slaves had to pass through many streets, stretching through a great part of the city, people of all classes and backgrounds were able to see this delightful procession. When the first of the slaves arrived at the gate of the first court of the palace, the gatekeepers, who had arranged themselves in order as soon as they saw the procession approaching, took him for a king and approached him to kiss the hem of his robe, but the slave, instructed by the demon, stopped them and said gravely, "We are only slaves. Our master will appear at the proper time."

Then this slave, followed by the rest, entered the second court, which was very spacious and in which the king's men always stood in order when the council was in session. Although the officers, who stood at the head of their troops, were magnificently dressed, they were eclipsed by the presence of the eighty slaves who carried 'Ala al-Din's present. Nothing in the king's palace seemed so beautiful and brilliant, and all the luster of his courtiers was nothing in comparison to what he saw at that moment.

As the king had been informed of the procession and the arrival of the slaves and had given orders to admit them, they were ushered into the audience hall, and they did so in good order, one part filing to the right and the other to the left. After they all had entered and had formed a great semicircle before the king's throne, the black slaves laid the basins on the carpet and all of them prostrated themselves, touching the carpet with their foreheads, and at the same time, the white slaves did the same. Then they all rose again, and the black slaves uncovered the basins, and they all stood with their arms crossed over their breasts, in great reverence.

Meanwhile, 'Ala al-Din's mother advanced to the foot of the throne and, after prostrating herself, said to the king, "My lord, my son 'Ala al-Din knows well that this present he sends to your majesty is very much below what Princess Badr al-Budur deserves; nevertheless, he hopes that your majesty will accept it and make it agreeable to the princess, with all the more confidence, since he has endeavored to meet the conditions that you were pleased to impose on him."

The king was in no condition to pay any attention to the compliments of 'Ala al-Din's mother. For as soon as he saw the forty gold basins, full to the brim of the most brilliant, lustrous, and precious jewels one has ever seen, and saw the eighty slaves, who, both by the comeliness of their persons and the surprising richness and magnificence of their dress, appeared like so many kings, he was so struck that he could not recover from his admiration. So instead of responding to the compliments of 'Ala al-Din's mother, he spoke to the grand vizier, who could not, any more than the king, understand where such a great profusion of riches could come from. He said to the grand vizier loudly, "Well, vizier, what do you think of him who sends me such a rich and extraordinary present, yet neither I nor you even know him? Do you think him unworthy of marrying my daughter Princess Badr al-Budur?" In spite of the grand vizier's envy and sadness to see a stranger preferred before his son to become the king's son-in-law, he did not dare to hide his sentiments. For it was too evident that 'Ala al-Din's present was more than enough to merit that he be received into such a high alliance; therefore, echoing the king's sentiments, he replied, "My lord, I am so far from thinking that the person who has made your majesty such a worthy present is unworthy of the honor you wish to do him, that I would dare to say that he merits even more, if I was not persuaded that there is no treasure in the world great enough to be put in balance with the princess, your majesty's daughter." At these words the lords of the court, who were present at the council, applauded in agreement.

The king did not hesitate any longer. He did not even think of finding out whether 'Ala al-Din possessed all the qualities appropriate to one who aspired to become his son-in-law. The sight alone of such immense riches and the diligence with which 'Ala al-Din satisfied the exorbitant demand he had imposed on him, without creating the slightest difficulty, easily convinced the king that 'Ala al-Din lacked nothing to render him as accomplished as the king wished. Therefore, to send 'Ala al-Din's mother back with all the satisfaction she could desire, he said to her, "Good woman, go and tell your son that I am waiting to receive him with open arms and to embrace him and that the sooner he comes to receive the princess, my daughter, from my hands, the greater pleasure he will do me."

As soon as 'Ala al-Din's mother departed, with the joy that a woman of her condition must feel, to see her son elevated, beyond her expectation, to such a high state, the king terminated the audience for that day and, rising from his throne, ordered that the princess's eunuchs should come and carry the basins to their mistress's apartment, where he went to examine them with her at his leisure. This order was carried out immediately, under the supervision of the chief eunuch. The eighty slaves, black and white, were not forgotten. They were conducted into the palace, and a little while later, the king, having described to the princess the slaves' magnificent appearance, ordered that they be brought before her apartment, so that she might see for herself through the shutters and realize that far from exaggerating, he had in fact told her much less.

Meanwhile, 'Ala al-Din's mother got home and showed, by her demeanor, the good news that she brought for her son. She said to him, "Son, you have every reason to be pleased, for you have reached the attainment of your desires, contrary to the expectations you have always heard me express. In order not to keep you too long in suspense, the king, with the approval of the whole court, has declared that you are worthy to possess Princess Badr al-Budur. He is waiting to embrace you and to conclude your marriage. You must now think of making some preparations for that meeting, so that you may live up to the high opinion he has formed of you, and after the wonders I have seen you do, I am convinced that nothing will be lacking. I must not forget to remind you again that the king waits for you impatiently; therefore, you must not lose any time in going to him."

'Ala al-Din, pleased with this news and full of thoughts of the object that had enchanted him, said very little to his mother and retired to his room. He took the lamp, which had till then answered all his needs and wishes, and as soon as he rubbed it, the obedient demon appeared immediately, as usual. 'Ala al-Din said to him, "Demon, I have called you to help me bathe immediately, and afterwards provide me with the richest and most magnificent suit ever worn by a king." No sooner had he finished speaking than the demon made him as invisible as himself and carried him to a bath of the finest and most beautiful marble of all kinds and all colors, where he was undressed, without seeing by whom, in a spacious and very clean hall. From the hall, he was led to the bath, which was of moderate heat, and there he was rubbed and washed with all sorts of scented water. After he passed through several chambers of different degrees of heat, he came out, completely different from what he had been before. His skin was fresh, white, and ruddy, and his body felt much lighter and more refreshed. When he returned to the hall, he did not find the suit he had taken off, for the demon had carefully replaced it with the one he had demanded, the magnificence of which amazed him. He got dressed, with the help of the demon, admiring each piece he put on, for everything was beyond anything he could have imagined. When he finished, the demon carried him back to his room and asked him whether he had any other command. 'Ala al-Din replied, "Yes, I want you to bring me, as soon as possible, a horse that surpasses in quality and beauty the best in the king's stables, with a saddle, housing, bridle, and other trappings worth a million dinars. I also want you to bring me at the same time twenty slaves, dressed as richly and smartly as those who carried the presents, to walk by my side and behind me, and twenty more like them to walk in two ranks before me. In addition, bring my mother six slave-girls to wait on her, each dressed at least as richly as the slave-girls of Princess Badr al-Budur, each carrying a complete suit as splendid and magnificent as that of a queen. I want also ten thousand pieces of gold, in ten purses. Go, and be quick." As soon as 'Ala al-Din finished giving these orders, the demon disappeared and soon returned with the horse, the forty slaves, ten of whom each carried a purse containing one thousand pieces of gold, and the six slave-girls, each carrying on her head a different suit for 'Ala al-Din's mother, wrapped up in a silver cloth, and he presented all of them to 'Ala al-Din.

Of the ten purses, 'Ala al-Din took four and gave them to his mother, telling her to use them for her needs, and left the other six in the hands of the slaves who brought them, ordering them to throw the money by the handfuls among the people, as they passed through the streets on their way to the king's palace. He ordered the six slaves to march before him with the others, three on the right and three on the left. Finally he presented the six slave-girls to his mother, telling her that they were hers to use as her slaves and that the suits they brought were for her. When 'Ala al-Din settled all these matters, he dismissed the demon, telling him that he would call him when he needed him, and the demon disappeared immediately. Now 'Ala al-Din's only thought was to respond to the desire the king had expressed to see him. He dispatched to the palace one of the forty slaves (I will not say the most handsome, for they were all equal), with an order to address himself to the chief of the officers and inquire when 'Ala al-Din might have the honor to come and throw himself at the king's feet. The slave did not take long to deliver his message and bring back the reply that the king was waiting for him impatiently.

'Ala al-Din immediately mounted his horse and marched in the order already described. Although he had never been on horseback before, he rode with such grace that the most experienced horseman would not have taken him for a novice. The streets through which he passed were almost instantly filled with innumerable bystanders, who made the air echo with their shouts of acclamation, admiration, and blessings, especially every time the six slaves who carried the purses threw handfuls of money into the air, to the right and left. These shouts of acclamation did not, however, come from those who pushed and bent down to pick up the money, but from a higher rank of people, who could not help expressing publicly the praise 'Ala al-Din deserved for his generosity. Those who knew him when he played in the streets as a grown-up urchin did not recognize him, and even those who had seen him recently hardly knew him, so much were his features altered, by virtue of the lamp, which had the power to procure by degrees for those who possessed it perfections in proportion to the state they attained by the right use of it. Much more attention was paid to 'Ala al-Din than to the pomp, which most people had seen on that same day, when the slaves marched, carrying the present. Nevertheless, the horse was especially admired by the connoisseurs, who were able to discern his beauties without being dazzled by the brilliance of the diamonds and other jewels with which he was covered.

As the news spread that the king was going to give Princess Badr al-Budur in marriage to 'Ala al-Din, without regard to his birth, no one envied his good fortune nor his elevation, for he seemed so worthy of it.

When he arrived at the palace, everything was prepared for his reception, and when he reached the second gate, he was about to dismount from his horse, following the custom observed by the grand vizier, the generals of the armies, and the governors of the provinces of the first rank, but the chief of the officers, who was ordered by the king to wait on him, prevented him and accompanied him to the audience hall and helped him to dismount, although 'Ala al-Din protested strongly, to no avail. Then the officers formed themselves in two rows at the entrance of the hall, and their chief put 'Ala al-Din on his right and, passing with him through the middle, led him to the king's throne.

When the king saw 'Ala al-Din, he was no less surprised to see him more richly and magnificently dressed than he himself had ever been than to see his handsome face, elegant figure, and a certain air of grandeur, very different from the mean aspect in which his mother had appeared before him. His surprise and amazement, however, did not hinder him from rising from his throne and descending two or three steps, quickly enough to prevent 'Ala al-Din from throwing himself at his feet, and to embrace him with all the demonstration of friendship. After this, 'Ala al-Din wanted again to throw himself at the king's feet, but the king held him by the hand and forced him to ascend and sit between him and the grand vizier.

Then 'Ala al-Din said, "My lord, as I receive the honor that your majesty, out of your goodness, is pleased to confer on me, permit me to say to you that I have never forgotten that I am your slave, that I know the greatness of your power, and that I recognize how much is my birth below the splendor and luster of the supreme rank to which I am being raised." He continued, "If there is any way by which I could have merited such a favorable reception, I confess that I owe it only to the boldness that pure chance inspired in me to raise my eyes, my thoughts, and my aspirations to the divine princess, who is the object of my wishes. I ask your majesty's pardon for my temerity, but I cannot dissemble that I would die of grief, if I should lose my hope of seeing them fulfilled." The king embraced him again and said, "Son, you do me wrong to doubt for a moment the sincerity of my promise. From now on, your life is too dear to me not to preserve it, by presenting you with the remedy that is at my disposal. I prefer the pleasure of seeing you and hearing you to all my treasures added to yours."

When the king finished, he gave a signal, and immediately the air echoed with the sound of trumpets, oboes, and drums, and at the same time he led 'Ala al-Din to a magnificent hall where a superb banquet was prepared. The king and 'Ala al-Din ate by themselves, while the grand vizier and the lords of the court, each according to his status and rank, waited on them. The king, who took such a great pleasure in looking at 'Ala al-Din that he never took his eyes off him, spoke with him on a variety of subjects, and throughout their entire conversation during the meal, 'Ala al-Din spoke with so much knowledge and wisdom on every topic that he confirmed the king in the good opinion he had of him.

After they finished the meal, the king sent for the chief judge of the capital and ordered him to draw up immediately a marriage contract between his daughter, Princess Badr al-Budur, and 'Ala al-Din. In the meantime, the king and 'Ala al-Din conversed on different subjects in the presence of the grand vizier and the lords of the court, who all admired the soundness of his wit, the great ease with which he spoke and expressed himself, and the refined and keen sentiments with which he enlivened his conversation.

When the judge finished drawing up the contract in the requisite manner, the king asked 'Ala al-Din whether he wished to stay in the palace and conclude the wedding ceremony that same day. 'Ala al-Din replied, "My lord, although I am impatient to enjoy your majesty's kindness, I beg of you to give me leave to postpone it until I build a palace to receive the princess in, according to her dignity and merit. For this purpose, I beg you to grant me a piece of land within the grounds of your palace, in order that I may come the more frequently to pay my respects to you. I will do all I can to have it finished with all possible diligence." The king said, "Son, take all the ground you deem proper. There is a large piece of land in front of my palace which is vacant and on which I myself had thought of building, but remember that I cannot see you soon enough united with my daughter, in order to make my joy complete." Then he again embraced 'Ala al-Din, who took his leave of him, with as much courtesy as if he had been bred and had always lived at court.

'Ala al-Din mounted his horse and returned home, in the same order he came, through the same throngs of people, who acclaimed him and wished him all happiness and prosperity. As soon as he dismounted, he retired to his own room, took the lamp, and called the demon, as usual. The demon did not tarry, but appeared and offered his services. 'Ala al-Din said to him, "Demon, I have every reason to congratulate myself in that you have carried out faithfully and punctually everything I have asked of you till now, by the power of this lamp, your mistress. But now, for the sake of the lamp, you must, if possible, show more zeal and more diligence than before. I demand of you to build me, as soon as you can, at a proper distance opposite the king's palace, a palace fit to receive my spouse Princess Badr al-Budur. I leave it to you to choose the materials, that is to say, porphyry, jasper, agate, lapis lazuli, and the finest marble of the most varied colors, and the rest of the building. I expect you to build at the top of the palace a large hall with a dome and four equal sides made entirely of alternate layers of heavy gold and silver and each containing six windows, the shutters of which, except one, which shall be left unfinished, shall be enriched artistically and symmetrically with diamonds, rubies, and emeralds, in a way the like of which has never been seen anywhere in the world. I also want an outer court in front of the palace, an inner court, and a garden, but above all, there should be, in a place that you shall point out to me, a treasury full of gold and silver coins. I also want in this palace kitchens, offices, storerooms, and a place to store fine furniture for all seasons, fit for the magnificence of the palace. Besides, there must be stables full of the finest horses, with their riders and grooms and hunting equipment, and there must be officers to supervise the kitchens and offices, as well as slave-girls to wait on the princess. You understand what I mean. Go, and come back when all is finished."

The sun had just set when 'Ala al-Din finished charging the demon with the construction of the palace of his imagination. The next day, at dawn, 'Ala al-Din, whose love for the princess did not let him sleep restfully, was hardly up, when the demon presented himself and said, "My lord, your palace is finished. Come and see if you are satisfied." No sooner had 'Ala al-Din expressed his strong desire to see it, than the demon transported him there instantly, and he found it so much beyond his expectation that he could not admire it well enough. The demon led him through every part, and everywhere he found nothing but neatness, richness, and magnificence, with officers and slaves all dressed according to their rank and function. The demon did not forget to show him, as one of the principal parts, the treasury, the door to which was opened by the treasurer and in which 'Ala al-Din saw heaps of purses, of different sizes, according to the amount of money they contained, piled up to the ceiling and arranged in a pleasing order. As they left, the demon assured him of the trustworthiness of the treasurer. Then he led him to the stables, where the demon showed 'Ala al-Din some of the finest horses in the world and the grooms busy in grooming them. He then led him through the storerooms, which were filled with all the necessary food and trappings for the horses.

After 'Ala al-Din inspected the entire palace from top to bottom, apartment after apartment, particularly the hall with the twenty-four windows, and found it so rich and magnificent and well-furnished, beyond his expectation, he said to the demon, "Demon, no one can be more satisfied than I, and I should be remiss to complain. There is only one thing lacking, which I forgot to mention, that is, to lay from the gate of the king's palace to the door of the apartment designed for the princess a carpet of the finest velvet for her to walk on, when she comes from the king's palace." The demon, saying, "I will return in a moment," disappeared, and a short time later, 'Ala al-Din was surprised to see what he desired carried out, without knowing how it was done. Then the demon reappeared and carried 'Ala al-Din home, just as the gatekeepers were opening the gate of the king's palace.

When the gatekeepers, who were used to an open view at the side where 'Ala al-Din's palace stood, opened the gates, they were very much surprised to find it obstructed and to see a velvet carpet that stretched from there to the gate of the king's palace. At first, they did not see very well what that obstruction was, but when they saw clearly 'Ala al-Din's superb palace, their surprise increased. The news of such an extraordinary wonder spread rapidly throughout the king's palace. The grand vizier, who arrived almost at the opening of the gate, was no less surprised then the other people by this new sight. He was the first to inform the king, and he tried to make him believe that it was all enchantment. But the king said, "Vizier, why do you think it to be an enchantment? You know as well as I do that it is 'Ala al-Din's palace, which I gave him, in your presence, permission to build for my daughter, the princess. After the manifestations we have seen of his riches, can we think it strange that he has built this palace in such a short time? He wanted to surprise us and make us see what miracles one can achieve with ready money, from one day to another. Confess with me that the enchantment you talk of comes from a little envy." The conversation ended, as it was time to go to the council.

When 'Ala al-Din had been carried home and had dismissed the demon, he found his mother up, dressing herself in one of the suits brought for her. By the time the king returned from the council, 'Ala al-Din prepared his mother to go to the palace with the six slave-girls who had been brought by the demon. He asked her, if she saw the king, to tell him that she came to have the honor to accompany the princess, toward evening, to her palace, when she was ready. So she departed, but although she and the slave-girls, who followed her, were dressed like queens, the crowd that watched them pass was not as large, because they were veiled and because an appropriate cloak concealed the richness and magnificence of their clothes. Meanwhile, 'Ala al-Din mounted his horse, and after leaving his paternal home forever, without forgetting the magic lamp, which was so helpful to him in attaining the height of happiness, he went to his palace, with the same pomp as on the previous day, when he went to present himself to the king.

As soon as the gatekeepers of the king's palace saw 'Ala al-Din's mother, they informed the king, and the order was immediately given to the bands of trumpets, drums, tambourines, fifes, and oboes which had been stationed at different parts of the terrace of the palace, and instantly the air resounded with fanfares and concerts, announcing the rejoicing to the whole city. The merchants began to adorn their shops with fine carpets and cushions, as well as boughs, and to prepare illuminations for the night. The artisans left their work, and all the people rushed to the great square between the king's palace and that of 'Ala al-Din. The latter drew their attention, not so much because they were used to see that of the king, but because there was no comparison between the two. But what amazed them most was to comprehend by what an unheard-of miracle they saw such a magnificent palace standing at a place that, the day before, had neither foundations nor building materials.

'Ala al-Din's mother was received in the palace with honor and introduced into Princess Badr al-Budur's apartment by the chief of the eunuchs. As soon as the princess saw her, she embraced her and seated her on her sofa, and after her waiting women finished dressing her and adorning her with the most precious jewels 'Ala al-Din had presented her with, a superb light meal was served. The king, who wished to spend as much time as possible with his daughter before she left him to go to 'Ala al-Din's palace, came to pay her his respects. 'Ala al-Din's mother had several times talked to the king in public, but he had never seen her without a veil, as she was then. Although she was somewhat advanced in years, one could still see from her face that she had been a beautiful woman when she was young. The king, who had always seen her dressed very plainly, not to say poorly, was surprised to find her as richly and magnificently dressed as the princess, his daughter. This made him think that 'Ala al-Din was equally prudent, intelligent, and wise in everything he did.

When it was night, the princess took leave of her father the king. Their adieus were tender and tearful. They embraced each other silently, and at last the princess left her own apartment and walked out, with 'Ala al-Din's mother on her left, followed by a hundred slave-girls, all dressed with striking magnificence. All the bands of musicians, which had not ceased playing since 'Ala al-Din's mother arrived, joined together and led the procession, followed by a hundred officers and an equal number of black eunuchs, in two rows, with their chief officers at their head. Four hundred of the king's young pages

marched on each side, each carrying a torch, and the light of the
torches, joined with the light of the illumination of the king's palace
and that of 'Ala al-Din, marvelously made the night like day. The
princess walked on the carpet, which was spread from the king's
palace to that of 'Ala al-Din, and as the bands of musicians who preceded the procession approached 'Ala al-Din's palace, they joined
those playing on the terraces, forming a concert, which, although
seemingly extraordinary and confusing, increased the pleasure, not
only of the great crowd that filled the square, but also of those who
were in the two palaces and indeed the entire city and far beyond.

At last, the princess arrived at the new palace, and 'Ala al-Din ran
with all imaginable joy to receive her at the entrance of the apartment
appointed for him. 'Ala al-Din's mother had taken care to point her
son out to the princess, in the midst of the officers who surrounded
him, and the princess found him so handsome that she was charmed
by him. 'Ala al-Din, approaching her and saluting her with great
respect, said to her, "Adorable princess, if I have the misfortune to
have displeased you by my boldness in aspiring to the possession of
such a lovely princess and daughter of my king, I should say that you
ought to blame your beautiful eyes and charms, not me." The princess
replied, "Prince, as I may now call you, I am obedient to the will of
my father the king, and it is enough for me to have seen you to say
that I obey him without reluctance."

'Ala al-Din, charmed with such an agreeable and gratifying
response, did not keep the princess standing after the long walk, to
which she was not accustomed, but took her by the hand, which he
kissed with a great demonstration of joy, and led her into a great hall,
lighted with an infinite number of candles, where, by the care of a
demon, a superb banquet was served. The plates were of heavy gold
and full of the most delicious foods. The vases, basins, and goblets,
with which the table was well furnished, were also of gold and of
exquisite workmanship, and all the other ornaments and embellish-
ments of the hall were perfectly in keeping with such great sumptu-
ousness. The princess, delighted to see so many riches assembled in
one place, said to 'Ala al-Din, "Prince, I thought that nothing in the
world was more beautiful than the palace of my father the king, but by
seeing this hall alone, I know that I was mistaken." 'Ala al-Din, leading her to the place appointed for her at the table, replied, "Princess, I
receive such great honesty, as I ought, but I know what I should
believe." As soon as she, 'Ala al-Din, and his mother sat down, a band
of the most harmonious instruments, accompanied by very beautiful
female voices, began a concert, which lasted without interruption to
the end of the meal. The princess was so delighted that she declared

that she never heard anything like it in the palace of her father the king. But she did not know that the musicians were fairies chosen by the demon, slave of the lamp.

When the meal ended and the table was taken away, a troupe of male and female demons followed the musicians and danced several kinds of figure dances peculiar to the country. They ended with a dancing man and woman, who performed with surprising agility, each showing in turn all the good grace and skill they were capable of. Near midnight, 'Ala al-Din, according to the custom of that time in China, got up and presented his hand to Princess Badr al-Budur to dance with him and bring the wedding ceremony to an end. They danced so elegantly that they were the admiration of the entire company. When they finished, 'Ala al-Din did not let go of the princess's hand, but led her into the apartment where the wedding bed was prepared. The princess's women helped to undress her and put her to bed, and Ala al-Din's attendants did the same for him, and then everyone retired. Thus ended the ceremonies and the celebrations of the wedding of 'Ala al-Din and Princess Badr al-Budur.

The next morning, when 'Ala al-Din woke up, his valets came in to dress him, and they put on him another suit, as rich and magnificent as the one he wore on his wedding day. Then he ordered one of his private horses and, mounting it, rode to the king's palace, surrounded by a large group of slaves. The king received him with the same honors as before, embraced him, and, after seating 'Ala al-Din near him on the throne, ordered breakfast. 'Ala al-Din said to him, "My lord, I beg your majesty to exempt me from this honor today. I came to ask you to do me the honor to come and take a meal at the princess's palace, with the grand vizier and the lords of the court." The king granted him this favor with pleasure, got up immediately, and, as it was not far, wished to go there on foot. So he went, with 'Ala al-Din on his right, the grand vizier on his left, and the lords of the court behind, preceded by the guards and the chief officers of his palace.

The closer the king approached 'Ala al-Din's palace, the more struck he was with its beauty, but he was much more amazed when he entered it, and he could not stop his exclamations of approbation at every room he saw. But when he came to the hall with the twenty-four windows, to which 'Ala al-Din had invited him to ascend, and saw the ornaments and, above all, the shutters adorned with diamonds, rubies, and emeralds, all large and perfectly proportioned stones, and heard from 'Ala al-Din that they were as rich on the outside, he was so amazed that for a while he stood motionless. When he recovered, he said to the grand vizier, who was standing near him, "Vizier, is it possible that there is such a superb palace in my kingdom and so close to my own, yet I do not find out about it till now?" The grand vizier replied, "Your majesty may remember that the day before yesterday, you granted 'Ala al-Din, whom you accepted as your son-in-law, permission to build a palace opposite your own and that, that very day, at sunset, there was no palace on the spot, and that, yesterday, I had the honor to be the first to announce to you that the palace was built and finished." The king said, "I remember, but I never imagined that this palace would be one of the wonders of the world. Where in all the world can one find a palace built of layers of heavy gold and silver, instead of stones or marble, with windows, the shutters of which are set with diamonds, rubies, and emeralds? Never in the world has anything like it been mentioned before."

The king wished to examine and admire the beauty of the twenty-four windows, but when he counted them, he found that only twenty-three were richly adorned, and he was very much astonished to see that the twenty-fourth was left unfinished. He said to the grand vizier, who made a point of being always by his side, "I am surprised that a hall so magnificent should be left imperfect here." The grand vizier replied, "My lord, 'Ala al-Din was apparently in a hurry and did not have enough time to finish this window, like the rest, but one may suppose that he has enough jewels and that he will have it done at the first opportunity."

At that moment, 'Ala al-Din, who had left the king to give some orders, returned to join him. The king said to him, "Son, this hall is the most worthy of admiration above all halls in the world, but there is one thing that baffles me, that is, to see this window left unfinished." He added, "Is it from forgetfulness, negligence, or lack of time that the workmen have not put the finishing touch to such a beautiful piece of architecture?" 'Ala al-Din replied, "My lord, it is for none of these reasons that your majesty sees this window in this condition. It was done by design, and it was by my orders that the workers left it untouched, for I wanted your majesty to have the glory to finish this hall and this palace at the same time, and I beg of you to approve of my good intentions, in order that I may remember your kindness and your favors." The king replied, "If you did it with this intention, I accept it willingly, and I will immediately give the orders to have it done." Accordingly, he sent for the jewelers who had the best precious stones and for the most skillful goldsmiths in the capital.

Then the king went out of this hall, and 'Ala al-Din descended with him, leading him into that hall in which he had entertained Princess Badr al-Budur on their wedding day. The princess came in a moment later, and received her father the king with an air that showed him how much she was satisfied with her marriage. Two tables were spread with the most delicious foods, all served on gold plates. The king sat at the first table and ate with his daughter the princess, 'Ala al-Din, and the grand vizier, while all the lords of the court sat at the second, which was very long. The king found the food delicious and declared that he had never eaten anything more exquisite. He said the same thing of the wine, which was indeed very fine. But what he admired most was four sideboards, full of a profusion of flagons, basins, and cups, all of heavy gold, set with jewels. He was also pleased with the bands of musicians, who were arranged in order and played inside the hall, while the sounds of trumpets, accompanied by drums and tambourines, resounded in the air, at a proper distance outside, producing a most delightful effect.

When the king rose from the table, he was informed that the jewelers and goldsmiths he had sent for had arrived. He went up again to the hall with the twenty-four windows, and when he was there, he showed the jewelers and goldsmiths, who had followed him, the window that was left unfinished, saying, "I sent for you to finish for me this window and make it as perfect as the others. Examine them, and do not waste any time in making this one just like the rest."

The jewelers and goldsmiths examined all twenty-three windows very carefully, and after they consulted together and agreed as to what each could contribute, they returned and presented themselves before the king. The palace jeweler spoke for them, saying to him, "My lord, we are ready to exert our care and industry to obey your majesty, but among us all, we cannot furnish enough jewels for such a great project." The king replied, "I have more than necessary. Come to my palace, and I will let you choose."

When the king returned to his palace, he ordered all his jewels to be brought out, and the jewelers took a great quantity, particularly of those ''Ala al-Din had given him as a present. Then they used them, but without seeming to make much progress. They came again several times for more, but after a whole month, they had not finished half of the work. They used all the jewels of the king, as well as those he had borrowed from the grand vizier, but all they could do with all this was to finish at most only half of the window.

''Ala al-Din, who knew that the king's endeavors to make this window like the rest were in vain and that he would never be able to have it done with any distinction, sent for the jewelers and asked them not only to stop their work, but also to undo what they had done and return all the jewels to the king, including those he had borrowed from the grand vizier. They undid in five hours the work that had taken them more than six weeks to achieve, and they departed, leaving 'Ala al-Din alone in the hall. He took out the lamp, which he carried with him, and rubbed it, and the demon appeared immediately. 'Ala al-Din said to him, "I ordered you to leave one of the windows of this

hall unfinished, and you have carried out my order. Now I have summoned you to tell you that I want you to make it like the others." The
demon disappeared, and 'Ala al-Din descended from the hall. When
he went up again, a few moments later, he found the window exactly
like the others, as he had wished.

Meanwhile, the jewelers and goldsmiths reached the palace and
were brought into the presence of the king. The first jeweler, presenting the jewels he had brought back and speaking for the others, said to
the king, "My lord, your majesty knows how much time we have spent
to finish, with all possible industry, the work that you have charged us
with. It was far advanced when 'Ala al-Din forced us not only to stop
the work, but also to undo what we had done and to bring you back
your own jewels and those of the grand vizier." The king asked them
whether 'Ala al-Din gave them any reason for doing this, and as they
answered that he had given them none, the king immediately ordered
a horse to be brought to him. When the horse was brought, he
mounted and rode to 'Ala al-Din's palace, with only a few attendants,
who accompanied him on foot. When he arrived, he dismounted at
the staircase that led up to the hall with the twenty-four windows and
went up to it, without giving 'Ala al-Din any advance notice. But it
happened that at that very moment, 'Ala al-Din was very opportunely
there, and he had just enough time to receive the king at the door.
The king, without giving 'Ala al-Din time to complain obligingly that
his majesty had not given him notice and had put him in a position
that forced him to fail in his duty, said to him, "Son, I come myself to
ask you the reason why you wish to leave imperfect a hall as magnificent and unique as this." 'Ala al-Din concealed the true reason, which
was that the king was not rich enough in jewels to afford such a great
expense; but in order to let him know how much this palace surpassed,
not only his own, but every palace in the world, even in that condition,
since he was unable to finish one of its smallest parts, said to him, "My
lord, it is true that your majesty saw this hall unfinished, but I beg of
you now to see if anything is lacking."

The king went directly to the unfinished window, and when he saw
that it was like the others, he thought that he was mistaken. So he
examined not only the two windows on each side, but also all the
other windows, one by one, and when he was convinced that the shutters, on which many workmen had spent so much time, were finished,
in such a short time, he embraced 'Ala al-Din and kissed him between
the eyes, saying in amazement, "Son, what a man you are to do such
surprising things in the twinkling of an eye! There is no one like you in
the whole world, and the more I know you, the more I admire you."
'Ala al-Din received the praises and acclamations of the king with a
great deal of modesty and replied, "My lord, it is a great honor for me

to merit your majesty's good will and approbation, and I assure you
that I will do all I can to deserve them more and more."

The king returned to his palace, as he came, without letting 'Ala al-
Din go with him. When he arrived, he found the grand vizier waiting
for him, and he described to him, still full of admiration, the wonder
he had just seen, in terms that left the grand vizier no doubt that the
thing was indeed as the king had described it, although he was more
confirmed in his belief that 'Ala al-Din's palace was nothing but the
effect of enchantment, as he had told the king, the first moment he
laid eyes on it. He started to repeat the same thing, but the king interrupted him, saying, "Vizier, you told me so once before, but I see that
you have not yet forgotten my daughter's marriage to your son." The
grand vizier, seeing clearly that the king was biased, and not wishing
to enter any disputes with him, left him to his opinion. Meanwhile the
king, as soon as he got up in the morning, went regularly to a room
from which he could see the entire palace of 'Ala al-Din, and he used
to go there many times during the day to contemplate it and admire it.

In the meantime, 'Ala al-Din did not confine himself to his palace.
He took care to show himself in town, several times a week, by going
to pray sometimes in one mosque, sometimes in another, or by paying
a visit from time to time to the grand vizier, who affected to pay his
respects to him on certain days, or by doing the principal lords of the
court, whom he often entertained in his palace, the honor to return
their visits. Every time he went out, he ordered two of the slaves who
walked, surrounding his horse, to throw handfuls of money in the
streets and the squares through which he passed and to which a great
crowd of people always flocked. Besides, no poor man came to his
palace gate without returning satisfied with the generosity he received
by 'Ala al-Din's orders. As 'Ala al-Din divided his time in such a way
that he went hunting at least once a week, sometimes in the vicinity of
the city, sometimes farther off, he also exercised his generosity on the
roads and in the villages. This generous disposition earned him a thousand blessings from the people, and it was common for them to swear
by his head. In short, without offending the king, to whom he paid his
respects very regularly, one may say that 'Ala al-Din, by his affable
manner and his generosity, won the affection of the people and that in
general he was more beloved than the king himself. In addition to all
these fine qualities, he showed such courage and zeal for the good of
the nation that one could not praise him well enough. He manifested
both qualities when a rebellion broke out near the borders of the kingdom, for no sooner had he learned that the king was levying an army
to quell the rebellion than he begged the king to put him in charge,
which he had no difficulty in obtaining. As soon as he was the head of
the army, he marched against the rebels, so expeditiously that the king

heard of the defeat, punishment, and dispersal of the rebels before he heard of 'Ala al-Din's arrival in the army. But although this success made his name famous throughout the kingdom, it did not alter his disposition, for he was as affable after his victory as before.

'Ala al-Din had been living in this manner for several years, when the African magician, who had unintentionally given him the means of raising himself to a high fortune, thought of him in Africa, where he had returned. Although he was till then convinced that 'Ala al-Din had died miserably in the subterranean place where he had left him, it came to his mind to find out precisely how he had died. As he was a great geomancer, he took out of a cupboard a covered square box, which he used in his geomantic observations. He sat on the sofa, set the box before him, and uncovered it. After he prepared and leveled the sand, with the intention of discovering how 'Ala al-Din had died in the subterranean place, he cast the points, drew the figures, and formed the horoscope. But when he examined it, he discovered that, instead of being dead in the subterranean place, 'Ala al-Din was out of it and was living in great splendor, being extremely rich, married to a princess, and respected and honored.

The African magician had no sooner found out by the rules of his diabolic art that 'Ala al-Din had arrived at this high fortune than his face burned red with rage, and he said to himself, "This miserable son of a tailor has discovered the secret and power of the lamp. I believed that his death was certain, yet here he is, enjoying the fruits of my labor and study. But I will prevent him from enjoying it much longer, or perish." He did not take long in deliberating on what action to take. So the next morning, he mounted a Barbary horse he had in his stable and set out on his journey, traveling from city to city and from province to province, without stopping, except to rest his horse, until he reached China and, soon after, the capital of the king whose daughter 'Ala al-Din had married. He took up lodgings in an inn and remained there the rest of the day and the night to rest from the fatigue of his journey.

The next morning, the first thing he did was to find out what people said of 'Ala al-Din, and, taking a walk through the town, he went into the best known and most frequented place, where people of distinction met to drink a certain kind of warm liquor, which he had drunk when he was there before. As soon as he sat down, a glass of it was poured and presented to him. He took it, listening to the conversation of people on each side, and heard them talking of 'Ala al-Din's palace. When he finished his drink, he approached one of them and took the opportunity to ask him specifically what was that palace of which they spoke so well. The man said, "From where do you come? You must have newly arrived, not to have seen or heard talk of Prince 'Ala al-

Din's palace." (He was called by no other title, ever since he married Princess Badr al-Budur.) He continued, "I will not say to you that it is one of the wonders of the world, but that it is the only wonder of the world, for nothing so rich, so grand, and so magnificent has ever been seen. You must have come from very far, not to have heard talk of it. Indeed, it must have been talked of all over the world, ever since it was built. See it, and judge for yourself whether I have not told you the truth." The African magician replied, "Forgive my ignorance. I arrived here only yesterday, and I did indeed come from very far, in fact the farthest part of Africa, which the fame of this palace had not yet reached when I left. For in view of the urgent business that brought me here, my sole aim was to get here as soon as possible, without stopping anywhere or making any acquaintances, and therefore I did not learn about it until you told me. But I will not fail to go and see it. My impatience to do so is so great that I am eager to satisfy my curiosity immediately, if you will do me the favor to show me the way to it."

The man was pleased to show him the way he must take to have a view of 'Ala al-Din's palace, and the African magician got up and left instantly. When he arrived and examined the palace closely, on all sides, he had no doubt that 'Ala al-Din had made use of the lamp to build it. Without dwelling on the inability of 'Ala al-Din, the son of a simple tailor, he knew that only the demons, the slaves of the lamp, the possession of which had eluded him, could have performed such wonders. Pierced to the quick at 'Ala al-Din's happiness and greatness, which he could hardly distinguish from those of the king, he returned to the inn where he lodged.

The question was to find out where the lamp was and whether 'Ala al-Din carried it with him, or whether he kept it somewhere else, and this he had to discover by an operation of geomancy. As soon as he entered his lodging, he took his square box and his sand, which he carried along with him whenever he traveled, and after he performed the operation, he discovered that the lamp was inside 'Ala al-Din's palace, and his joy was so great at this discovery that he was beside himself and said, "I will have the lamp, and I defy 'Ala al-Din to stop me from taking it from him and making him sink to his original meanness, from which he has taken such a high flight."

It was 'Ala al-Din's misfortune that at that time he had gone hunting for eight days, of which only three had expired, and the African magician found out about it by the following means. After he performed the operation that gave him so much joy, he went to the inn's caretaker, on the pretext of having a chat with him, and the caretaker, who liked to talk, did not need much prodding. The magician then told him that he had seen 'Ala al-Din's palace, and, after describing to him, with exaggeration, the features that had seemed the most amazing and most striking to him and all the world, he added, "But my curiosity goes beyond all this, and I will not be satisfied until I see the person to whom this wonderful edifice belongs." The caretaker replied, "That will not be difficult. There is hardly any day, when he is in town, on which he does not give the opportunity, but he has been outside the city on a long hunting trip, which will last five more days."

The African magician did not wish to inquire any further. He took leave of the caretaker and, returning to his room, said to himself, "This is the time to act, and I should not let this opportunity slip by." He went to the shop of a maker and seller of lamps and said to him, "Master, I need a dozen copper lamps; can you supply me with them?" The lamp seller told him that he did not have enough, but that if he waited till the next day, he would have them any time he wished. The magician consented and asked that they should be clean and polished, and, after promising that he would pay him well, he returned to the inn.

The next day, the magician received the twelve lamps and paid the man the asking price, without haggling. He put them in a basket that he had brought for that purpose, and, with the basket hanging on his arm, headed to 'Ala al-Din's palace and began to cry out, "Who would like to exchange old lamps for new ones?" As he came nearer, the children, who were playing in the square and who heard him from a distance, rushed to surround him and jeer at him, thinking him to be a madman, and the passersby laughed at what they considered to be his folly, saying, "He must have lost his mind to offer new lamps for old ones." But he was not taken aback by the jeers of the children or by what was said about him, and in order to promote his merchandise, he continued to cry out, "Who would like to exchange old lamps for new ones?" He repeated this so often, walking back and forth in the square, in front of the palace and around it, that Princess Badr al-Budur, who was at that time in the hall with the twenty-four windows, hearing a man cry something, but being unable to distinguish his words because of the jeers of the children who followed him and who kept increasing in number, sent down one of her slave-girls, who went close to him to find out what that noise was.

The slave-girl soon returned, and went into the hall with a loud burst of laughter, and she kept laughing so heartily that the princess could not prevent herself from laughing when she saw her. She asked her, "Well, foolish one, will you tell me what you are laughing at?" The slave-girl replied, still laughing, "Princess, who can prevent himself from laughing to see a madman, with a basket on his arm, full of

fine new lamps, asking, not to sell them, but to exchange them for old
ones? The children have surrounded him so closely that he can hardly
move, and it is their cries of mockery at him that you hear."

Hearing this, another slave-girl said, "Speaking of old lamps, I don't
know whether the princess has observed that there is an old one on
the cornice, and whoever owns it will not be sorry to find a new one in
its place. If the princess wishes, she may have the pleasure to try
whether this fool is indeed foolish enough to exchange a new lamp for
an old one, without taking anything for it." The lamp of which the
slave girl spoke was the magic lamp that 'Ala al-Din had made use of
to raise himself to a high position. He himself had put it on the cornice, before he went hunting, for fear of losing it, a precaution he
always took on such occasions. But neither the slave-girls, the eunuchs,
nor the princess herself had ever noticed it during his absence. When
he was not on a hunting trip, he always carried it with him. One may
say that the precaution 'Ala al-Din took was all right, but he should
have at least locked up the lamp. This is true, but other people have
made similar mistakes before and will continue to make them to the
end of time.

Princess Badr al-Budur, who was not aware of the great value of
the lamp and of 'Ala al-Din's great interest, not to speak of her own, in
keeping it safe from everyone, joined the pleasantry and bid a eunuch
to take it and make the exchange. The eunuch obeyed, went down,
and, as soon as he was outside the palace gate, saw the African magician and called to him. When he came, the eunuch showed him the
old lamp, saying, "Give me a new lamp in exchange for this." The
African magician had no doubt that this was the lamp he wanted.
There could not have been any others like it in the palace, where all
the utensils were either gold or silver. He snatched it from the
eunuch's hand, and, after thrusting it as far as he could in his breast,
offered him his basket and told him to choose whichever lamp he
pleased. The eunuch chose one, left the magician, and carried the new
lamp to Princess Badr al-Budur. The exchange was no sooner made
than the square rang again with the cries of the children, who shouted
even louder than before, mocking what they thought to be his folly.

The African magician let the children shout as much as they
pleased and, not wishing to stay any longer near 'Ala al-Din's palace,
walked, leaving it far behind, without making any noise, that is to say,
without crying or speaking any longer of exchanging new lamps for
old ones, for he wanted no other save the one he carried off, and his
silence made the children leave him alone and let him go.

As soon as he was out of the square between the two palaces, he
escaped through the least frequented streets, and since he had no
more need for the lamps or the basket, he set them down in the mid-

dle of a street when he saw that there was nobody there. Then he entered another street and walked quickly until he came to one of the city gates, and, pursuing his way through the suburbs, which extended far, he bought some provisions before he left the vicinity of the city and got into the fields. Then he turned from the road and went to a remote hidden place, where he stayed, waiting for the proper moment to achieve the aim he had come for. He did not regret leaving the horse behind at the inn where he had taken lodgings, for he thought himself well compensated by the treasure he had acquired.

He spent the rest of the day in that place until the darkest time of the night, when he pulled the lamp out of his breast and rubbed it. At that call, the demon appeared and said, "What do you wish? Here I am, ready to obey you, as your slave and the slave of all those who have the lamp in their hands." He replied, "I command you to transport me immediately, with the palace which you or the other slaves of the lamp have built, as it is, with all the people in it, to such and such a place in Africa." The demon did not reply, but with the assistance of the other demons, the slaves of the lamp, transported him and the entire palace, in a very short time, to the designated place in Africa, where we will take leave of the magician, the palace, and Princess Badr al-Budur, to describe the surprise of the king.

As soon as the king got up in the morning, he went as usual to the room with the view, to have the pleasure of contemplating and admiring 'Ala al-Din's palace. But when he looked in that direction, instead of the palace, he saw an empty space, such as it had been before the palace was built. He thought that he was mistaken and rubbed his eyes, but he saw nothing more than he did the first time, even though the weather was fine, the sky clear, and the daylight, which was beginning to appear, had made all objects very distinct. He looked through the two openings on the right and left and saw nothing more than he had formerly been used to see out of them. His amazement was so great that he stood for some time, looking at the spot where the palace had stood, but where it was now no longer to be seen. He could not comprehend how so large and striking a palace as that of 'Ala al-Din, which he saw only the day before and had seen almost every day ever since he gave 'Ala al-Din permission to build it, could have vanished, without leaving a trace behind. He said to himself, "Certainly, I am not mistaken. It did stand there. If it had collapsed, the materials would have lain in heaps, and if the earth had swallowed it up, there would have been some mark left. How then could it have vanished?" Although he was convinced that the palace was gone, he stayed there for some time to see whether he might not be mistaken. At last, he retired to his apartment, looking behind him one more time before he left the room. Then he ordered that the grand vizier be brought to him in all haste and, in the meantime, sat down, his mind agitated by so many conflicting thoughts that he did not know what to think.

The grand vizier did not make the king wait long. He came in such great haste that neither he nor his men noticed, as they passed by, that 'Ala al-Din's palace was no longer there; neither did the gatekeepers, when they opened the palace gate. When the grand vizier approached the king, he said to him, "My lord, the haste in which your majesty has sent for me leads me to believe that something very extraordinary has happened, since you know that this is council day and that I must not fail to report to my duty there in a few moments." The king replied, "Indeed, it is very extraordinary, as you say, and you will agree that it is so. Tell me, where is 'Ala al-Din's palace?" The grand vizier replied, in amazement, "My lord, I thought, as I passed by, that it stood in its usual place. Buildings as substantial as that do not change place so easily." The king said, "Go into that room, and tell me if you see it."

The grand vizier went into the room and had the same experience as the king. When he was well assured that 'Ala al-Din's palace was no longer where it used to be and that there was not a trace of it left, he returned to the king, who asked him, "Well, have you seen 'Ala al-Din's palace?" The grand vizier replied, "My lord, your majesty may remember that I had the honor to tell you that that palace, which was the subject of your admiration, with all its immense riches, was only the work of magic, wrought by a magician, but your majesty would not pay any attention." The king, who could not dispute the grand vizier's claims, flew into a great rage, because he could not deny his incredulity, and cried out, "Where is that imposter, that rascal, so that I may have his head cut off?" The grand vizier replied, "My lord, it has been some days since he came to take leave of your majesty. He ought to be sent for, to ask him what became of his palace, for he must surely know." The king said, "This would be treating him with too much indulgence. Go and give orders to a detachment of thirty of my horsemen to bring him back to me in chains." The grand vizier went to convey the king's order to the horsemen, instructing their commanding officer in what manner to take 'Ala al-Din, in order that he might not escape them. The horsemen rode out and, about five or six leagues from the city, met him, as he was hunting in the direction of the city. The commanding officer approached 'Ala al-Din and told him that the king, who was impatient to see him, had sent them to inform him and ride back with him.

'Ala al-Din, who did not have the slightest suspicion of the true reason that had brought this detachment of the king's guards, continued on his way back to the city. But when he was about half a league away, the horsemen surrounded him, and the commanding officer said to him, "Prince 'Ala al-Din, it is with great regret that I must inform you of the king's order to arrest you and bring you back to him as a criminal. I beg you not to take it ill that we are performing our duty, and to forgive us."

'Ala al-Din, who felt himself innocent, was very much surprised at this declaration and asked the officer whether he knew what crime he was accused of. The officer replied that neither he nor his men knew. 'Ala al-Din, seeing that his own men were considerably inferior in number to the detachment, even if they were farther off, dismounted and said to the officer, "Here I am. Carry out your order, but I can tell you that I am not aware of being guilty of any crime against the king or against the state." A very large and long chain was immediately put around his neck and tied around his body, in such a way as to bind his arms. Then the officer rode at the head of the horsemen, while a horseman, holding the end of the chain and riding behind him, led 'Ala al-Din, who was obliged to follow him on foot, to the city.

When the horsemen entered the suburbs, the people who saw 'Ala al-Din led as a state criminal had no doubt that his head was going to be cut off. As he was generally beloved, some took swords, some took other weapons, while those who had none gathered stones and followed the detachment. Some horsemen who rode in the rear turned around with threatening looks, in order to disperse them. But soon the crowd grew so large that the horsemen decided on a maneuver, thinking that they would be lucky if 'Ala al-Din was not rescued before they reached the king's palace. To prevent this, as the streets varied in width, they took care to cover the space by spreading out or closing in. In this manner, they arrived at the palace square and drew up a line, facing the armed rabble, until the officer and the horseman who led 'Ala al-Din went through the gate, which the gatekeepers shut immediately, to prevent the people from following in.

'Ala al-Din was brought before the king, who was waiting for him, attended by the grand vizier, on the balcony. As soon as the king saw him, he commanded the executioner, who had been ordered to be there, to cut off his head, without hearing him or getting any explanation from him. The executioner seized 'Ala al-Din, took off the chain fastened around his neck and his body and, after laying down on the ground a leather mat stained with the blood of an infinite number of criminals he had executed, made him kneel on his knees and tied a bandage over his eyes. Then the executioner drew his sword, took his measures to strike the blow, by flourishing the sword in the air and trying it three times, and waited for the king to give the signal to cut off 'Ala al-Din's head.

At that moment, the grand vizier, who perceived that the crowd, which had overpowered the mounted palace guard and filled the square, were scaling the walls in several places and were beginning to tear them down, in order to force their way in, said to the king, before he gave the signal, "My lord, I beg your majesty to consider what you are going to do, for you will risk your palace being stormed, and if any mishap occurs, it may be fatal." The king replied, "My palace forced? Who can have the audacity?" The grand vizier replied, "My lord, if your majesty will cast your eyes toward the walls of your palace and toward the square, you will discover the truth of what I say."

When the king saw the animated and aggressive mob, his fear was so great that he instantly commanded the executioner to put his sword in the scabbard and remove the bandage from 'Ala al-Din's eyes, to release him. At the same time, he ordered the guards to declare to the men that the king had pardoned him and that they might withdraw. Then all the men who had already scaled the palace walls and had seen what happened, abandoned their plan and descended quickly, full of joy that they had saved the life of a man they truly loved. They gave the news to those who were around them, and it soon spread throughout the entire crowd assembled in the square, and when the guards proclaimed the same thing from the top of the terraces, it became known everywhere. The justice the king had done 'Ala al-Din by pardoning him disarmed the mob and put an end to the tumult, and everyone returned home quietly.

When 'Ala al-Din found himself free, he looked toward the balcony and, seeing the king, cried out to him, in a moving manner, "My lord, I implore your majesty to add one more favor to the one you have already done me, to let me know my crime." The king replied, "Your crime? Don't you know it? Come up here, and I will show you." 'Ala al-Din went up, and when he presented himself, the king, saying, "Follow me," walked ahead of him, without looking back at him, and led him to the room with the view. When he reached the door, the king said to him, "Enter. You ought to know where your palace stood. Look everywhere, and tell me what has become of it."

'Ala al-Din looked around, but found nothing. He saw clearly the spot of ground his palace had occupied, but since he could not guess how it could have disappeared, this extraordinary and surprising event threw him into such a great bewilderment and confusion that he could not reply with a single word. The king, growing impatient, asked 'Ala al-Din again, "Where is your palace, and where is my daughter?" Then 'Ala al-Din, breaking his silence, said to him, "My lord, I see very well, and I admit that the palace I have built is no longer in the place where it was. I see that it has disappeared, and I cannot tell your majesty where it may be, but I can assure you that I had no part in this." The king replied, "I am not so much concerned about what happened to your palace. I value my daughter a million times more, and I want you to find her for me, or I will cut off your head, and nothing will stop me." 'Ala al-Din replied, "My lord, I implore your majesty to grant me forty days for this endeavor, and I give you my word that if in that time I do not succeed, I will offer my head at the foot of your throne, so that you may dispose of it as you please." The king replied, "I grant you the forty days you ask for, but do not think of abusing the favor I am doing you by thinking that you can escape my resentment, for I will find you in whatever corner of the earth you may be."

'Ala al-Din went out of the king's presence in great humiliation and in a state worthy of pity. He crossed the courts of the palace, with his head hanging down, without daring to lift up his eyes in his confusion. The principal officers of the court, who had been his friends and whom he had never disobliged, instead of going up to him to console him and offer him shelter in their houses, turned their backs on him, as much to avoid seeing him as to avoid being recognized by him. But had they approached him to give him some words of comfort or offer him some help, they would not have recognized him, for he hardly recognized himself, being no longer in his right mind, as was evident when, as soon as he left the palace, he, without knowing what he was doing, inquired from door to door and from all passersby he met whether they had seen his palace or whether they could give him any news of it. These inquiries made everybody believe that 'Ala al-Din was mad. Some laughed at him, but the most sensible of them, and particularly those who had any connection of business or friendship with him, truly pitied him. He stayed in the city for three days wandering from one place to another, without eating anything, save what people gave him out of charity, and without coming to any resolution.

At last, as he could no longer stay in that unhappy condition in a city in which he had formerly cut such a fine figure, he left it and took the road to the country. He avoided the main roads, and after crossing several fields, in a terrible uncertainty, he finally, as night approached, came to the side of a river. There, he was overcome by despair and said to himself, "Where shall I go to look for my palace? In what province, country, or part of the world shall I find it and find my dear princess, whom the king demands of me? I will never succeed. I should therefore better free myself from so much fruitless labor and from the bitter grief that preys on me." He was going to throw himself into the river, following the resolution he had made, but being a good Muslim, true to his religion, he thought that he should not do it without performing his prayers. Wishing to prepare himself, he went to the river bank to wash his hands and face, according to custom. As the bank was sloping and wet, because the water beat against it, he slid down and would have fallen into the river, had he not held on to a rock that jutted about two feet above the ground. Fortunately for him, he was still wearing the ring the African magician had put on his finger before he went down into the subterranean place to get the precious lamp that was taken from him. In holding onto the rock, he rubbed the ring against it so hard that instantly the same demon who had appeared before him in the subterranean place where the African magician had confined him, appeared again and said, "What do you wish? Here I am, ready to obey you, as your slave and the slave of those who have the ring on their finger, I and the other slaves of the ring."

'Ala al-Din, pleasantly surprised at an apparition he so little expected in his despair, said, "Demon, save my life a second time, either by telling me where the palace is or by transporting it instantly back to where it was." The demon replied, "What you demand of me is not in my power, for I am only the slave of the ring. You must address yourself to the slave of the lamp." 'Ala al-Din said, "If this is so, then I command you by the power of the ring to transport me to the place where my palace is, wherever it may be, and to set me down under Princess Badr al-Budur's windows." No sooner did he utter these words than the demon transported him to Africa, to the middle of a meadow, where his palace stood, at a little distance from a large city, and set him down exactly under the windows of Princess Badr al-Budur's apartment, where he left him. All this was done in an instant.

Despite the darkness of the night, 'Ala al-Din recognized very well his palace and Princess Badr al-Budur's apartment, but since it was late, and all was quiet in the palace, he retired at some distance and sat down at the foot of a tree. There, full of hope and reflecting on his good fortune in having been delivered from the danger of losing his life, which he owed to pure chance, he found himself in a much more peaceful state than when he was arrested and led before the king. He mused for some time on these agreeable thoughts, but as he had not slept for five or six days, he could not resist the drowsiness that came upon him and at last fell asleep where he was, at the foot of the tree.

The following day, as soon as the dawn began to break, 'Ala al-Din was pleasantly awakened by the warbling of the birds, not only those that had roosted in the tree under which he had spent the night, but also all those perched in the thick trees of his palace garden. When he cast his eye on that admirable edifice, he felt an inexpressible joy to be on the verge of being master of it again and possess once more his dear Princess Badr al-Budur. He got up and, approaching her apartment, walked for some time under her windows, in the expectation that she might be up and that he might be able to see her. During this time, he asked himself what was the cause of his misfortune, and after

deep reflection, he no longer doubted that it was caused by his having
left the lamp out of his sight. He blamed himself for his negligence
and the little care he took of it, to be a single moment without it. But
what puzzled him most was that he could not imagine who was so
jealous of his happiness. He would have soon guessed, had he known
that he was in Africa, but the demon, the slave of the ring, had said
nothing about it, nor had 'Ala al-Din asked him.

That morning Princess Badr al-Budur rose earlier than she had
done ever since her abduction and transfer to Africa by the treachery
of the African magician, whose sight she was forced to endure once a
day, because he was now the master of the palace, but she had always
treated him so harshly that he did not dare to reside in it. As she was
dressing, one of her women, looking through the shutters, saw 'Ala al-
Din and ran to inform her mistress. The princess, who could not
believe the news, went immediately to the window and opened the
shutters. The noise the princess made in opening the window made
'Ala al-Din raise his head, and when he recognized her, he saluted her
very joyfully. The princess said to him, "In order not to lose any time,
someone has already gone to open the secret door for you. Enter and
come up." Then she shut the window.

The secret door, which was just under the Princess's apartment, was
opened, and 'Ala al-Din went up. It is impossible to express the joy of
this husband and wife at seeing each other again, after a separation
they thought would last forever. They embraced several times and
showed all the marks of love and tenderness one can imagine, after
such a sad and unexpected separation. After their embraces, which
were mixed with tears of joy, they sat down, and 'Ala al-Din said, "For
God's sake, Princess, before we talk of anything else, I beg of you, in
your own interest and that of the king, your revered father, as well as
mine in particular, to tell me what has become of the old lamp I had
put on the cornice of the hall with the twenty-four windows, before I
went hunting." The princess replied, "Alas, dear husband, I strongly
suspected that our misfortune came from that lamp, and what grieves
me most is that I have been the cause of it." 'Ala al-Din said,
"Princess, do not blame yourself, since it is entirely my fault, for I
ought to have taken better care in guarding it. Let us now think only
of repairing the damage, and for a beginning, do me the favor of
telling me what has happened and into whose hands it has fallen."

Princess Badr al-Budur related to him how she had exchanged the
old lamp for a new one (which she ordered to be brought, in order
that he might see it), and how on the following night she had perceived the palace transported and how, in the morning, she had found
herself in the unknown country, which, she was told, was Africa, a face
she heard from the mouth of the traitor who had transported her there

by his magic art. 'Ala al-Din interrupted her, saying, "Princess, you have already informed me who the traitor is, by telling me that you and I are in Africa. He is the most perfidious of all men, but this is neither the time nor the place to give you a full account of his evil acts. I beg you only to tell me what he has done with the lamp and where he has put it." The Princess replied, "He carries it carefully, wrapped up in his breast, and I can assure you of this, because he pulled it out before me and showed it to me as a trophy." 'Ala al-Din said, "My princess, do not be displeased that I trouble you with so many questions. They are equally important both to you and to me. But to come to what most particularly concerns me, tell me, I entreat you, how such a wicked and perfidious man has been treating you?" The princess replied, "Ever since I have been here, he comes once every day to see me, and I am convinced that the little satisfaction he gets from his visits dissuades him from bothering me more often. All his talk with me has centered on persuading me to break the commitment I have pledged to you and to take him for a husband, by trying to make me believe that I ought not to entertain any hope of ever seeing you again, saying that you were dead and that my father the king had had your head cut off. He said, to justify himself, that you were ungrateful and that you owed your good fortune solely to him, adding a thousand other things, which I will not repeat. But as he received no answers from me but tears and agonized complaints, he was forced to retire with no more satisfaction than when he came. I have no doubt, however, that his intention is to allow me time to overcome my grief, expecting that I might later change my mind, and if I persisted in my resistance to him, to use violence in the end. But your presence, dear husband, has removed all my worries."

'Ala al-Din interrupted her, saying, "I am confident that it is not in vain, since your worries are over, and I think that I have found the means of delivering you from your enemy and mine. But in order to do this, it is necessary for me to go to the city. I will return toward noon, and then I will acquaint you with my plan and what you shall do to contribute to its success, but I should caution you in advance not to be surprised, if you see me dressed in different clothes, and I ask you to give orders not to let me wait too long at the secret door, but to open it at the first knock." The princess promised that he would be waited for at the door and that it would be opened promptly.

When 'Ala al-Din descended from the princess's apartment and went out through the same door, he looked around and saw a peasant on the road to the country. As the peasant had already gone beyond the palace and was at some distance, 'Ala al-Din hurried after him, and when he overtook him, he proposed to him to exchange their clothes, pressuring the peasant until he agreed. The exchange was

done behind a hedge, and when they parted, 'Ala al-Din took the road
to the city. When he entered the gate, he took the street that led from
it, and after crossing the most busy streets, he came to that part of the
town where each sort of merchant and artisan had their particular
street. He went into that of the druggists and, entering the largest and
best-stocked shop, asked the druggist whether he had a certain powder
'Ala al-Din named.

The merchant, who judged 'Ala al-Din by his clothes and thought
that he was poor and did not have enough money to pay him, told
him that he had it, but that it was expensive. 'Ala al-Din, who guessed
what the merchant was thinking, pulled out his purse and, showing
him his gold coins, asked for half a dram of the powder. The merchant weighed it, wrapped it up, and, giving it to him, asked him for a
piece of gold. 'Ala al-Din put the money in his hand, and without
spending any more time in the city, except to eat something, returned
to his palace. He did not wait at the secret door, for it was already
open. When he went up to Princess Badr al-Budur's apartment, he
said to her, "Princess, the aversion you feel for your abductor, as you
have told me, may make it difficult for you to do what I am going to
propose to you. But allow me to tell you that it is proper that you dissemble and even violate your feelings, if you wish to deliver yourself
from his persecution and give the king, your father and my lord, the
satisfaction of seeing you again." 'Ala al-Din continued, "If you therefore wish to do what I propose, begin now by putting on one of your
most beautiful suits, and when the African magician comes, do your
best to give him the best reception possible, without affectation or
strain and with an open countenance, yet in such a manner that if
there remains any sign of affliction, he may think that it will go away
with time. During the conversation, let him think that you are making
efforts to forget me. In order that he may be the more fully convinced
of your sincerity, invite him to have supper with you, and indicate to
him that you will be pleased to taste some of the best wine of his country. He will not fail to go to fetch you some. During his absence, when
the table is laid, put this powder into one of the cups similar to the
one you are accustomed to drink out of and, setting it apart, ask the
slave-girl who serves you your drink to bring it to you, full of wine,
upon a signal you agree on with her. Ask her not to make a mistake.
When the magician returns and you sit to eat, and when you have
eaten and drunk as much as you please, let her bring you the cup with
the powder, and change cups with him. He will think this favor to be
so great that he will not refuse you and will even drink the cup empty,
but no sooner will he have finished it, than you will see him fall backward. If you have any aversion to drinking from his cup, you may only
pretend that you are drinking, without fear of being discovered, for

the effect of the powder is so quick that he will not have enough time to notice whether you are drinking or not."

When 'Ala al-Din finished, the princess said, "I confess that I am forcing myself in consenting to make the magician the advances that I see to be necessary for me to make, but what can one not resolve to do against a cruel enemy! I will therefore follow your advice, since my peace, no less than yours, depends on it." After 'Ala al-Din and the princess agreed on these measures, he took leave of her and went out to spend the rest of the day in the vicinity of the palace, waiting for the night to come before returning to the secret door.

Princess Badr al-Budur remained inconsolable since her separation not only from her dear husband, whom she loved and continued to love more out of inclination than duty, but also from her father the king, whom she cherished and who loved her tenderly, and she had, ever since that painful separation lived in great neglect of her person. She had even, one may say, forgot the neatness so becoming to persons of her sex, particularly after the first time the African magician visited her, and she found out from some of her women who recognized him that it was he who had taken the old lamp in exchange for a new one, an infamous ploy that rendered him abhorrent. But, the opportunity to wreak on him the vengeance he deserved, and to take it sooner than she dared hope for, made her resolve to acquiesce to 'Ala al-Din's request. Therefore, as soon as he was gone, she sat down at her dressing table and was groomed by her women in a most attractive style and dressed in the suit richest and most suitable to her purpose. She wore a belt of gold, set with the finest and largest diamonds, and a pearl necklace with six pearls on each side, so well proportioned to the one in the middle, which was the largest and the most valuable, so much so, that the greatest kings and queens would have considered themselves lucky to have a necklace of the size of two of the smallest of her pearls. Her bracelets, which were of diamonds intermixed with rubies, reinforced marvelously the richness of the belt and the necklace. When Princess Badr al-Budur was completely dressed, she looked in the mirror and, following her women's advice, made adjustments, and when she saw that she lacked no charm to flatter the foolish passion of the African magician, she sat down on the sofa, waiting for him to come.

The African magician soon came at the usual hour, and as soon as the princess saw him enter the hall with the twenty-four windows where she was waiting for him, she got up in all her beauty and charm and motioned him with her hand to the most prestigious place, where she wished him to sit, before sitting down herself. This was a mark of civility she had never shown him before. The African magician, dazzled more by the luster of the princess's eyes than the brilliance of the jewels with which she was adorned, was very much surprised, and the majestic and gracious air with which she received him, so contrary to her former rebuffs, confounded him. At first, he wanted to sit at the end of the sofa, but as he saw that the princess was not going to sit down unless he sat where she wished, he complied.

When he was seated, the princess, to relieve him from his embarrassment, spoke first, looking at him in such a manner as to make him believe that he was no longer odious to her, as she had shown before. She said, "You are doubtlessly amazed to see me so much altered today from what I used to be, but you will no longer be surprised when I tell you that my temperament is so opposed to sadness and melancholy, to griefs and worries, that I strive to put them out of my mind as soon as possible, when I perceive that their subject is past. I have reflected on what you told me of 'Ala al-Din's fate, and from what I know of my father's temper, I am as convinced as you are that 'Ala al-Din could not escape the terrible effects of his rage. If I persist in mourning him all my life, all my tears will not bring him back. For this reason, after I have paid all the duties my love requires of me, even while he is in his grave, it seems to me that I ought to endeavor to find ways of consoling myself. These are the reasons behind the change you see in me. To cast off sadness entirely, I have resolved to make a beginning and, convinced that you very much wish to keep me company, I have ordered a supper to be prepared, but since I have only Chinese wines, and since I am in Africa, I have a desire to taste some of the wine produced here, and I believe that, if it exists, you will get some of the best."

The African magician, who had looked on the happiness of coming so soon and so easily into Princess Badr al-Budur's good graces as impossible, told her that he could not find words strong enough to express to her how much he appreciated her favors. But the sooner to put an end to a conversation from which he would not have been able to extricate himself had he proceeded any further, he changed the subject to the wines of Africa, which she had initiated, and said to her that of all the advantages Africa can be proud of, that of producing excellent wines is one of the principal ones, particularly in that part of the country where she was. He said that he had a seven-year-old barrel that was never opened and that it is not praising it too much to say that it surpassed the most exquisite wines in the world, adding, "If my princess will give me leave, I will go and fetch two bottles and return immediately." The princess said, "I should be sorry to put you to that trouble. It is better to send for them." The African magician replied, "It is necessary that I go myself, for nobody but I knows where the key to the storeroom is, and nobody but I knows the secret of unlocking the door." The princess said, "If this is so, go then and come back quickly, for the more time you take, the greater will be my impatience to see you again. We will sit down to supper as soon as you return."

The African magician, full of hope of his anticipated happiness, did not run, but rather flew, to fetch the seven-year-old wine, and returned very quickly. The princess, who had no doubt that he would hurry, put with her own hand the powder 'Ala al-Din had given her in the cup set apart and prepared the table. They sat down at the table opposite to each other, in such a way that the magician's back was turned toward the sideboard. The princess offered him some of the best dishes at the table and said, "If you please, I will entertain you with singing and music, but since we are only two, you and I, it seems to me that conversation may be more agreeable." The magician looked on this choice as a new favor.

After they ate a few bits, the princess called for some wine and drank the magician's health, and then said to him, "You were right to praise your wine, for I have never tasted any so delicious." He replied, holding in his hand the cup that had been presented to him, "My wine acquires a new virtue by your praise of it." The princess said, "Then drink my health. You will find that I know wines." He drank to her health and, returning the cup, said, "I consider myself happy to have reserved this wine for such a good occasion. I too confess that I have never before drunk any so excellent in so many ways."

After they ate and drank three cups each, the princess, who had succeeded in charming the African magician by her civility and obliging manners, at last gave the signal to the slave-girl who was serving the wine, bidding her to bring her cup filled to the brim with wine and likewise to fill the magician's cup and present it to him. When they both had their cups in their hands, she said to him, "I do not know what you do here, when you love each other and drink together, as we are doing now. Back home in China, the lover and his beloved exchange cups and drink each other's health." So saying, she offered him the cup that was in her hand and held out the other hand to receive his. The African magician hastened to make this exchange, with all the more pleasure, since he looked on this favor as the most certain indication that he had completely conquered the princess's heart, and this raised his happiness to its utmost. Before he drank, he said, with his cup in his hand, "Princess, we Africans are by no means so refined as the Chinese in enlivening the art of love with such grace notes, and having been instructed in a lesson I was ignorant of, I now know to what extent I should appreciate the favor done me. I will never forget it, lovely princess, for, by drinking out of your cup, I have found the life that your cruelty, had it continued, would have made me despair of."

Princess Badr al-Budur, who began to be exasperated with the talk of the African magician, interrupted him, saying, "Let us drink first, and then you may say what you wish afterward," and at the same time, brought the cup to her mouth, hardly touching it with her lips, while the African magician, eager to drink his wine first, drank it all, without leaving a drop. In finishing it, he had bent his head back, to show his eagerness, and he remained in this state for some time, while the princess kept her cup at her lips until she saw that his eyes began to turn and he fell on his back, lifeless.

The princess had no need to order someone to go and open the door for 'Ala al-Din. As soon as the word was given that the African magician had fallen on his back, her women, who had stationed themselves at some paces from each other, from the hall to the foot of the stairs, opened the door. 'Ala al-Din went up, entered the hall, and saw the African magician stretched backward on the sofa. Princess Badr al-Budur got up and ran to him to express her joy by embracing him, but he stopped her, saying, "Princess, it is not time yet. Do me a favor by retiring to your apartment, and let me be left alone here, while I endeavor to transport you back to China as quickly as you were brought from there."

As soon as the princess and her slave-girls and eunuchs were out of the hall, 'Ala al-Din shut the door and, going to the body of the African magician, who lay lifeless, opened his vest and pulled out the lamp, which was wrapped up in the manner the princess had described to him. He unwrapped it, and as soon as he rubbed it, the demon appeared, and after he made his usual compliments, 'Ala al-Din said to him, "Demon, I have summoned you, in order to command you, on behalf of the lamp, your good mistress, to see to it that this palace be immediately carried back to China, to the same part and the same spot from where it was brought here." The demon indicated with a nod that he was going to obey and disappeared. Immediately, the palace was transported to China, and its removal was only felt by two very mild shocks, the one when it was lifted up, the other when it was set down, both occurring at a very little interval from each other.

'Ala al-Din went down to the princess's apartment and, embracing her, said, "Princess, I can assure you that your joy and mine will be complete tomorrow morning." As the princess had not yet finished her supper, and 'Ala al-Din was hungry, the princess bade the food, which was served but hardly touched, be brought down from the hall with the twenty-four windows. The princess and 'Ala al-Din ate together and drank of the African magician's good old wine, and after a conversation, which must have been very satisfying, they retired to their apartment.

From the time of the disappearance of 'Ala al-Din's palace and of Princess Badr al-Budur, her father the king was inconsolable at what he imagined was the loss of his daughter. He hardly slept night or day, and instead of avoiding everything that could prolong his affliction, he, on the contrary, sought it assiduously. Thus, whereas before he used to go every morning into the room with the view to enjoy that agreeable sight, he now went there many times a day, to renew his tears and to plunge himself deeper and deeper into the most profound grief, by the thought that he would never again see what had given him so much pleasure and that he had lost what was the most dear to him in the world.

The morning 'Ala al-Din's palace was brought back to its place, it was barely there when the king went into the room with the view. When the king entered, being withdrawn into himself and in deep grief, he cast his eyes sadly toward that part of the square where he expected to see nothing but empty air and did not notice the palace. But when he perceived that that vacancy was filled up, he thought at first that it was the effect of the fog, but, looking more carefully, he realized that it was without doubt 'Ala al-Din's palace. Then joy and gladness replaced pain and sadness. He returned hurriedly to his apartment and ordered a horse to be saddled and brought to him, and as soon as it was brought, he mounted and rode out, thinking that he could not ride fast enough to get to 'Ala al-Din's palace.

'Ala al-Din, who foresaw what would happen, rose that morning at daybreak, and as soon as he took out from his closet one of his most magnificent suits and put it on, he went up to the hall with the twenty-four windows, from where he saw the king coming. He went down just in time to receive the king at the foot of the great staircase, and helped him to dismount. The king said to him, " 'Ala al-Din, I cannot speak to you, unless I see and embrace my daughter." 'Ala al-Din led the king to the apartment of Princess Badr al-Budur, who had been told by 'Ala al-Din that she was no longer in Africa, but in China, in the capital of her father the king, and next to his palace, and had just finished dressing herself. The king embraced her several times, with his face bathed in tears, and the princess, on her part, showed him all the signs of her extreme joy at seeing him again. It took the king some time before he could speak, for so great was his emotion to recover his dear daughter, after he had given her up for lost.

At last he spoke, saying, "I would like to believe, daughter, that your joy to see me again makes you seem so little changed, as if no misfortune has befallen you. Yet I am convinced that you must have suffered a great deal, for one cannot be suddenly transported with an entire palace, as you have been, without great fright and terrible anguish. I would like you to tell me all about it and to conceal nothing from me."

The princess, who was very pleased to satisfy the king's demand, said, "My lord, if I seem so little changed, I beg your majesty to consider that I received a new life only yesterday morning by the presence of 'Ala al-Din, whom I had looked on and mourned as lost to me, and whom the happiness of seeing and embracing has almost brought me back to my former state. But my greatest pain was to be torn off from your majesty and my dear husband, not only because of my feeling for my husband, but also because of my anxiety that he, though innocent, should feel the painful consequences of your anger, to which I knew he was exposed. I suffered only a little from the insolence of my abductor, who made unpleasant speeches, for I always knew, by my power over him, how to put a stop to them, and I was as little constrained as I am now.

"As to my abduction, 'Ala al-Din had no part in it. I alone, though very innocent, am to blame for it." To persuade the king of the truth of what she said, she told him in detail how the African magician disguised himself as a seller of lamps and offered to exchange new lamps for old ones; how she amused herself by exchanging 'Ala al-Din's lamp, unaware of its secret and its importance; how, after the exchange, the palace and she herself were lifted up and transported to Africa, with the African magician, who was recognized by two of her slave-girls and by the eunuch who made the exchange of the lamp, when, after the success of his audacious enterprise he had the audacity to pay her the first visit and to propose marriage to her; how he persecuted her till 'Ala al-Din's arrival, and how the two of them took measures together to take from him the lamp that he carried with him; and finally how they succeeded, particularly by her dissimulation in inviting him to have supper with her and giving him the cup with the powder, adding, "The rest I leave to 'Ala al-Din to relate to you."

'Ala al-Din had little more to tell the king, but said, "When the secret door was opened, I went up into the hall with twenty-four windows and saw the African magician lying dead on the sofa, as a result of the violent effect of the powder. As it was not proper for the princess to stay there any longer, I begged her to go down into her apartment, with her slave-girls and her eunuchs. As soon as I was alone, I took the lamp out of the magician's breast and made use of the same secret he used to remove the palace and abduct the princess. By that means, the palace was returned to its former place and I had the happiness to bring back the princess to your majesty, as you had commanded me. I do not wish to impose on your majesty, but if you wish to take the trouble to go up into the hall, you will see the magician punished as he deserves."

The king, to be completely assured of the truth, got up instantly and went up into the hall, and when he saw the African magician dead and his face already turned livid by the violent effect of the poison, he embraced 'Ala al-Din with great tenderness and said to him, "Son, do not be displeased at my action against you, for I was driven to it by paternal love, and I deserve to be forgiven my excessive reaction." 'Ala al-Din replied, "My lord, I do not have the slightest reason to complain of your majesty's conduct, since you did only what you were forced to do. This magician, this infamous creature, this basest of men, was the sole cause of my misfortune. When your majesty has leisure, I will give you an account of another wicked action he took against me, which was no less sinister than this and from which I was saved only by the grace of God in a very peculiar way." The king replied, "I will take an opportunity, and very soon, to hear it, but for now, let us think only of rejoicing and getting rid of this odious object."

'Ala al-Din ordered the magician's corpse to be removed and thrown on the dunghill for the birds and beasts to feed on. In the meantime, the king ordered the tambourines, the drums, the trumpets, and other musical instruments to announce the public rejoicing and proclaimed a feast of six days to celebrate the return of the princess and 'Ala al-Din with his palace. Thus 'Ala al-Din escaped for the second time the almost inevitable danger of losing his life. But this was not the last, for he was to face it a third time, as I shall now relate.

The African magician had a younger brother, who was no less skilled than he in magic. One may even say that he surpassed him in villainy and pernicious schemes. They did not always live together, or in the same city, but often when one was in the east and the other was in the west, they did not fail to inform each other, by geomancy, in which part of the world and in what condition they were and whether they needed each other's assistance.

Some time after the African magician had failed in his attempt against 'Ala al-Din's happiness, his younger brother, who had not heard from him for a year and who was not in Africa, but in a far-off country, wanted to know in what part of the world his mother was, how he did, and what he was doing. As he, like his brother, always carried his geomantic square instrument with him wherever he went, he took it out, prepared the sand, cast the points, drew the figures, and formed the horoscope. On examining each figure, he discovered that his brother was no longer living, that he had been poisoned and died suddenly, that this had happened in one of the capitals of China, situated in such and such a place, and finally that the person who had poisoned him was not a man of high birth and was married to a princess, a king's daughter.

When the magician found out in this way his brother's sad fate, he did not waste any time in useless regrets, which could not restore his brother to life again, but resolving immediately to avenge his death, he mounted a horse and set out to China, traversing plains, rivers, mountains, deserts, and a vast tract of land, without stopping. At last, after an incredibly arduous journey, he reached China and, a little time thereafter, the capital he discovered by geomancy. Certain that he was not mistaken and that he had not taken it for another country, he stopped there and took a lodging.

The next day, he went out and, walking in the city, not so much to see its fine sights, which were indifferent to him, but to take the proper measures to carry out his pernicious plan, he entered the most frequented places and listened to what was being said. In a place where people went to divert themselves with different kinds of games, and where some played while others chatted, exchanging news and discussing the affairs of the day or their own affairs, he heard talk of a woman called Fatima, who had withdrawn from the world, and of her virtue, piety, and the wonders and even miracles she performed. As he thought that this woman might be of use to him in his plan, he drew one of the men aside and asked him to give him more information, particularly who that holy woman was and what sort of miracles she performed. The man said to him, "What, have you never seen her or heard about her? She is the admiration of the whole town, for her fasting, her austerity, and her exemplary conduct. Except for Mondays and Fridays, she never goes out of her little cell, and on the days on which she comes to town, she does an infinite deal of good, and there is not a person with a headache who is not cured by a touch of her hands."

The magician wished to hear no more on the subject, but only asked the man in which part of town was the cell of this holy woman. After the man told him, and he conceived and decided on his detestable plan, of which I will speak soon, he, in order to know the way with more assurance, watched all her steps the first day she went out after he had made his inquiry, without losing sight of her till evening, when he saw her reenter her cell. When he had fully marked the place, he went into one of those places where, as was mentioned earlier, they served a certain kind of hot liquor and where anyone might spend the night if he wished, particularly in the great heat, when the people of that country preferred to sleep on a mat rather than in a bed. About midnight, after he paid the proprietor for the little he owed, he went out and headed directly to the cell of Fatima the holy woman, a name by which she was known throughout the entire city. He had no difficulty in opening the door, which was fastened only with a latch, and entered, closing it behind, without making any noise. When he was inside, he saw Fatima by moonlight lying in the open on a sofa covered only with a miserable mat, with her head leaning against the wall. He went up to her, and pulling out a dagger he carried on his side, awakened her. When poor Fatima opened her eyes, she was very much surprised to see a man about to stab her. With his dagger clapped at her breast, ready to be plunged into her heart, he said to her, "If you cry or make the slightest noise, I will kill you. Get up and do what I tell you."

Fatima, who had slept in her clothes, got up, trembling with fear. The magician said to her, "Don't be afraid. All I want is your clothes. Give them to me, and take mine." They made the exchange, and after the magician put on her clothes, he said to her, "Color my face like yours, to make me look like you, and in such a way that the color will not come off." Seeing that she was still trembling, to assure her and to encourage her to do what he wished, he said to her, with more confidence, "I tell you again not to be afraid, and I swear by God that I will spare your life." Fatima made him come into a corner of her cell, lighted her lamp and, dipping a brush into a certain liquid in a jar, brushed his face with it, assuring him that it would not come off and that his face was exactly the same color as hers. Then she put her own headdress on him, with a veil, showing him how to use it to hide his face as he went through the town. Finally, after she put around his neck a long rosary, which hung down in front to the middle of his body, and gave him the stick she used to walk with, she gave him a mirror and said, "Look, and you will see that you cannot resemble me any better." The magician found himself as he had wished, but he did not keep the oath he solemnly swore to the good Fatima. In order not to leave any blood, instead of stabbing her, he strangled her, and when he saw that she was dead, he dragged her body by the feet and threw it in a cistern by the cell.

Thus disguised as Fatima the holy woman, the magician, after he had committed that horrible murder, spent the rest of the night in the cell. The next morning, one or two hours after sunrise, even though it was not a day on which the holy woman used to go out, he went out of the cell, convinced that nobody would question him about it and that, even if someone did, he would know how to respond. As one of the first things he had done upon his arrival was to find out where 'Ala al-Din's palace was situated, where he had intended to play his role, he went directly there.

As soon as the people saw what they thought to be the holy woman, a great crowd gathered around the magician. Some asked for his blessing, others kissed his hand, and others, more reserved, kissed only the hem of his gown, while others, whether they had a headache or wished to be protected from one, bent their heads before him, in order that he might touch them with his hands. He did so, muttering some words in the guise of prayer, and imitated the holy woman so well that everybody took him for her.

After stopping frequently to satisfy such people, who received neither good nor ill from this touch of the hands, he came at last to the
square before 'Ala al-Din's palace, where, as the crowd grew greater,
the eagerness to get to him increased accordingly. The strongest and
most zealous shoved their way to make room for themselves, and this
caused such quarrels that their noise was heard at the hall with the
twenty-four windows, where Princess Badr al-Budur was sitting.

The princess asked what caused that noise, and as no one could tell
her, she asked someone to go and find out and report to her. Without leaving the hall, one of the slave-girls looked through one of the
shutters and came back to tell her that the noise came from a crowd of
people who gathered around the holy woman, to be cured of the
headache by the touch of her hands. The princess, who had for a long
time heard a great deal of the holy woman but who had never seen
her, was curious to see her and converse with her. As she gave some
indication of this, the chief of the eunuchs, who was present, told her
that it was easy to bring the woman to her, if she so wished, and that
all she had to do was to command it. The princess consented, and he
immediately sent four eunuchs to bring the pretended holy woman.

As soon as the crowd saw the eunuchs come out of the gate of 'Ala
al-Din's palace and head toward the disguised magician, they dispersed, and the magician, finding himself alone and perceiving that
the eunuchs were coming for him, advanced to meet them, overjoyed
to see his deceit working so well. One of the eunuchs said, "Holy
woman, the princess wishes to see you. Follow us." The fake Fatima
replied, "The princess does me a great honor," and followed the
eunuchs, who had already headed toward the palace.

When the magician, who, under a holy garment disguised a wicked
heart, was ushered into the hall with the twenty-four windows and saw
the princess, he began with a prayer that contained a long enumera-
tion of vows and good wishes for her health, her prosperity, and the
fulfillment of everything she might desire. Then he deployed all his
false and hypocritical rhetoric, to insinuate himself into the princess's
favor, under the cloak of great pity. This was very easy to do, since
the princess, who was good by nature, believed that everyone was as
good as she, especially those who devoted themselves to serving God
in solitary retreat.

When the false Fatima finished his long harangue, the princess said
to him, "Good mother, I thank you for your good prayers. I have
great confidence in them and hope that God will grant them. Come
and sit beside me." The false Fatima sat down with affected modesty.
Then the princess, resuming her conversation, said, "Good mother, I
ask you for one thing, which you must do for me, and I beg of you
not to refuse me, that is, to stay with me, to discuss your way of life, so

that I may learn by your good example how I should serve God." The false Fatima replied, "I beg you not to ask me for what I cannot consent to, without distracting myself and neglecting my devotions and prayers." The princess said, "This should not cause you any problem, since I have several apartments that are not occupied. You shall choose the one you like best and shall perform your devotions as freely as if you were in your own cell."

The magician, whose sole aim was to gain access to 'Ala al-Din's palace, where it would be much easier for him to carry out his pernicious plan, under the auspices and protection of the princess, than if he had been forced to go back and forth between the palace and the cell, did not press much to excuse himself from accepting the obliging offer of the princess. He said to her, "Princess, whatever resolution a poor wretched woman like me may have made to renounce the pomp and grandeur of this world, I dare not presume to resist the wish and command of such a pious and charitable princess." When the princess heard this reply, she got up and said, "Rise, and come with me, so that I may show you the unoccupied apartments I have and you may make your choice." He followed Princess Badr al-Budur, and from among all the apartments she showed him, he chose the one that seemed to him to be the least neat and worst furnished, saying hypocritically that it was too good for him and that he accepted it only to comply with her wishes.

The princess wanted to take the imposter back to the hall with the twenty-four windows, to have him dine with her, but since, in order to eat, he would have had to uncover his face, which he had always kept veiled, and fearing that the princess might discover that he was not Fatima the holy woman, as she had believed, he begged her earnestly to dispense with him, telling her that she ate nothing but bread and a few dried fruits, and asked her to let him eat his little meal in his apartment. She agreed, saying, "Good mother, you may be as free as if you were in your own cell. I will have dinner brought to you, but remember that I expect you as soon as you have finished your meal."

After the princess finished dining, and the false Fatima was informed of it by one of the eunuchs, the magician did not fail to rejoin her. The princess said to him, "Good mother, I am delighted to have with me a holy woman like you, who will bless this palace. Speaking of this palace, what do you think of it? But before I show it to you, room by room, tell me first what you think of this hall in particular." Upon this question, the false Fatima, who, the better to play his part, had till then affected to bow his head down, without even looking sideways, at last raised it and, surveying the hall from one end to the other, reflected for a while and said to the princess, "This hall is truly admirable and very beautiful; however, as far as a solitary being like me, who is not acquainted with what the world considers beautiful, can judge, it seems to me that this hall lacks only one thing." The princess asked, "What is it? Tell me; I entreat you. For my part I have always believed and heard it said that it lacked nothing, but if it does, it should be remedied." The false Fatima replied, with great guile, "Princess, forgive me the liberty I have taken, but my opinion, if it has any importance, is that if a Rukh's egg is suspended from the middle of the dome, this hall would have no parallel in the four quarters of the world, and your palace would be the wonder of the universe." The princess asked, "What kind of bird is the Rukh, and where can one get an egg?" The false Fatima replied, "Princess, it is a bird of prodigious size which inhabits the peak of Mount Caucasus. The architect who built your palace can get you one."

After Princess Badr al-Budur thanked the false Fatima for what she believed to be her good advice, she conversed with her on other subjects, but she did not forget the Rukh's egg, which she planned on mentioning to 'Ala al-Din, as soon as he returned from the hunt. He had been gone for six days, and the magician, who knew that, wanted to take advantage of his absence, but 'Ala al-Din returned that same evening, just after the false Fatima had taken leave of the princess to retire to her apartment. As soon as he arrived, he went up directly to the princess's apartment, which she had just entered, and saluted her and embraced her, but she seemed to receive him coldly. He said, "My princess, I do not find you as cheerful as you are usually. Has something happened during my absence to displease you and cause you any trouble or dissatisfaction? For God's sake, do not hide it from me, for there is nothing in my power I will not do to dispel." The princess replied, "It is a trifling matter that gives me so little concern, that I did not think it would show on my face and make you notice, but since, contrary to my intention, you have noticed some alteration, I will not hide from you the cause, which is of little consequence. I have always believed, as you have, that our palace was the most superb, the most magnificent, and the most perfect in the world. But I will tell you now what has occurred to me, after I had carefully examined the hall with the twenty-four windows. Do you not find, as I do, that it would leave nothing to be desired, if a Rukh's egg was suspended from the middle of the dome?" 'Ala al-Din replied, "Princess, it is enough for me that you think that a Rukh's egg is lacking, to find the same fault. You shall see by my diligence to remedy the matter that there is nothing I will not do for your sake."

'Ala al-Din left Princess Badr al-Budur that very moment and went up into the hall with the twenty-four windows, and after pulling out from his breast the lamp, which he always carried with him, wherever he was, ever since the danger he had run into when he neglected to take this precaution, he rubbed it, and when the demon immediately appeared before him, he said to him, "Demon, there lacks a Rukh's egg to be suspended from the middle of the dome. I command you, in the name of the lamp which I am holding, to repair this deficiency." 'Ala al-Din had no sooner spoken these words than the demon uttered such a loud and terrible cry, that the hall shook, and 'Ala al-Din staggered and almost fell down. The demon said to him with a voice that would have made the most steadfast man tremble, "What! Wretch, is it not enough that I and my companions have done everything for you, but you ask me, out of an unparalleled ingratitude, to bring you my master and to hang him from the middle of the dome? This attempt deserves that you, your wife, and your palace be immediately reduced to ashes. But you are lucky that you are not the author of this request and that it does not come directly from you. The real author is the brother of the African magician, your enemy whom you have exterminated as he deserved. He is in your palace, disguised in the clothes of Fatima the holy woman, whom he strangled, and it is he who had suggested to your wife to make the pernicious demand you have made of me. His intention is to kill you, therefore you should take care of yourself," and as soon as the demon finished, he disappeared.

'Ala al-Din did not miss a single word of what the demon had said. He had heard talk of Fatima the holy woman and knew how she supposedly cured the headache. He returned to the princess's apartment and, without speaking a word of what had happened to him, sat down, saying that he was suddenly seized with a headache and putting his hand on his forehead. The princess immediately ordered that the holy woman be fetched and in the meantime told 'Ala al-Din how that holy woman came to the palace and how she gave her an apartment.

The false Fatima arrived, and as soon as he entered, 'Ala al-Din said to him, "Come here, good mother. I am glad to see you here at such an opportune time. I am suffering from a violent headache, which has just seized me, and I ask for your help, being confident in your good prayers and hoping that you will not refuse me the favor you have done to so many of those who suffer from this affliction." So saying, he got up, but held his head down, while the false Fatima advanced toward him, with his hand holding the dagger he had in the belt under his gown. 'Ala al-Din, observing him, seized his hand before he drew it, pierced him to the heart with his own dagger, and threw him down on the floor, dead.

The princess cried in surprise, "My dear husband, what have you done? You have killed the holy woman!" 'Ala al-Din replied without emotion, "No, my princess, I have not killed Fatima, but a villain who would have killed me, if I had not prevented him." He explained, adding, "This wicked man you see here has strangled Fatima, whom with regret you accused me of killing, and has disguised himself in her clothes, in order to murder me. In order that you may know him better, he is the brother of the African magician." Then he told her how he came to know these particulars, and afterwards ordered the corpse to be removed.

Thus was 'Ala al-Din delivered from the persecution of the two brothers who were magicians. A few years later, the king died in very old age, and as he did not have any male children, Princess Badr al-Budur, as the legitimate heir, succeeded him and transferred the supreme power to 'Ala al-Din. They reigned together for many years and left behind an illustrious progeny.

THE STORY OF
QAMAR AL-ZAMAN AND HIS TWO
SONS,
AMJAD AND AS'AD

A long time ago, there lived a king called Shahraman, who commanded many troops and had many attendants and guards. Although he was old and decrepit, God had not yet blessed him with a son. He ruminated on this, mourned, and worried. One day, he complained to one of his viziers, saying, "I am afraid that if I die, the kingdom will be lost, for I have no son to rule it after me." The vizier replied, "Perhaps God will yet provide for this; o King, place your trust in God, make your ablutions, perform two prayers, then sleep with your wife, and you may get what you wish." The king slept with his wife, and she conceived at once, and when she completed her months, she gave birth to a male child who was like the full moon on a dark, cloudless night. Shahraman named him Qamar al-Zaman and was overjoyed with him, and they decorated the city for seven days and beat the drums and sent messengers out to announce the happy news. Then the nurses and attendants took him and reared him until he was fifteen years old.

He was extremely handsome and elegantly built, and his father loved him so much that he could not part from him day or night. One day he complained to one of his viziers of the excess of his love for his son and said, "O Vizier, I fear for my son Qamar al-Zaman the accidents of fate and misfortunes of life, and I would like him to marry in my lifetime." The vizier replied, "O King, marriage is laudable, and it is not a bad idea for your son to marry in your lifetime." King Shahraman said, "Fetch me my son Qamar al-Zaman." Qamar al-Zaman came and bowed his head shyly before his father, who said to him, "Qamar al-Zaman, I wish you to marry and to rejoice in you during my lifetime." Qamar al-Zaman replied, "Father, I have no wish to marry, nor am I inclined to women, for I have read tales of their guile and heard verses on their cunning. As the poet says,

> If you would know of women and their ways,
> I am a doctor who well knows the lot.
> If a man age or if he lose his wealth,
> His friendship they forsake and love him not.

"Or as another says,

> Resisting women is obeying God,
> For they will not thrive who lend them their ears.
> They will hinder them on perfection's way,
> Though they may study for a thousand years."

When he finished reciting these verses, he said, "Father, marrying is something I will never do, even if I have to die." When King Shahraman heard his son's reply, the light became darkness before his eyes, and he was extremely distressed at his son's disobedience to his wishes, yet out of love for him, he did not press him nor provoke him, but spoke gently to him, treated him courteously, showed him favors, and did all that which brings love to the heart.

He waited a whole year, while Qamar al-Zaman increased every day in loveliness and seductive charm and became perfect in eloquence and grace. All beholders were ravished by his beauty, and every wafting breeze told of his gentle charm. He was a temptation to lovers and a paradise to longing hearts, with a sweet speech, a face that puts the full moon to shame, a cheek like the anemone, and a slender, elegant figure like a willow branch or a bamboo wand. He was all beauty and seductive charm, like him of whom the poet said,

> When he appeared, they said, "May he be blessed,
> And glory be to God Who fashioned such a one."
> Above all lovely men he was the king,
> And they his subjects all, excepting none.
> The nectar of his mouth tasted so sweet,
> And like a row of pearls his white teeth shone.
> He garnered all the beauty of the world,
> Leaving all mortals helpless and undone.
> And on his cheek beauty for all to see,
> Proclaimed, "No one is beautiful but he."

When another year passed, King Shahraman called his son and said to him, "Son, will you listen to me?" Qamar al-Zaman knelt before his father, in modesty and reverence, and said, "Father, how could I refuse to listen to you, when God has commanded me to obey you and not contradict you?" King Shahraman said to him, "Son, I wish you to marry and to rejoice in your marriage during my lifetime and make you king before I die." When Qamar al-Zaman heard his father's words, he bowed his head for a while, then raised it and said, "Father, this is something I will never do, even if I have to die. I know that God has commanded me to obey you, but for God's sake do not ask me to marry, and do not think that I will ever marry, as long as I live. For I have read the books, both of the ancients and the moderns, and I know all the misfortunes and disasters and calamities that have happened to them through the guile and intrigue of women, which know no bounds. How well has the poet put it, when he said,

> He whom the whores have well entrapped,
> Cannot escape their snare,
> And though he builds a thousand forts
> And citadels to spare
> And fortifies them all with lead
> He'll build them all in vain,
> For women betray every man,
> Near and far; that is plain.
> With fingers dyed with henna red,
> With tresses sweet of show,
> And with eyes beautified with kohl,
> They make one drink of woe.

"And how well another poet put it, when he said,

> Women, though chaste supposed to be,
> Are carrion to vultures.
> Tonight they ope their heart to you,
> Tomorrow, their arms and legs to others.
> You live with them, as you would live
> In a travelers' inn,
> And in the morning you depart,
> And another comes in."

When King Shahraman heard these words from his son and understood their meaning, he made no reply, out of his great love for him, but treated him with even greater favor and kindness.

As soon as the audience was over, King Shahraman summoned his vizier and said to him in private, "Vizier, what shall I do about my son, Qamar al-Zaman? For when I consulted you about marrying him, before making him king, you advised me to do so and to propose marriage to him, but when I did, he disobeyed me. Tell me what is the best course now." The vizier replied, "O King, I advise you to wait another year, and if after that you wish to speak to him of marriage, do not speak to him privately, but do it on a day of state, when all the princes and viziers are present and all the troops are standing before you. Then send for your son Qamar al-Zaman, and when he comes, address him on the subject of marriage, in the presence of all the princes, the viziers, the chamberlains, the deputies, the officers of state, and the captains and all the troops, for he will be embarrassed before them and will not be able to oppose you in their presence." When King Shahraman heard these words he felt very happy, approved of the vizier's advice, and bestowed on him a magnificent robe of honor.

King Shahraman waited another year, and every day Qamar al-Zaman increased in comeliness and beauty, in perfection and splendor until he was by now twenty years old. God had clad him with the robe of beauty and crowned him with the crown of perfection. His eyes were more enchanting than Harut's, and his glances were more seductive than Maghut's. His cheeks were shining red, his eyelashes scorned the keen-edged sword, his fair forehead vied with the shining moon, and his black hair resembled the dark night. His waist was finer than gossamer, his hips fuller than two hills of sand, so that the heart was troubled with their softness, and the waist complained of their weight. In short, his beauties ravished everyone, and he was like him of whom the poet said,

> By his soft cheeks and by his smiling mouth,
> By his beguiling eyes so keen, so fair,
> By his sharp glances and his tender sides,
> By his white forehead and his jet-black hair,
> By eyebrows that have robbed my eyes of sleep
> And made me subject to their mighty will,
> By lovely sidelocks that curl, coil, and charm
> And all rejected lovers with their beauty kill,
> By the soft myrtle of his rosy cheeks,
> By his carnelian lips and mouth of pearls,
> Which sends the fragrance of its honey breath
> Sweeter than wine which in its sweetness purls.
> By his charming, tender, and slender waist,
> And hips that quiver while they move or rest,
> By his open hand and his truthful tongue
> And high birth and esteem which are his share.
> By these I swear that his life-giving breath
> Gives the musk being and perfumes the air,
> That the sun pales before him, and the moon
> Is nothing but a paring of his nail; I swear.

King Shahraman followed the advice of the vizier and waited another year until a festival day arrived, and all the princes and the viziers and the chamberlains and the officers of state and the captains together with all the troops were assembled. Then the king sent for his son Qamar al-Zaman, who, when he came in, kissed the ground before his father three times, and stood with his hands clasped behind his back. His father said, "Son, I have summoned you this time before this assembly, with all the troops present before me, in order to give you a command, in which you should not oppose me. I wish to marry you to a daughter of one of the kings and rejoice in you before my death." When Qamar al-Zaman heard these words, he bowed his head for a while, then raised it, looking at his father and, being moved by the ignorance and folly of youth, replied, "As for me, I will never marry, even if I have to die; as for you, you are a man of great age and little sense. You have already asked me twice before to marry, and each time I refused." Then he unclasped his hands from behind his back and rolled up his sleeves, before his father, in his rage. The king was mortified, for this had happened before the officers of state and the troops assembled for the festival, but he quickly recovered his royal dignity and cried out at his son, making Qamar al-Zaman tremble, and, calling to the guards, commanded them to seize him. When they seized him, the king commanded them to bind his hands behind his back, and they did so and led him before the king. He stood with his head bowed down in apprehension and fear, and his brow and face covered with sweat, in his great embarrassment, while his father cursed and reviled him, saying, "Damn you, you son of a whore and nursling of sin, how dare you give me this reply before my men and troops? But till now, no one has corrected you. Don't you know that what you have done, had it proceeded from one of my meanest subjects, would have been disgraceful even in him?" Then the king commanded the guards to unbind Qamar al-Zaman and to imprison him in one of the towers of the castle.

The attendants, therefore, went immediately to the hall in the tower and swept it and wiped its pavement. Then they set up a bed for Qamar al-Zaman, on which they put a mattress, a leather cover, and a pillow, and they placed a large lantern and a candle, for that hall was dark even in the daytime. Then the guards brought Qamar al-Zaman in and stationed a eunuch at the door. Qamar al-Zaman threw himself on the bed, sad and depressed, blaming himself and regretting his unfair conduct toward his father, when regret was useless. He said to himself, "May God curse marriage and curse all girls and women—deceitful creatures! I wish that I had listened to my father and married, for it would have been better for me than being in this prison."

Meanwhile, King Shahraman sat on his throne till sundown, when he retired with the vizier and said to him, "Vizier, you were the cause of all that has happened between me and my son, by the advice you gave me. What do you advise me now?" The vizier replied, "O King, leave your son in prison for a period of fifteen days; then summon him and command him to marry, and he will not disobey you again." The king accepted the vizier's advice and lay down to sleep, full of anxiety for his son, for he loved him very dearly and had no other son. He used to lie without sleep every night until he put his arm under Qamar

al-Zaman's neck, and then he slept. So he passed that night, troubled
and full of misgivings about his son, turning over from side to side, as
if he lay on burning coals, so that he could not sleep a wink all night.
His eyes ran over with tears, and he repeated the words of the poet,

> My night is long, while the slanderers sleep,
> And my restless heart aches with parting's pain.
> I ask, while my night is prolonged by care,
> "When will the light of day return again?"

And the words of another,

> When I beheld the Pleiades' distracted look
> And lethargy over the polestar shed,
> And the Great Bear's maids in mourning unveiled,
> I was convinced that their morning was dead.

As for Qamar al-Zaman, when night came, the eunuch set the
lantern before him and lighted the candle, placing it in a candlestick.
Then he brought him some food. Qamar al-Zaman ate a little, while
he sat reproaching himself for his ill manners toward his father King
Shahraman, saying to himself, "Don't you know that Adam's son is
the hostage of his tongue and that a man's tongue is what casts him
into perils?" He kept reproaching and blaming himself until his eyes
filled with tears, and his heart burned with pain, regretting dearly
what his tongue had uttered against his father and repeating the following verses,

> For one slip of his tongue the youth is put to death
> But when the man missteps, he does not die,
> For the slip of the mouth leads to his doom,
> While the slip of the foot heals by and by.

When Qamar al-Zaman finished eating, he asked for water to wash
his hands, and he washed them clean of the food that adhered to
them. Then he made his ablutions and performed his sundown and
nightfall prayers and then sat on the bed, reciting the Koran. He
recited the chapters of "The Cow," "The Family of Imran," "Yasin,"
"The Compassionate," "Blessed Be the King," and "The Two Incan-
tations," and concluded with a prayer to God to protect him from evil.

Then he lay in bed on a mattress stuffed with ostrich down and
covered on both sides with satin from Ma'din. When he wished to
sleep, he took off all his clothes, except for a shirt of delicate wax cloth
and a blue headcovering of the cloth of Mirv, appearing that night
like the full-orbed moon. He then covered himself with a sheet of silk
and fell asleep, with the lighted lantern at his feet and the burning candle at his head. He slept through the third part of the night, not know-

ing what lay in store for him and what God, who knows all secrets, had decreed to befall him.

As it happened, the tower was ancient and had been deserted for many years, save for a she-demon who inhabited a Roman well inside it. She was a descendant of Satan the accursed, and her name was Maimuna, daughter of al-Dimiryat, one of the well-known kings of the demons. While Qamar al-Zaman slept, the she-demon came out of the Roman well, intending to soar up in the air, in order to eavesdrop on heaven, but when she reached the top of the well, she unexpectedly saw a light shining in the tower and was extremely surprised, for she had lived there for a great many years without seeing anything like this before. Thinking that there must be a reason behind that light, she advanced toward it and saw that it came from the hall, at whose door she found the eunuch asleep. She entered the hall and saw a bed, on which slept someone in the form of a man, with a candle burning at his head and a lantern lighted at his feet. The she-demon Maimuna marveled at the sight and advanced toward the bed, little by little, and, folding her wings, stood over the bed, removed the sheet from Qamar al-Zaman's face, and looked at him. She stood for a long time, gazing in amazement at his beauty and grace, for his face was lustrous, beaming with a light that outshone the light of the candle, his cheeks were red, his eyebrows were like arched bows, his eyelids languorous, his dark eyes seductive, and his scent like wafting musk. He was like him of whom the poet said,

> I kissed him and forthwith his cheeks turned red,
> And his eyes, my torment, gleamed dark and bright.
> If the critics say an equal exists,
> Say to them, heart, "Bring him before my sight."

When Maimuna, daughter of al-Dimiryat, saw him, she glorified God and said, "Blessed be God the best of creators," for she was one of the true-believing demons. She continued to gaze at Qamar al-Zaman's face for a long time, proclaiming the unity of God and envying Qamar al-Zaman's face for his beauty and grace. She said to herself, "By God, I will never harm him nor let anybody hurt him, and from every evil I will protect him with my life, for this beautiful face deserves that people should only look at it and glorify God. But how could his people neglect him in this ruined place, for if any of our evil demons came to him now, they would destroy him!" Then she bent over him and kissed him between the eyes and, drawing the sheet, covered his face with it.

Then she spread her wings and, leaving the hall behind, flew up into the air and kept soaring upward until she came near the lowest heaven, when she heard the sound of wings beating the air. She flew toward the sound, and when she came near the source, she found that it came from a demon called Dahnash and she pounced on him like a hawk. When Dahnash saw her and knew that she was Maimuna, the daughter of the king of the demons, he feared her, began to tremble, and implored her, saying, "I conjure you by the Supreme Named and by the noble talisman engraved on the seal of Solomon to treat me kindly and hurt me not." When she heard Dahnash's words, she felt tenderness toward him and said to him, "You have conjured me by a mighty oath, but I will not let you go unless you tell me where you have come from at this hour." He said, "O my lady, I have come from the furthest end of China and from the Islands, and I will acquaint you with a wonderful thing I saw tonight. If you find my words to be true, let me go, and write me a note in your own hand that I am your freed slave, so that none of the demons, whether of the air or earth, flyers or divers, may challenge me." Maimuna replied, "Tell me, Dahnash, what is it that you saw tonight? Tell me, and don't lie to me, thinking that you can escape from me by lying. I swear by the inscription on the seal of Solomon, son of David (peace be on him) that if what you say is not true, I will pluck out your feathers with my own hands and tear your skin and break your bones." The demon Dahnash, son of Shemhurish the Flyer, said, "O my lady, if what I saw is not true, do with me what you wish." Then he proceeded, saying, "I have come tonight from the Interior Islands of China, which belong to King Ghaiur, Lord of the Seas and the Islands and the Seven Palaces, and I have seen a daughter of his, than whom God has created none more beautiful in our time. I don't know how to describe her to you, for my tongue is unable to do it properly, but I will touch on some of her charms, as well as I can. Her hair is like the nights of separation and forsaking, and her face is like the days of union and love. Well has the poet described her when he said,

> She spread three locks of her lovely black hair
> One night, and showed four nights in the one night,
> And with her face welcomed the full-orbed moon,
> And showed two moons at once shining with light.

"She has a nose as aquiline as the edge of the polished sword, cheeks like purple wine or red anemones and lips like coral or carnelian. The water of her mouth is sweeter than wine and its taste quenches the torments of fire. Her agile tongue is moved by great intelligence; her bosom is a temptation to all who see it (Glory be to him who created and finished it!); and her arms are round and smooth, like those of which the enamored poet said,

> Her wrists, were they not by her bracelets slowed,
> Would have out of their sleeves like liquid flowed.

"She has breasts which are like two perfume jars of ivory, lending their luster to the moon, a belly with folds like the folds of delicate, white Egyptian linen, leading to a waist, slender beyond imagining, over hips like hills of sand, which force her to sit, when she tries to rise, and awaken her when she sleeps. As the poet said,

> Her hips hang heavy from a slender waist,
> And thus afflict us both and tyrannize.
> They make me stand up, when I think of them,
> And force her to sit, when she tries to rise.

"They are borne by thighs like two pillars of pearl, braced only by the grace of the sheik that nestles between. And she has feet, the handiwork of the Judge and Protector, so slender that one wonders how they can carry what is above them. Other charms I omit, for neither words nor signs can do them justice.

"The father of this girl is a mighty king and an impetuous horseman, who crosses the sea to wage war by night or day, never shying away from battle or fearing death, for he is a despotic tyrant and an oppressive conqueror. He is lord of armies, provinces, islands, cities, and villages. His name is Ghaiur, King of the Seas and the Islands and the Seven Palaces. He loves his daughter, whom I have described to you, very dearly, and because of his great love for her, he collected the treasures of all the kings and built her seven palaces, each of a particular kind, the first of crystal, the second of marble, the third of Chinese iron, the fourth of onyx and other stones, the fifth of silver, the sixth of gold, and the seventh of jewels. He filled the seven palaces with rich furnishings and vessels of gold and silver and all utensils that kings may require and bade his daughter, whose name is Princess Budur, to live in each palace by turn for a certain period of the year.

"When her beauty became known, and her fame spread, all the kings sent to her father to ask for her hand in marriage, but when he consulted her on the matter, she expressed aversion and said, 'Father, I have no wish to marry at all, for I am a sovereign princess who rules over men, and I do not wish any man to rule over me.' But the more reluctance she showed to marry, the more grew the eagerness of the suitors to have her, and all the kings of the Inner Islands of China sent her father offerings and rare gifts, with letters asking for her hand in marriage, and he repeated the proposals to her many times, but she refused and said angrily, 'O father, if you mention marriage one more time, I will take a sword, put its hilt in the ground, and its point on my chest and lean on it until it goes through my back and kills me.' When her father heard her words, the light turned to darkness before his eyes, and his heart ached for her, for fear that she would kill herself, and he was tormented and perplexed, not knowing how to deal with her and with the kings who sought her hand. He said to her, 'If

you absolutely refuse to marry, refrain then from going in and out.'
He then confined her to her quarters, commanding ten old female
attendants to guard her, and forbade her from going to the seven
palaces, pretending that he was angry with her. Then he sent letters to
all the kings, informing them that she had been afflicted with insan-
ity."

The demon Dahnash added, "My lady, it is now a year since she
has been confined. I go to her every night, gaze at her, contemplating
her face for a long time, and kiss her between the eyes, while she lies
asleep. But because of my love for her, I never mount her or do her
any harm, for her beauty is so great that everyone who sees her is jealous even of himself. I conjure you, my lady, to go back with me and
see her beauty, elegance, and grace, and if after that you still wish to
punish me or imprison me, do what you wish, for the command is
yours." Then he bowed his head toward the earth and dropped his
wings. The she-demon Maimuna laughed at him and, spitting in his
face, said, "What is this girl you speak of, for she is nothing but a pot
of piss? What would you say if you saw my beloved? By God, I
thought that you devil had some wonderful tale or some extraordinary news. This night, I saw a young man whom, if you saw even in
your dream, you would be stunned, and your mouth would water."
Dahnash asked, "What is the story of this young man?"

She said, "Dahnash, the same thing that happened to your beloved
has happened to this young man, for his father commanded him again
and again to marry, but he refused until his father became angry with
him and imprisoned him in the tower, where I live. When I came out
tonight, I saw him." Dahnash said to her, "My lady, show me this
young man, so that I can see for myself whether or not he is more
beautiful than my beloved Princess Budur, for I don't believe that she
has an equal in this age." She replied, "You are lying, you devil, you
most unfortunate demon and vilest of devils, for I am certain that my
beloved has no equal in this world. Are you mad to compare your
beloved with mine?" He said, "For God's sake, my lady, go back with
me and look at my beloved, and after that I will return with you and
look at yours." Maimuna said, "Damn you, we have to do it your way,
you sly devil, but I will not go with you, and you will not come with
me, unless we place a bet. If your beloved, whom you praise highly,
proves more beautiful than mine, you will win, and if my beloved,
whom I praise highly, proves more beautiful than yours, I will win."
Dahnash replied, "O my lady, I accept your condition gladly. Come
then with me to the islands." But Maimuna said, "My beloved is closer
to us than yours; he is here beneath us. Descend with me to look at my
beloved, and afterwards we will go to yours." Dahnash replied, "I hear
and obey."

Then they flew down and alighted in the hall inside the tower, and

Maimuna, making Dahnash stand beside the bed, drew the sheet from Qamar al-Zaman's face, which shone and beamed and glowed. Maimuna looked at him and, turning to Dahnash immediately, said, "Look at him, devil, and don't be the most disgusting madman. I am a female, and I am fascinated by him." Dahnash looked at him and stood contemplating a while. Then he shook his head and said to her, "By God, my lady, you are excused, but the female is different from the male. By God, your beloved bears the closest resemblance to mine in beauty, elegance, and grace, as if they were made from the same mold." When Maimuna heard these words, the light turned to darkness before her eyes, and she struck him on the head with her wing, with a blow so hard that it almost killed him. She said, "I swear by the light of his face that you shall go at once, you devil, and carry your beloved and bring her quickly here, so that we may lay them together, look at them, as they lie asleep side by side, and see who is the more beautiful of the two. If you don't follow my command immediately, you devil, I will shower you with my lethal sparks and burn you and scatter you in pieces in the desert, making you an example to every passerby." Dahnash replied, "My lady, you will be obeyed, even though I know that my beloved is more beautiful and charming than yours."

Then he flew away immediately, and Maimuna flew with him to guard him. They were absent for an hour; then they returned, carrying the girl, who was wearing a delicate venetian shirt laced with gold and embellished with the most wonderful embroidery, with the following verses inscribed on the cuffs,

> Three causes prevent her from visiting,
> Fear of the spy and envier who harms,
> And her own beauties: her ambergris scent,
> Her shining brow, and the sound of her charms.
> Grant she doffs her jewels and hides her brow
> With her sleeves, how can she hide that scent, how?

They descended with the girl and laid her beside the young man, and when they uncovered their faces, they looked very much alike, as if they were twins or only brother and sister. They were a temptation to the pious, as the poet eloquently said,

> O heart, be not to one alone confined
> For you will be confused, meek, and doting.
> Rather love all the fair, and you will find,
> If one disdains, another is forthcoming.

Maimuna and Dahnash looked at them for a while; then Dahnash said, "My beloved is more beautiful," and Maimuna replied, "Mine is more beautiful. Damn you, Dahnash, are you blind? Don't you see his beauty, elegance, and grace? Listen to what I will say of my beloved, and if you are a true lover, match me in her praise." Then she kissed Qamar al-Zaman several times and recited the following poem,

> What respite from rebuke for loving you,
> And for a fine shape what consolation?
> Your dark eyes cast their charm and captivate
> And fill the burning heart with chaste elation,
> With Turkish looks, which even more than steel,
> When sharply honed, my soul they pierce and tear.
> I bear the heavy burden of your love,
> When I'm too weak even a shirt to wear.
> My nature has become my love for you,
> And that for others is only a show.
> My wasting body is thin like your waist.
> Were my heart like yours, I would not say no.
> Woe to me from a moon with every grace,
> Whose fabled beauties all men fascinate.
> Some rail, "Who is he for whose love you pine?"
> I say, "Look, and his charms enumerate."
> Learn, o hard heart of his, from his soft shape,
> So that he may perhaps relent and bend.
> Your eyes, my prince of beauty, conquer me,
> And your eyebrows my heart unfairly rend.
> He lies who says, "Joseph all beauty owns,"
> For Joseph is only of you a part.
> I terrify the demons, when we meet,
> But when I meet you, with fear beats my heart.
> Daunted, I try to keep away from you,
> But my love is greater than all my tries.
> Your hair is black, your brow is shining bright,
> Your shape is slender, brilliant are your eyes.

When Dahnash heard Maimuna's verses, he was moved with great admiration and delight and said, "You have sung with tender verses the praises of your beloved, with whom you are obsessed; now it is my turn to praise my beloved to the best of my ability." Then he approached his beloved Budur and kissed her between the eyes and, looking at her and at Maimuna, recited the following verses,

> I haunt the valley where we used to meet,
> But I am slain and far is her abode.
> I am drunk with love, and the teardrops dance,
> As the cameleer sings upon the road.

I search for love and happiness and know
That happiness is only in Budur.
Say, of which of her charms should I complain the most?
Let me enumerate; so listen and be sure:
Her sword-like glances, her lance-like figure,
Or mail-like woven sidelocks of her hair?
She said, as I queried every bedouin
And townsman, searching for her everywhere,
"My dwelling is your heart; look for me there."
I said, "Alas for me, for my heart is not here."

When he finished reciting his verses, Maimuna said, "Bravo, Dahnash! But which of the two is the more beautiful?" Dahnash replied, "My beloved Budur is more beautiful than yours."

They continued to contradict each other until Maimuna shouted at him and was about to strike him. But he humbled himself and spoke meekly, saying, "You are not one to evade the truth. Let us forget our claims, for each of us insists that his beloved is more beautiful. Rather, let us find someone who will judge fairly between us, and we will abide by his judgment." Maimuna replied, "I agree." Then she struck the floor with her foot, and there arose from it a mangy, one-eyed demon. His eye was slit upright on his face, his head bore seven horns and four locks of hair hanging to the ground, his hands were like pitchforks, his claws like those of a lion, his legs like those of an elephant, and his hoofs like those of an ass. When he came out and saw Maimuna, he kissed the ground before her and, clasping his hands behind his back, said to her, "What do you wish, o mistress, o daughter of the king?" She said to him, "Qashqash, I want you to judge between me and this devil Dahnash." Then she told him the story from beginning to end, and when she finished, the demon Qashqash looked at the young man and the girl and saw them lying asleep, with the arm of each under the neck of the other, and looking alike in beauty and grace. He marveled at their beauty and charm, and after gazing at them for a long time, he turned to Maimuna and Dahnash and recited the following verses,

Cleave to the one you love and ignore calumny,
For those who envy never favor love.
Two lovers in one bed, no fairer sight
Has Mercy's Lord created from above.
Bosom to bosom in each other's arm,
They lie in bliss, clad in their own delight,
For when two hearts unite in love's embrace,
The world and all its chatter seem so trite.
Therefore, if ever you your true love find,

O rare occasion, you should never part,
And you who chide the lovers for their love,
Why not, instead, reform the wicked heart?
O Lord of Mercy, join us two, I pray,
Before we die, if only for one day.

Then Qashqash turned to Maimuna and Dahnash and said to
them, "By God, none of them is more or less beautiful than the other.
They bear the strongest resemblance to each other in beauty and
charm and elegance and perfection, even though one is male and the
other female. But I have another idea. Let us awaken each of them in
turn, without the other's knowledge, and whichever shows more love
for the other will be judged to be the lesser in beauty and grace."
Maimuna said, "This is an excellent idea. I accept," and Dahnash
said, "I too accept."

Then Dahnash turned himself into a flea and bit Qamar al-Zaman
on a soft spot on the neck. Qamar al-Zaman reached with his hand
and scratched the place of the smarting bite and, moving sideways,
felt something lying beside him, with a breath sweeter than musk and
a body softer than butter. He was startled and amazed and, sitting up,
looked at the person lying beside him and found that it was a girl who
looked like a shining pearl or an opulent dome, with a slender body,
five feet tall, a high bosom, and rosy cheeks. She was like her of whom
the poet said,

She shines like a moon and bends like a willow bough
And breathes like ambergris and like a gazelle gazes.
Grief seems to love my heart, and when she parts,
It finds home in my heart's lonely mazes.

When Qamar al-Zaman looked at Princess Budur, the daughter of
King Ghaiur, and saw her beauty and grace as she slept beside him,
wearing a venetian shirt, without pants, a kerchief embroidered with
gold and jewels, and a necklace inlaid with gems, beyond the means of
any king, his reason was confounded, and the heat of instinct began to
stir within him, as God aroused in him the desire to make love to her.
Saying to himself, "What God wills shall be, and what he wills not,
shall not," he turned her over and untied the collar of her shirt, revealing her belly and her breasts. When he saw them, his love and desire
redoubled, and he shook her and moved her, in order to awaken her,
saying, "Sweetheart, wake up and look on me; I am Qamar al-
Zaman," but she did not wake up, nor even move her head, for Dahnash had made her sleep heavy. He thought for a while and said to
himself, "If my guess is right, this is the girl whom my father wishes me
to marry, the one I have been refusing for three years. In the morning,

God willing, I will go to my father and ask him to marry me to her, and I will not let half the day pass before I possess her and enjoy her beauty and charm." Then he bent over Budur to kiss her, and Maimuna shook with embarrassment, while Dahnash jumped with joy. But when he was about to kiss her on the mouth, he felt embarrassed before God and turned his head away, saying to himself, "I should be patient, for perhaps my father, when he was angry with me and imprisoned me here, brought me this bride in order to test me, and ordered her to lie beside me and not to appear awake when I attempted to awaken her, charging her to let him know whatever I did to her. Perhaps he is hiding somewhere, where he can see, without being seen, everything I do to this girl, and in the morning he will chide me saying, 'How could you say that you had no wish to marry, while you kissed and embraced this girl?' I had better refrain, lest I be found out by my father. I will not look at her or touch her at this time, but I will take from her something that will be a souvenir of her and a token between us." Then Qamar al-Zaman lifted her hand and took from her little finger a ring worth a great deal of money, for it was set with a very precious gem, inscribed all around with the following verses,

> Do not think that I have your vows forgot,
> No matter how long is your cruel disdain.
> Have pity master, and grant me my wish,
> That I may kiss your cheeks and lips again.
> Although you go beyond the bounds of love,
> By God, I will always with you remain.

He placed the ring on his own little finger, turned his back to her, and went to sleep.

When Maimuna saw this, she was glad and said to Dahnash and Qashqash, "Have you seen my beloved Qamar al-Zaman and how he has abstained from this girl? This is the result of his perfect character, for see how he looked at this girl and saw her beauty and charm, yet he did not embrace her nor caress her with his hand, but instead turned his back to her and went to sleep." They replied, "We have witnessed his perfect behavior."

Then Maimuna turned herself into a flea and, entering the clothes of Budur, Dahnash's beloved, crept up her leg, then her thigh, and continued until she reached a spot four inches below the navel and bit her there. Budur opened her eyes and, sitting up, saw a young man lying beside her and breathing heavily in his sleep, with cheeks like anemones, eyes that put to shame the maids of paradise, and a mouth like the seal of Solomon, whose sweet water is more healing than treacle. He was like him of whom the poet said,

From Zainab and Nawar I'm drawn away
By a rose on the myrtle of a cheek.
Being in love with a tunic-clad fawn,
I no longer the bangles-wearing seek,
In private and in public he's my friend,
Unlike a woman who is seen by none.
You who blame my leaving Hind or Zainab,
When my excuse is as clear as the sun,
Do you wish me to become a slave's thrall,
A cloistered slave, one kept behind a wall?

As soon as Princess Budur saw Qamar al-Zaman, she fell passionately in love with him and said to herself, "Shame on me! This young
man is a stranger whom I do not know; how come he is lying beside
me in the same bed?" Then she looked at him closely and, noting his
beauty and grace and coquettish charm, said to herself, "By God, this
young man is as beautiful as the moon, and my heart is torn with love
and longing for his beauty and grace. Shame on me! Had I known
that it was he who had asked for my hand from my father, I would
not have refused him but would have married him and enjoyed his
beauty." Then she gazed in his face and said, "O my lord, my sweetheart, and light of my eyes, awake from your sleep and enjoy my
beauty and charm," and she shook him with her hand. But the she-
demon Maimuna pressed on his head with her wings and cast a heavy
sleep on him, so that he might not awake. Princess Budur kept shaking
him and said, "By my life, listen to me! Wake up from your sleep and
look at the narcissus and the green, enjoy my belly and navel, and
dally with me and play with me from now till morning. O my lord, sit
up and lean against the pillow and do not sleep." But Qamar al-
Zaman did not reply or respond but continued to breathe heavily in
his sleep. She added, "Why are you so conceited with your beauty and
grace and coquettish charm? Just as you are beautiful, I too am beautiful. Why do you behave this way? Have they taught you to ward me
off, or has the wretched old man, my father, forbidden you to speak to
me tonight?" Qamar al-Zaman's eyes flickered open for a moment,
and her love intensified, as God inflamed her heart. One look at him
was followed by a thousand sighs, her heart fluttered, her being
yearned, her body trembled, and she said to him, "O my lord, my
beloved, sweetheart, speak to me, answer me, and tell me your name,
for you have made me lose my mind," while Qamar al-Zaman continued to sleep soundly, without uttering a word. She sighed and said,
"Why are you so conceited?" Then she shook him and, turning his
hand over, saw her ring on his little finger. She gasped and said to him
flirtatiously, "Ah, ah, by God, I love you, and you love me, but you

turn away from me out of coquetry; you came to me while I was asleep, and I do not know what you did to me, but I will not take off my ring from your finger." Then she opened his shirt and, bending over him, kissed him on the neck and searched for something to take from him, but found nothing. And when she saw that he was without pants, she placed her hand under his shirt and felt his legs, and as his skin was very smooth, her hand slipped and touched his penis, and her heart ached and pounded with desire, for the lust of women is greater than the lust of men, and she felt embarrassed. Then she took his ring from his finger and put it on her own and kissed his mouth and hands and every spot on his body. Then she took him in her lap, embraced him, with one arm under his neck and the other under his armpit, and fell asleep.

When Maimuna saw this, she was very happy and said to Dahnash, "Did you see, devil, how your beloved behaved out of passion for my beloved, and how my beloved comported himself with coquettishness and pride? There is no doubt that my beloved is more beautiful than yours; nevertheless, I pardon you." Then she wrote him a certificate of manumission and, turning to Qashqash, said, "Carry Dahnash's beloved, and help him take her back to her place, for most of the night has passed, and I am late." Dahnash and Qashqash went to Princess Budur and, lifting her, flew with her back to her palace and put her back in her bed, while Maimuna stayed alone with Qamar al-Zaman, gazing on him as he slept, until the night was almost over when she went her way.

When it was dawn, Qamar al-Zaman awoke from his sleep and looked right and left but did not find the girl with him and said to himself, "What does this mean? It seems that my father wanted to make me desire marriage with the girl that was with me and took her away by stealth to intensify my desire." Then he called out to the eunuch who was sleeping at the door and said to him, "Get up, damn you!" The eunuch got up, still dazed from sleep, and brought him the basin and ewer. Qamar al-Zaman entered the toilet and relieved himself; then he came out, made his ablutions, and after he performed his morning prayer, sat repeating the praises of God. Then he looked up, and when he saw the eunuch standing in attendance before him, he said to him, "Hey, Sawwab, who came here and took the girl from my side, while I was asleep?" The eunuch said, "What girl, my lord?" Qamar al-Zaman said, "The girl who was sleeping beside me last night." The eunuch was troubled and said, "There has been neither girl nor anyone else with you last night. How could she have come in, when I was sleeping at the door, and the door was locked? By God, my lord, neither man nor woman came in to you." Qamar al-Zaman said to him, "You are lying, you wretched slave. Do you too presume to trick me and refuse to tell me what happened to the girl who slept beside me and who took her away from me?" The eunuch was upset and said, "By God, my lord, I have seen neither girl nor boy." Qamar al-Zaman was angered by the eunuch's words and said to him, "Devil, they have taught you deceit. Come here!" He came up to Qamar al-Zaman, who seized him by the collar and threw him to the ground, causing him to fart. Then Qamar al-Zaman knelt on him, kicked him, and choked him until he fainted. Then he tied him to the well-rope and, letting him down the well, plunged him into the water, then pulled him up and plunged him in again. Qamar al-Zaman kept plunging him in and pulling him up, while he screamed and called for help, for it was severe winter weather, and Qamar al-Zaman kept saying to him, "Devil, by God, I will not pull you out of this well until you tell me what happened to the girl and who took her away while I was asleep."

Finally, the eunuch said, "My lord, take me out of the well, and I will tell you the truth." So Qamar al-Zaman pulled him out of the well, almost unconscious from the beating and water and cold and torture and fear of drowning. His clothes were all wet, he shook like a reed in a storm, and his teeth chattered. As soon as he found himself on the land, he said to Qamar al-Zaman, "My lord, let me go and take off my clothes, wring them out, spread them in the sun, and put on others. Then I will come back quickly and tell you the story of the girl." Qamar al-Zaman said, "Wretched slave, by God, had you not tasted death, you would never have told the truth. Go and take care of yourself, and after that come back quickly and tell me the story of the girl."

The eunuch went out, hardly believing in his safe escape, and he kept running until he came in to King Shahraman, the father of Qamar al-Zaman, whom he found, with the vizier beside him, discussing Qamar al-Zaman, and heard him saying, "I did not sleep last night because of my worry about my son Qamar al-Zaman, for I fear that something may happen to him in that old tower. What good was there in imprisoning him?" The vizier replied, "Do not worry about him. By God, nothing bad will happen to him. Leave him in prison for a month until he relents." As they spoke, in came the eunuch in that plight and said to the king, "My lord the King, your son has gone mad and has done this to me, saying that a girl had spent the night with him and stolen away and demanding that I tell him what happened to her, but I know nothing of the matter." When King Shahraman heard what the eunuch said about his son, he cried out, "O my son!" He was extremely angry at the vizier, who had been a cause of this, and said to him, "Go and find out what is the matter with my son."

The vizier stumbled out, in his fear of the king, and hastened with the eunuch to the tower. It was by now plain daylight, and when he came in to Qamar al-Zaman, he found him sitting on the bed, reading the Koran. He saluted him and, sitting beside him, said, "My lord, this wretched slave has told us something that has troubled us and angered the king." Qamar al-Zaman asked, "Vizier, what has he told you about me, to trouble my father, when in truth he has troubled none but me?" The vizier said, "He came to us in a sorry plight and said something about you, which is far from the truth and a lie that is not proper to repeat. May God preserve your youth, your sound mind, and your eloquent tongue, and may He forbid anything base to proceed from you." Qamar al-Zaman asked, "Vizier, what has this wretched slave told you?" The vizier replied, "He told us that you had gone mad and told him that there was a girl with you last night. Did you tell him that?" When Qamar al-Zaman heard this, he was very angry and said to the vizier, "It is obvious that you instructed the servant to do what he did and asked him not to tell me what happened to the girl who spent last night with me. Vizier, you are more sensible than this servant. Tell me forthwith where that beautiful girl who slept in my lap last night has gone, for you are the ones who sent her to me and commanded her to sleep in my lap. I slept with her till the morning, but when I awoke, I did not find her. Where is she now?" The vizier said, "My lord, Qamar al-Zaman, may God preserve you! By God, we sent no one to you last night. You slept alone, with the door locked on you and the servant sleeping behind it, and neither girl nor anyone else came in to you. Return to your senses, my lord, and do not trouble your mind." Qamar al-Zaman said angrily, "Vizier, that girl is my beloved, the beautiful one with the black eyes and the red cheeks, whom I embraced last night." The vizier was astonished and said to him, "Did you see that girl last night with your eyes, while you were awake or asleep?" Qamar al-Zaman replied, "Wretched old man, do you suppose that I saw her with my ears? No, I saw her with my eyes while I was awake, turned her over with my hand, and spent half of the entire night looking at her beauty and grace and coquettish charm, but since you people instructed her not to speak, she pretended to be asleep, and I slept beside her till the morning, when I awoke and did not find her." The vizier said, "My lord, Qamar al-Zaman, perhaps you saw this in your sleep, and it is nothing but confused dreams or fancies caused by eating a mixture of different kinds of food, or an insinuation by the wicked devils." Qamar al-Zaman said, "Wretched old man, do you too mock me and tell me that this is perhaps the result of confused dreams, when this servant admitted her presence and said that he would soon come back to me and tell me her story?" Then Qamar al-Zaman got up instantly and, seizing the vizier's beard, which was long, twisted it around his hand, yanked him off the bed, and threw him on the floor. The vizier felt as if he was dying from the pain caused by the pulling of his beard, while Qamar al-Zaman kept kicking him and pummeling him on the back of the head until he almost killed him. The vizier said to himself, "If the slave saved himself from this mad young man by a lie, it is all the more reason that I too should save myself by a lie. Let me do it; otherwise, he will kill me, for he is mad, and there is no doubt about it."

Then he turned to Qamar al-Zaman and said, "Forgive me, my lord, for it was your father who had instructed me to conceal you from the affair of the girl. But now I am weak and weary of the beating, for I am an old man, and I am too weak to bear it. Give me a respite, and I will tell you the story of the girl." Qamar al-Zaman stopped beating him and said, "Why did you not tell me about the girl, without the beating and the humiliation? Get up, wretched old man, and tell me about her." The vizier said, "Are you asking about that girl with the beautiful face and elegant body?" Qamar al-Zaman replied, "Yes, vizier, tell me who brought her to me and let her sleep beside me, and tell me where she is now, so that I may go to her myself. If my father King Shahraman did this to me to test me with that beautiful girl, with a view of marrying her, I consent to the marriage. He did this to me, inflaming my love for the girl, then taking her away from me, only because I refused to get married. Now I consent, and again consent. Tell that to my father, vizier, and advise him to marry me to that girl, for I desire none but her, and I love none but her. Hurry to my father, advise him to hasten my marriage, and come back as soon as you can."

The vizier could hardly believe his escape from Qamar al-Zaman until he went in to King Shahraman, who said to him, "Vizier, why are you upset, and who has abused you and terrified you?" The vizier replied, "I bring you news." The king asked, "What is it?" The vizier said, "Your son Qamar al-Zaman has gone mad." When the king heard this, the light turned to darkness before his eyes and said, "Vizier, describe to me my son's madness." The vizier said, "I hear and obey," and he told him what his son had done. The king said to him, "Vizier, I will reward you for the news of the madness of my son with the cutting of your head and forfeiture of your property, you the most wretched of viziers and most wicked of princes, for I know that you have been the cause of my son's madness by the wretched advice you gave me from beginning to end. By God, if my son has been hurt or afflicted with madness, I will nail you to the dome and let you taste death."

Then he got up and, taking the vizier with him, went to the tower where Qamar al-Zaman was imprisoned. When they entered, Qamar al-Zaman jumped off the bed, kissed his father's hands and, drawing back, stood before him a while, with his hands behind his back and his head bowed down. Then he raised his head and, with tears streaming down his cheeks, recited the following verses,

> If I have sinned against you in the past,
> Or done anything loathsome against you,
> I do repent, and your ample mercy
> Includes him who does for your pardon sue.

When the king heard this, he embraced his son, Qamar al-Zaman, and, seating him beside him on the bed, looked at the vizier angrily and said, "O dog of a vizier, why do you tell me such things about my son and frighten me about him?" Then he turned to his son and asked, "Son, what is today called?" Qamar al-Zaman replied, "Father, today is Saturday, and tomorrow is Sunday, and the day after that is Monday, and after that is Tuesday, then Wednesday, then Thursday, then Friday." The king said to him, "O my son Qamar al-Zaman, God be praised for your safety. What is the name of this month in Arabic?" Qamar al-Zaman replied, "It is Thu al-Qa'da, followed by Thu al-Hejja, then Muharram, then Safar, then Rabi' al-Awwal, then Rabi' al-Thani, then Jamadi al-Awwal, then Jamadi al-Thani, then Rajab, then Sha'ban, then Ramadan, then Shawwal." The king was very glad and, spitting in the vizier's face, said to him, "Wretched old man, why do you claim that my son Qamar al-Zaman has gone mad, when in fact none has gone mad but you?" The vizier shook his head and was about to reply, but it occurred to him to wait a little and see what would happen next.

The king said to his son, "Son, what is this you have been saying to the servant and the vizier that you spent last night with a beautiful girl? What about the girl?" Qamar al-Zaman laughed at his father's words and replied, "Father, I have no strength to endure any further mockery; therefore, do not add a single word of it, for I am exasperated by what you have been doing to me, and I now consent to marry, father, but on condition that you marry me to the girl who spent last night with me, for I am certain that you are the one who sent her to me and made me long for her, and afterward you sent for her before dawn and took her away from me." The king said, "O my son, may God preserve you and preserve your mind from madness! What girl do you claim I sent you last night and afterward sent for and took her from you before dawn? By God, son, I know nothing about this. For God's sake, tell me whether this is a confused dream or a hallucination caused by food, for you slept last night, troubled and worried about the thought of marriage (may God curse marriage and its existence and him who advised it). There is no doubt that you were disturbed by the thought of marriage and saw in your dream a beautiful girl embracing you, and you believed that you really saw her, but all of this, my son, is nothing but the delusion of dreams." Qamar al-Zaman said, "Stop this talk, and swear to me by God the Creator, the Omniscient, the Destroyer of the mighty and Annihilator of kings that you had no knowledge of the girl or her whereabouts." The king said, "By the Almighty God, the God of Moses and Abraham, I had no knowledge of that, and it was probably a confused dream that you saw in your sleep." Qamar al-Zaman said to his father, "I will give you an example to prove to you that I saw this when I was awake, by asking you whether it has ever happened that anyone dreamt that he was fighting in a fierce battle and afterward awoke from his sleep and found himself holding a sword stained with blood?" His father replied, "By God, my son, such a thing has never happened." Qamar al-Zaman said, "Then I will tell you what happened to me last night. It seems that I awoke from my sleep in the middle of the night and saw lying beside me a girl, whose figure and looks were like mine, and I embraced her and held her with my hand and took off her ring and put it on my finger, and she took off my ring and put it on her own finger. I abstained from her in deference to you, thinking that you had sent her and hid yourself somewhere to see what I would do. For this reason, I was too embarrassed to kiss her on the mouth in your presence, supposing that you were testing me and making me desire marriage. When I awoke from my sleep at dawn, I found no trace of the girl and no explanation about her, and this was the cause of what happened between me and the servant and the vizier. How could all this be a lie, when the matter of the ring is true? Were it not for the ring, I would have thought that it was a dream. This is her ring on my little finger at this moment. Look at the ring, O King, and see how valuable it is." Then he handed the ring to his father.

The king took it and turned it over, then, turning to his son, said, "There is a great and deep mystery behind this ring. What happened to you with that girl last night is a puzzle, and I do not know how this intruder came in upon us, nor who caused all this, except the vizier. For God's sake, son, be patient, and God may relieve you of this distress and bring you great comfort. As the poet said,

> Perhaps my fate will his own bridle turn
> And bring good fortune, o my fickle fate,
> Replacing past ills with present good deeds,
> My needs to answer and my hopes elate.

Son, now I am certain that you are not insane, but no one can solve your problem save God." Qamar al-Zaman said to his father, "For God's sake, father, search after that girl and bring her quickly back to

me; otherwise, I will die of grief." Then, looking at his father, he
recited passionately the following verses,

> If your vow of reunion be not true,
> At least in sleep your longed-for visit make.
> They said, "How can a ghost in a dream visit one
> Who is deprived of sleep and lies awake?"

When he finished these verses, he looked at his father with submis-
sion and dejection, and, with tears streaming from his eyes, recited the
following verses,

> Beware her beautiful bewitching eyes,
> For the smitten can't his heart extricate;
> Nor be deluded by her tender words,
> For passion does the mind intoxicate,
> So soft she is that if the rose touches her cheek,
> It makes her cry, and her eyes with tears flow,
> And if the breezes pass by while she sleeps,
> They pick her scent and with her fragrance blow.
> Her necklaces echo the music of her feet,
> While on her wrists the bracelets speechless sit,
> And when her anklet her earrings wishes to kiss,
> The eyes of love does not her merits miss.
> One critic sees my love and censures me,
> But seeing without insight is a vain enterprise.
> God curse you, critic, for you are not fair;
> To such a beauty pay homage all eyes.

When Qamar al-Zaman finished reciting these verses, the vizier at
last said to the king, "O King of the age, how long will you remain
sequestered with your son from your troops? Your absence from the
officers of the state may cause disorder in the kingdom. When the wise
man is afflicted with a malady, he must seek to cure the cause. It is
my advice that you remove your son to the pavilion in the palace overlooking the sea and retire there with him, appointing two days of the
week, namely Thursday and Monday, for the procession and the
assembly, when you will be attended by the princes and viziers and
chamberlains and deputies and the officers and chief men of the state
and captains, together with the rest of your troops and subjects. On
those two days, they will present you with their cases, and you will
answer their needs and judge between them and take and give and
issue your commands. The rest of the week, you will spend with your
son, Qamar al-Zaman, and you will continue this way until God grant
you and grant him relief. O King, do not think yourself safe from the

accidents of fate or the calamities of life, for the wise man is always on guard. How well the poet put it, when he said,

> You thought well of the days when they were good,
> Oblivious to the ills fate brings to one.
> You were deluded by the peaceful nights,
> Yet in the peace of night does sorrow stun.
> O people, who have been favored by fate,
> The turns of fate you should anticipate.

When the king heard the vizier's advice, it impressed him as sound and beneficial to him and, fearing disorder in the state, he at once gave orders that his son be removed to the pavilion in the palace over-looking the sea. The access to it was over a causeway, sixty feet wide, in the middle of the sea. Around it were windows overlooking the sea, its floor was paved with colored marbles, and its ceiling was painted with the richest colors and decorated with gold and lapis lazuli. They spread silk carpets for Qamar al-Zaman, covered its walls with bro-cade, and hung curtains bespangled with jewels. Qamar al-Zaman sat there, languishing with passion, depressed, sleepless, emaciated in body, and pallid in color. His father the king sat at his head, grieving for him, and every Monday and Thursday he gave the viziers and princes and chamberlains and deputies and officers of state and any of his troops and subjects who wished to see him permission to come in to him in the pavilion. And they came in to perform their tasks, stay-ing with him till the end of the day, when they departed, and he returned to his son, with whom he stayed day and night. Thus he lived for some time.

As for Princess Budur, the daughter of King Ghaiur, Lord of the Seven Islands and Seven Palaces, by the time the two demons trans-ported her back and laid her in her bed, only three hours were left of the night. When it was dawn, she awoke from her sleep and, sitting up, looked to the right and left but did not find her beloved, who had been lying in her lap. At that moment, she lost her mind, shook with agita-tion, and uttered a loud cry, which awakened all her servants, nurses, and attendants, who came in to her, and their chief advanced toward her and asked, "O my lady, what has happened to you?" Princess Budur replied, "Wretched old woman, where is my beloved, the beau-tiful young man who slept in my lap last night? Tell me, where has he gone?" When the attendant heard these words, the light turned to darkness before her eyes, and she was terrified of the princess's power and said, "O my lady Budur, what unseemly talk is this?" Princess Budur said, "Damn you, old woman, where is my beloved, the beauti-ful young man, with the shining face and the black eyes and the joined eyebrows, who spent the night with me from nightfall till near day-break?" The attendant replied, "By God, I saw neither young man nor anyone else. For God's sake, my lady, stop this unseemly jesting, lest we be all undone, for your father may hear it, and who will deliver us from his hand?" Princess Budur said, "A young man spent last night with me, and he had the most beautiful face." The attendant said, "May God preserve your mind! There was no one with you last night." Princess Budur looked at her hand and, seeing instead of her own ring, Qamar al-Zaman's ring on her finger, said to the attendant, "Damn you, deceitful woman! Do you lie to me, tell me that no one spent last night with me, and swear by God falsely?" The nurse said, "By God, I never lied to you nor swore falsely." That reply enraged Princess Budur, who drew a sword, struck the nurse with it, and killed her. The eunuch and the maids and attendants cried out at her and, running to her father, acquainted him with the situation.

The king came immediately to his daughter and asked her, "O daughter, what is the matter with you?" She said, "O father, where is the young man who was sleeping by my side last night?" She looked to the right and left in a frenzy, and tore her dress all the way to the hem. When her father saw this, he ordered the servants and attendants to seize her, and they seized her and bound her and, putting an iron collar around her neck, chained her to a window of the palace.

When her father saw what happened to Princess Budur, he was depressed, for he loved her and could not bear to see her in that condition. He therefore summoned the astrologers, the doctors, and the magicians and said to them, "Whoever cures my daughter of her condition, I will marry him to her and give him half of my kingdom, and whoever fails to cure her, I will strike off his head and hang it over her palace gate." So the king struck off the head of whoever went in to her and did not cure her, and hung each head over the palace gate until he beheaded forty doctors because of her. So everyone stayed away from her, and all the doctors failed to cure her, and her malady puzzled the men of science, as well as the men of magic. In the meantime, whenever Princess Budur felt the intensity of love and the fire of passion, she wept and recited verses like the following,

> My love for you, my moon, is but my foe;
> The thought of you at night, a friend, does with me
>   dwell.
> I spend the dark night with fire in my breast,
> That burns and blazes like the fire of Hell.
> I am afflicted by longing and love,
> And malady and pain that none can quell.

And the following,

> "May peace be on you wherever you are,"
> These words I said to those for whom I long.
> I say, "Peace on you," not bidding adieu
> But welcome that my love does e'er prolong.
> I love you and I love your dear abode,
> But the road to my wish is hard and long.

When she finished reciting those verses, she wept until her eyes smarted and her cheeks wilted. In this plight she lived for three years.

It happened that she had a foster-brother, whose name was Marza-wan and who had been absent from her all this time, traveling in far countries. He loved her with a great love surpassing that of brothers, and when he came back, he went to see his mother and inquired about his foster-sister, Princess Budur. His mother said to him, "O my son, your sister has been afflicted with madness and has spent the past three years with an iron collar around her neck, and all the doctors have failed to cure her." When Marzawan heard this, he said, "I must go to see her; perhaps I will discover what ails her and be able to cure her." His mother replied, "Yes, you must go to see her, but wait till tomorrow, so that I may find a way." Then she went to the palace of Princess Budur and, meeting the eunuch, gave him a present and said, "I have a married daughter who was brought up with Princess Budur, and when the princess became ill, she became concerned about her. I would like to ask you a favor, to let her see the princess for a while then return as she came, and no one will ever know about it." The eunuch said, "This is not possible except at night. After the king comes to see his daughter and leaves, come in with your daughter." The old woman kissed the eunuch's hand and went home.

The following day, as soon as it was dark, she dressed her son Marzawan in women's clothes and, taking him by the hand, entered the palace and went to the eunuch, after the king had departed from his daughter. When the eunuch saw her, he got up and said, "Go in, but don't stay too long." When they went in, Marzawan saw Princess Budur in that condition, and he saluted her, after his mother had taken off his women's clothes. Then he took out the books he had brought with him and lighted a candle, and when Princess Budur saw him, she recognized him and said to him, "O my brother, you have been traveling, and we have not had any news of you." He said, "This is true, but God has brought me back safely. I had intended to travel again, and nothing would have prevented me, save the news of your illness, which made my heart ache for you and brought me here, in order that I might discover what ails you and be able to cure you."

She said to him, "Brother, do you think it is madness that ails me?"
Then she pointed to him and recited the following verses,

> They said, "The one you love has made you mad with love."
> I said, "Such madness is only the lover's bliss.
> Yes, I am mad, bring me the cause of it,
> And if he cure me, blame me not for this."

When he heard this, Marzawan realized that she was in love and
said to her, "Tell me your story, and perhaps God will show me a way
to deliver you from your plight." She said, "O brother, listen to my
story. I awoke from my sleep one night, in the last third of the night
and, sitting up, saw beside me a most beautiful young man, whose
beauty no tongue can describe, as if he were a willow bough or bamboo wand. I thought that my father had ordered him to lie beside me,
in order to tempt me by him, for he had consulted me about marriage
when the kings asked him for my hand, but I refused. That thought
prevented me from awakening him, fearing that if I embraced him,
he would tell my father. When I awoke in the morning, I saw his ring
on my finger, in place of my own. O my brother, I was taken with him
at first sight, and because of my great love and longing for him, I have
not been able to sleep and have done nothing but cry and shed heavy
tears and recite verses night and day." Then she wept profusely and
recited the following verses,

> Love has banished my pleasures and delights,
> For that fawn in my heart enjoys to play.
> To him the blood of lovers is a trifling thing;
> For him my poor soul aches and pines away.
> I'm jealous for him of my sight and thought,
> Thus I fear myself, as part watches part.
> His eyelashes their deadly arrows shoot
> And find their way and dart into the heart.
> Will I see him again before I die?
> Only if there is luck in this sad life.
> I try to hide my feelings, but my tears
> Reveal to the spy my anguish and strife.
> He is so close, yet he is hard to get,
> So far, yet I can him never forget.

Then she said, "O my brother, how will you help me in my affliction?" Marzawan bowed his head a while wondering and not knowing
what to do; then he raised it and said to her, "I believe everything you
have told me, though the story of that young man puzzles me, but I
will travel through every country and search for your cure. Perhaps

God will accomplish it through me. Be patient and stop worrying."
He bade her farewell, praying that she might be granted endurance,
and left her, while she repeated the following verses,

> Your image in my thought does like a pilgrim fare,
> Though from my dwelling how distant you are!
> My wishes bring you closer to my heart,
> But from the watcher's eye lightning is far.
> O leave me not, for you are my eyes' light,
> And in your absence all is darkness in my sight.

Marzawan returned to his mother's house, where he spent the
night, and in the morning, he prepared himself for his journey and
departed. He traveled for a whole month from island to island and
from city to city, asking for information that might help him find a
cure for his sister's ailment, and everywhere he went, he heard it said
that Princess Budur, daughter of King Ghaiur, had been afflicted by
madness. He continued his search until he came to a city called al-
Tayrab, where he heard that Qamar al-Zaman, son of King Shahraman, was sick and that he was suffering from melancholy and
madness. When Marzawan heard this, he asked some of the people
of the city the name of the prince's capital and was told that it was in
the Khalidan Islands and that it was a whole month's journey by sea
and six by land.

Marzawan embarked in a ship ready to set out to the Khalidan
Islands, and they sailed with a fair wind for a whole month until they
saw the city, but when they approached the harbor and were about to
touch the shore, a strong wind blew, carrying away the yard, casting
the sails in the sea, and overturning the ship with everyone on board.
Each looked to himself, and Marzawan was drawn by the force of the
current and conveyed beneath the king's palace in which was Qamar
al-Zaman. It happened, as had been foreordained, that the princes
and viziers were there in attendance on King Shahraman, who was
sitting with the head of his son Qamar al-Zaman in his lap, while a
servant whisked the flies away from him. Qamar al-Zaman had spent
two days without eating or drinking or speaking. The vizier was standing at his feet, near the window overlooking the sea. When he raised
his eyes, he saw Marzawan at his last gasp, on the verge of drowning
in the current. Feeling sorry for him, the vizier approached the king
and, bending his head toward him, said, "I beg your leave to go down
to the palace courtyard and open the gate, in order to save a man who
is about to drown in the sea and deliver him from his plight. Perhaps
God, on this account, will deliver your son." The king replied, "All
that has happened to my son has been caused by you, and it may be
that if you save this drowning man, he will discover the situation, see

my son in this condition, and gloat over our plight. I swear by God that if this man comes up, sees my son, and proceeds to divulge any of our secrets to anyone, I will strike off your head before his, for you, vizier, are the cause of all that has happened to us, from beginning to end. Do as you wish."

The vizier went out, opened the courtyard gate, and walked twenty steps on the causeway until he reached the water and saw Marzawan at the point of death. He stretched his hand toward him and, seizing him by the hair of his head, pulled him unconscious out of the water, with his body full of water and his eyes bulging. The vizier waited until Marzawan came to himself. Then the vizier took off Marzawan's clothes and dressed him with others, putting on his head one of his page's turbans. Then he said to him, "I have been the means of saving you from drowning. Do not be the means of my death and yours." Marzawan asked, "How so?" The vizier replied, "Because you are now about to go up and pass among viziers and princes, all sitting silently, because of Qamar al-Zaman, the king's son." When Marzawan heard the name of Qamar al-Zaman, he realized that this was he about whom he had been hearing, but he said, "Who is Qamar al-Zaman?" The vizier replied, "He is the son of King Shahraman. He is lying restlessly, sick in bed, not knowing night from day. His wasting body is on the verge of death, for he spends the day on fire and the night in torment, and we have despaired of his life and are certain of his impending death. Beware of looking at him or anywhere else, except where you place your feet; otherwise you and I will lose our lives." Marzawan said, "For God's sake, tell me more about this young man whom you have described to me, and tell me the cause of his sickness." The vizier replied, "I do not know any cause, except that his father, three years ago, asked him to marry, but he refused. One morning he awoke and claimed that he had seen lying beside him a girl of such beauty as to dazzle the mind and defy description. He told us that he had taken her ring off her finger and put it on his own and put his ring on her finger, but we do not know the mystery behind this affair. For God's sake, son, come up with me into the pavilion, but do not look at the king's son; then go on your way, for the king is full of rage against me." Marzawan said to himself, "By God, this is what I wanted."

He followed the vizier until they entered the pavilion. The vizier sat at the feet of Qamar al-Zaman, but Marzawan proceeded until he stood before Qamar al-Zaman and looked at him. The vizier was about to die of fright and winked to him with his eyes to go away, but Marzawan pretended not to see him and kept looking at Qamar al-Zaman and, realizing that the prince was the object of his search, said, "Praise be to God who has made his figure like hers, his complexion

like hers, and his cheeks like hers." Qamar al-Zaman opened his eyes
and listened, and when Marzawan saw that he was listening to his
words, he recited the following verses,

> I find you joyful, plaintive, full of song,
> Delighting in describing beauty's lot.
> Are you in love or by some arrows pierced;
> This is the mark of one in the heart shot.
> Pour me out the wine and of Tena'um
> And Suleyma and Rabab sing the praise.
> I am jealous of the dress that covers her hips,
> Her soft and delicate hips, and there stays.
> I envy the cup that kisses her mouth,
> When her lips caress the fortunate one.
> Think not that I am slain by the keen sword,
> No, I am by the arrows of her eyes undone.
> Ah, when we met, I saw her fingers red,
> As if with blood-red dye they had been dyed.
> She said, inflaming my poor heart with love,
> Speaking like one whose love she could not hide.
> "Slowly, this is no red dye I have used,
> Accuse me not of falsehood and deceit.
> When you were lying fast asleep in bed,
> My arms and hands were bare and indiscreet,
> And when we parted, I shed tears of blood
> And wiped them and my blood my fingers stained."
> Had I for passion wept before she did
> I would have, ere regret, relief attained.
> But she before me wept and made me weep
> And say, "The winner of the race deserves the praise."
> Blame not my love, for my love's name I swear
> That she torments and sets my heart ablaze.
> I wept for one whose charm so graced her face
> That no Arab or foreigner could like her be.
> Lukman's wisdom she has and Joseph's loveliness
> And David's tuneful voice and Mary's chastity,
> While I have Jacob's grief and Jonah's stifled sighs
> And Job's misfortunes and Adam's sorry plight.
> Yet slay her not, although I die of love,
> But ask her who to shed by blood gave her the right.

When Marzawan recited these verses, the words descended like
balm on Qamar al-Zaman's heart, and turning his tongue in his
mouth, he said, motioning with his hand, "Let this young man sit by
my side." When the king heard these words from his son, he was

extremely happy, for he had been angry at Marzawan and determined to strike off his head. He seated him by the side of his son and, addressing him courteously, asked him, "From what country are you?" Marzawan replied, "From the Interior Islands, the kingdom of King Ghaiur, Lord of the Seas and the Islands and the Seven Palaces." King Shahraman said to him, "Perhaps my son's relief will be at your hand." Then Marzawan turned to Qamar al-Zaman and whispered in his ear, "Take heart and be cheerful and happy. As for her on whose account you are in this plight, ask not for her condition on your account. You suppressed your feelings and fell sick, but she expressed them and raved, and now she is imprisoned and in the worst of plights, with an iron collar around her neck. But, God willing, your healing both will be at my hand." When Qamar al-Zaman heard this, he revived and came to himself, and he motioned to his father the king to help him sit up, and the king, who was exceedingly happy, helped his son sit up. He then dismissed all the princes and viziers, while Qamar al-Zaman sat reclining between two cushions. Then the king gave orders to perfume the pavilion with saffron and to decorate the city, saying to Marzawan, "By God, son, this is an auspicious occasion," and he treated him very courteously and called for food for him, and when they brought it, Marzawan ate, and Qamar al-Zaman ate with him. They passed the night together, and the king remained with them, in his great joy at the recovery of his son.

On the following morning, Marzawan and Qamar al-Zaman discussed the affair, and Marzawan said, "I am acquainted with the girl you met, and her name is Princess Budur, the daughter of King Ghaiur." Then he related to him all that had happened to her from beginning to end and informed him of her great love for him, adding, "All that has happened to you with your father has happened to her with her father. You are without doubt her beloved, and she is yours. Take heart, and be resolute, for I will take you to her and unite you both. As one of the poets says,

> If lover reject lover
> And persist in his disdain,
> I will, as does the pivot
> Of scissors, unite the twain."

He continued to encourage Qamar al-Zaman until he began to eat and drink regularly, felt revived, and recovered. Marzawan kept conversing with him, amusing him, cheering him, and reciting verses to him until he entered the bath, and when he did so, his rejoicing father gave orders to decorate the city again, bestowed robes of honor, gave alms, and freed those who were in the jails.

Marzawan then said to Qamar al-Zaman, "The sole purpose of my journey here is to deliver Princess Budur from her predicament. Now we have to devise a strategy to go to her, for your father cannot bear to part from you. Tomorrow, ask your father's permission to go hunting in the desert. Then take with you a pair of saddlebags full of money, ride a swift horse, and take with you a spare one. I will do likewise. Say to your father, 'I would like to divert myself in the desert, to hunt and enjoy the open country. I will spend only one night there. Do not worry about me.' " Qamar al-Zaman rejoiced in Marzawan's plan and, going in to his father, asked his permission to go hunting, repeating what Marzawan had told him to say. His father gave his permission and said to him, "Stay no more than one night, and tomorrow come back to me, for you know that you are my only bliss in life, and I can hardly believe in your recovery from your recent illness." Then he recited the following verses to his son,

> If I had every blessing in the world
> And all the kingdom of the Persian king,
> If I see not your person with my eyes,
> All this will not be worth an insect's wing.

Then he equipped Qamar al-Zaman and Marzawan, giving orders that they be furnished with six horses, as well as a dromedary to carry the money and a camel to carry the food and water. His father bade him farewell, pressed him to his breast, and said to him, "For God's sake, do not be absent from me more than one night, for even then I will be deprived of sleep." Then he recited the following verses,

> Your presence with me is my greatest joy;
> Your absence is destructive pain within.
> My life for yours, if my offense is love,
> Then you are right, and serious is my sin.
> Do you, like me, suffer the fire of love,
> Which burns within and is to Hell akin?

Qamar al-Zaman, who had forbidden his attendants from going with him, and Marzawan mounted their two horses and, taking with them the dromedary, which carried the money, and the camel, which carried the food and water, entered the desert. They rode the first day till sunset, when they dismounted, ate and drank, fed their beasts, and rested a while. Then they mounted again and rode for three days. On the fourth day, they came to a spacious tract in which there was a thicket, where they dismounted. Then Marzawan took the camel and one of the horses, slaughtered them, and cut the flesh to pieces and stripped the bones. Then he took Qamar al-Zaman's shirt, trousers, and cassock, tore them in pieces, stained them with the blood of the horse, and threw them in a spot at the crossroads. Then, after they

ate and drank, they continued their journey. Qamar al-Zaman asked
Marzawan the reason for what he had done, and he explained to him,
saying, "When your father finds that you did not return the following
day, he will ride and follow our track, and when he sees the blood and
your clothes torn and bloodied, he will assume that something has
happened to you at the hand of robbers or a wild beast of the desert.
He will then give up all hope of you and return to the city, and by this
strategy we will achieve our purpose." Qamar al-Zaman said, "What
you did is excellent." Then they journeyed many days and nights, during which the tears never left Qamar al-Zaman's eyes, until they
approached their journey's end, when he rejoiced and recited the following verses,

> Will you disdain a lover who never forgets
> And spurn him, after love with love you paid?
> May I be by rejection punished if I lied;
> May I your favor lose if I your love betrayed.
> No sin have I committed to deserve your wrath,
> And if I sinned, I for your pardon pray.
> 'Tis fortune's wonder that you me disdain,
> But fortune brings new wonders every day.

When Qamar al-Zaman had finished reciting these verses, the
islands of King Ghaiur appeared before him, and he was overjoyed
and thanked Marzawan for his endeavors. They entered the city, and
Marzawan lodged Qamar al-Zaman in an inn, where he rested for
three days from the fatigue of the journey. Then he took him to the
bath, dressed him in the attire of a merchant, and provided him with
a set of instruments, as well as a divination tablet and an astrolabe of
gold. Then he said to him, "My lord, go and stand beneath the palace
of the king and call out 'I am the scribe, the calculator, the astrologer.
Where is he who seeks to consult me?' When the king hears you, he
will summon you and take you to his daughter, your beloved, and
when she sees you, she will recover, and her father will rejoice at her
recovery, marry her to you, and divide his kingdom with you, for this
has been his own condition."

Qamar al-Zaman, following Marzawan's instructions, went out of
the inn, dressed in merchants' attire and carrying with him the afore-
mentioned instruments, and he walked until he stood beneath the
palace of King Ghaiur and called out, "I am the scribe, the calculator,
the astrologer. I am he who calculates, who knows what is hidden,
who divines the answers, and who writes charms. Where is the
seeker?" When the people of the city, who had not seen a fortune-
teller or an astrologer for a long time, heard him, they assembled
around him and gazed at him and, wondering at his beauty and

youthful charm, said to him, "Sir, for God's sake, don't do this to
yourself, in your ambition to marry the daughter of King Ghaiur. See
for yourself these hanging heads, for their owners have all been killed
because of this, all led by their ambition to their destruction." But
Qamar al-Zaman paid no attention to their words. On the contrary,
he raised his voice and called out again, "I am the scribe and calculator. I help the seeker to fulfill his wish," while the people continued in
their attempt to dissuade him until they were angry at him and said,
"You are nothing but a foolish arrogant young man. Have pity on
your youth, beauty, and charm," but Qamar al-Zaman cried out, "I
am the calculator and astrologer. Where is the seeker?"

While the people were attempting to dissuade him, King Ghaiur
heard their shouting and clamor and said to the vizier, "Go down and
bring me this astrologer." The vizier went down and brought back
Qamar al-Zaman, who, when he came in to the king, kissed the
ground before him and recited the following verses,

> Eight glorious elements are met in you:
> Knowledge and piety, munificence and fame,
> Wisdom and eloquence, honor and victory;
> To serve you thereby, fortune to you came.

When King Ghaiur saw him, he made him sit beside him, treated
him courteously, and said, "For God's sake, son, do not call yourself
an astrologer, and do not submit yourself to my condition, for I have
bound myself that whoever goes in to my daughter and does not cure
her, I will strike off his head, and that whoever cures her, I will marry
her to him. Do not be deluded by your beauty, elegance, and grace,
for by God, by God, if you do not cure her, I will strike off your head."
But Qamar al-Zaman replied, "I accept your condition." Then King
Ghaiur asked the judges to bear witness and handed him to the
eunuch, saying, "Take him to Princess Budur."

The eunuch took him by the hand and proceeded with him
through the corridor, but Qamar al-Zaman hurried ahead of him,
while the eunuch followed him, saying, "Hey, don't hasten to your
own destruction, for, by God, I have never seen an astrologer in such
a hurry to destroy himself, except you. You don't know the calamities
that await you." But Qamar al-Zaman turned his face away from the
eunuch and recited the following verses,

> I know your beauties, but helpless I stand
> To do justice to them, not knowing what to say.
> If I compare you to the sun, you always shine,
> While the sun always sets and fades away.
> Your beauties are so perfect they defy
> Description and the eloquent dismay.

The eunuch made Qamar al-Zaman stand behind the curtain that hung over the door, and Qamar al-Zaman asked, "How do wish me to proceed? Shall I treat and cure your mistress from here, or go in and cure her inside the curtain?" The eunuch wondered at his question and said, "It would be more to your credit to cure her from here." So Qamar al-Zaman sat behind the curtain and, taking out the inkwell and pen, wrote on a sheet of paper the following, "He whose affliction is deprivation, his cure is fulfillment. Miserable is he who has despaired of his life and become certain of his demise, whose grieving heart there is no one to comfort or help, whose sleepless eye finds no relief from distress, whose day is on fire and whose night is in torment, whose body has wasted, and whose beloved has sent him no messenger." Then he wrote the following verses,

> I write you with a heart devoted to your name
> And wounded eyelids shedding tears for you
> And body with the dress of leanness clad
> By grief, as it does long and waste and rue.
> To you I now complain of painful love,
> And my forbearance has become outworn.
> Then be generous, merciful, and kind,
> For my heart is with love to pieces torn.

And beneath these verses he wrote the following sayings, "The cure of hearts is union with the beloved; he whose beloved rejects him, God is his physician, if either of us betrays, may the betrayer fail; and no one is more charming than a lover faithful to a disdainful beloved." Then at the bottom of the letter he wrote, "From the distracted lover, the distraught lover, the one afflicted by longing and love, the captive of passion and desire, Qamar al-Zaman, son of Shahraman, to the peerless of her age and most beautiful maid of Paradise, Princess Budur, daughter of King Ghaiur. By night I am sleepless, by day perplexed, wasting with love and passion and pain, full of sighs and tears, the slave of love, the victim of passion, tormented by desire, and befriended by sickness. I am the restless one whose eyes never sleep and the lover whose tears never dry. The fire of my heart is ever burning, and the flame of my desire is ever blazing." Then in the margin he wrote the following admired verses,

> Peace from the stores of God's grace from above
> On her who holds my life and has my love.

He also wrote the following verses,

> Grant me some word of yours that you may
> Show me pity or bring my heart some peace.
> My love and longing for you make me bear

The torment of my lowly state with ease.
God keep the lover whose abode was far,
Whose secret I have guarded everywhere.
Now fortune has turned kind to me at last
And cast me on her soil and brought me near.
When I saw Budur in bed by my side,
My life's moon shined, for her sun light supplied.

Then he sealed the letter and in the place of the address wrote the
following verses,

Ask of my letter what my pen has writ;
Its characters will show my love and pain.
My hand writes, while my tears flow, and desire
Does to the paper of sickness complain.
My tears continue to flow down my cheeks,
And if they cease, my blood this page will stain.

And he added the following verses,

The day we met, I took a ring of thine.
I send it back to you, please send me mine.

For he had enclosed Princess Budur's ring in the letter.

Then he handed the letter to the eunuch, who took it and went in
with it to Princess Budur. She took it from his hand and, opening it,
found in it her very ring, and when she read it and understood its con-
tents, she realized that her beloved was Qamar al-Zaman and that it
was he who was standing outside the curtain. She jumped with joy
and, feeling extremely happy, recited the following verses,

Long have I rued the day of severance,
And long, long have my eyes shed tears of pain.
And vowed that should fortune unite us two,
I would never mention that word again.
Now joy has so overwhelmed me that it has brought
To my sad tearful eyes tears of relief.
Tears have become a habit to you, eyes.
So that you always weep whether in joy or grief.

As soon as Princess Budur finished reciting these verses, she set her
feet to the wall and pulled with all her strength on the iron collar until
she broke it from her neck and snapped the chains. Then she rushed
out and, throwing herself on Qamar al-Zaman, embraced him passionately, kissed his mouth, like a pigeon feeding its young, and said,
"O my lord, is this true, or is it a dream? Has God indeed granted us
reunion?" Then she thanked God and praised Him for reuniting her
with him, after she had despaired.

When the eunuch saw her in that condition, he went running to King Ghaiur and, kissing the ground before him, said, "O my lord, this astrologer is the wisest of all astrologers, for he has cured your daughter, and he did it from behind the curtain, without even going in to her." The king asked him, "Is this true?" And the eunuch replied, "O my lord, come and see how she has broken the iron chains and rushed to the astrologer, hugging him and kissing him." The king arose and went in to his daughter. When she saw him, she stood up, covered her head, and recited the following verses,

> I like not the toothstick, for when I mention it,
> It sounds as if I am saying, "other than you."
> But I like the tree whence it comes, whose name
> Sounds as if I am saying, "I see you."

The king rejoiced at her recovery and kissed her between the eyes, for he loved her dearly. Then he addressed Qamar al-Zaman courteously and asked him from which country he had come. Qamar al-Zaman informed him about himself, saying that his father was King Shahraman. Then he related to him all that had happened between him and Princess Budur from beginning to end and how he had taken her ring from her finger and she had put on his ring. King Ghaiur marveled and said, "Your story must be recorded in books and read after you, generation after generation." Then he forthwith summoned the judges and witnesses and performed the marriage contract between Princess Budur and Qamar al-Zaman and gave orders to decorate the city for seven days. The city was decorated, and a banquet was prepared, and the troops put on their best uniforms, and the messengers announced the happy news. The people praised the Almighty God for having caused Princess Budur to fall in love with a handsome young man who is the son of a king. Then they unveiled her to him, and the two looked alike in beauty, elegance, and coquettish charm. Then he went in to her and slept with her that night and fulfilled his desire, and she too enjoyed his beauty and grace, and they slept in each other's arms till the morning. On the following day, the king prepared a banquet, covering the tables with all kinds of food, and invited visitors from the Inner Islands and Outer Islands, for an entire month.

After a while, Qamar al-Zaman began to think of his father, and he saw him in a dream, and his father was saying to him, "Why do you treat me in this way?" and reciting the following verses,

> The moon has by his absence racked my soul
> And to watch his own stars, my eyelids charged,
> Yet stay, O heart, for he may yet return,
> And forebear, soul, the pain he has discharged.

When Qamar al-Zaman saw his father reproaching him in the dream, he awoke in the morning, feeling sad, and told his wife Princess Budur about it. Then he went with her to see her father and, telling him what had happened, asked his permission to depart. The king gave his permission, but Princess Budur said, "O father, I cannot bear to part from him." Her father replied, "Very well, go with him," bidding her to stay a whole year and visit him annually thereafter. She kissed his hand, and Qamar al-Zaman did likewise.

The king proceeded to equip his daughter and her husband for the journey, providing them with horses and dromedaries, as well as a litter for his daughter, and loaded the dromedaries and mules with gear and provisions. On the day of departure, he bestowed on Qamar al-Zaman a magnificent gold robe, adorned with jewels, presented him with a great sum of money, and charged him to take care of his daughter. Then he accompanied them on their journey until they reached the farthest limits of the Islands, when he bade Qamar al-Zaman good-bye. Then he entered his daughter's litter, began to embrace her and weep and recited the following verses,

> Be patient you who wish to part;
> For to embrace is lovers' joy
> And fortune's nature is deceit,
> And at the end does love destroy.

Then he left his daughter and, coming up to Qamar al-Zaman, bade him farewell again and kissed him. The he bade them proceed and returned to his capital with his troops.

Qamar al-Zaman and his wife Princess Budur journeyed with their retinue for a whole month, after which they stopped at a spacious meadow, abounding with grass, where they pitched their tents and ate and drank and rested. Then Princess Budur went to sleep, and when Qamar al-Zaman went in, he found her asleep, clad in a transparent silk dress of apricot color and a golden head cover, adorned with jewels. The breeze had lifted her dress up to her breasts, revealing her navel and her snow-white belly with its folds, each of which contained a pound of benzoin ointment. His love and desire for her stirred within him, and he recited the following verses,

> If I was asked, while the flames raged about
> And set my heart and soul on hellish fire,
> Which would you rather have, the one you love,
> Or water cold?" I'd say, "Her I desire."

He desired her and put his hand to the ribbon of her pants, but when he pulled it loose, he saw, knotted to the ribbon, a blood-red jewel engraved with two lines of unfamiliar characters. He marveled at that and said to himself, "If she had not attached a great importance to this jewel, she would not have tied it to the ribbon of her pants and hidden it in her most precious part, in order to guard it. I wonder what she does with it and what is the secret behind it."

He took the jewel outside the tent to look at it in the light. As he was examining it, a bird swooped down and, snatching it from his hand, flew off with it and alighted on the ground, at a little distance. Fearing for the jewel, Qamar al-Zaman ran after the bird, while it kept flying just ahead of him from valley to valley and from hill to hill, until night descended and it grew dark, when the bird roosted on a high tree. Qamar al-Zaman stood under the tree, feeling perplexed, and faint from hunger and fatigue and giving himself up for lost. He wanted to turn back but did not know the way, for all was dark. So he said to himself, "There is no power and no strength save in God the Almighty, the Magnificent," and went to sleep under the tree in which the bird roosted.

When he awoke in the morning, the bird rose and flew from the tree. He followed it, and it flew slowly before him at the same speed at which he walked. Qamar al-Zaman smiled and said to himself, "By God, this is a strange thing. This bird yesterday flew at the same speed at which I ran, and today, knowing that I am tired and unable to run, it flies at the same speed at which I walk. This is strange, but I must follow this bird, and whether it leads me to my life or to my death I will follow it wherever it goes, for in any event it lives only in an inhabited part."

Qamar al-Zaman walked, while the bird flew above him, roosting on a tree every night, and he kept following it for ten days, during which he fed on the vegetation of the land and drank the water of the streams, until he came to the outskirts of a populous city. Suddenly, the bird darted into the city and disappeared in a wink from Qamar al-Zaman, who did not know where it had gone. He wondered and said to himself, "God be praised for preserving me and bringing me to this city." Then seating himself by some water, he washed his face, as well as his hands and feet and rested for a while, reflecting on his former comfort and his present distance from home and on his hunger and weariness, and recited the following verses,

> I tried to hide my love, but I could not,
> And sleeplessness has now replaced my sleep.
> I cried out with a heart oppressed by care,
> "O fate, destroy and of me nothing keep";
> My soul is between toil and peril deep.
> If love's lord had only been fair to me
> Sleep would not have been banished from my eyes.

O lady, pity one who has offered to love
His health, his wealth, his pride a sacrifice.
Be kind to him and his love recognize.
The railers chided me for you, but I
heeded them not and closed my ears and mind.
They said, "You love a slender one," and I
Replied, "I chose her, yes, and left the rest behind.
Enough, for when fate strikes, the eyes are blind."

When Qamar al-Zaman finished reciting these verses and felt rested, he entered the city, not knowing where to go. He walked through the entire city, without meeting any of its inhabitants, until, having entered by the land gate, he went out from the sea gate, for the city was on the shore of the sea. He kept walking until he came to the city orchards. He made his way among the trees and stood by the gate of one of the orchards, where the gardener came out and welcomed him, saying, "Thank God that you have escaped the people of this city. Come into this orchard quickly, before any of them sees you." Qamar al-Zaman entered the orchard, perplexed, and asked the gardener, "What is the story of the people of this city?" and the gardener replied, "The inhabitants are Magians, but, for God's sake, tell me how you came to this city, and what is the reason for your coming to our country?"

Qamar al-Zaman related to the gardener all that had happened to him, and the gardener marveled exceedingly and said to him, "O my son, the Muslim countries are far from here, a four-month voyage by sea and a whole year's journey by land. We have a ship that sails every year with merchandise to the nearest of the Muslim countries. It goes from here to the Ebony Islands, then to the Khalidan Islands, whose ruler is called King Shahraman." Qamar al-Zaman reflected for a while and concluded that the best course of action was to stay with the gardener and work as his assistant for one-fourth of the crop. He asked the gardener, "Will you take me as your assistant in this orchard for one-fourth of the crop?" The gardener replied, "I hear and obey," and he clad him with a blue vest reaching to the knees and taught him how to direct the water among the trees. So he conducted the water and hoed the grass, and as he watered the trees, he wept bitterly and recited verses on his beloved, night and day. Among them were the following,

Will you the promise you have made fulfill
And follow words with deeds in all fidelity?
Passion has made me sleepless, while you sleep;
Sleepers and sleepless lack equality.
We vowed to hide our passion from the world,

But the traitor enticed you, and you broke the vow.
Beloved, whether angry or content,
You are always my wish, whatever happens now.
There's one who holds captive my aching heart;
Would that she had pity on my sore plight.
Not every heart is, like my own, enthralled by love;
No, nor every eye the bitter tears blight.
You wronged me, saying, "It was love that did."
This is the case indeed, and what you say is true.
You have forgotten one whose vow endures,
Although his heart does burn with love and rue.
If my opponent is my judge in love,
To whom shall I complain about my foe?
Were it not for my ardent need for love,
My heart would not have suffered enslavement and woe.

This was what happened to Qamar al-Zaman; as for his wife, Princess Budur, the daughter of King Ghaiur, she awoke and looked for her husband Qamar al-Zaman but did not find him, and when she saw her pants open and, feeling the knot of the ribbon, found it untied and the jewel missing, she said to herself, "O God, this is strange. Where is my beloved? It seems that he has taken the jewel and gone, without knowing its secret power. I wonder where he has gone; it must have been some extraordinary matter that drew him away, for he cannot bear to be without me even for an hour. May God curse the jewel and its very existence." Then she reflected and said to herself, "If I go out and tell the attendants that my husband is missing, they will be emboldened with me; therefore, I must find some strategy." Then she put on some of Qamar al-Zaman's clothes and a turban like his and veiled the lower part of her face and, placing a maidservant in the litter, she came out of the tent and called to the pages, who brought her a horse. She mounted and ordered them to load the animals, and they did so and departed, none discovering her identity, for she resembled Qamar al-Zaman so much that no one doubted that she was he himself. She journeyed with her retinue many days and nights until they came in sight of a city overlooking the sea. She stopped outside the city and pitched the tents to rest there, and when she asked the name of the place, she was told that it was called the City of Ebony and that its king was called Armanus who has a daughter named Hayat al-Nufus.

Soon King Armanus sent out a messenger to find out about the king who had encamped outside his city. When the messenger arrived and inquired, they told him that it was the son of a king who had strayed from the road, on his way to the Khalidan Islands and their king, Shahraman. The messenger returned and told King Armanus, who went out with his officers of state to meet the newly arrived prince. When he approached the tents, Princess Budur and he dismounted and saluted each other. Then he led her into the city and took her to his palace, where he ordered that the tables be spread. Then he ordered that she be transferred to the guest-house, where she stayed for three days, after which he came to see her. That day she had gone to the bath, and her face shone like the full moon, enchanting and ravishing all beholders. She was wearing a robe of silk, embroidered with gold and adorned with jewels. When he came in, he said to her, "O my son, I have become an old man, and I am no longer able to govern. I have not been blessed with a son, but I have one daughter, whose face and body resemble yours in beauty and grace. Will you be willing to live in my country? I will marry you to my daughter and give you my kingdom." Princess Budur bowed her head, and her forehead perspired in embarrassment, and she said to herself, "What shall I do, being a woman? If I refuse and depart, he may send after me troops to kill me, and if I consent, I may be compromised. I have lost my beloved Qamar al-Zaman, and I don't know what is become of him; therefore, I see no solution, save to consent and stay here until God accomplishes what must be." Then she raised her head and said to the king submissively, "I hear and obey." The king rejoiced and sent out a proclamation throughout the Ebony Islands to hold a festival and decorate the houses. Then he assembled the chamberlains, and deputies and princes and viziers and officers of state and judges of the city and abdicated, naming Princess Budur in his place and investing her with the royal robes. Then all the princes came in to pay her homage, without doubting that she was a young man, and all who looked on her almost wetted their pants when they saw her surpassing beauty and grace.

After Princess Budur was made king, and the drums were beaten to announce the happy event, King Armanus proceeded to equip his daughter Hayat al-Nufus for the wedding, and a few days later, they brought Princess Budur in to her, and the two looked like two moons joined together or two suns shining at the same time. The attendants closed the doors and let the curtains down, after they had lighted the candles and prepared the bed for them. When Princess Budur found herself with Princess Hayat al-Nufus, she recalled her beloved Qamar al-Zaman and, feeling very sad, wept and recited the following verses,

> You who have left me with a pining heart,
> No life is left in me, consumed with care.
> My smarting eyes of sleeplessness complained
> Till with tears wasted; would that they sleepless were.

> When you parted, your lover did abide,
> But ask her how she did your absence bear.
> Were it not for my ceaseless tears, my fire
> Would have consumed the earth and left naught there.
> To God I do complain about a lover lost,
> One who pities not my love and despair.
> My only sin against him is my love,
> And in love, some men joy, some sorrow share.

When Princess Budur finished reciting these verses, she sat beside Princess Hayat al-Nufus and, kissing her on the mouth, rose immediately to make her ablutions and perform her prayer, and she prayed until Princess Hayat al-Nufus fell asleep. Then Princess Budur joined her in bed, turning her back to her till the morning, then she got up and went out. Soon the king and his wife came in to their daughter and asked her how she did, and she told them what had passed and the verses she had heard.

In the meantime, Princess Budur sat on the throne, and all the princes and officers of state and captains and troops came in to her to congratulate her on ascending the throne, kissing the ground before her and calling down blessings on her. She responded courteously, smiled to them, bestowed robes of honor, and augmented the fiefs of the princes, and all the people and troops loved her and prayed for the continuation of her reign, thinking all the while that she was a man. She sat in the audience hall, ordering and interdicting, dispensing justice, releasing those who were in prison, and repealing customs duties, till nightfall.

Then she withdrew to her apartment and found Princess Hayat al-Nufus seated. Princess Budur sat down beside her, patted her on the back, caressed her, kissed her between the eyes, and recited the following verses,

> My ceaseless tears do my secret reveal;
> My wasting body does my love betray.
> I labor to hide it, but parting's pains
> My soul's sorry plight to the spies display.
> You have departed and have left behind
> A frail body and soul about to die.
> You have made your dwelling place in my heart,
> While my tears flow and lacerate my eye,
> My sore eye that suffers the pain of love,
> Rejecting sleep and shedding ceaseless tears.
> My life is ransom for the distant one,
> And my yearning for him always appears.
> My foes think I have his absence foreborn,

Such notion I'll ne'er entertain or heed,
Spoiling their expectation and surmise,
For Qamar al-Zaman is my only need.
His are the virtues, all gathered in one,
As none beside him, past and present, none.
In clemency and in largesse he has surpassed
E'en Mu'awiya and Za'ida's son.
Were not verse limited, boring in time,
I would, to praise his beauties, spare no rhyme.

Then Princess Budur rose and, wiping her tears, made her ablution and kept praying until sleep overcame Princess Hayat al-Nufus. Then Princess Budur came and lay beside her till the morning. Then she arose, and after performing the morning prayer, she sat on the throne, ordering and interdicting and judging and dispensing justice. Meanwhile, King Armanus came in to his daughter and asked her how she did, and she told him all that had passed and repeated to him the verses Princess Budur had recited, adding, "O father, I have never seen anyone more sensible and more bashful than my husband, but he only weeps and sighs." Her father replied, "Daughter, have patience with him for this third night, and if he does not take your virginity and consummate the marriage, I know what course to pursue with him. I will depose him and banish him from our country." He resolved with his daughter to follow this course of action and was determined to carry it out.

At nightfall, Princess Budur rose from the throne and, returning to her chamber in the palace, saw the candles lighted and Princess Hayat al-Nufus sitting there, and she recalled her husband and what had happened to them in such a short time and wept and sighed, again and again, and recited the following verses,

I swear my tidings spreads and fills the sky,
Just as on Nejad's hills the shining sun.
His gesture speaks, but what, no one can tell
And thus my yearning grows and of respite has none.
I hate fair patience since I fell in love;
Have you a lover who hates his love seen?
He has afflicted me with deadly looks,
Which have, of all afflictions the most lethal been.
He shook his ringlets down, as he removed the veil,
And thus his charms I saw both white and black.
My sickness and my health are in his hands;
To the lovesick only the cause can bring health back.
His girdle madly loves his slender waist,
And his hips in envy refuse to rise.

His forelock o'er his brow is like the night,
Illumined through and through by the sunrise.

When Princess Budur finished reciting these verses and was about to get up to perform her prayer, Hayat al-Nufus clung to the hem of her robe and said, "O my lord, aren't you embarrassed toward my father, to neglect me after all the favors he has done you?" When Princess Budur heard these words, she sat down again and asked, "O my dear, what do you mean?" Hayat al-Nufus replied, "What I mean to say is that I have never seen anyone as conceited as you. Is every beautiful person so conceited? I am not saying this to make you desire me, but I am saying it out of fear for you from King Armanus, for he has resolved that if you don't take my virginity and consummate the marriage tonight, he will depose you and banish you from his country; he may even become more enraged and kill you. I am advising you out of compassion for you, my lord, and it is up to you to decide." When Princess Budur heard this, she bowed her head, puzzling over what to do, and said to herself, "If I disobey him, I will perish, and if I obey him, I will be exposed. But I am now king of all the Ebony Islands, and they are under my rule, and I will never be reunited with Qamar al-Zaman, except in this place, for there is no way by which he can return to his country but by the Ebony Islands. Therefore, I will commit my case to God, for He knows best what to do." Then she said to Hayat al-Nufus, "O my dear, my neglect of you and abstaining from you have not been voluntary." Then she told her all that had happened to her from beginning to end, revealed herself to her, and said, "For God's sake, keep my secret until God reunites me with my beloved Qamar al-Zaman, and after that let whatever happens happen."

When Hayat al-Nufus heard the story, she was extremely surprised. She felt pity for Princess Budur, prayed to God to reunite her with her beloved Qamar al-Zaman, and said to her, "O sister, fear nothing, and be patient until God accomplishes what must be." Then she recited the following verses,

Only the faithful does a secret keep;
None but the best can hold it unrevealed.
I keep a secret in a well-shut house,
Of which the key is lost and the lock sealed.

Then she said, "O sister, the breast of the brave is the secret's grave. I will not divulge your secret." Then they prayed and, embracing, slept till near the call of the morning prayer, when Hayat al-Nufus got up and, taking a chicken, slaughtered it and smeared herself with its blood. Then she took off her pants, and cried out. The women of her family went in to her, and her waiting women let out trilling cries of joy. Soon her mother came to see her, asking her how she did, and she stayed with her till evening. Meanwhile, Princess Budur went to the bath and washed herself, and after performing her morning prayer, went to the audience hall and sat on the throne, governing her subjects. When King Armanus heard the trilling cries of joy, he asked about the cause, and when he was told that his daughter's marriage had been consummated, he rejoiced and felt relieved and made a great banquet.

To return to King Shahraman, after his son departed with Marzawan on his excursion to hunt and trap, he waited for him, and when night fell and he did not return, he was perplexed and could not sleep. He was extremely worried and anxious to see his son, and scarcely had the day dawned when he rose. He waited for his son till noon, and when Qamar al-Zaman did not come, he felt the pang of separation and ached with pity for his son and wept until his clothes were wet with tears and recited in agony the following verses,

> I disagreed with those who worship love
> Until I tasted its bitter and sweet
> And swallowed its bitter cup to the dregs,
> Humbling myself to bondsman and elite.
> Time made a vow to separate us two,
> A vow he has fulfilled and made it true.

Then he wiped off his tears and ordered all his troops to march on a long journey. They mounted and departed with the king, who rode out with a heart full of fire and grief for his son. He divided his troops into six groups, on the right and left and in front and behind, and said to them, "Tomorrow, we shall meet at the crossroads." The groups separated, each heading in a different direction, and rode all that day and night until, at noon of the following day, they met at the crossroads. Here four roads met, and they did not know which road Qamar al-Zaman had taken until they saw the torn clothes, the mangled flesh, and the traces of blood scattered everywhere. When King Shahraman saw this, he uttered a great cry from the depths of his heart, exclaiming, "O my son!" and he beat his face, plucked his beard, and tore his clothes, feeling convinced that his son was dead. He wept and wailed, and his troops wept with him, all of them being certain that Qamar al-Zaman had perished. They threw dust on their heads and wept and wailed until it was dark and they were exhausted. The king sighed in anguish and recited the following verses, with an aching heart and with anguished sighs,

> Blame not the mourner in his sorry state,
> For longing is torment enough and fire.

> He weeps in anguish and unequaled pain,
> And his yearning reveals his inner pyre.
> Alas for one who loves, whose grief has sworn
> never to let his eyes be without tears,
> A lover who has lost a brilliant moon,
> Who used to shine high above all his peers.
> He was offered the brimming cup of death,
> When he left home, on his departure day.
> He left his land and journeyed to his death,
> Before he could to his own brothers farewell say.
> I am now stricken with the sense of loss,
> Longing, and loneliness, love's painful price.
> He left us suddenly and went away,
> When God welcomed him to His Paradise.

King Shahraman returned with the troops to his capital, feeling certain that his son had perished and thinking that he had either been murdered by a highwayman or devoured by a wild beast. He proclaimed that all the people in the Khalidan Islands should wear black, in mourning for his son, Qamar al-Zaman, and built a monument he called the House of Sorrows where, except for Monday and Thursday, when he governed his subjects and troops, he spent the whole week mourning for his son and lamenting with verses, like the following,

> The day I have you is the day I crave;
> The day you leave me is the day I die.
> Were I to live in fear of promised death,
> I'd rather be with you than my life save.

Or,

> My life is ransom for the absent one
> Who left my heart the torment and the blight.
> Let gladness then await its lawful time,
> For I have divorced all joy and delight.

Meanwhile, Princess Budur remained as king in the Ebony Islands, and the people would point to her and say, "There is the son-in-law of King Armanus." She spent every night with Hayat al-Nufus, expressing to her her longing for her husband Qamar al-Zaman and describing to her his beauty and grace. As for Qamar al-Zaman himself, he continued to live with the gardener in the orchard, weeping day and night and reciting verses, lamenting the lost happy days, while the gardener kept consoling him, saying, "By the end of the year, the ship will sail to the land of the Muslims."

One day, he saw people assembling together and wondered at this, and the gardener came to him and said, "Son, stop working today, and don't water the trees, for today is a feast day, on which people visit each other. Rest and keep an eye on the orchard, for I wish to find the ship for you, in order to send you to the land of the Muslims, since there is only a little time left." Then the gardener left the orchard, while Qamar al-Zaman remained alone, feeling depressed and weeping, and he wept until he fell into a swoon. When he came to himself, he got up and wandered in the orchard, reflecting upon what fate had done to him and on his long separation from his wife. In his distraction, he stumbled and fell on his face, hitting his forehead against the root of a tree, and his blood flowed and mingled with his tears. He wiped away the blood, dried up his tears and, having bandaged his forehead with a rag, resumed his aimless wandering in the orchard.

He turned up his eyes toward a tree and saw two birds fighting. One of them overcame the other and pecked at its neck until it separated the head from the body. Then it flew away with the head, while the other bird fell dead on the ground in front of Qamar al-Zaman. Soon two big birds swooped down, and one stood at the neck of the dead bird and the other at its tail and, folding their wings, stretched their necks toward it and wept. When Qamar al-Zaman saw the birds weeping for their companion, he wept at his separation from his wife. Then they dug a hole, in which they buried the dead bird, and flew up in the sky. After a while, they returned, bringing with them the bird that had killed the other. They alighted with it on the grave of the slaughtered bird and, crouching on it, killed it. Then they cut open its belly, tore out its entrails, and spilled its blood on the grave of the slaughtered bird. Then they strewed its flesh, tore its skin, and, pulling out all the innards, scattered them in different places. All this happened while Qamar al-Zaman watched in amazement. Then he happened to cast a glance at the spot where the two big birds had killed the other and saw something shining. He approached it and saw that it was the bird's craw. He took it and opened it and found in it the jewel that was the cause of his separation from his wife. When he saw it and recognized it, he was so overcome with joy that he fell into a swoon, and when he recovered, he said to himself, "This is a good sign and an omen of my reunion with my beloved." He then examined it and passed it over his eyes and tied it to his arm, anticipating something good to happen. He walked in the orchard, waiting for the gardener to return, until it was night, and when he failed to return, Qamar al-Zaman slept in his usual place.

In the morning, he arose and, girding his waist with a fiber rope, took a hoe and basket and went out to do his work in the orchard. Soon he came to a carob tree and struck its roots with the hoe. The blow resounded, removing the earth and uncovering a trapdoor. He raised it and found an opening, into which he descended and found a large, ancient hall from the time of Thamud and 'Ad, and in it he found twenty jars full of red gold. He said to himself, "Toil has departed, and joy and happiness have returned." Then he climbed out to the orchard and, replacing the trapdoor, resumed his task of conducting water to the trees.

He continued to work till the end of the day, when the gardener returned and said, "Son, I have good news about your return to your country, for the merchants have prepared themselves for the journey, and in three days' time, the ship will sail to the City of Ebony, which is the first of the Muslim cities. After you reach it, you will travel by land for six months until you reach the Khalidan Islands and King Shahraman." Qamar al-Zaman was glad to hear this, and he kissed his hand and said, "Father, just as you have given me good news, I too have good news for you," and he told him about the hall. The gardener too was glad and said, "Son, I have been in this orchard for eighty years, without finding anything, while you have been with me here less than a year and have found this. It is God's gift to you to reverse your ill fortune and help you return to your family and join the one you love." Qamar al-Zaman replied, "No, you must share it with me." Then he took the gardener to the hall and, showing him the twenty jars of god, took ten and gave him ten.

The gardener said to him, "Son, fill for yourself large jars with the large olives in this garden, for they are not to be found anywhere except in our country, and the merchants export them to all parts. Put the gold in the jars and cover it with the olives; then close them and take them to the ship." Qamar al-Zaman proceeded immediately and filled fifty large jars, placing the olives over the gold and hiding the jewel in one of them. Then he closed them and sat to chat with the gardener. He felt certain of his speedy reunion with his family and said to himself, "When I reach the Ebony Islands, I will journey from there to my father's country and inquire about my beloved Budur. I wonder whether she has returned to her home or went to my father's country, or whether something has happened to her on the way."

Qamar al-Zaman then sat, waiting for the days to pass, and he related the story of the birds to the gardener, who marveled at it. Then they went to sleep, but when they awoke in the morning, the gardener felt ill and remained so for two days, and on the third day, he became so ill that they despaired of his life. Qamar al-Zaman grieved for him, and while he was in this state, the captain and the sailors came and inquired about the gardener, and he told them about the gardener's illness. Then they asked him, "Where is the young man who wishes to sail with us to the Ebony Islands?" Qamar al-Zaman replied, "He is

the servant before you." Then he asked them to carry the jars to the
ship, and they did so, saying to him, "Hurry up, for the wind is favorable." He said, "I hear and obey." He then carried his provisions to
the ship and returned to bid the gardener farewell, but he found him
in the agonies of death. Qamar al-Zaman sat at his head until he died.
Then he closed the gardener's eyes, prepared his body, and buried
him. Then he went to the ship but found that it had spread its sails
and departed, and it continued to cleave the waves until it disappeared
from his sight. He was confounded and perplexed and returned to the
orchard, feeling so sad and depressed that he threw dust on his head.
A little later, he leased the orchard from its owner and hired a man to
assist him in watering the trees. Then he went to the trapdoor and,
descending to the hall, filled fifty large jars with the rest of the gold
and placed the olives over it. Then he went and inquired about a ship,
and when he was told that it sailed only once a year, his anxiety and
regret for what had happened increased, especially for the loss of the
jewel that belonged to Princess Budur. And he kept weeping and reciting poetry day and night.

Meanwhile, the ship sailed with a fair wind until it reached the
Ebony Islands. It so happened, as had been foreordained, that
Princess Budur was sitting at the window, and when she saw the ship
cast anchor by the shore, her heart throbbed. She rode down to the
port with the princes and the chamberlains and stopped by the ship, as
the sailors were carrying the goods to the storehouses. She summoned
the captain and asked him what he had with him, and he replied, "O
King, I have with me in this ship drugs and powders and cosmetics
and ointments and plasters and rich fabrics and other precious merchandise and wealth, more than can be carried by horses or camels.
Among the goods are different kinds of perfumes and spices, as well as
aloeswood, tamarind, and choice olives, the like of which is not found
here." When she heard this, she felt a desire for olives and asked the
captain, "How much olives do you have?" He replied, "I have fifty
jars full. Their owner is not with us, but the king may take whatever he
wishes." She said, "Bring them ashore, so that I may look at them."
He called to the sailors, who brought out the jars, and she opened one
and, looking at the olives, said to the captain, "I will take all fifty jars
and pay you their price, whatever it may be." The captain said,
"These olives have no value in our country, but their owner tarried
behind, and he is a poor man." She asked, "What is their price?" He
replied, "A thousand dirhams." She said, "I will take them for a thousand dirhams."

Then she gave orders to carry the jars to the palace, and when night
came, she asked for one of the jars. There was no one in the room but
herself and Hayat al-Nufus. She opened the jar and, placing a dish

before her, poured some olives in it, and there fell into the dish a heap of red gold. She exclaimed to Hayat al-Nufus, "This is nothing but gold!" Then she examined all the jars and found that they were all full of gold and that all the olives altogether would not fill even one jar. She searched among the gold and found the jewel. She took it and examined it and found that it was the jewel that was attached to the ribbon of her pants which Qamar al-Zaman had taken. As soon as she recognized it, she screamed with joy and fell down in a swoon. When she recovered, she said to herself, "This jewel was the cause of my separation from my beloved Qamar al-Zaman, but now it is an omen of good fortune," and she told Hayat al-Nufus that its recovery was an omen of their reunion.

In the morning, she sat on the throne and summoned the captain, and when he came and kissed the ground before her, she asked him, "Where did you leave the owner of these olives?" He replied, "O king of the age, we left him in the country of the Magians, where he works as a gardener." She said to him, "If you do not bring him, you cannot imagine what harm will happen to you and your ship." Then she gave orders to seal the storehouses of the merchants, saying to them, "The owner of these olives is an offender who owes me money, and if he does not come, I will kill you all and confiscate your merchandise." The merchants went to the captain and promised to pay him the cost of going and returning a second time, saying, "Deliver us from this tyrant."

The captain embarked and spread the sails, and God granted him safe passage until he reached the island. He landed at night and went up to the orchard. When he knocked at the gate, Qamar al-Zaman was sitting in the orchard, feeling weary of the tedious night, thinking of his beloved, and weeping over what had happened to him. He opened the gate, and as soon as he went out, the sailors seized him, carried him to the ship, and, spreading the sails, departed. They sailed many days and nights, while Qamar al-Zaman remained ignorant of what had prompted their conduct. When he asked them the cause, they finally said, "You are an offender against the King of the Ebony Islands, the son-in-law of King Armanus. You have stolen money from him, you unlucky one." He replied, "By God, in all my life I have never entered that country, nor am I familiar with it."

They continued their voyage until they came to the Ebony Islands and took him up to Princess Budur, who, as soon as she saw him, recognized him and said, "Leave him with the attendants to take him to the bath." Then she released the merchants and bestowed on the captain a robe of honor worth ten thousand dinars. Then she went in to Hayat al-Nufus and told her what had happened, saying, "Keep this a secret until I accomplish my purpose and do a thing that shall be recorded and read after us by kings and commoners." Meanwhile, the attendants took Qamar al-Zaman to the bath and dressed him in the attire of kings, and when he came out of the bath, feeling revived, he looked like a willow wand or a star whose light puts the moon and sun to shame. He went to Princess Budur who, when she saw him, restrained herself until she would accomplish her purpose. Meanwhile, she bestowed on him slaves and servants and camels and mules, as well as a large sum of money, and she kept promoting him from rank to rank until she made him treasurer and put him in charge of all the treasures of the state. She treated him courteously, showed him favor, and informed the princes of his special status, and they all loved him. Every day she raised his allowances, while he remained in the dark as to the cause of these honors. Having acquired so much wealth, he gave liberally, and he served King Armanus so well that the king and all the princes and the people, great and small, loved him and swore by his life.

But all this time, he kept wondering at the cause of the honors showered on him by Princess Budur and said to himself, "By God, there must be a reason behind this affection. This king's excessive generosity toward me may hide some ill purpose. I must therefore ask his permission and leave his country." Then he went to Princess Budur and said to her, "O King, you have bestowed on me great favors, but your favors will not be complete unless you permit me to depart and take back from me all you have given me." Princess Budur smiled and said, "What makes you wish to depart and expose yourself to peril, when you are enjoying such great favor and prosperity?" Qamar al-Zaman replied, "O King, if there is no special reason behind these favors, then they are the wonder of wonders, especially since you have conferred on me positions befitting maturer men, while I am only a boy." Princess Budur said to him, "The reason is that I love you for your surpassing beauty and grace, and if you grant me my desire, I will grant you more favors, make you more prosperous, and appoint you vizier, just as the people made me king, in spite of my young age. Nowadays, there is nothing strange in the primacy of children. Bravo for the poet who said,

> Our time and Lot's are both alike,
> Advancing boys is what we like."

When Qamar al-Zaman heard this, he felt embarrassed and blushed until his cheeks seemed on fire, and he said, "I have no need of favors that lead to sin. I will live poor in wealth but rich in virtue and honor." Princess Budur replied, "I am not deceived by your piety, which arises from your conceit and coquettishness. Bravo for the poet who said,

> When I mentioned our vow of love, he said,
> 'How long will you wage this painful debate?'
> But when I showed him a dinar, he said
> 'How can one flee such a decisive fate?' ' "

When Qamar al-Zaman heard this and understood its meaning, he said, "O King, I am not used to such doings, nor can I, being young, bear such a burden, which is too heavy even for those older than I to bear." When she heard this, Princess Budur smiled and said, "It is wonderful how error springs from faulty reasoning. Since you are young, why are you afraid of committing sin and doing forbidden things? You are not of age yet, and the offenses of a child are neither blamed nor punished. You are trying to find excuses, whereas you should give in. Therefore, you should no longer show resistance or distaste for what God has foreordained. I myself have more reason than you to fear falling into error. The poet put it well, when he said,

> When my penis got big, the young boy said,
> 'Thrust it inside as bravely as you can.'
> I said, ' 'Tis not lawful,' but when he said,
> 'It is for me,' I fucked the little man.

When Qamar al-Zaman heard these words, the light turned to darkness before his eyes, and he said, "O King, you have many beautiful women and slave-girls who are matchless in this age. Will they not suffice you without me? Do whatever you desire with them and leave me alone." Princess Budur replied, "What you say is true, but they cannot heal the burning desire and torment of one who loves you, and when one's nature and inclination are perverted, they do not listen or follow advice. Stop arguing and listen to what the poet said,

> Don't you see the different fruits in the stores?
> Some men buy figs, and some buy sycamores.

"And what another said,

> Of girls whose anklets are silent, whose girdles ring,
> Some claim fulfillment, some of want complain.
> You'd have me be a fool and you in them forget,
> But I such bad apostasy disdain.
> No, by the whiskers that mock all their curls,
> All women from you will lure me in vain.

"And another,

> Unique in beauty, your love is my faith,
> And of all creeds my only creed and way.

I have forsaken women, so much for your sake
That people say I am a monk today.

"And another,

From Zainab and Nawar I'm drawn away
By a rose on the myrtle of a cheek.
Being in love with a tunic-clad fawn,
I no longer the bangles-wearing seek.
In private and public he is my friend,
Unlike a woman, who is seen by none.
You who blame my leaving Hind or Zainab,
When my excuse is as clear as the sun,
Do you wish me to become a slave's thrall,
A cloistered slave, one kept behind a wall?

"And another,

Do not compare a young boy to a girl,
Nor heed the spy who says that you have gone astray.
Far different is the girl whose feet are kissed,
From a deer who kisses the earth, far different, aye.

"And another,

My life your ransom, I have chosen you
Because you neither menstruate, no, nor give birth.
Did I desire with girls to copulate,
I would with my brood overcrowd the earth.

"And another,

When she urged me to do what I could not,
She said to me, in rage and wounded pride,
'If you fuck me not as a man his wife,
Blame me not if horns on your head you see.
Your penis seems as soft as melting wax,
And when I rub it, it goes limp on me.'

"And another,

She said when I refused to sleep with her,
'How you persist in your folly, you fool!
If you reject my cunt as Mecca to your cock,
I will then show you a more pleasing tool.'

"And another,

She offered me a tender cunt,
But I replied, "This will not do."

> She drew back, saying, "He who turns
> From it is to his faith untrue.
> And fucking frontwise nowadays
> Is out of fashion, as you see."
> Then turned around and a rump
> Like a lump of silver showed me.
> 'Bravo!' I said, 'My lady dear,
> You who have made my pain abate,
> Bravo! You who are more endowed
> And wider than a royal gate.'

"And another,

> Men pardon crave with lifted hands,
> Women, with their legs lifted high.
> O what a pious piece of work
> Which God will raise, deep down to lie."

When Qamar al-Zaman heard these verses, he became convinced that there was no escape from compliance with her will and said, "O King of the age, if you must do it, promise me that you will do it to me only once, although it will not heal your corrupt appetite. After that, never ask me to do this again, so that God may purge me of my corruption." She replied, "I promise and hope that God will forgive us both and in his mercy blot out our mortal sins, for the sphere of God's forgiveness is not so narrow as not to include us and absolve us of the excess of our transgressions and bring us to the light of righteousness out of the darkness of error. The poet has excellently put it, when he said,

> People suspect us of an evil thing
> And with their hearts and souls in that persist.
> Let us fulfill their thought and free them from their sin.
> Against us, then repent and afterwards desist."

Then she gave him oaths and assurances, swearing by the First Cause, that this thing will take place between them only once, even though her desire for him may drive her to perdition and death. He went with her, on this condition, to her bedroom, in order that she might quench the fire of her lust, saying, "There is no power and no strength save in God the Almighty, the Magnificent." He opened his trousers, feeling extremely embarrassed and shedding tears in fear. She smiled, took him with her to bed, and said, "After tonight, you will experience nothing offensive again." Then she bent over him, kissing and embracing him and wrapping her leg around his, and said to him, "Put your hand between my thighs and touch the fellow, so that it may get up from prostration." He wept and said, "I am not good at this sort of thing." But she said, "By my life, if you obey me, there will be something in it for you." So he put out his hand with trepidation and found her thighs softer than butter and finer than silk and, feeling pleasure in touching them, moved his hand all over until he came to a dome full of blessings and life and said to himself, "Perhaps this king is a hermaphrodite, being neither male nor female." So he said to her, "O King, you don't seem to have a tool like other men. What then moved you to carry on like this?" When Princess Budur heard this, she laughed until she fell on her back and said, "O my darling, how quickly you have forgotten the nights we spent together!" Then she revealed herself to him, and he recognized her as his wife Princess Budur, the daughter of King Ghaiur, Lord of the Islands and the Seas. So he embraced her, and she embraced him and he kissed her, and she kissed him, and they made love, celebrating with the words of the poet,

> When a soft, curving shape led him to my embrace,
> As if he were by a thick vine entwined
> And with its softness softened his hard heart,
> He yielded, though at first he had declined.
> Fearing detection by the watchful spies.
> He came with caution's armor, the spy to defeat,
> His waist complaining of his hips that weighed,
> As heavy as a camel's load, upon his feet.
> He came, with the sword of his glances girt
> And clad with the mail of his dusky hair.
> His fragrance brought me news of his approach,
> And like a bird uncaged, I flew to meet him there.
> I laid my cheeks for his sandals to tread,
> And their dust, salve-like, healed my ailing eye.
> I hugged him and I raised the banner of our love
> And loosed the knot of my luck gone awry
> And held festivities, and in reply
> Delight came unalloyed and crystalline.
> The moon handseled the mouth with star-like teeth,
> Like bubbles dancing on the face of wine.
> I tasted in the prayer niche of delight
> What would make even a sinner repent.
> I swear by the signs of his glorious face
> That I'll never forget the sign God sent.

Then Princess Budur related to Qamar al-Zaman all that had happened to her from beginning to end, and he did likewise. Then he began to remonstrate with her, asking, "What made you treat me like this tonight?" She replied, "Do not reproach me, for I only did it in jest, to increase the pleasure and joy."

When it was morning and the sun shone, she sent for King Armanus, the father of Princess Hayat al-Nufus, and acquainted him with the truth of the case and told him that she was the wife of Qamar al-Zaman. She related to him their story and the cause of their separation from each other and informed him that his daughter Hayat al-Nufus was still a virgin. When Armanus, King of the Ebony Islands, heard the story of Princess Budur, the daughter of King Ghaiur, he marveled exceedingly and ordered that it be written in letters of gold. Then he turned to Qamar al-Zaman and said, "O Prince, will you marry my daughter Hayat al-Nufus and be my son-in-law?" Qamar al-Zaman replied, "I must consult Princess Budur first, for I owe her an unlimited debt of gratitude." When he consulted her, she said, "This is an excellent idea. Marry her, and I will be her maidservant, for I am indebted to her for her kindness and help and favors, especially since we are her guests here, and her father has overwhelmed us with his generosity." When Qamar al-Zaman saw that Princess Budur favored the proposal and that she was not jealous of Hayat al-Nufus, he agreed with her on this matter and repeated to King Armanus that she favored the idea and that she would become a maidservant to Hayat al-Nufus.

When King Armanus heard this, he was overjoyed, and he went out and, sitting on the throne, summoned all the viziers and princes and chamberlains and officers of state and related to them the story of Qamar al-Zaman and his wife, Princess Budur, from beginning to end, adding that he wished to marry his daughter Hayat al-Nufus to Qamar al-Zaman and to make him king over them, instead of his wife, Princess Budur. They all replied, "Since Qamar al-Zaman is the husband of Princess Budur, who was king over us before him while we thought that she was the son-in-law of King Armanus, we all accept him as king over us, and we will always be his obedient servants." When King Armanus heard their reply, he was overjoyed, and he immediately summoned the judge and witnesses and the chief officers of the state and performed the marriage contract between Qamar al-Zaman and his daughter Hayat al-Nufus. Then he celebrated with festivities and sumptuous banquets and bestowed rich robes of honor on all the princes and high officers of the army and gave alms to the poor and needy and released many prisoners. The people rejoiced at the accession of Qamar al-Zaman, wishing him abiding prosperity, happiness, honor, and renown. As soon as Qamar al-Zaman became king, he repealed the customs duties and released the rest of the prisoners. He conducted himself in a praiseworthy way toward his people and lived with his wives in happiness and delight and fidelity and cheerfulness, spending one night with each in turn. He lived in this manner for a long time. His worries and sorrows were gone, and he forgot his father King Shahraman and the sway and the privilege he enjoyed with him.

The Adventures of Qamar al-Zaman's Two Sons, Amjad and As'ad

In time, God the Almighty blessed Qamar al-Zaman with two sons by his two wives, and they were like two shining moons. The elder was the son of Queen Budur, and his name was Prince Amjad; and the younger was the son of Queen Hayat al-Nufus, and his name was Prince As'ad, and he was more handsome than his brother. They were brought up with all love and care, taught fine manners, and instructed in penmanship and science and the arts of government and horsemanship until they attained perfection and the height of beauty and grace by the time they were seventeen, so that both men and women were ravished by their charms. They grew up together, always in each other's company, eating together and drinking together and never separating from each other even for an hour, and all the people envied them their togetherness. When they reached manhood and became accomplished men, their father, whenever he went on a journey, seated them in turn in the audience hall, where each of them judged among the people for one day at a time.

It happened, as unalterable fate and divine decree would have it, that Queen Budur fell in love with As'ad, son of Queen Hayat al-Nufus, and the latter fell in love with Amjad, son of Queen Budur. Each of them used to play with the other's son, kissing him and pressing him to her bosom, while his mother thought that this was out of motherly love, until the two women were madly in love, and passion took complete possession of their hearts, so that when the other's son came to see one of them, she would press him to her bosom and hang onto him, wishing that he would never leave. When this went on, and they found no way to fulfill their desire, they refused to eat and drink and forsook the pleasure of sleep.

One day, the king went out to hunt and trap, bidding his two sons to administer justice in his place, taking turns one day at a time, as usual. The first day was the turn of Prince Amjad, the son of Queen Budur. While he sat in judgment, ordering and forbidding, appointing and deposing, giving and denying, Queen Hayat al-Nufus took a sheet of paper and wrote him a letter in poetic prose, suing for his favor and declaring her true feeling, to the effect that she was in love with him, that she was wholly devoted to him, and that she wished to enjoy him. She wrote, "From the miserable lover, the neglected one, whose youth is wasted and whose torment is prolonged by your love. Were I to acquaint you with all my afflictions and sorrows, my ardent love, my sighs and tears, my lacerated, grieving heart, my ceaseless cares and constant sorrow, and my suffering in my burning desire, deprivation, and sadness, they would be too many to count and too hard to describe in a letter. The earth and heaven have become too narrow for me; I am on the verge of death, and I suffer the horrors of dissolution. My desire and the torment of neglect and deprivation are ever-increasing, and you are my only hope and trust. Were I to describe my yearnings, no paper would be enough." After this, she wrote the following verses,

> If I described my passion and desire
> And lovesickness and absence of all mirth,
> Nor pen nor paper would be left to use,
> Nor any ink would be found on this earth.

She then folded the letter in a piece of precious silk, heavily perfumed with musk and ambergris, and, putting her priceless hair ribbons with the letter, wrapped them up in a handkerchief and gave it to a eunuch, bidding him take it to Prince Amjad.

The eunuch went, not knowing what lay in store for him, for He who knows all secrets orders all events according to His will. When he went in to Prince Amjad, he kissed the ground before him and handed him the handkerchief with the letter. Prince Amjad took the handkerchief and, unfolding it, saw the letter, and when he read it and understood its meaning, he realized that his stepmother was unfaithful to his father, Qamar al-Zaman, and that she was intent on committing adultery. He was, therefore, very angry, and he railed at women for their conduct, exclaiming, "God curse treacherous women, who are deficient in sense and religion." Then he drew his sword and said to the eunuch, "Damn you, wicked slave, how dare you carry this adulterous message from your master's wife? By God, there is no good in you, o black without and within, o foul of face and vile of nature." Then he struck him on the neck, severing his head from his body, and, folding the letter back in the handkerchief, put it in his pocket and went to his mother and told her what had happened, cursing her and reviling her and saying, "Each one of you is worse than the other. By the Great God, did I not fear to commit a breach of good manners against my father Qamar al-Zaman and my brother Prince As'ad, I would go in to her and strike off her head, as I did to her eunuch." Then he left Queen Budur and went out, in a state of extreme rage.

When Queen Hayat al-Nufus heard what he had done to her eunuch, she reviled him and cursed him and planned treachery against him. He spent the night, sick with anger, grief, and concern, and unable to eat or drink or sleep.

The following morning, Queen Hayat al-Nufus felt ill because of what Prince Amjad had done, while his brother Prince As'ad went out and sat in the audience hall, instead of his father, to judge among the people, ordering and forbidding, appointing and deposing, and giving and bestowing, until late afternoon. At that very time, Queen Budur sent for a wily old woman and, disclosing her feelings to her, wrote a letter to Prince As'ad, her stepson, complaining in poetic language of her extreme love and desire for him. She wrote, "From her who pines with love and longing, to the best of mankind in form and disposition, him who is conceited with his beauty and complacent in his coquettishness, who disdains the one who desires him and who refuses to show favor to the submissive and abject, to him who is disdainful and indifferent, to Prince As'ad who is endowed with surpassing beauty, splendid grace, moon-bright face, shining brow, and dazzling light. This is my letter to him whose love has consumed my body and reduced me to skin and bone. My patience is at an end, and I do not know what to do. I am beset by desire and sleeplessness, and patience and sleep have deserted me. I keep a mournful vigil, burning with love and desire and racked by sickness and pain. Even though the torment of the love-stricken pleases you, may my life be ransom for yours, and may God preserve you and protect you from harm." After this, she wrote the following verses,

> Fate has decreed that I should fall in love
> With you whose charms do shine like the full moon.
> To you all eloquence, beauty, and grace,
> Above all men, are given as your boon.
> It pleased you to torment me with your love;
> Be merciful; throw me a glance again.
> Yet dying for you is indeed a bliss,
> For he who lives and loves not lives in vain.

Then she added the following,

> To you, o As'ad, I complain of love.
> Have pity on one whose heart is on fire.
> How long will longing keep toying with me,
> And sleeplessness, and worry and desire?
> O my sole wish, 'tis strange that I sometimes
> Burn in the fire, sometimes in the sea churn.
> O critic, stop railing and flee from love

Which causes the eyes to shed tears and burn.
How oft I mourn your absence with the cries of love,
But all my cries have been in vain, indeed.
You have afflicted me with hard disdain,
O you my doctor, give me what I need.
And you, critic of love, your railing cease,
Lest you be afflicted with my disease.

Then Queen Budur perfumed the letter with pungent musk and, wrapping it in her hair ribbons, which were of Iraqi silk adorned with oblong emerald pendants and jewels and pearls, gave it to the old woman and ordered her to give it to her stepson Prince As'ad.

The old woman, wishing to please her, went immediately to Prince As'ad, who was alone when she entered. She handed him the letter and waited a long time for the answer. After he read the letter and understood its meaning, he wrapped it again in the ribbons and put it in his pocket, feeling extremely angry and cursing treacherous women. He got up and, drawing his sword from its scabbard, struck the old woman on the neck, severing her head from her body. Then he went to his mother Hayat al-Nufus and found her sick in bed, as a result of what had happened to her with Prince Amjad. He cursed her and reviled her, then went to Prince Amjad and told him what had happened between him and his mother Queen Budur and how he had killed the old woman who had brought him the letter, adding, "O my brother, by God, were it not for my respect for you, I would have gone to her immediately and struck off her head." His brother Prince Amjad replied, "Brother, by God, yesterday, while I was sitting on the throne, the same thing happened to me, for your mother sent me a letter with similar intent." Then he told him all that had happened between him and Queen Hayat al-Nufus, adding, "Brother, by God, were it not for my respect for you, I would have gone to her and done to her what I had done to the eunuch." They spent the rest of the night in grief, conversing and cursing treacherous women and agreeing to keep the matter secret, lest their father Qamar al-Zaman should hear of it and kill the two women.

The following morning, the king returned with his men from the hunt and entered his palace, where, dismissing the princes, he went to see his two wives, whom he found very sick in bed. They had agreed on a plot to destroy their sons, for they had disgraced themselves before them, and feared the consequences of their error. When the king saw them in that condition, he asked, "What is the matter with you?" They got up and, kissing his hand, reversed the situation, saying to him, "O King, your two sons, who have been reared enjoying your bounty, have cheated you and disgraced you with your wives." When Qamar al-Zaman heard what his two wives said, the light turned to darkness before his eyes, and he was beside himself with rage. He said to them, "Explain this matter to me." Queen Budur said, "O King of the Age, your son As'ad has been recently sending me letters soliciting me to commit adultery, while I kept dissuading him in vain. When you went to the hunt, he attacked me, drunk and with a drawn sword in his hand, and killed my eunuch. Fearing that he would kill me as he killed my servant if I resisted, I let him rape me. If you do not avenge me on him, o King, I will kill myself with my own hand, for I do not wish to live after this foul deed." Queen Hayat al-Nufus too told him a similar story, saying, "The same thing happened to me with your son Amjad," and, weeping and wailing, added, "If you do not avenge me on him, I will tell my father, Armanus." Then they both wept bitterly before their husband.

When Qamar al-Zaman heard the same story from his two wives and saw both of them weeping, he believed that what they said was true, and he was so angry that he rushed out, intending to kill his two sons. On his way, he met his father-in-law, King Armanus, who, on hearing of his return from the hunt, had come to greet him and, seeing him fuming with anger and his sword in his hand, asked him what was the matter with him. Qamar al-Zaman told him what his sons had done, adding, "I am now going to them to kill them in the most horrible way and make a terrible example of them." His father-in-law, King Armanus, was likewise enraged against them and said, "Bravo! May God never bless them or any sons who do such deeds against their fathers. But, son, the proverb says, 'He who does not heed the end, fortune will not be his friend.' They are your sons in any event, and it is not proper for you to kill them with your own hand, lest you be tormented and regret killing them when regret will be to no avail. But send them with one of the Mamluks to kill them in the desert, out of your sight."

Qamar al-Zaman saw that his father-in-law was right. So he sheathed his sword and went back and, sitting on the throne, summoned his treasurer, who was a very old man, wise in the ways of the world and the vicissitudes of fortune. When he came in, he said to him, "Go in to my two sons, Amjad and As'ad, bind their hands firmly behind their backs, put each of them in a chest, and place them on a mule. Then ride with them into the middle of the desert, put them to death, and fill two bottles with their blood and bring them to me quickly."

The treasurer said to him, "I hear and obey," and went immediately to Amjad and As'ad, whom he met on the way, coming out from the vestibule of the palace. They had put on their richest clothes and were on their way to greet their father and congratulate him on his safe return from the hunt. When the treasurer saw them, he seized them and said, "Sons, I am a slave under orders, and your father has given me an order; will you obey it?" They said, "Yes." He then bound their hands behind their backs, put each of them in a chest, and, placing them on the back of a mule, went with them out of the city. He rode with them in the desert until near midday, when he halted in a waste and desolate spot. He dismounted and, setting down the two chests, opened them and took out Amjad and As'ad. When he looked at them, he wept bitterly for their beauty and grace. Then he drew his sword and said to them, "My lords, by God, it grieves me to harm you, but I am excused in this case, for I am a slave under orders, and your father King Qamar al-Zaman has commanded me to strike off your heads." They said to him, "O Prince, do what our father has commanded you, for we submit to what the Almighty and Glorious God has decreed for us, and you are absolved of our blood," and they embraced and bade each other farewell. Then As'ad said to the treasurer, "For God's sake, uncle, do not make me suffer the sight of my brother's anguish and agony. Kill me first, for it is easier for me." Amjad said the same thing to the treasurer and begged him to kill him first, saying, "My brother is younger than I. Don't make me suffer his anguish." And they wept bitterly, and the treasurer wept with them. Then they again embraced and bade each other farewell, saying to each other, "All this comes from the cunning of the two treacherous women, your mother and mine; it is the reward of my behavior toward your mother and yours toward mine. There is no power and no strength save in God the Almighty, the Magnificent; we are God's and to Him we return." Then As'ad embraced his brother, and sighed and recited the following verses,

> O Refuge and Comfort of the oppressed,
> Always ready to help them in their need,
> My only hope is the knock at Your door,
> And if You turn me back who then will heed?
> O You who grants when He says "Let there be,"
> Grant my wish, for all good is Yours, indeed.

When Amjad heard the weeping of his brother, he too wept, pressed him to his bosom, and recited the following verses,

> O You, whose blessings have been more than one,
> Whose ample favors on me countless stand,
> I have not suffered any blow of fate,
> But You have come to take me by the hand.

Then he said to the treasurer, "I beg you, in the name of the one Lord, the Omnipotent, the Protector, to kill me before my brother

As'ad and put an end to my anguish." But As'ad wept and said, "No, I will die first." Then Amjad said, "Let us embrace each other, so that the sword may kill us both at one stroke." They embraced, face to face, and clung to each other, while the treasurer bound them with ropes, as he wept. Then he drew his sword and said, "By God, my lords, it grieves me to kill you. Do you have any last wish for me to fulfill or any commission to carry out or any message to convey?" Amjad replied, "We do not have any wish, except to ask you to place me above my brother As'ad, so that the blow may fall on me first. When you finish killing us and return to the king, and he asks you, 'What did you hear them say before they died?' say to him, 'Your two sons salute you and say that you do not know whether they are guilty or innocent and that you have killed them without investigating their case or ascertaining their guilt.' Then repeat to him the following verses,

> Women are devils, made to make us rue.
> May God protect us and their harm forestall.
> They are the cause of mischief among men
> And all evil on earth and in heaven, yes all.

Amjad added, "This is all we desire of you, except that you be patient with us while I recite a few lines to my brother." Then he recited the following verses,

> We have examples in the kings
> Who have before us gone.
> How many men, both great and small,
> Have that same journey done.

When the treasurer heard this, he wept bitterly until his beard was drenched with tears, while As'ad's eyes filled with tears, as he recited the following verses,

> Fate, after they are gone, afflicts us with their trace,
> And weeping is not for the shape but soul.
> May God protect us all from wayward fate,
> And may the law of change defy its sad control.
> It wreaked its malice on ibn-Zubair,
> Respecting not his refuge in the Holy Place.
> Would that, when it ransomed 'Umru with Kharija,
> It did 'Ali with anyone replace.

And with his tears flowing down his cheeks, As'ad recited the following verses,

> Perfidious fortune's nature is to cheat,
> Play dirty tricks, and take men by surprise.

The false mirage is but her shining teeth;
The gloomy night is the kohl of her eyes.
My offense against her (may she be cursed)
Is the sword's when the hero from the battle flies.

Then he sighed deeply and recited the following verses,

O you who seek this vile world, you should know
It is a snare of death and pit of woe,
A home which, if it makes one laugh today,
Will make him weep tomorrow. Let it to Hell go.
Its raids are endless, its prisoner
Can never free himself e'en if he death bestride.
How many glory in its vanities
Until they swell with overweening pride;
Then it turns against them and stabs to pay them back.
Its deadly blows are sudden, when they come,
Though time may seem slow and waiting fate slack.
Then prize your life, lest it should in this world
Pass uselessly, a lie and empty show,
And sever all relation with the world,
And you will find truth and peace here below.

When As'ad finished reciting the verses, he embraced his brother so hard that they seemed to be one body, and the treasurer drew his sword and was about to strike them, when his horse started and fled into the desert. It was a horse worth one thousand dinars, with a saddle worth a great sum of money. So the treasurer threw down his sword and went after his horse. He kept running after him, until the horse entered a wood and made his way into the middle of it, and he followed him there, trying to catch him. Then the horse began to strike the ground and raise the dust with his hoofs, while snorting and neighing in his fury, for as it happened there was in this wood a ferocious, hideous lion, with blazing eyes and a grim, terrifying look. The treasurer turned and saw the lion coming toward him, with no way to escape and no sword to fight with. He said to himself, "There is no power and no strength save in God the Almighty, the Magnificent. I have fallen in this predicament only because of my sin against Amjad and As'ad. This journey has been unfortunate from the start."

Meanwhile, the heat became intense for Amjad and As'ad, and they were so thirsty that their tongues hung out, and they cried for relief, but there was no one to relieve them. They said, "We wish that we were put to death and relieved of this torment. We wonder where the horse has gone, and where the treasurer has followed him and left us bound. Had he come back to us and killed us, it would have been easier for us than this torment." As'ad said, "Brother, be patient, and the relief of the Almighty and Glorious God will come to us, for the horse did not run away, save out of kindness to us, and no harm has befallen us save this thirst." Then he shook himself and strained right and left until he freed first himself from the bonds; then he freed his brother. He took the treasurer's sword and said to his brother, "By God, we will not depart from here until we find out what has happened to the treasurer." So they began to follow his tracks, which led them to the wood, and they said to one another, "The horse and the treasurer have not gone beyond this wood." As'ad said to his brother, "Wait here, while I enter the wood and search it." But Amjad replied, "I will not let you enter it alone. We will both go in, so that if we escape safely, we shall escape together, and if we perish, we shall perish together." So the two entered and found the lion standing over the treasurer, who lay beneath him like a sparrow, raising his hands to heaven and supplicating God. When Amjad saw him, he took the sword and, rushing to the lion, struck him between the eyes and killed him.

The lion fell to the ground, and the treasurer got up in amazement and, when he saw Amjad and As'ad, the sons of his master, standing there, he threw himself at their feet and said to them, "By God, my lords, it is wrong of me to put you to death; may the man who would kill you perish. I will give my life for you." He then came up immediately to them, embraced them, and asked them how they managed to loosen their bonds and come to him. They told him that they had become thirsty, that one of them had loosened his bonds and freed the other, because of the purity of their hearts, and that they had followed his tracks until they found him. When he heard this, he thanked them for their deed and went with them out of the wood, where they said to him, "O Uncle, do our father's bidding." But he replied, "God forbid that I should harm you. I will take your clothes and clothe you with mine. Then I will fill two bottles with the lion's blood, return to the king, and tell him that I have put you to death. As for you, fare over the lands, for God's earth is wide. It will be hard for me to part from you, my lords!" All of them wept, and the two young men took off their clothes and put on his. Then he tied up the clothes of each in a wrapper and, filling two bottles with the lion's blood, put the two wrappers before him on the horse, bade them farewell, and headed back to the city.

He rode until he went in to the king and kissed the ground before him. The king saw his pale face and rejoiced, thinking that it was because of the murder of his sons, although in truth it was because of the adventure with the lion. He asked him, "Have you done your task?" The treasurer replied, "Yes, my lord," and gave him the two bundles of clothes, and the two bottles of blood. Then the king asked him, "What did you see in their conduct, and did they charge you with anything?" The treasurer replied, "I found them patient and resigned to their fate. They said to me, 'Our father is not to blame. Give him our salutation and tell him that we absolve him of our murder and our blood, but we charge you to repeat to him these lines,

> Women are devils, made to make us rue.
> May God protect us, and their harm forestall.
> They are the cause of mischief among men
> And all evil on earth and in heaven, yes all.' "

When the king heard what the treasurer said, he bowed his head for a long time and knew that this meant that they had been put to death unjustly. Then reflecting on the perfidy of women and the calamities they cause, he opened the two bundles and began to turn over his son's clothes and weep. Soon, he found in As'ad's pocket a letter in the handwriting of his wife Budur, together with her hair ribbons. He unfolded the letter, read it, and, understanding its meaning, realized that his son As'ad had been wronged. Then he found in Amjad's pocket a letter in the handwriting of his wife Hayat al-Nufus, together with her hair ribbons. He unfolded the letter, read it, and realized that he too had been wronged. He wrung his hands and said, "There is no power and no strength save in God the Almighty, the Magnificent. I have put my two sons to death unjustly," and he began to beat his face and cry out, "O my sons! O my eternal grief!" Then he ordered a monument to be built, with two tombs, each inscribed with the name of his son, and he called the monument the House of Sorrows. There, he threw himself on Amjad's tomb, weeping and groaning and lamenting, and recited the following verses,

> O moon that has vanished beneath the earth,
> And for whose loss, the stars of heaven weep,
> O bough, after whose loss, no one his eyes
> Will on his graceful, curving body keep.
> I bereft my eyes of you, jealous of myself,
> And I'll never see you again until Doomsday.
> Now my eyes are sleepless and full of tears,
> Mourning your absence since you went away.

Then he threw himself on As'ad's tomb, crying, lamenting, and shedding tears, and recited the following verses,

> How I have wished to share sad death with you,
> But God has willed events against my will.
> My grief makes all I see black in my eyes
> And blots out their black pupils, as with tears they fill.

I weep with ceaseless tears and ulcered heart,
Infected with my grief, and rant and rave.
How hard it is for me to see you lie,
Where lie alike both nobleman and knave.

Then he abandoned his friends and companions and forsook his women and all those dear to him, secluding himself in the House of Sorrows, where he spent his time weeping for his sons.

Meanwhile, Amjad and As'ad walked in the desert for a whole month, eating of the plants of the earth and drinking of the rain pools, until they came to a sprawling mountain of black stone where the road divided into two, one fork going over the mountain and the other passing through it. They took the former and followed it for five days, but saw no end to it and became very tired, for they were not used to walking in mountains or anywhere else. At last, despairing of coming to the end of the road, they went back and took the road that passed through the mountain. They followed it all that day till nightfall, at which time, As'ad, feeling exhausted from walking, said to his brother, "O my brother, I cannot go any further, for I am very weak." Amjad replied, "O my brother, hang on, for God may send us relief." So they walked on for part of the night, until As'ad, becoming totally exhausted, said, "O my brother, I am worn out from walking," and fell to the ground, weeping. So Amjad carried him and went on, walking for a while and sitting to rest for a while, until dawn, when they reached the mountaintop and found a stream of running water coming out of a spring, beside which stood a pomegranate tree and a prayer niche. They could hardly believe their eyes. They sat by the spring and, having drunk of its water and eaten some pomegranates from that tree, they slept there until it was broad daylight. Then after washing themselves at the spring and eating some pomegranates, they slept again until late afternoon. They wanted to continue their journey, but As'ad was unable to proceed because his feet were swollen. So they remained there for three days until he rested. Then they proceeded and journeyed over the mountain for many days, feeling parched with thirst, until they saw a city in the distance.

When they saw the city, they rejoiced and walked toward it, and when they came near it, they thanked the Almighty God, and Amjad said to As'ad, "Brother, sit here, while I go to this city and find out more about it, so that we may know where we are in God's wide world and what lands we have traversed in crossing this mountain. Had we not journeyed through it, we would not have reached this city in a whole year. God be praised for our safety." But As'ad replied, "By God, brother, none shall go to this city but myself. I will offer myself for you; besides, if you leave me and go down I will worry about you, and I cannot bear your absence from me." Amjad said, "Go then, but do not tarry."

As'ad descended from the mountain, taking some money with him, and left his brother to wait for him. He walked at the foot of the mountain until he entered the city. As he passed through its streets, he met a very old man, with a long beard parted in two and flowing down on his breast. He carried a walking staff in his hand and was richly dressed, with a big red turban on his head. When As'ad saw him, he wondered at his dress and his appearance and, advancing toward him, saluted him and asked, "Sir, which is the way to the market?" When the old man heard his question, he smiled in his face and said, "Son, you seem to be a stranger." As'ad replied, "Yes, uncle, I am a stranger." The old man said, "Son, your coming brings cheer to our country and your absence, sadness to your home and family. What do you want from the market?" As'ad replied, "Uncle, I have a brother whom I have left on the mountain, and we have been journeying for three months from a distant country until we approached this city. So I came here to buy some food and take it back to my brother, so that we may nourish ourselves." The old man said, "O my son, rejoice in your good fortune, for today I am having a banquet with many guests, and I have prepared the finest and the most delicious dishes that the heart desires. Will you come with me to my place, so that I may give you what you desire, without charging you for it. I will also tell you about this city. God be praised, son, that it was I who have met you and not someone else." As'ad replied, "As you wish, but hurry, for my brother is waiting and wondering about me."

The old man took As'ad by the hand, smiling in his face and saying to him, "Glory be to Him who has saved you from the people of this city." Then he walked with him through a narrow alley until they came to a spacious house. When they entered, As'ad found himself in a hall in which were forty very old men seated in a ring around a lighted fire, to which they were doing worship and prostrating themselves. When he saw this, he shuddered, though he did not know what they were. Then the old man said to the company, "O Elders of the Fire, what a blessed day this is." And called out, "O Ghadban!" And in came a black slave, with a grim face, flat nose, stooping figure, and hideous shape. The old man signaled to the slave, who bound As'ad immediately. Then he said to him, "Take him to the underground chamber, and leave him there, and tell that slave-girl so and so to torture him day and night and to give him a loaf of bread and a cup of brackish water morning and evening." The slave took him to the underground chamber, while the old men said to each other, "When the day of the Fire Festival comes, we will sacrifice him on the mountain as an offering to propitiate the Fire." Soon the slave-girl went down to him and beat him severely until he bled from every limb and fainted. Then she set at his head a loaf of bread and a cup of brackish water and left.

In the middle of the night, As'ad came to himself, and found himself bound and smarting from the beating, and he wept bitterly, and when he recalled his former state of power and dominion and privilege and happiness, he lamented, sighed, and recited the following verses,

> Stop by the ruins of our former home,
> And ask them to inform you of your fate.
> Fortune, the separator, has severed our loves,
> Yet the spite of our foes does not abate.
> A mean woman has tortured me with whips,
> Feeling against me full of spite and hate.
> May our good Lord unite us two again,
> Protect us and our foes annihilate.

Then he groped behind his head and, finding a loaf of bread and a cup of brackish water, ate a piece to stay his hunger and drank a little of the water, and he remained sleepless all night because of the swarms of bugs and lice. When it was morning, the slave-girl came down to him again and took off his clothes, which were drenched with blood and stuck to him, so that his skin came off with them. He screamed and moaned and cried out, "O Lord, if this is your pleasure, increase it upon me. You are not unmindful of him who has oppressed me; avenge me on him!" Then he groaned and recited the following verses,

> O take your mind off your present affairs,
> And place your trust in the Almighty's will
> For a hardship may ease or may get worse,
> And an ultimate good may come from present ill.
> God does what He pleases; gainsay Him not,
> And good fortune will be yours, and your pain, forgot.

As soon as As'ad finished reciting these verses, the slave-girl fell on him with blows until he fainted, and, throwing him a loaf of bread and a cup of brackish water, departed and left him alone, bleeding from every limb. He lay bound in chains, far from his friends, feeling sad and lonely, and yearning for his brother and his former privileged life. He lamented, groaned, wept, and recited the following verses,

> Slow down, o fate, how long will you oppress
> Me wrongly and trample upon my friends!
> Is it not time that your hard heart of stone
> Pities me and my long estrangement ends?

You have brought ruin on my friends and me
And made my foes exult over my plight,
My sad estrangement and my loneliness.
And my longing, rejoicing at the sight.
My loss of friends was not enough for them,
Nor my sore eyes, nor my torment and grief,
But I must languish in a narrow cell,
Where gnawing my hands is my sole relief
And tears that fall as if from rain-charged clouds
And ardent passion like a raging fire
And memories and yearnings and sad thoughts
And sobs and sighs and groans and galled desire.
I suffer longing and destroying grief,
Fallen to raging passion a weak prey,
Without a soul that, pitying my plight,
To ease my pain visits of mercy pay.
Is there a true friend with a tender heart
To pity my torments and lack of sleep
And share my grief and with me the long vigil keep?
My endless torments make endless my night,
As I burn with anxiety and care.
The bugs and flies enjoy my blood like wine,
Poured by a sweet-mouthed, slender-waisted fair.
The crawling lice play with my body now,
As with an orphan's goods a godless judge does play.
My house is but a cell three cubits wide,
Wherein in chains I suffer night and day,
My tears my wine, chains music, thoughts dessert,
And cares the bed on which myself I lay.

When he finished reciting his poem, he lamented, groaned, and wept, longing for his brother and former life.

Meanwhile, his brother Amjad waited for him till noon, and when he failed to return, he felt the pangs of separation, his heart fluttered, and he wept bitterly, exclaiming, "Ah, my grief! I was terribly worried that we would be separated." Then he descended from the mountain, with the tears running down his cheeks, entered the city, and went to the market. There, he asked the people the name of the city, and they told him that it was called the City of the Magians and that its inhabitants worship the Fire, instead of the Omnipotent King. Then he inquired about the City of Ebony, and they told him that it was a year's journey by land and six months by sea and that its former king was Armanus who married his daughter to a man called Qamar al-Zaman and made him king in his place, adding that the new king was just, loyal, munificent, and generous. When Amjad heard his father's name, he yearned for him, and he lamented and groaned and wept. Not knowing where to go, he bought something to eat and sat in a secluded place, but when he was about to eat, he recalled his brother and began to weep and ate only a little morsel to stay his stomach. Then he got up and walked in the city, seeking news of his brother, until he saw a Muslim tailor sitting in his shop. He sat down with him and told him his story, and the tailor said, "If he has fallen into the hands of one of the Magians, you are not likely to see him again. Yet God may reunite you with him. In the meantime, brother, will you stay in my house?" Amjad replied, "Yes," and the tailor was very pleased. So Amjad stayed with him for some time, while the tailor consoled him, encouraged him, and taught him his craft until he became expert at it.

One day, he went to the seashore and washed his clothes. Then he entered the bath and, putting on clean clothes, went out and walked in the streets to enjoy the sights of the city. Soon, he found himself face to face with a girl of unequaled beauty, elegance, and grace. When she saw him, she lifted her veil and, winking to him flirtatiously, recited the following verses:

> I saw you coming and cast down my eyes,
> O slender one, as if you were the sun.
> You are the fairest of all living men
> And fairer still as time goes by, o paragon!
> If beauty were divided into fifths,
> One part would be Joseph's, or less than one;
> The rest would be your very own. May all
> Men be your ransom, yes, all, saving none.

When he heard that, he was pleased and felt attracted to her, for love stirred within him. So he winked back to her and recited the following verses:

> Above the cheek-rose are the deadly thorns
> Of her lashes; who will then touch it dare?
> Since the mere look unleashed a deadly war,
> To touch that rose I tremble and forebear.
> Tell her the tyrant, who tempts with her charms,
> She would have been fairer, had she been fair.
> The lifting of the veil is safer for her charms,
> For she provokes the more when she the veil does wear.
> The eye looks at the sun, when veiled with mist,
> But cannot look at it when it is bare.
> The honey is protected by the bees themselves;

So ask the camp guards why they guard her there.
If killing me is what they wish, let them
Withdraw and leave us to our own affair.
Their swords are not deadlier than the fair with the mole,
When she with her looks does my heart ensnare.

When she heard this, she sighed deeply and, winking to him, recited the following verses,

'Tis you who have resorted to disdain,
Not I. Then give me love, for fulfillment is near.
O you, whose shining brow is the daylight,
Whose black locks made therein the night inhere,
You have seduced me as an idol does,
And have ensnared me as you did of yore.
No wonder then that my heart with passion should burn,
For fire is the due of those whom idols adore.
You sell someone like me for nothing, without price;
If you must sell, exact a price and more.

When Amjad heard this, he said to her, "Will you come to my place, or shall I go with you to yours?" She bowed her head bashfully and repeated the words of the Almighty, "Men shall have the preeminence over women, for God has preferred these over those." Amjad understood that she wished to go with him, and felt obliged to find a place, for he was too embarrassed to take her to the tailor's house. He walked ahead of her, while she followed him from street to street and from place to place until she got tired and asked, "O my lord, where is your house?" He replied, "Not very far from here." Then he turned aside with her into a nice street and walked until he came to the end of it and found that it was a dead end. He said to himself, "There is no power and no strength save in God the Almighty, the Magnificent." He looked up toward the upper end of the street and saw a large closed door with two benches in front. So he sat on one bench, and she sat on the other and asked him, "My lord, what are you waiting for?" He bowed his head for a while, then he raised it and said, "I am waiting for my Mamluk who has the key, for I asked him to prepare for me food and drink and the wine accoutrements by the time I come out of the bath." Then he said to himself, "Maybe she will get tired of waiting and go on her way, leaving me here."

But she waited a while and said, "My lord, your Mamluk is taking a long time, while we are waiting here in the street." So saying, she took a stone and went up to the lock. He said to her, "Don't be hasty; be patient until he comes." But she paid no attention to him and, striking the lock with the stone, broke it in half, and the door opened. He said

to her, "What possessed you to do this?" She replied, "My lord, what
harm is done? Is not this your house?" He said, "Yes, but there was no
need to break the lock." Then she entered the house, leaving Amjad
confounded, not knowing what to do for fear of the people of the
house. She said to him, "Why don't you come in, o my lord, o light of
my eyes and darling of my heart?" He replied, "I hear and obey. It is
just that my Mamluk is already late, and I don't know whether he has
done what I asked him to do or not." He followed her, in a state of
extreme anxiety, fearing the people of the house, and found himself
in a handsome hall furnished with cupboards and benches covered
with silk and brocade. It was surrounded by four recessed rooms with
raised floors, and in the middle stood a costly fountain, by which were
arranged dishes set with precious stones and filled with fruits and aro-
matic flowers, as well as wine cups and a candlestick holding a candle. The place was full of chests and precious stuffs. There were chairs
set in it, and on every chair there was a wrapping cloth, and on each
cloth there was a purse full of pieces of gold. The house attested to the
prosperity of its owner, for its floor was paved with marble.

When Amjad saw all this, he was confounded and said to himself, "I
am a lost man. We are God's and to God we return." As for the girl,
when she saw the place, she was overjoyed and said to him, "By God,
my lord, your Mamluk has not failed you, for he has swept the place,
cooked the food, and prepared the fruits. Indeed, I come at the best of
times." But he paid no attention to her, for he was absentminded from
worry, fearing the people of the house. She said to him, "My lord, why
are you standing like this?" Then she sighed and, giving him a kiss
that resounded like the cracking of a walnut, said, "My lord, if you
have a rendezvous with another woman, I will gird myself and serve
her." Amjad laughed in anger and sat down, panting and saying to
himself, "What a wretched death I will face when the owner of the
house returns!" The girl sat beside him, jesting and laughing, while he
sat anxious and frowning, thinking a thousand thoughts and saying to
himself, "The owner of this house will certainly come, and what shall
I say to him? He will kill me without a doubt." Soon she rose and,
tucking up her sleeves, took a table, set on it some food, and began to
eat, saying to Amjad, "Eat, my lord." He approached the table to eat,
but he had no appetite and kept looking toward the door until the girl
ate her fill. Then she removed the table and, setting on the dessert,
began to eat of the dried fruits. Then she brought the wine service
and, opening the jar, filled a cup and gave it to Amjad, who took it,
saying to himself, "Alas, what will happen to me if the owner of the
house comes and sees me?"

He sat with the cup in his hand and his eyes fixed on the door when
suddenly the owner of the house came in. He was a Mamluk, one of

the prominent men of the city, for he was Master of the Horse to the king. He had that hall prepared for his private pleasure, ready to entertain whomever he wished. That day, he had invited a boy friend with whom he was in love and had prepared the entertainment for him. The name of this Mamluk was Bahadir. He was generous, beneficent, charitable, and obliging.

When he came in and saw the hall door open, he approached it slowly and quietly and, sticking his head in, saw Amjad and the girl with the dish of fruits and the wine service before them. At that moment, Amjad was holding the wine cup, with his eyes fixed on the door, and when his eyes met Bahadir's, he turned pale and began to tremble. Bahadir, seeing him pale and shaken, put his finger on his lip and signaled, meaning, "Keep silent and come to me." Amjad put the wine cup down and got up. The girl asked him, "Where are you going?" And he motioned with his head that he wished to urinate and went into the corridor, barefooted. When he saw Bahadir, he knew that he was the owner of the house; so he hurried to him and, kissing his hands, said to him, "For God's sake, my lord, before you hurt me, listen to what I have to say." Then he told him his story from beginning to end, from the time he was forced to leave his home and country to the time he was obliged to enter the house, saying that it was the girl who had broken the lock, entered the house, and done all these deeds.

When Bahadir heard Amjad's explanation and knew that he was the son of a king, he felt pity and compassion for him and said, "Listen, Amjad, and do what I tell you, and I will guarantee your safety, but if you disobey me, I will kill you." Amjad replied, "Command me as you wish. I will never disobey you, for I am deeply indebted to your manly generosity." Bahadir said, "Go back to the hall and sit down in your place calmly, and I will soon come to you. When I enter, scold me and curse me and ask me the reason for my delay till now. By the way, my name is Bahadir. Don't accept any excuses from me, but rise and beat me, and if you show pity for me, I will kill you. Go back and enjoy yourself, and whatever you desire of me will be immediately before you. Spend tonight here, as you please, and tomorrow you may go your way. I am doing this to honor you as a stranger, for I love strangers and hold myself bound to honor them." Amjad kissed his hand and went back to the hall, his fair face flushed, and as soon as he entered, he said to the girl, "O my lady, you have brought cheer to this place; this is a blessed night." She replied, "It is wonderful of you to treat me so cordially!" Amjad said, "By God, my lady, I was worried that my Mamluk Bahadir had robbed me of some jewel necklaces, each worth ten thousand dinars. When I went out now to look for them, I found them in their place. But I still don't know why he is gone till now, and I must punish him for it." The girl was satisfied with his explanation, and they drank, sported, and enjoyed themselves till near sunset.

Then Bahadir came in to them, having changed his clothes, girded himself, and put on a pair of shoes of the kind worn by servants. He saluted, kissed the ground before Amjad, and stood with his hands clasped behind his back and his head bowed down, as one acknowl- edging his guilt. Amjad looked at him angrily and asked, "Why are you so late, you most wretched slave?" Bahadir replied, "O my lord, I was busy washing my clothes and did not know that you were here, for our appointment was for the evening, not for the daytime." Amjad shouted at him, saying, "You are lying, you most wretched slave. By God, I must beat you." Then he rose and, laying Bahadir on the floor, took a stick and beat him gently. But the girl rose, and, snatching the stick from Amjad's hand, fell on Bahadir with such hard blows that the tears ran from his eyes, and he ground his teeth together and cried for help, while Amjad cried out to her, saying, "Stop it," and she replied, "Let me satisfy my anger at him." At last, Amjad snatched the stick from her and pushed her away from Bahadir, who got up and, wiping off his tears, stood there for some time, waiting on them. Then he swept the hall and lighted the lamps, and every time he went in and out, the girl reviled him and cursed him, while Amjad said to her angrily, "For God's sake, leave my servant alone, for he is not used to such a treatment."

They continued to eat and drink, while Bahadir waited on them until it was midnight, and being exhausted from the work and the beating he fell asleep, snoring and snorting, in the middle of the hall. The girl, who was intoxicated by then, said to Amjad, "Get up, take the sword hanging there, and cut off this slave's head. If you don't, I will kill you." He asked her, "Why do you wish to kill my slave?" She replied, "Our delight will not be complete without his death. If you don't kill him, I will do it myself." Amjad said, "For God's sake, don't do it." Saying, "I must," she took the sword and, drawing it, approached Bahadir, intending to kill him, but Amjad said to himself, "This man has been good to us, sheltered us, done us a favor, and made himself my servant. How can I reward him by killing him? This shall never be." Then he said to the girl, "If my slave must be killed, it is more fitting that I kill him, rather than you." Then he took the sword from her and, raising his hand, struck her on the neck and sev- ered her head from her body. The head fell on Bahadir, who awoke and, sitting up, saw Amjad standing with the bloodstained sword in his hand and the girl lying dead. He asked Amjad for an explanation, and he told him what had happened, adding, "She insisted on killing you, and this is her reward." Bahadir rose and, kissing Amjad's head, said, "I wish that you had forgiven her. Now there is nothing to be done but to get her out of here immediately, before daylight." Then he girded himself, wrapped the girl in a cloak and, placing her in a basket, carried her and said to Amjad, "You are a stranger here, and you don't know anyone. Wait for me here, and if I return, I will do you a great service, and I will endeavor to find out what happened to your brother. If I don't return by sunrise, assume that I am finished and that is the end of it, except that this house shall be yours with all the wealth and stuffs it contains."

He carried the basket out of the hall and, passing through the market streets, took the way leading to the sea, where he planned to get rid of the girl. But when he was almost there, he turned and found himself surrounded by the chief of the police and his officers. When they recognized him, they wondered and, opening the basket, found the murdered girl. So they seized him and kept him in chains till the morning, when they took him with the basket to the king and reported the case to him. When the king heard their report, he was extremely angry and said to him, "Damn you, do you always kill people and throw them in the sea and take all their possessions? How many have you killed already?" But Bahadir stood with his head bowed to the ground before the king, who cried out, "Damn you, who killed this girl?" Bahadir replied, "O my lord, I killed her, and there is no power and no strength save in God the Almighty, the Magnificent." The king was enraged and ordered that he be hanged. So the executioner and the chief of the police descended with him at the king's command and paraded him through the streets and markets of the town, while a crier preceded them, bidding the people to watch the execution of Bahadir, Master of the Horse to the king.

Meanwhile, Amjad waited till sunrise, and when Bahadir failed to return, he said, "There is no power and no strength save in God the Almighty, the Magnificent. I wonder what has happened to him." While he sat wondering, he heard the crier bidding the people to watch the execution of Bahadir, who was to be hanged at noon, and when he heard this, he wept and said, "We are God's and to Him we return. He risked his own death for me, her murderer. By God, this must never be." He then went out of the house and, locking it up, made his way through the city until he came to Bahadir and, standing before the chief of the police, said to him, "O my lord, don't hang Bahadir, for he is innocent. By God, no one killed her but I."

When the chief of the police heard this, he took him, together with Bahadir, and went up to the king and told him what Amjad had said. The king looked at Amjad and asked him, "Did you kill the girl?" Amjad replied, "Yes." The king said, "Tell me why you killed her, and be truthful." Amjad said, "O king, my story is so strange and extraordinary that were it written with needles on the corners of the eye, it would be a lesson to those who wish to consider." Then he told his story to the king, acquainting him with all that had happened to him and his brother from beginning to end. The king was filled with wonder and said to Amjad, "I know now that you are not to blame. Will you become my vizier?" Amjad replied, "I hear and obey." And the king bestowed on him and on Bahadir magnificent robes of honor and gave him a handsome house, with servants and officers and whatever was needed, and allocated him stipends and supplies and charged him to search for his brother As'ad. So Amjad began to perform his duty as vizier, administering and doing justice, appointing and deposing and receiving and giving. He also sent a crier to cry his brother throughout the city, and he made proclamation in the streets and markets for many days, but he heard no news nor found any trace of As'ad.

In the meantime, the Magians continued to torture As'ad, day and night, for a whole year, until the day of their festival drew near, when the old man, whose name was Bahram, prepared himself for his voyage and fitted out a ship. Then he put As'ad in a chest and locking it, carried him to the ship. It so happened, according to fate and divine decree, that at that very time, Amjad was standing looking at the sea, and when he saw the men carrying the gear to the ship, his heart throbbed, and he ordered his pages to bring him his horse. He mounted with a company of his men, rode down to the seashore and, stopping by the Magian's ship, ordered his men to board the ship and search it. The men dismounted and searched the entire ship but found nothing and returned and told him. So he mounted again and rode back to his house, feeling depressed. As he entered, he happened to glance at the wall and saw written there the following verses,

> Dear ones, if you are absent from my sight,
> Your presence in my heart and thought I keep.
> You went away and left me languishing
> And robbed my eyes of sleep and went to sleep.

When he read these verses, he recalled his brother and wept.

Meanwhile, Bahram the Magian embarked in the ship and called out to the sailors, ordering them to hurry and loosen the sails. They did so and departed, and they continued to sail many days and nights, and every other day, Bahram took As'ad out and gave him a little food and water until they drew near the Mountain of Fire, when suddenly a wind blew against them, and the sea became boisterous, causing them to stray from their course until they came to a city built on the seashore, with a castle with windows overlooking the sea. The ruler of that city was a woman called Queen Marjana. The captain of the ship said to Bahram, "Master, we have strayed from our course, and we must enter this city to rest, and after that, let God do what He wills." Bahram said to him, "This is an excellent idea, and I will act according to it." The captain asked, "If the queen sends to inquire, what shall we tell her?" Bahram replied, "I have this Muslim with us. So we will dress him in the attire of Mamluks and take him with us, and when she sees him, she will think him to be a Mamluk, and I will say to her that I am an importer and trader in Mamluks and that I had with me many Mamluks, but I have sold them all, except this one." The captain replied, "This is a good idea."

Soon, they reached the city and slackened the sails, and as soon as they cast anchor, Queen Marjana came down with her guards and, stopping by the ship, called out to the captain, who disembarked and kissed the ground before her. She asked him, "What do you carry in your ship, and whom do you have with you?" He replied, "O Queen of the Age, I have with me a merchant who deals in slaves." She said, "Bring him to me," and Bahram came out, followed by As'ad, dressed in the garb of a Mamluk, and when Bahram came up to her, he kissed the ground before her. She asked him, "What is your business?" And he replied, "I am a slave dealer." Then she looked at As'ad, thinking him to be a Mamluk, and asked him, "What is your name?" And he replied with a voice choking with tears, "My name is As'ad." She felt tenderness toward him and asked, "Can you write?" He replied, "Yes." Then she gave him a pen and a sheet of paper and said, "Write something for me to see." So he wrote the following verses,

> How can God's creature alter His decree?
> How can he respite from his sentence get?
> He bound him, cast him in the sea, and said,
> "Beware, beware, don't let yourself get wet."

When she read this, she felt compassion for him and said to Bahram, "Sell him to me." He replied, "O my lady, I cannot sell him, for I have sold all my slaves except this one." Queen Marjana said, "I will certainly take him, either by sale or as a gift." Bahram said, "I will neither sell him nor give him as a gift." But she seized As'ad and took him up to the castle. Then she sent Bahram a message, saying, "If you don't sail from our city tonight, I will confiscate your goods and destroy your ship." When he received the message, he was very unhappy and said, "This voyage has been unfortunate." Then he prepared himself and, taking whatever he needed, waited for the night to proceed on his voyage, and said to the sailors, "Take provisions for yourselves and fill the water skins, so that we may set sail at the end of the night." So the sailors went about, preparing themselves for the voyage.

Meanwhile, Queen Marjana took As'ad into the castle, opened the windows overlooking the sea, and ordered her handmaids to bring food. So they brought it, and after she and As'ad ate, she ordered them to bring the wine, and they brought it, and she drank with As'ad. And the Almighty and Glorious God filled her heart with love for As'ad, and she began to fill the cup and give it to him to drink until he was intoxicated. Soon, he rose and went out of the hall, wishing to relieve himself, and, seeing a door open, he went through and walked until he came to a large garden, full of fruits and flowers. He sat under a tree and relieved himself. Then he went up to a fountain in the garden, lay there on his back and, lulled by the breeze, slept into the night.

Meanwhile, when it was night, Bahram called out to the sailors, saying, "Loosen the sails, and let us depart." They replied, "We hear and obey, but wait until we fill our water skins." They disembarked with the water skins and went around the castle and, finding nothing but the garden walls, they climbed over and descended into the garden and followed the tracks that led to the fountain. When they reached it, they found As'ad lying on his back, and when they recognized him, they rejoiced. So they carried him, after they filled their water skins and, jumping with him over the wall, hurried back to Bahram the Magian and said to him, "We bring you good news, which is cause for celebration with drums and trumpets, for you have attained your wish and fulfilled your desire; we have found your captive whom Queen Marjana took from you by force, and we have brought him with us." And they threw As'ad down before him. When Bahram saw him, his heart leapt with joy, and he was pleased and relieved. Then he rewarded the sailors and ordered them to loosen the sails quickly. So they did so, and heading for the Mountain of Fire, they sailed till the morning.

Meanwhile, after As'ad went down, Queen Marjana waited for him for some time, and when he did not return, she proceeded to search for him but did not find him. Then she lighted the candles and ordered her handmaids to search for him. Then she herself went down, and when she saw the garden door open, she knew that he had gone there. So she went into the garden and, finding his slippers lying by the fountain, searched every part of the garden till the morning, but found no sign of him. Then she inquired about the ship and was told that it had set sail during the first third of the night. So she realized that the sailors had taken him with them, and this grieved her and made her extremely angry. She ordered that ten great ships be made ready immediately and, preparing herself for battle, embarked in one of them, with her troops carrying their fine gear and their weapons. They loosened the sails, and she said to the captains, "If you overtake the Magian's ship, I will give you robes of honor and money, but if you don't, I will kill you all." So the seamen were filled with hope and great fear.

They sailed for three days and nights until, on the fourth day, they sighted the ship of Bahram the Magian, and before the day ended, they had it surrounded. At that time, Bahram had taken As'ad out and was beating and torturing him, while As'ad, who was in great pain, cried out for help and relief, but there was no one to help him or relieve him. Soon, Bahram happened to look up and saw that the ships had surrounded his, as the white of the eye surrounds its black. He was certain of destruction, and he sighed and exclaimed, "Damn you, As'ad, this is all your doing." Then he took him by the hand and ordered the sailors to throw him into the sea, saying, "By God, I will kill you before I die." The sailors took him by his hands and feet and threw him into the middle of the sea. But the Almighty and Glorious God, desiring to save him and prolong his life, caused him to rise again, and he beat with his hands and feet until God helped him and sent him relief, and the waves bore him away from the Magian's ship and cast him on the shore. He landed, hardly believing in his escape, and, taking off his clothes, he wrung them and spread them out to dry and sat naked, weeping over his captivity and his misfortunes and repeating the following verses,

> O God, my patience and resources fail me now,
> Seized by depression, as I try in vain.
> O Lord of lords, to whom should a wretched
> Like me, but to his Mighty Lord complain?

Then he rose and, putting on his clothes, began to wander, not knowing where he was coming or going. He walked day and night, eating of the plants of the earth and the fruits of the trees and drinking the water of the streams, until he came in sight of a city. He rejoiced and hurried toward it, but before he could reach it, the night descended, and the gate was shut. As it happened, this was the very city in which he had been a prisoner and his brother Amjad was vizier to the king. When he saw that the gate was shut, he turned back and walked in the direction of the cemetery. When he reached it, he found a tomb without a door, and he entered it and went to sleep, with his face in his sleeve.

Meanwhile, when Queen Marjana overtook Bahram the magian, he destroyed her ships by his guile and sorcery and returned safely to his city. He landed from the ship and headed directly home, feeling happy, and as fate and divine decree would have it, he walked through the cemetery and saw that the tomb in which As'ad was sleeping was open. He wondered and said to himself, "I must look into this tomb."

When he looked, he found As'ad sleeping there, with his face in his sleeve, and when he looked in his face he recognized him and exclaimed, "Are you still alive?" Then he took him to his house where he had the underground chamber prepared for the torture of Muslims. He took As'ad down to that chamber, put heavy shackles on his feet, and put him in the charge of a daughter of his named Bustana, bidding her to torture him day and night until he should die. Then he beat him severely and, locking the door on him, gave the keys to his daughter.

Bustana went down to beat him, but when she saw that he was a handsome, charming young man with a sweet face, arched eyebrows, and black eyes, she fell in love with him and asked him, "What is your name?" He replied, "My name is As'ad." She said, "May you be happy and happy be your life. You don't deserve torture, and I see that you have been unjustly treated." Then she undid his shackles and proceeded to cheer him with conversation. She asked him about the Islamic religion, and he told her that it was the true and right faith and that our Lord Muhammad was the author of dazzling miracles and manifest signs and that the worship of the Fire was unprofitable and harmful. Then he acquainted her with the tenets of Islam, and she was persuaded, and the love of the faith entered her heart and mixed with her love of As'ad, as God the Almighty had willed, and she professed the two articles of the faith and became one of the blessed. After that, she gave him food and drink, conversed and prayed with him, and fed him with chicken broth until he recovered and regained his strength.

One day, as she stood at the door of the house, she heard the crier proclaiming aloud, "Whoever has with him a handsome young man, of such and such description, and bring him forth, he shall have all the wealth he demands, but whoever has him and fails to bring him forth, he will be hanged at the door of his house, and his property shall be plundered." When Bustana heard this, she knew that As'ad was the person they were looking for, for he had already told her all that had happened to him. She went back to him and told him the news, and he took her with him and went to the mansion of the vizier, and as soon as he saw him, he exclaimed, "By God, this is my brother Amjad," and threw himself on him. Amjad likewise recognized him and threw himself on him, and they embraced each other and fell into a swoon, while Amjad's Mamluks stood around them.

When they recovered, a little later, Amjad took his brother and went up with him to the king and told him his story, and the king ordered Amjad, his vizier, to plunder Bahram's house. So Amjad sent a company of men who went to Bahram's house and plundered it and brought his daughter to Amjad, who received her with great honor.

Then As'ad described to his brother all the torture he had suffered and the acts of kindness Bahram's daughter had done him, and Amjad, therefore, treated her with increased honor. Then Amjad in turn related to his brother all that had happened to him with the girl and how he had escaped hanging and become vizier. They then complained to each other of the pain they had suffered because of their separation. Then the king sent for Bahram the Magian and ordered that his head be struck off. But Bahram said, "O most mighty king, are you determined to put me to death?" The king replied, "Yes." Bahram said, "Be patient with me for a moment." Then he bowed his head a little while and, raising it again, professed the articles of the faith to the king and became a Muslim. They all rejoiced at his conversion, and Amjad and As'ad related to him all that had happened to them. He said to them, "My lords, prepare yourselves for the journey, and I will take you back." At this they rejoiced and wept bitterly, but he said to them, "Don't weep, my lords, for in a short time you will be reunited with your family, as were Ni'ma and Nu'am." They asked him, "What happened to Ni'ma and Nu'am?" He said:

[The Tale of Ni'ma and Nu'am]

It is told, but God knows best, that there lived in the city of Kufa a man called al-Rabi' ibn-Hatim. He was one of its prominent people, a man of great wealth and prosperous circumstances, and God had blessed him with a son whom he called Ni'mat-Allah. One day, while he was in the slave dealers' mart, he saw a female slave offered for sale, with a wonderfully beautiful and charming little girl on her arm. He beckoned to the broker and asked him, "What is the price of this female slave and her daughter?" The broker replied, "Fifty dinars." Al-Rabi' said, "Write the sale contract and take the money and give it to her owner." Then he gave the broker the money, together with his commission, and took the woman and child and went home.

When his wife saw the female slave, she asked her husband (who was the son of her father's brother), "Cousin, what is this woman?" He replied, "I bought her for the sake of the little girl on her arm, for when she grows up, there will be none like her and none more beautiful in Arab or in foreign lands." Then his wife asked the slave, "What is your name, slave-girl?" She replied, "My name is Taufiq," and she asked her, "And what is the name of your girl?" She replied, "Sa'ad." His wife said, "You are right. You are fortunate, and fortunate is he who has purchased you." Then she asked her husband, "Cousin, what name will you give her?" He replied, "Any name you choose." She said, "We will call her Nu'am." He said, "This is fine."

Little Nu'am was brought up with Ni'ma, al-Rabi's son, in the same cradle, and each grew more beautiful than the other. The boy used to call her sister, and she used to call him brother. When they reached the age of ten, al-Rabi' said to his son Ni'ma, "Son, Nu'am is not your sister, but your slave whom I bought in your name, while you were still in the cradle. From now on, don't call her sister." Ni'ma said to his father, "If this is the case, I will marry her." Then he went in to his mother and told her about it, and she said, "Yes, son, she is your slave." Ni'ma then slept with her and fell in love with her.

They lived together for four years, and in all of Kufa there was not a single girl more beautiful or charming than Nu'am. She had grown up, having read the Koran, as well as the works of science, learned all kinds of musical instruments, and excelled in playing music and singing, surpassing everyone in her time. One day, as she sat with her husband Ni'ma in the wine chamber, she took the lute and, tuning it, sang the following verses,

> Since you are my dear lord, by whose bounty I live,
> A sword by which I strike the neck of adverse fate,
> I need neither Amru nor Zaid but you
> If I find myself in a narrow strait.

Ni'ma was moved with great delight and said to her, "By my life, Nu'am, sing to us with the tambourines and other instruments." So she sang the following verses to a lovely melody,

> By him who holds me captive in his hand,
> In love I will cross my envier, I swear,
> My censors I will vex and only you obey,
> And I will sleep and all pleasures forswear
> And will bury you in my breast, so deep
> That even my heart will not be aware.

Ni'ma exclaimed, "O Nu'am, this is excellent!"

While they led a most happy life, al-Hajjaj sat in his governor's mansion, saying to himself, "I must maneuver to take this girl whose name is Nu'am and send her to the Commander of the Faithful Abd-al-Melik ibn Marwan, for there is none in his palace who matches her singing and her beauty." Then he called for an old stewardess and said to her, "Go to the house of Ni'ma ibn-al-Rabi', get together with the girl Nu'am, and try to steal her away, for there is none like her on the face of the earth."

The old woman consented to do his bidding, and the following morning, she put on clothes of wool, threw around her neck a rosary of thousands of beads, and, taking in her hand a walkingstaff and a water bottle of Yemen, proceeded to Al-Rabi's house, exclaiming as she went, "Glory and praise be to God; there is no god but God; God is great; there is no power and no strength save in God the Almighty, the Magnificent." She continued with her glorification and impreca- tion of God, while her heart was full of guile and deceit, until she reached the house of Ni'ma ibn-al-Rabi', at the hour of the noon prayer. She knocked at the door, and the doorkeeper opened it and asked, "What do you want?" She replied, "I am a poor devout woman, and the time of the noon prayer is upon me, and I wish to pray in this blessed place." The doorkeeper said, "Old woman, this is the house of Ni'ma ibn-al-Rabi', not a mosque or a place of worship." She replied, "I know that there is no mosque or place of worship like the house of Ni'ma ibn-al-Rabi', but I am a stewardess from the palace of the Commander of the Faithful, and I have come to wor- ship and to see the sights." But the doorkeeper said, "You cannot come in." They kept arguing until she grabbed him, saying, "Shall someone like me, who is admitted to the houses of princes and promi- nent men, be denied entry to the house of Ni'ma ibn-al-Rabi'?" At that moment Ni'ma happened to come out and, hearing what she said, laughed and asked her to enter.

The old woman entered and followed Ni'ma until he brought her to Nu'am, whom she saluted in the best of manners, and when she looked at her, she marveled at her great beauty and said to her, "O my lady, I commend you to the protection of God who made you and your lord alike in beauty and grace." Then she stood up at the prayer niche and proceeded to perform her prayers, prostrating herself and supplicating God until the day departed and darkness descended. At last, Nu'am said to her, "O mother, rest your feet a while." The old woman replied, "O my lady, he who seeks the world to come, must toil in this world, and he who toils not in this world, will not enter the dwelling of the righteous in the world to come." Then Nu'am brought her food and said, "Eat of my food and pray to God to forgive me and have mercy on me." The old woman replied, "My lady, I am fasting, but you are a young woman, and eating and drinking and mirth are more suitable to you. God the Almighty will forgive you, for He says that none shall be saved, except those who repent and believe and do righteous deeds." Ni'ma sat for a while, conversing with the old woman. Then Nu'am said to Ni'ma, "My lord, entreat this old woman to stay with us a while, for piety is marked on her face." He said to her, "Give her a room where she may do her devotions without being disturbed, so that the Almighty and Glorious God may benefit

us by the blessing of her presence and keep the two of us together."
And the old woman spent the night there, praying and reciting the
Koran.

In the morning she went in to Ni'ma and Nu'am and, wishing them
good morning, said, "God be with you!" Nu'am said to her, "O
mother, where are you going? My master has ordered me to give you
a room where you may do your devotions." The old woman replied,
"May God preserve him and continue His blessings on you both; for
the time being, I would like the two of you to tell the doorkeeper not to
prevent me from coming in to you. God the almighty willing, I will
visit the holy places and pray for you both at the close of my prayer
and devotion, every day and night." Then she went out of the house,
leaving Nu'am in tears, being ignorant of the reason for which she
had come.

The old woman went back to al-Hajjaj, who asked her, "What news
do you bring?" She replied, "I have seen the girl, and indeed, in this
day, there is none lovelier." Al-Hajjaj said, "If you do what I have
asked you, I will reward you amply." She said to him, "I ask of you a
month's time." He replied, "Very well, I give you a month." Then she
began to pay frequent visits to Ni'ma and Nu'am, morning and
evening, and they treated her with increasing kindness, and everyone
in the house welcomed her. One day, when the old woman was alone
with Nu'am, she said to her, "By God, my lady, when I visit the holy
places, I pray for you, and I wish that you will go with me to see the
religious elders who come there, so that they may pray to God to grant
you your wishes." Nu'am replied, "For God's sake, mother, take me
with you." The old woman said, "Ask your mother-in-law for permission, and I will take you with me." So Nu'am said to her mother-in-
law, "O my lady, ask my master to let me go one day with you and my
mother the old woman to pray and supplicate God with the poor in
the holy places." When Ni'ma came home and sat down, the old
woman approached him to kiss his hands, but he did not let her. Then
she invoked blessings on him and departed. The following day, the
old woman came, when Ni'ma was not in the house, and, approaching Nu'am, said to her, "We prayed for you yesterday, but come with
me now and divert yourself and return before your master comes
home." Nu'am said to her mother-in-law, "For God's sake, give me
permission to go out with this pious woman to watch the holy men in
the holy places and return quickly before my master comes home."
Ni'ma's mother replied, "I am afraid that he will find out." The old
woman said, "By God, I will not let her even sit down, but she will
watch standing on her feet and will not tarry."

So the old woman took the girl by guile and carried her to the mansion of al-Hajjaj and, putting her in a private chamber, informed al-

Hajjaj of her arrival. He went in to her, and when he looked at her, he saw her to be the loveliest woman of her day, the like of whom he had never seen before. When Nu'am saw him, she veiled her face from him, but he did not leave her until he called his chamberlain and ordered him to take fifty horsemen, mount the girl on a swift drome-dary, ride to Damascus, and deliver her to the Commander of the Faithful abd-al-Melik ibn-Marwan. He also wrote the caliph a letter, saying to the chamberlain, "Give him this letter, take the answer, and come back quickly." The chamberlain put the girl on a dromedary and journeyed with her, while she wept all the way at her separation from her master, until they reached Damascus. The chamberlain asked for permission to see the Commander of the Faithful, who granted him permission, and he went in to him and informed him about the girl.

The caliph appropriated a private chamber for her. Then he went to the harem and said to his wife, "Al-Hajjaj has bought for me a girl who is a descendent of the ancient kings of Kufa, for ten thousand dinars, and he has sent me this letter with her." His wife said, "May God multiply His blessings on you." Then the caliph's sister went in to Nu'am, and when she saw her, she said to her, "He is not disap-pointed who has you in his house, even if your price is a hundred thousand dinars." Nu'am said, "O cheerful one, to which king does this palace belong, and what city is this?" The caliph's sister replied, "This is the city of Damascus, and this palace belongs to my brother, the Commander of the Faithful Abd-al-Melik-ibn-Marwan," adding, "It seems that you don't know this." Nu'am replied, "By God, my lady, I had no knowledge of it." The caliph's sister said, "Didn't he who sold you and received your price tell you that it was the caliph who bought you?" When Nu'am heard this, she wept and lamented and said to herself, "I have been tricked. If I speak up, nobody will believe me. So I will be silent and patient, for I know that God's deliv-erance is near." Then she bowed her head bashfully, and her cheeks were reddened from the exertion of travel and the heat of the sun. The caliph's sister left her and on the following day returned with clothes and jewel necklaces and dressed her.

Then the Commander of the Faithful came in to her and sat beside her. His sister said to him, "Look at this girl in whom God has per-fected beauty and grace." The caliph said to Nu'am, "Remove the veil from your face," but she did not. So even though he did not see her face, he saw her wrists and fell in love with her, and he said to his sister, "I will wait for three days until you cheer her up, before I go into her." Then he went out, leaving Nu'am worried about herself and sad because of her separation from her master Ni'ma. When night came, she felt sick with fever. She did not eat or drink, and she looked pale, and her charms faded. When they informed the caliph about her condition, he grieved for her, and he brought in the physicians and the sages to examine her, but no one could offer a remedy for her.

Meanwhile, her master Ni'ma came home and, seating himself on his bed, called out, "Nu'am!" But she did not answer. So he got up quickly and called out again, but no one came to him, for every woman in the house hid herself, in fear of him. He went to his mother and saw her sitting with her hand on her cheek. He asked her, "Mother, where is Nu'am?" She replied, "Son, she is with one who is more trustworthy than myself with her. She went out with the pious old woman to visit the poor." He said, "Since when has she been accustomed to do this? When did she go?" His mother replied, "She went out early in the morning." He asked, "Why did you give her permission to go?" She replied, "Son, she was the one who persuaded me to do it." He said, "There is no power and no strength save in God the Almighty, the Magnificent." Then he left the house in a daze and, going to the chief of the police, said to him, "Did you trick me and take my slave-girl from my house? I will certainly journey and complain against you to the Commander of the Faithful." The chief of the police asked him, "Who took her?" Ni'ma replied, "An old woman with such and such a description, dressed in wool garments and carrying a rosary of thousands of beads." The chief of the police said, "Tell me who the old woman is, and I will get you back your slave-girl." Ni'ma said, "Who knows the old woman?" The chief of the police replied, "And who knows what lies hidden, save God the Almighty, the Magnificent?" He knew that she was al-Hajjaj's wily henchwoman. Ni'ma said to him, "No one has the responsibility to get back my slave-girl but you. I will let al-Hajjaj judge between us." The chief of the police said, "Go to whomever you wish."

So Ni'ma, whose father was one of the prominent men of Kufa, went to al-Hajjaj's mansion, and as soon as he arrived, the chamberlain went in to al-Hajjaj and informed him of the case. Al-Hajjaj said, "Bring him to me," and when he stood before him, al-Hajjaj asked him, "What is the problem?" And Ni'ma explained to him. Al-Hajjaj said, "Bring me the chief of the police, and I will order him to search for the old woman." When the chief of the police arrived, al-Hajjaj said to him, "I want you to search for the slave-girl of Ni'ma ibn-al-Rabi'." The chief of the police said, "No one knows what lies hidden, save the Almighty God." Al-Hajjaj said to him, "You must send horsemen and look for the girl in all the roads and towns." Then turning to Ni'ma, he said, "If you don't get your slave-girl back, I will give you ten slave-girls from my house and ten from that of the chief of the police." Then he said to the chief of the police, "Go and look for the girl," and the chief went out.

Ni'ma returned home, feeling depressed and desperate. He was by now only fourteen years old, and there was not a hair on his face. He secluded himself and wept and lamented till the morning, when his father came to him and said, "Son, al-Hajjaj has tricked us and taken the girl away, but God sends relief from hour to hour." But Ni'ma's grief increased, so that he did not know what he said or who came to see him, and he fell ill and his condition deteriorated until his father despaired of him, for all the physicians who came to see him said, "There is no cure for him but the girl."

One day, his father heard of a skilled Persian physician, said to be accomplished in medicine, astrology, and geomancy. Al-Rabi' called for him, and when he came, he seated him beside him, treated him courteously, and said to him, "Examine my son." The physician said to Ni'ma, "Give me your hand." Ni'ma gave him his hand, and he felt his joints, looked in his face and laughed and, turning to al-Rabi', said, "Your son's only ailment is in his heart." Al-Rabi' replied, "You are right, doctor. Apply your skill to all aspects of the case and tell me, without hiding anything from me." The Persian said, "He is in love with a girl who is either in Basra or in Damascus, and his only remedy is reunion with her." Al-Rabi' said, "If you reunite them, I will give you what will make you rejoice, and you will live all your life in prosperity and happiness." The Persian said, "This is easy and speedily accomplished." Then he returned to Ni'ma and said, "You will be all right; so cheer up and relax." Then he said to al-Rabi', "Give me four thousand dinars of your money," and al-Rabi' took out the money and gave it to the Persian, who said to him, "I would like your son to journey with me to Damascus, and, God willing, I will not return from there but with the girl." Then he turned to Ni'ma and asked him, "What is your name?" Ni'ma answered, "Ni'ma," and he said to him, "Sit up, and trust in the Almighty God to reunite you with your girl." When Ni'ma sat up, he said to him, "Take heart, and be cheerful, and eat and drink to fortify yourself for the journey, for we set out for Damascus this very day."

Then the Persian set about preparing whatever he needed for the journey, having taken from Ni'ma's father altogether ten thousand dinars, as well as horses and camels and other beasts of burden to carry the baggage. Ni'ma bade his father and mother farewell and journeyed with the physician to Aleppo, but they heard no news of Nu'am there. So they continued until they arrived in Damascus, where, three days later, the Persian rented a shop and, decorating the shelves with gilding and costly ornaments, stocked them with precious chinaware and covers. Moreover, he placed before him glass bottles containing all kinds of ointments and potions surrounded by cups of crystal and, putting on a physician's attire, sat in his shop with an astrolabe before him. Then he dressed Ni'ma in a silk shirt and gown and girded his waist with a silk kerchief, embroidered with gold, and he made Ni'ma sit before him and said to him, "Ni'ma, from this day on, you are my son. So call me by no other name but father, and I will call you son." Ni'ma replied, "I hear and obey."

The people of Damascus began to congregate before the Persian's shop, gazing at the beauty of Ni'ma and the elegance of the shop and its wares, while the physician spoke in Persian with Ni'ma, who likewise answered him in Persian, for he had learned it, as was usually the case with the sons of prominent families. The Persian became famous among the people of Damascus who began to come to him and describe their ailments, for which he gave them remedies. Moreover, they brought him the urine of the sick in jars, and he would examine it and say, "He whose urine this is is suffering from such and such an ailment," and the patient would say, "This is true." He continued to minister to the people of Damascus, who flocked to him until his fame spread throughout the city and into the households of its prominent people.

One day, as he sat in his shop, an old woman approached him, riding on an ass, with a saddle of brocade adorned with jewels. She stopped at the shop and, pulling the ass's bridle, motioned to him, saying, "Hold my hand." He held her hand, while she dismounted and said, "Are you the Persian physician who came from Iraq?" He replied, "Yes." She said, "I have a sick daughter," and brought out a bottle of urine. After he examined it, he asked her, "Tell me her name, in order that I may calculate her horoscope and learn the best hour for taking the medicine." She replied, "O Persian, her name is Nu'am." When he heard the name, he proceeded to calculate and write on his hand and soon said to her, "My lady, I cannot prescribe any medicine for her unless I know in which country she was brought up, because of the difference in climate, and how old she is." The old woman replied, "She is fourteen years old, and she was brought up in the city of Kufa, in Iraq." He asked, "And how many months has she been in this country?" The old woman replied, "She has been here only a few months." When Ni'ma heard this and the name of his girl, his heart throbbed. The Persian said to her, "Such and such remedies will be suitable for her." The old woman said to him, "Then give them to me with the blessing of the Almighty God," and threw him ten dinars. He turned to Ni'ma and ordered him to prepare the drugs, while the old woman looked at him and exclaimed, "O my son, you look just like her. May God protect you!" Then she asked the Persian, "Persian, is this your Mamluk or your son?" The Persian replied, "He is my son." Ni'ma put the drugs in a box and, taking a paper, wrote the following lines,

If Nu'am grant me a glance, I care not
If Su'ad her favors grant or Juml prove unkind.
They said, "Forget her and you'll have twenty like her."
But I'll never forget her, never her like find.

Then he slipped the paper inside the box and, sealing it, wrote on the lid in Kufie characters, "I am Ni'ma ibn-al-Rabi' of Kufa." Then he placed the box before the old woman, who took it and, bidding them farewell, went to the caliph's palace.

There, she went to Nu'am and, putting the box before her, said, "O my lady, there has come to our city a Persian physician, and I have never seen one more skillful in medicine. When I showed him the bottle and mentioned your name, he knew your ailment and prescribed the remedy. Then he ordered his son to prepare this medicine for you. There is not in all Damascus a lovelier, more charming, or better dressed young man than this son of his, nor is there a shop like his." Nu'am took the box, and when she found the names of her master and his father written on the lid, she changed color and said to herself, "Undoubtedly, the owner of this shop has come in search of me." Then she said to the old woman, "Describe to me this young man." The old woman replied, "His name is Ni'ma, he is finely dressed, he is perfectly handsome, and he has a mark on his right eyebrow." Nu'am said, "Give me the medicine, with the blessing and help of the Almighty God." She took the medicine and swallowed it, laughing, and said, "This is a blessed medicine." Then she searched in the box, and found the paper. So she opened it and read it, and when she understood its meaning, she was sure that it was written by her master, and she rejoiced and became cheerful. When the old woman saw her laughing, she said to her, "This is a blessed day," and Nu'am replied, "Yes, stewardess. Now I would like some food and drink." So the old woman said to the female attendants, "Bring the trays of fine foods to your mistress." They brought the food, and she sat to eat.

At that moment, Abd-al-Melik-ibn-Marwan came in, and when he looked at Nu'am and saw her sitting and eating, he rejoiced. The stewardess said to him, "O Commander of the Faithful, congratulations for the recovery of your slave. A physician has come to the city and I have never seen one more knowledgeable about ailments and their remedies. I brought her some medicine from him, and she took it only once and recovered, O Commander of the Faithful." The caliph said to her, "Take a thousand dinars and use it for her complete recovery." Then he went out, rejoicing at Nu'am's recovery. The old woman went back to the physician's shop with the thousand dinars and gave them to him, telling him that she was a female slave of the caliph and giving him a paper Nu'am had written. The physician took it and gave it to Ni'ma, who, when he looked at it, recognized the handwriting and fell into a swoon. When he recovered, he opened the paper and found written in it, "From the duped slave-girl who is robbed of her happiness, and separated from the darling of her heart. Your letter has reached me, and it has cheered me and gladdened my heart, as the poet says,

> The letter reached me. Long live the fingers
> That wrote until it was with perfume fraught.
> 'Twas as if Moses was to his mother restored,
> Or Joseph's coat was to blind Jacob brought."

When Ni'ma read these verses, his eyes flowed with tears, and the old woman asked him, "Son, why do you weep? May God protect your eyes from tears!" The Persian said, "O my lady, how should he not weep, when she is his slave-girl, and he is her master Ni'ma ibn-al-Rabi' of Kufa? Indeed, her recovery depends on seeing him, for her only ailment is her love for him. Take the thousand dinars for yourself (and you will receive from me more than this), and look on us with compassion, for we have no way to remedy the situation except through you." The old woman asked Ni'ma, "Are you really her master?" Ni'ma replied, "Yes." She said, "You are telling the truth, for she never stops mentioning you." Then Ni'ma related to her what had happened from beginning to end, and the old woman said to him, "Young man, you will be reunited with her through none but me."

Then she mounted and returned immediately and, going to the girl, looked in her face, laughed, and said, "O my daughter, you are justified in weeping and falling sick on account of your separation from you master Ni'ma ibn-al-Rabi' of Kufa." Nu'am said, "The veil has been lifted, and the truth has been revealed to you." The old woman said, "Cheer up and relax, for, by God, I will bring you together, even if it costs me my life." Then she returned to Ni'ma and said to him, "I went to your slave-girl and found that she longs for you more than you do for her, for the Commander of the Faithful wishes to visit her, but she refuses to receive him. If you have determination and courage, I will take a risk and bring you together, by devising a strategy to get you into the caliph's palace, where you will meet her, for she cannot go out." Ni'ma said to her, "May God reward you." Then she bade him good-bye and went to Nu'am and said to her, "Your master is dying of love for you, and he wishes to meet with you. What do you say?" Nu'am replied, "I too am dying of love and wish to meet with him."

So the old woman put a woman's suit and some ornaments and jewelry in a wrapper and, going to Ni'ma said to him, "Take us to some place where we can be by ourselves." He took her to a room behind the shop, where she dressed him like a slave-girl, made up his face, styled his hair, put bracelets on his wrists, and bedecked him with the finest ornaments that girls wear until he looked like one of the maids of Paradise. When she saw how he looked, she exclaimed, "Blessed be God, the best of Creators. By God, you are more beautiful than the girl!" Then she said to him, "Walk with your left shoulder forward, and swing your hips." He walked in front of her, as she instructed him, and when she saw that he knew how to walk like a woman, she said, "Wait until I return to you tomorrow night and, God the Almighty willing, take you into the palace. When you see the chamberlains and eunuchs, don't be afraid, but bow your head and speak to no one, for I will speak for you, and may God grant us success."

The following day, the old woman returned to him and took him up to the palace. She entered before him, and he followed her, and the chamberlain was about to prevent him from entering, but the old woman said to him, "O most wretched slave, this is the slave-girl of Nu'am, the caliph's favorite. How dare you prevent her from entering?" Then she said to Ni'ma, "Enter, girl." Ni'ma walked with her until they came near the door leading to the inner court of the palace. The old woman said to him, "Ni'ma, summon your determination and courage, and enter the court. Turn to the left, count five doors, and enter the sixth, for it is the door of the place prepared for you. Don't be afraid, and if anyone speaks to you, don't answer." Then she proceeded with him until they came to the doors, where the eunuch assigned to guard them met them and asked her, "Who is this slave-girl?" The old woman replied, "Our mistress wishes to buy her." The eunuch said, "No one enters without the permission of the Commander of the Faithful. Go back with her, for I will not let her enter. These are my orders." The old woman said, "O chief chamberlain, use your head. Nu'am is the slave-girl of the caliph, who loves her and who is happy at her recovery, and she wishes to buy this slave-girl. Don't prevent her from entering, lest Nu'am hears about it and gets angry with you and causes your head to be cut off." Then she said to Ni'ma, "Enter, girl; don't mind the chamberlain, and don't tell your mistress that he tried to prevent you from entering." Ni'ma bowed his head and entered, but, instead of turning to the left, he turned to the right by mistake, and instead of counting five doors and entering the sixth, he counted six and entered the seventh.

When he was in, he found himself in a place carpeted with brocade and hung with silk curtains embroidered with gold. There were censers of aloewood, ambergris, and pungent musk, and at the upper end was a couch covered with brocade. Ni'ma sat on the couch, thinking about his situation, unaware of what God had destined for him, when suddenly the caliph's sister entered, followed by her maid. When she saw the young man, she thought that he was a slave-girl and, approaching him, asked, "Who are you, girl, and why are you here?" Ni'ma did not reply, and she said, "If you are one of my brother's favorites, and he is angry with you, I will intercede on your behalf." But again Ni'ma did not reply. So she said to her maid, "Stand at the door, and don't let anyone enter." Then she went up to him and gazed on his beauty and said, "Young lady, tell me who you are, what is your name, and why are you here, for I have never seen you in our palace before." When Ni'ma again did not reply, she got angry and, putting her hand to his chest, found no breasts, and she was about to pull aside his outer garment, in order to find out who he was, but he said to her, "O my lady, I am your slave, and I throw myself at your mercy; buy me and protect me." She said, "You will not be harmed, but who are you, and who brought you into my chamber?" Ni'ma replied, "O Princess, my name is Ni'ma ibn-al-Rabi' of Kufa, and I have risked my life for my slave-girl Nu'am whom al-Hajjaj took by trickery and sent here." She said to him again, "You will not be harmed." Then she called to her maid and said to her, "Go to Nu'am's chamber."

The old stewardess had gone to Nu'am's chamber and asked her, "Has your master come to you?" Nu'am replied, "No, by God." She said, "He has probably missed his way and entered another chamber by mistake." Nu'am exclaimed, "There is no power and no strength save in God the Almighty, the Magnificent! Our appointed hour has come, and we are going to perish." As they sat pondering, the princess's maid came in and, saluting Nu'am, said to her, "My mistress invites you to her entertainment." Nu'am replied, "I hear and obey." The old woman said to Nu'am, "Perhaps you master is with the caliph's sister, and the affair is exposed." Nu'am rose and went immediately into the caliph's sister, who said to her, "Here is your master, sitting with me. It seems that he entered my chamber by mistake, but God the Almighty willing, no harm will come to either of you." When Nu'am heard this from the Caliph's sister, her fear subsided, and she advanced to her master Ni'ma, and when he saw her, he got up, and each of them pressed the other to their bosom and fell into a swoon.

When they recovered, the caliph's sister said to them, "Sit here until we find a way out of this predicament." They replied, "We hear and obey. Our fate is in your hands." She said, "By God, I have nothing but goodwill toward you." Then she said to her maid, "Bring the food and the beverage," and when she did so, they ate until they had their fill. Then they sat to drink, passing the cups around, until they forgot their sorrows. But Ni'ma said, "I wonder what is going to happen next." The caliph's sister asked him, "Ni'ma, do you love your slave-girl Nu'am?" He replied, "O my lady, it is my love for her that has driven me to risk my life." Then she said to Nu'am, "Nu'am, do you love your master Ni'ma?" Nu'am replied, "O my lady, it is my love for him that has made me ill and wasted my body." The princess said, "By God, you love each other, and may no one separate you. Cheer up and rejoice." They were happy to hear this, and Nu'am asked for a lute, and when it was brought, she tuned it and sang the following verses to a melody that delighted her audience,

> When the traitors labored to part us two,
> Although we gave them no cause for foul play,
> And on our ears waged war with poisoned darts
> And my protectors and aids drove away,
> I fought them with your eyes, and with my tears and soul—
> With the sword, the torrent, and the fire, aye.

Then she handed the lute to her master Ni'ma and said, "Sing to us," and he tuned it and sang the following verses to a melody that delighted his audience,

> Were it not freckled, the full moon would look like you
> And were it not eclipsed, would shine like you the sun.
> I wonder, but of wonders love is full,
> Passion and joy and sorrows, all in one,
> When I go to her, short does seem my way,
> But long it seems when I journey away.

When he finished his song, Nu'am filled a cup and gave it to him, and he drank it. Then she filled another and gave it to the caliph's sister, who drank it and, taking the lute, tuned it and sang the following verses,

> Passion torments my breast, and in my heart,
> Sorrow and grief are dwellers, there to stay.
> My wasting body is for all to see,
> For racked by love, I pine and waste away.

Then she gave the lute to Ni'ma, who tuned it and sang the following verses,

> O you to whom I gave my soul and who
> Tormented it, and free it I could not,
> Redeem a lover from perdition now,
> For this is his last breath and death his certain lot.

They continued to sing and drink to the sweet sound of the strings, full of joy and merriment, when suddenly the Commander of the

Faithful came in. As soon as they saw him, they stood up and kissed the ground before him. When he looked at Nu'am and saw her with the lute in her hand, he said to her, "O Nu'am, praise be to God who has cured you of your affliction and pain." Then looking toward Ni'ma, who was dressed as described before, he asked, "Sister, who is this girl sitting beside Nu'am?" His sister replied, "O Commander of the Faithful, she is one of your concubines, a close friend of Nu'am who does not eat or drink without her." Then she recited the poet's saying,

> Two opposites met, each with beauty lit,
> And beauty shines more brightly 'gainst its opposite.

The caliph said, "By the Great God, she is as beautiful as Nu'am. Tomorrow, I will give her a chamber next to Nu'am's and send her furniture and clothes and everything suitable, in honor of Nu'am." Then his sister called for food and placed it before her brother, who ate and remained sitting with them. Then he filled a cup and made a sign to Nu'am to sing for him. So she took the lute, after she had drunk two cups, and sang the following verses,

> When my cup companion pours out for me
> Three cups overbrimming with bubbling wine,
> I strut with pride all night, as if the Prince
> of the Faithful were a subject of mine.

The Commander of the Faithful was filled with delight, and he filled another cup and, giving it to Nu'am, asked her to sing again. She drank it off, tuned the strings, and sang the following verses,

> O most noble of men in this our present age,
> Whom no one his equal to be can claim,
> O matchless in munificence and dignity,
> O Lord and King, in everything, high is your fame.
> O sovereign over all kings of the world,
> And without grudging give of your largesse,
> May God preserve you and spite all your foes
> And crown your life with triumph and success.

When the caliph heard these verses from Nu'am, he said to her, "Bravo, Nu'am! How excellent is your language and how eloquent you are!"

They continued to enjoy themselves until midnight, when the caliph's sister said, "O Commander of the Faithful, I would like to tell you a story I have read of a certain person of rank." The caliph asked, "What is it?" She said, "O Commander of the Faithful, there lived in the city of Kufa a young man called Ni'ma ibn-al-Rabi', and he had a slave-girl whom he loved and who loved him. They had been brought up together in the same cradle, and when they reached puberty, they fell in love with each other, but life dealt them with misfortunes and treated them unfairly and decreed their separation. For some schemers tricked her out of the house and stole her from him, and the man who stole her sold her to a king for ten thousand dinars. The girl loved her master as much as he loved her. So he left his home and family and journeyed in search of her. He tried to find a way to get to her, devoting his whole being and risking his life, until he finally succeeded. But no sooner had they sat together than in came the king who had bought her from the man who stole her, and he hastily ordered that they be put to death, without granting them the opportunity for a fair trial. O Commander of the Faithful, what do you say of this king's unjust conduct?" The caliph replied, "This is a strange story! It behooved this king to pardon when he was able to punish, for he should have considered three factors in their case: first, that they loved one another; second, that they were in his house and at his mercy; third, that a king should be deliberate in judging people, especially in matters in which he is personally involved. This king, therefore, did not behave like a king." His sister said, "By the Lord of the heaven and earth, ask Nu'am to sing, and listen to her words." He said to Nu'am, "Sing for us," and she sang the following verses to a moving melody,

> Fate has betrayed, as it is wont to do,
> Smiting the hearts, kindling disquieting woe,
> And parting lovers after they have been
> Together, and causing their tears to flow.
> We were together, and my life was bliss,
> For fortune kept us in each other's sight.
> I will then mourn in sorrow for your loss
> And shedding blood and tears, weep day and night.

When the Commander of the Faithful heard these verses, he was moved with great delight, and his sister said to him, "Brother, he who passes a sentence on himself, must carry it out and follow his words with deeds, and you have passed a sentence on yourself." Then she said to Ni'ma, "Stand up, Ni'ma, and you too Nu'am." They both stood up, and the caliph's sister said, "This girl, standing before you, is the stolen Nu'am, whom al-Hajjaj ibn-Yusuf al-Thaqafi stole and sent to you, lying in what he claimed in his letter, namely, that he had bought her for ten thousand dinars. And this young man is her master Ni'ma ibn-al-Rabi'. I beg you in the revered name of your noble forefathers to pardon them and give each as a gift to the other, so that God may reward you on their account, for they are at your mercy, and they have eaten of your food and drunken of your drink, and I am interceding for them and begging you for their lives." The caliph said, "You are right; I have passed that sentence and I never pass a sentence and revoke it." Then he asked Nu'am, "Nu'am, is this your master?" She replied, "Yes, Commander of the Faithful." He said, "Fear no harm, for I give you each as a gift to the other." Then he said, "Ni'ma, how did you find out where she was and who led you to this place?" Ni'ma replied, "No Commander of the Faithful, listen to my story, for by your noble forefathers, I will not hide anything from you." Then he related to the caliph all that had happened to him and what the Persian physician and the stewardess had done and how she had brought him into the palace and he had mistaken the doors. The caliph marveled exceedingly and said, "Bring me the Persian." So they brought him, and the caliph made him one of his chief officers, bestowed on him a robe of honor, and gave him a handsome reward, saying, "He who has managed so well must be made one of our chief officers." He also treated Ni'ma and Nu'am kindly, bestowing favors on them, as well as on the stewardess. They remained with him in joy and contentment for seven days. Then Ni'ma asked him for permission to return with Nu'am to Kufa, and he granted them permission. So they set out on their journey, and Ni'ma was reunited with his father and mother, and they lived together a most happy life until they were overtaken by the sunderer of companies and terminator of delights.

The Conclusion of
the Story of Qamar al-Zaman

Amjad and As'ad marveled exceedingly at Bahram's story, saying, "This is extraordinary!" They passed the night together, and the following morning, they rode to the palace and asked for an audience with the king, who received them courteously. As they sat talking, they heard the people of the city shouting and crying one to another and calling for help, and the chamberlain came in and said to the king, "Some king has encamped with his troops before our city, and they are brandishing their weapons, and we do not know what their purpose is." When the king acquainted his vizier Amjad and his brother As'ad with what he had heard from the chamberlain, Amjad said, "I will go to him and find out what he wants."

He went out of the city and found the king attended by numerous troops and mounted Mamluks. When they saw him, they knew that he was an envoy from the king of the city. So they took him and brought him before the king, and when he stood and kissed the ground before him, he saw that the person was a woman, with a veil covering the lower part of her face. She said to him, "I have nothing to demand from you except a beardless Mamluk. If I find him with you, no harm will come to you, but if I don't, I will wage a fierce battle against you." Amjad asked, "O Queen, what is the description of this Mamluk and what is his story and what is his name?" She replied, "His name is As'ad, and my name is Marjana. He came to me with Bahram the Magian, and when he refused to sell him to me, I took him from him by force, but he attacked him and stole him from me at night. As for his description, it is such and such." When Amjad heard this, he realized that the person in question was his brother As'ad and said to her, "O Queen of the age, God be praised for sending us deliverance. This Mamluk is my brother." Then he told her his story and all that had happened to them in exile, explaining to her the cause of their departure from the Ebony Islands. Queen Marjana marveled at that and rejoiced at finding As'ad and bestowed a robe of honor on his brother Amjad, who returned to the king and told him what had taken place, and they all rejoiced. Then the king, together with Amjad and As'ad, went down to meet Queen Marjana, and when they went in, they sat and talked.

While they were engaged in conversation, they saw the dust suddenly rise until it covered the countryside, and when it subsided, a while later, they saw multitudinous troops like the swelling sea, all equipped and armed, heading for the city, which they surrounded as a ring encircles the little finger and stood with their swords drawn. Amjad and As'ad exclaimed, "We are God and to Him we return. This great army is undoubtedly an enemy. If we don't make an alliance with Queen Marjana, they will take the city from us and kill us. We have no recourse but to go to them and find out what they want." So Amjad went out of the gate of the city, passing by the army of Queen Marjana, and when he reached the troops, he found out that they belonged to King Ghaiur, Lord of the Seas and Islands and the Seven Palaces and the father of his mother Queen Budur. When Amjad entered in the king's presence, he kissed the ground before him and delivered the message. The king replied, "My name is King Ghaiur, and I have come on a journey in search of my daughter Budur, of whom fortune has bereft me, for she left me and never returned, nor have I heard any news of her or her husband Qamar al-Zaman. Do you have any news of them?" When Amjad heard this, he bowed his head, reflecting, until he was convinced that this was his grandfather, his mother's father. Then he raised his head and, kissing the ground before the king again, told him that he was the son of his daughter Budur. When the king heard that Amjad was his grandson, he threw himself on him, and they both began to weep. Then King Ghaiur said, "O my son, God be praised for having preserved you and allowed me to meet you." Then Amjad told him that his mother Budur and his father Qamar al-Zaman were well and that they lived in a city called the City of Ebony. He also told him that his father had been angry with him and with his brother and had ordered the treasurer to put them to death and that the treasurer had had pity on them and spared them. The king said to him, "I will take you and your brother back to your father and reconcile you with him, and I will remain with you." Amjad kissed the ground before him, and the king bestowed on his grandson a robe of honor.

Amjad returned to the king of the Magians, smiling, and told him about King Ghaiur, and he marveled exceedingly. Then he sent King Ghaiur the offerings of hospitality, horses and camels and sheep and fodder. He did the like to Queen Marjana and acquainted her with what had happened, and she said, "I, too, will accompany you with my troops and endeavor to bring about your reconciliation."

At this moment, they saw the dust rise again, covering the countryside and making the day dark, and beneath it, they heard calls and cries and the neighing of horses and saw glittering swords and brandished spears. When this army drew near the city and saw the two other armies, they beat the drums, and the king of the Magians said, "This has been indeed an auspicious day. God be praised for having brought harmony between us and these two armies, and God willing, we will have peace with this army, too." Then he said to Amjad, "Go with your brother As'ad and find out about this army, for I have never seen a more massive one." The two brothers opened one of the city gates, which the king had closed for fear of the surrounding troops, and they proceeded until they reached the army that had just arrived and found that it belonged to the king of the Ebony Islands and that it was headed by their father Qamar al-Zaman. As soon as they saw him, they kissed the ground before him and wept, and when he saw them he threw himself on them and pressed them to his bosom, weeping bitterly. Then he apologized to them and told them of the terrible desolation he had suffered after their separation. Amjad and As'ad acquainted their father with King Ghaiur's arrival, and Qamar al-Zaman mounted with his chief officers and rode with Amjad and As'ad toward King Ghaiur's army. When they drew near, one of the princes rode forward and told King Ghaiur that Qamar al-Zaman had arrived. So he came out to meet him, and they all joined company, marveling at what had happened and how all of them met at this one place. Then the people of the city made banquets with all kinds of food and sweets and offered them horses and camels and sheep and fodder and whatever the troops needed.

Soon, they saw the dust rise again, covering the countryside, and felt the earth tremble under the horses' hoofs and heard the drums sound like a storm and saw a whole army equipped with weapons and coats of mail, all dressed in black. In their midst rode a very old man, also dressed in black, whose beard flowed down over his breast. When they saw these prodigious troops, the king of the Magians said to the other kings, "Praise be to God the Almighty; by whose permission you have met, all on the same day and found that you know each other, but this is a mighty army that covers the countryside." They said to him, "Fear not, for we are three kings, each with a large army, and if they prove to be enemies, we will fight them with you, even if they were three times larger."

Soon, an envoy from the approaching army came to the city, and when he was brought into the presence of Qamar al-Zaman and King Ghaiur and Queen Marjana and the King of the Magians, he kissed the ground before them and said, "The king my master comes from the land of the Persians. Many years ago, he lost his son, and he is searching for him in every country. If he finds him with you, no harm will come to you, but if he does not, he will wage war against you and destroy your city." Qamar al-Zaman replied, "That will not happen, but how is your master called in the land of the Persians?" The envoy said, "He is called King Shahraman, Lord of the Khalidan Islands, and he has levied these troops in the lands he passed through, while searching for his son." When Qamar al-Zaman heard what the envoy said, he uttered a loud cry and fell into a swoon. When he recovered, a while later, he wept bitterly and said to his sons Amjad and As'ad and to their chief officers, "Sons, let us go with the envoy and salute your grandfather King Shahraman and give him the good news about me, for he is still mourning my loss and wearing black for my sake." Then he related to the other kings all that had happened to him in his youth, and they all marveled. Then they accompanied Qamar al-Zaman, and went with him to his father. Qamar al-Zaman saluted him, and they embraced each other and fell down in a swoon, from extreme joy. When they recovered, the other kings saluted him, and he related to his son all that had happened to him.

Then they married Marjana to As'ad and sent her back to her kingdom, charging her not to interrupt her correspondence with them. Then they married Amjad to Bustana, Bahram's daughter, and they all went to the City of Ebony. When they arrived, Qamar al-Zaman saw his father-in-law, King Armanus, privately, and related to him all that had happened to him and how he had been reunited with his two sons, and the king rejoiced and congratulated him on his safe return. Then King Ghaiur went in to his daughter Queen Budur and greeted her and satisfied his yearning for her. He stayed in the City of Ebony

for a whole month, then returned with his troops to his country, taking
his daughter and his grandson Amjad with him, and as soon as he settled down in his kingdom, he seated Amjad to govern in his place.
Meanwhile, Qamar al-Zaman seated his son As'ad to govern in his
place in the city of his grandfather Armanus, who was pleased with
him. Then Qamar al-Zaman prepared himself and journeyed with his
father King Shahraman to the Khalidan Islands. When they arrived,
the city was decorated, and the drums continued to beat for an entire
month, in celebration of the happy event, and Qamar al-Zaman rule
in place of his father until they were overtaken by the sunderer
companies and destroyer of delights.